SPOTLIGHT

SPOTLIGHT

Carole Bellacera

A Tom Doherty Associates Book
New York

SPOTLIGHT

Copyright © 2000 by Carole Bellacera

Lyrics for "Eclipsed Summer" by Stephen Goggin
used by permission of Stephen Goggin.

This book is printed on acid-free paper.

A Forge Book
Published by Tom Doherty Associates, LLC
175 Fifth Avenue
New York, NY 10010

www.tor.com

Forge® is a registered trademark of Tom Doherty Associates, LLC.

Design by Jane Adele Regina

ISBN-0-312-87451-0

First Edition: July 2000

Printed in the United States of America

0 9 8 7 6 5 4 3 2 1

To Frank, my husband and best friend

ACKNOWLEDGMENTS

Thanks to Stephen Goggin of Waterford, Ireland, for creating the great lyrics for "Eclipsed Summer" and for taking me to Windmill Lane Studios. I never would've found it myself. To Aisling and Liam Clifford of Dublin, who showed me Ireland from a native's point of view. To Frank, Leah, and Stephen for their continued love and support. To Betty Norton and Susie Mosley Fuson for always lending an ear. To Pam Doctor for being my unofficial publicist in my home state of Indiana. To my agent, Jill Grosjean, and my brilliant editor, Stephanie Lane, for always being there for me.

SPOTLIGHT

PROLOGUE

January 30, 1972
Derry, Northern Ireland

RAIN MISTED the street as ten-year-old Devin O'Keefe pushed his way through the throng. In his right hand he carried an unwieldy sign that had been clumsily painted with five words: NO INTERNMENT. RELEASE CONOR O'KEEFE. It was a sentiment he believed with all his young heart, but he was tired and the sign had grown heavy since he'd joined the anti-internment march several kilometers out of town. They'd reached the middle of the Bogside, the Catholic ghetto where no sane Protestant dared venture for fear of becoming a target in the gunsights of the Provisional IRA.

As the marchers swept past the expressionless British soldiers dressed in battle fatigues and armed with Enfields, a new spirit of camaraderie seemed to pass through the crowd. Devin felt it. It was like an invisible current of electricity surging from one marcher to the next. *Oh, how proud Da would be if he could see me now!*

But his father wouldn't be seeing any of this. He'd been lifted by the Brits five months ago and locked up in the H-Blocks, the jail for political prisoners.

Along both sides of the road, Irish Catholics stood in the rain and cheered the crowd, some of them joining the march. Even priests and nuns were among the throng, many of them carrying banners like Devin's. A few faces along the roadside were implacable, some apprehensive, but most were jubilant. In America, Martin Luther King, Jr., had gathered blacks and whites alike to march upon Washington. Now, the Irish Catholics were doing the same, marching to Derry to win freedom for the oppressed.

Devin stood on tiptoe, searching the crowd for his brother, Glen, and his friend Pearse. His sign brushed a matronly woman's beehive; she glowered at him. "Watch where you be goin', laddie." She smelled of cheap perfume and sour body odor.

"Sorry, mum. Excuse me, I must get through." He'd spied the black head of Glen up ahead. "Wait up, Glen!" Eagerly, he jostled his way through the crowd. His sixteen-year-old brother hadn't wanted him to tag along today, but Devin was determined to be a part of this historical march for freedom and justice. Stay home with his mum and sisters? No bloody way.

"Glen!"

At the sound of his name, the tall, slender teenager turned. A pained expression crossed his face when he saw Devin. "Jaysus, Devin. Now, didn't I tell you to stay home?"

Next to him, Pearse laughed. "Since when does Devy listen to *you?*"

Devin brushed past the last of the marchers to reach him. "Bugger you," he said, grinning up at him. "I came anyway."

Glen's brown eyes glimmered with worry. "You hardheaded little imp. Can you never do as I tell you? There could be trouble here today."

Devin shifted the heavy sign to his left hand and held it higher. "I have to do my part for Da. You know that. Sure, maybe this will make the Brits release him. And all the other prisoners as well."

Pearse nudged Glen. "Ah, give the little squirt a break, Glennie. Sure, his heart's in the right place."

Glen stared at his little brother for a moment, then his eyes softened. His hand fastened on the boy's arm. "All right. Stay with us, then. But don't be doin' anything foolish."

Devin grinned. He knew Glen didn't really mind that he'd come. After all, it was for Da.

Glen gave him a sidelong glance. "I thought by leaving you the guitar, it would keep you busy for a time."

"It did. I made up a new song." Devin threw him a teasing grin. "It's about Rosalie." He waited for the blush to spread over his brother's cheeks, and when it did, he laughed. "Ah, she *is* a nice piece of crumpet, isn't she, now?"

Pearse laughed, shooting a knowing look at Glen. "She is that!"

Glen glared at Devin. "Make up all the songs you'd like about Rosalie O'Connor. It's nothing to me. Anyway, what made you leave my guitar and come join the march?"

Just as Devin opened his mouth to answer, the peaceful Sunday afternoon exploded in chaos. Gunfire. Devin spun in the direction it came from, his eyes searching for the source. But before he could see anything, Glen—or someone—shoved him hard in the middle of his back. He fell to the ground, his face and hands grinding into the pavement. Terrified screams erupted around him. Devin tried to move, but his brother held him securely to the ground. Glen's savage, suddenly adult voice growled into his ear: "Bloody hell! Keep your head down, Devin."

Devin obeyed. Seconds later, he heard a dull thump and felt Glen flinch. A soft sigh whispered from his brother's lips, just inches from Devin's ear. Devin's bowels tightened as an ice-cold fear ate its way through his insides. He knew what this meant.

"*No!*" With renewed strength, he struggled up. Glen's limp body rolled away. His lifeless eyes stared at Devin, still showing the surprise he must've felt as the bullet entered his head just above the right temple. For a moment, Devin felt weightless, as if his body hovered above the still form of his brother, watching with a detached sort of curiosity. Then reaction set in. It was as if a leaden pipe had plowed a hole through his stomach. He gasped for breath, reaching a shaking hand toward the ominous trickle of blood oozing from Glen's wound.

"Glennie. Jaysus, Glen." Devin crouched on his knees, his hands touching Glen's face, brushing his black hair away from his forehead. His skin was still warm. He *was* still alive, wasn't he? Nothing could happen that fast, could it? "Blessed Mary, Mother of God . . ." Devin's voice broke. He couldn't go on. He bit his trembling bottom lip and leaned in to his brother. "I'll get help for ya. Just hang on, Glen. Ya got to."

Devin scrambled to his feet, eyes darting frantically. "Help me! *Pearse!* Glen's been hit!"

His voice was lost in a swirling vortex of activity. Desperately, he peered around. Where was Pearse? Wasn't there someone who could help him?

All around him, the marchers huddled on the ground, cowering from bullets still whizzing through the air. He didn't see Pearse anywhere. Had he been hit, too? Amid hysterical screams, Devin heard someone murmuring the Lord's Prayer.

A hand reached out and grabbed his ankle. "Help me . . ."

Startled, Devin looked down. It was the woman he'd bumped against only minutes before; her beehive was now matted with blood. Everywhere he looked, he saw blood. Even the air was rank with it.

"Devin! *Get down!*"

Blankly, he turned to look in the direction of the panicked voice. Pearse was stumbling toward him, motioning frantically, but Devin could only stare at him in numbed confusion. Blood covered the older boy's jeans and black shirt in paintlike splotches.

Suddenly, a hot white fire speared Devin's upper left arm. In slow motion, he could feel himself falling. He could not protect himself from the impact with the concrete; it scraped his cheek, imbedding bits of dirt and gravel under his skin. Another searing pain shot through his nose, driving needlepoints into his skull. But it was nothing compared to the agony in his arm. Groaning, he lifted his head and saw blood from his smashed nose dripping onto the street. He sat up, shaking his head groggily. Almost immediately, everything dimmed; he slumped to the ground. His hand moved to the painful left arm and came back covered with blood. In amazement, he gazed at the crimson liquid. So much blood. Funny, Glen hadn't bled like this. There had been only that one little round hole.

Devin's head swam. In the distance, he heard the singsong whine of a siren growing closer. The rain fell harder now, its cool wetness a balm against his flushed face. His mind drifted as he stared up into the scudding gray clouds. The dull throb in his arm faded.

Suddenly, Pearse appeared above him, peering down anxiously. Then he began to pull on his body, dragging him away. It hurt. Oh, Lord Jesus, it hurt. Finally, mercifully, Pearse stopped tugging on him and knelt down at his side. He ripped at his shirt and quickly tied a strip of cloth around Devin's bleeding wound. *A black armband.* Did Pearse know about Glen, then?

Tears welled in his eyes. "They killed him, Pearse. They killed Glen," he whispered. "Why are they shooting at us, Pearse?"

"Hush, now. Save your strength. You're still losing blood."

It was true. His vision blurred, and Pearse's voice faded in and out. Devin bit his lip so hard he tasted blood. He couldn't pass out now. He had to make his brother's friend understand.

"Pearse, please, I . . ." He grasped the older boy's hand, hot tears spilling down his face.

"What is it, Dev?" Pearse cradled him, bewildered tears in his blue eyes. His image wavered, growing close and then fading away.

Devin felt the curtain of darkness around him. No. He wouldn't give in. Not until he had the chance to make Pearse understand. Despite the pain that sliced through to his very fingertips, he struggled up onto his elbow so his weakened voice could be heard. "Pearse, I don't care if I burn in hell," he whispered. "I'm going to make those bastards pay for what they did to Glen!"

PART ONE

Fonda

1

July 1985
Newark, New Jersey

FONDA BLAYNE reached for her fourth cup of coffee, took a sip, and grimaced. Cold. She hadn't touched it in twenty minutes because she'd been so involved in scribbling notes about the "Live Aid" concert. Hard to believe she was sitting here watching it on TV instead of actually being there. But that's what happens, she told herself, when you end up as an entry-level staff writer on one of the most popular rock music magazines in America. You sit home while more privileged writers get to go off on exciting assignments. But someday . . .

Fonda stared blankly at her notebook, thinking about "someday" until the MC's voice caught her attention by announcing Madonna. From the bathroom of her small apartment, she heard the shower tap turn off. She waited for a moment until she was sure Kari had stepped out from behind the glass doors, and then called out, "Kari! She's on."

A heavily accented masculine voice spoke through the bathroom door. "Madonna?"

A moment later, the door opened and a tall, well-built man in his mid-thirties padded into the room, a damp towel wrapped around his middle. His electric blue eyes zeroed in on the TV screen and he grinned, revealing straight white teeth. "Oh, *ja!* Come to me, baby."

Fonda shook her head, a wry smile on her lips. "What *is* it you find so sexy about her?"

"What? Are you kidding? Look at her!"

"I am. And I just don't get it."

On screen, Madonna was joking about her unauthorized nude photos in *Penthouse.*

Fonda rolled her eyes. "Gee, maybe if I wore my bra on the outside of my clothes and skipped washing my hair for a month, I could keep you from going into work on Saturdays."

Kari reached down and tangled his hand in her mass of light brown hair. "Don't you change a thing about yourself, babe. I said she was sexy, but that doesn't mean I'd sleep with her. It's purely a professional observation." He bent down and kissed Fonda soundly on the lips. His blue eyes were warm when he pulled away. "Good morning."

"Good morning, Mr. Jarlsberg." Fonda touched his damp face. His thinning blond hair was swept back, revealing a broad fore-head beaded with water. "You're dripping on me."

"So?" He kissed her again. "I wish I could stay. But as you'll find out someday, being an editor of a major magazine is *more* than a full-time job."

"If I climb that high."

"Oh, you will. Believe me, I see ambition in those lovely hazel eyes of yours. I predict you'll have your own magazine within a decade. Thank God, I won't have to worry about you competing with me and my new European mag."

"Right." Fonda grinned. "I'm sure you'd be shaking in your boots if you stayed in America."

He squatted down in front of her, his face growing serious. "God, I'm going to miss you. Are you sure you won't change your mind and come to Sweden with me?"

"You know I can't do that." Fonda traced a finger down his shoulder to his hard bicep, still damp from the shower. "Much as I want to be with you. But America is my home, and I'm starting to work my way up at *Spotlight.* I just don't want to start over somewhere else."

"You know I'll give you a good position at *Pop Musikk.* You'll be able to work your way up there much quicker."

Fonda shook her head. "And have everyone say I got where I

was because we're sleeping together? I don't think so. No, Kari. I thought you'd accepted my decision."

"I have. But I keep hoping you'll change your mind. We have something good together, you and I."

"Yes, it's called friendship . . . combined with sexual attraction. But it's not enough." Fonda bit her lip, wishing he wouldn't do this. From the TV, Madonna's sweet little-girl voice sang "Like a Virgin."

"*Ja,* I know. But you can't blame me for trying." He stood up. "I'll go get dressed now."

On his way to the bedroom, Kari dropped the towel from his midsection. Fonda's eyes followed the line of his brawny shoulders to where his body narrowed at the small of his back. A strip of white revealed where the line of his surfer-style swim trunks had hugged his attractive rear. She shook her head, thinking she must truly be crazy to let a man like that go back to Sweden without her.

He disappeared into the bathroom. With a melancholy sigh, Fonda turned to the TV screen where Madonna was just finishing her set.

Kari was such a special guy. She wished she *were* in love with him. Only a year ago, they'd started out as boss and employee, the editor of *Spotlight* magazine and the newly hired staff writer, but their relationship had quickly developed into friendship. Then, five months later, after the annual Christmas party, they'd surprised themselves by becoming lovers and had been together ever since. But Fonda didn't kid herself. Even though they knew each other's bodies intimately, they were still more friends than lovers.

When the opportunity arose for the handsome Swede to return to his native country to start up the European version of the rock magazine he edited, he'd suddenly proclaimed himself in love with her. Fonda knew better. Oh, there was love of a sort between them, but it wasn't the all-encompassing kind. She'd seen that kind of love between her twin brother, Michael, and his wife, Maggie. It was out there. Question was, would she ever find it?

A commercial break gave Fonda the opportunity to get a Pepsi from the fridge. Her craving for caffeine hadn't been quenched by her morning coffee, but it was growing too hot in the small apartment to drink more. It looked like it would be another hot and humid New Jersey day.

When she returned to the small living room, she saw that the telecast had switched to the concert at Wembley Stadium in London. They were announcing a new Irish group called "O'Keefe." As the camera fixed upon the four members of the band, Fonda was immediately caught by their clean-cut look. Except for the drummer, who had shimmery shoulder-length blond hair, the other three guys wore their hair in neat graduated lengths, layered short on top and longer in the back. They were dressed conservatively in jeans, dark T-shirts, and boots. A far cry from some of the new metal groups today with their Spandex, chains, and leather.

As the lead singer began the first song, the camera focused on him, and Fonda was arrested by the gravelly quality of his voice and the wiry grace of his body as he moved about on stage. But it was his intense brown eyes that captured her and held her transfixed. What a stage presence he had! How come she'd never heard of these guys before?

"Kari, come here. You've got to see this."

"I'm shaving, babe," he called from the bathroom.

Fonda's eyes remained glued to the TV. "You ever heard of O'Keefe from Ireland?"

"They sound vaguely familiar." Kari's reply was muffled as if he'd buried his face in a towel. "I must've heard something."

"Come here and see this lead singer. He's great!"

There was a grunt from the bathroom, then, "I can hear them. They sound good."

"Yeah, but you've got to *see* them. This guy has the audience in the palm of his hand. I've never seen such charisma."

"I'll take your word for it. I'm late."

O'Keefe segued into a second song without acknowledging the enthusiastic applause from the first. Fonda found her foot bouncing to its thundering drumbeat. These guys were fantastic!

They had a sound that was definitely unique. Not an easy trick to accomplish these days.

O'Keefe's second song ended to even more tumultuous applause than the first. When the noise died a bit, the lead singer spoke into the mike: "This next song is called 'Belfast Girl.'"

O'Keefe began to play a slow ballad, a melody that had the unmistakable flavor of Celtic music. The love in his voice as he sang of his Belfast girl came through loud and clear.

Fonda felt another tide of melancholy rush over her. Was she the only person in the world who couldn't fall in love? What was *wrong* with her?

As O'Keefe's lead singer finished the lilting song about his Belfast girl, Fonda found herself envying this unknown woman across the ocean. Whoever she was, she was a very lucky lady. *What would it be like to have a man love you so much he immortalized that love in the lyrics of a song?*

Fonda sighed and slumped in her chair. That was something she'd probably never know.

"WELL, THAT'S it, then. Unless anyone has anything else?"

Kari closed his notebook and began to move his chair back to get up from the conference table.

"Uh . . . I have something I'd like to discuss," Fonda said.

Six pairs of eyes fastened upon her as if she were an anomaly of science. She felt her face redden. It wasn't easy being the lowest-ranking employee at the weekly editorial meeting. Most of the time, she just took her notes and remained silent. But today was different. Today, she had a great idea.

She kept her gaze fixed on Kari. "I'd like you to send me to Ireland to interview O'Keefe."

"O'Keefe?" said Adam Bragg, the art director. He was a tall, skinny chain-smoker with red hair and a beard. "What the hell is that?" he asked, his teeth clenched around a Camel.

Fonda resisted the urge to fan the smoke away from her direction. Instead, she spoke directly to Kari. "Remember the Irish group on Live Aid, Saturday? You came in just as they were finishing."

"Oh, *ja.*" Kari rubbed his chin thoughtfully, his blue eyes musing. "I don't know, Fonda. They're very obscure."

"So?" Fonda fired back. "The more reason to get an interview now. Before they get big. And believe me, they *will* get big."

Corey Newton, the executive editor, twisted the diamond stud in his left ear, his blue eyes bored. "Oh, well—if *Fonda* is so sure they'll be big, then we should go for it." He gave a little grin. "After all, she was right on the money with . . . what was the name of that three-man pretty-boy group last fall who lucked out with a Top Ten hit? What was it you said about them, Fonda? Something about America's version of the Bee Gees?"

Fonda smiled sweetly at him. *May your nose hairs grow and get tangled in your teeth, Newton.* She turned back to Kari. "Okay, so I was wrong about Question Mark. But this is different. Kari, I have a feeling about O'Keefe. There's something very different about the lead singer. He's arresting."

Corey cleared his throat and ran a manicured hand over his blond bristle. "A feeling? What *is* this feeling, Fonda? Woman's intuition?"

Fonda concentrated on counting to ten before responding. How on earth was she going to survive at this magazine when Corey Newton took over? He was such an insolent jerk. For a moment, she entertained the idea of actually going to Sweden with Kari. At least there, she'd have some input in the magazine's editorial content. Here, with Newton at the controls, she'd be lucky to be able to caption her own photos. Still, she knew she wouldn't go to Sweden. She loved the energy of working at an established music magazine. There were so many perks—the occasional trips to Los Angeles to interview famous faces, the excitement of living near New York, attending Broadway plays or simply gazing at the skyline outside her apartment window. No, she could never leave.

"Call it what you like, Corey. But remember this. I'd bet my career that within five years, O'Keefe will be superstars." Her eyes returned to Kari. "That's why I want to interview them now. So we can get the jump on everyone else."

Sheryl Mitchell, the associate editor, pushed her red-framed glasses up on her nose with an index finger and pursed her ruby lips. "You know, experts in L.A. are predicting the trend in rock is switching from Europe to America again. I think we should keep that in mind before we start saturating our pages with unknown Irish bands."

"I'm talking *one* interview," Fonda said through clenched teeth. "Not saturation."

Sheryl shrugged her elegant shoulders and returned to nibbling on the end of her pen.

"Well, perhaps we should table this for now," Kari said. "It's lunchtime. Thanks, everyone. You've been doing a great job."

Papers rustled and notebooks slammed shut. Conversation rose with a low murmur and swelled to a buzz as chairs were pushed back and the editorial staff filed out of the conference room. Fonda sat stiffly, staring down at her notebook where she'd printed in block letters: O'KEEFE. Damn! Why did they have to be so obstinate? *If this magazine were mine* . . . How many times had that thought passed through her mind? How many more times would it come before she got any respect?

A hand clamped down on her shoulder.

"I'm sorry, Fon. I know how disappointed you are."

She glared up into Kari's sympathetic blue eyes. "Thanks for your support. I hope you didn't *strain* anything."

He pulled out the chair next to her and sat down. "Love, I'm leaving in less than a month. It's not my magazine anymore. I'm a . . . what is it you call your president when another one has been elected and the first one no longer has any power?"

"A lame duck," she said glumly.

"*Ja.* That's what I am. Your fight is with Corey. And here's my advice. Keep fighting for what you want. Make yourself a presence here, be a thorn in his side if you have to. I guarantee you, if you keep turning in great copy and those extraordinary photos that scream out 'Fonda,' he'll have no choice but to go along with you. You just have to hang in there, babe. But of course, if you choose not to, there's always Sweden."

Fonda smiled and reached out to touch his bristled jaw. "You are such a wonderful man. Do you have any idea how much I'm going to miss you?"

He grabbed her hand and kissed each finger one by one. "*Ja,* I think so."

Fonda had to blink quickly to hold back sudden tears that threatened. Why was it that everyone important to her always had to leave? First Michael when he'd chosen to go to the police academy instead of accompanying her to college, and now Kari. Would anyone ever stay?

2

FONDA STOOD under the muted glow of the safe-light, and with a pair of tongs, pulled the contact sheet from the tray of fixing solution. A shiver of excitement zipped through her. Her fingers trembled slightly as she placed the sheet of mini-photos onto the viewing board above the tray of second hypo, the more potent fixing solution used in developing prints. She took a deep breath and reached above her to switch on the 150-watt viewing light positioned to where its glow centered directly on the contact sheet.

"Oh, yes, yes, *yes!*" She danced around the tiny darkroom, barely able to suppress a cheer of exhilaration. Her prints from the Jackson Browne concert were beyond her wildest expectations.

It was after two in the morning. She had to be in the office at eight-thirty, but at the moment, sleep was the last thing on her mind. There was no way she could've put off developing the contact sheets. With one glance, she could now examine the entire roll of film and choose the best from which she'd make prints. But how would she ever choose? They were great, all of them, the best concert footage she'd shot yet. She'd captured the vibrancy, the combustible energy of the night, from the frenzy of the crowd to the sweat pouring off Browne's face. It was all there, every nuance of his concert at the Meadowlands.

The shrill ring of the phone broke the silence. Fonda's heart jumped and began to race. She dried her hands on the towel tucked into the belt of her jeans. Phone call at two in the morning? Definitely one for the answering machine. But she'd better monitor it just in case it was some kind of emergency.

Fonda stepped into the bedroom and waited for the answering machine to pick up. After the fourth ring, the machine clicked and she heard her own voice.

"Hi. I'm not available to take your call right now. Please leave your name and phone number and I'll get back to you as soon as I can."

"Fonda? Pick up if you're there. It's important."

Her brow furrowed, and quickly, she grabbed the phone. "Dad? Is that you?" It sounded like him, yet his voice was choked and muffled. An icy hand of fear clutched her heart. "Dad, has something happened to Mom?" Her eyes darted to the fluorescent hands of the travel alarm on the table. It was just after one o'clock in the morning in Indiana. Way too late for a social call. Besides, Dad didn't make social calls.

"Fonny . . ."

Fonda felt the blood drain from her face. He hadn't called her that since she was a preschooler. Her hand tightened on the phone. She tried to speak, but her voice wouldn't come. *Oh, Mom. Don't be sick! Don't have cancer! Don't be . . .* She wouldn't allow herself to even think of it.

"It's . . . it's bad news, honey. You'd better come home. Michael . . ." His voice broke into sobs. Outside, an ambulance passed, its siren moaning as if in sympathy with her father's anguish.

Fonda sank to the bed. On the wall opposite her, a framed photo of John Fogerty, her first cover-shot for *Spotlight*, wavered in front of her eyes. *Not Michael. Dear God, not Michael.*

"He was on duty." Her father resumed control of his voice. "A drug stake-out on the Lower East Side."

Fonda managed to draw in a deep breath. *Okay. You can deal with this. Michael has been hurt, but he'll get through it.*

"He took a bullet, Fonny."

The light from the bedside table flickered, or so it seemed to Fonda. Her teeth clenched. *Steady, girl. He's been shot, but he's in the hospital. Probably in intensive care, but they'll take care of him there. It will be a long haul, and it won't be easy, but we'll all get through it.* She thought of Maggie, seven months pregnant. In her last letter, she'd been bubbling with talk of the nursery decor, breastfeeding, and layettes. *She* would be strong. Fonda would have to follow her example.

"Fonny, you're going to have to be brave, girl. Michael died on the operating-room table. They tried, but they couldn't bring him back."

His tinny voice floated across the wire, fading in and out like incoming waves of surf. Only bits and pieces registered in her brain.

Breakdown in the system . . . backup SWAT team delayed . . . trauma helicopter dispatched . . . massive blood loss . . . cardiac arrest during surgery . . . Maggie in premature labor under sedation in the same hospital where Michael died.

Her twin brother dead.

"The funeral service is set for Saturday." Her father went on, his voice flat, numbed. "Let me know when your flight gets in and I'll pick you up at the airport."

You can't do that, Fonda wanted to say. *Michael always picks me up.* She dropped the phone and began to sob.

"Michael—Michael—Michael—"

IT WAS cool for July, almost perfect football weather. The afternoon sun splashed a pool of dappled light onto the olive green carpet of the family room. The leaves on the oak tree outside the window played a shadow dance on the beige wall, quivering and shivering in the brisk wind. Except for the monotonous *tick-tock* of the grandfather clock in the corner, it was silent inside the house where Fonda grew up, but outside, the afternoon was rent by occasional firecracker pops from yesterday's Independence Day celebration. Fonda jumped each time one exploded nearby. The sound reminded her of gunfire.

Still dressed in the slim black dress she'd bought for Michael's funeral, she sat on the sofa and stared blankly out the window. She wished she could cry, but now, even that was impossible. Besides, she'd been crying almost continuously for the last three days and that had done nothing to dislodge the stone wall of pain that entombed her. It was still so hard to believe—even the sight of Michael's coffin being lowered into the freshly turned earth had a surreal quality about it. As she'd stood at the graveside, she couldn't shake the feeling of something left behind. She found herself searching for his face in the crowd, even though she knew it wouldn't be there. There were even times when she'd turn to speak to him, like the moment when she'd caught a glimpse of their eighth-grade English Lit. teacher. "Look, Mike, Mrs. Swanson!" Michael had always been a favorite of hers. On the other hand, Fonda had been the bane of her existence. A memory of a blackboard message flashed in her mind. "Mrs. Swanson wears falsies!" Fonda's handiwork.

You were the good twin, Michael. Why couldn't it have been me instead?

Poor Maggie. Still in the hospital under sedation, trying desperately to hold onto the only part of Michael she had left. Fonda had tried to pray for her, pray that the premature labor would stop. Maggie deserved that much, a healthy baby to give her reason to go on. But Fonda found she couldn't pray. For the first time in her life, she felt as if God weren't listening.

A rustle of movement came from the doorway behind her. She turned to see Jessie enter. Her younger sister's face was sheet-pale, yet her freckles glared like stars on a clear night. She'd changed from her somber gray dress back into shorts and a T-shirt. The shirt was emblazoned with the initials: ISPD. Fonda supposed it had been a gift from Michael. How could she wear it when it was the Indiana State Police Department that had brought about his death?

Jessie went directly to the TV and switched it on. "It's too damn quiet in here."

Fonda knew Jessie expected to be admonished for her language, but she couldn't summon the energy to do it. Jessie, at twelve, was shaping into a lovely young girl. Doted on by Mom and enjoying an easygoing relationship with Dad such as had been nonexistent for Fonda and Michael, Jessie was a bright, and for the most part, cheerful girl. But Michael's death had devastated her just as it had Fonda. His cruel murder had stolen her innocence; the world was no longer the safe place it had been. At the burial, she'd clung to Dad's hand as if it was a lifeline, staring down into Michael's grave, her eyes dark and wounded in her white heart-shaped face.

Dad. At the thought of him, Fonda allowed the anger to sweep over her yet again. It had been building in her since that horrible night of the phone call. Didn't anyone else feel it? When she looked at her parents, all she saw was grief. No anger on her mother's part. No guilt on her father's. Didn't they realize if it weren't for Dad's influence, Michael would be with them now?

Or was she the only one to see that?

Jessie sat down on the sofa next to her, closer than she normally would. Fonda put her arm around the shaken girl, wondering how she could possibly give comfort when she needed it so desperately herself. Michael had been the glue that had held their family together. Even the normally aloof Sandy had been devastated by his sudden death. In the first trimester of her third pregnancy, Fonda's older sister and her taciturn husband, Brian, had been the first to leave the graveside. Sandy's face had been an ashen shade of gray. Sandy, who'd never suffered morning sickness in the past, had been led away by Brian to lie down in the back of the station wagon until the nausea passed.

Fonda's eyes fastened on the TV. Something wasn't right. It took her fogged brain a moment to grasp it. Her hand tightened on Jessie's thin shoulder.

"You're watching CNN."

Jessie gave a slight shrug. Her eyes remained fixed upon the TV screen. "I don't care what's on. I just need to hear some voices."

Fonda nodded. Perhaps that was the secret. Listen to other voices so you could block out the ones inside your head. On the TV, a dapper man spoke in a cultured British accent.

"Yesterday's bombing in a Belfast department store has claimed another victim. Fourteen-year-old Laird Kingsley, who was pulled from the rubble in critical condition, died from his injuries in a Belfast hospital early this morning. Two suspects affiliated with the IRA are in custody. A third suspect died during the explosion when the bomb apparently detonated too early."

Jessie jumped up from the sofa and flew over to the TV. Violently, she jammed the channel selector to a higher number. The screen flickered and stopped on a heavy metal singer dressed in black leather and chains. He was screeching into a microphone at the top of his lungs. Jessie stood motionless, staring at the creature. Even from across the room, Fonda could see she was trembling.

"I'm so *sick* of hearing about death!"

Jessie adjusted the volume so the din from the heavy metal band was even louder.

"Jessie, come here."

White-faced, Jessie turned. Fonda patted the cushion of the sofa. "Come and sit down, hon."

With a stifled sob, Jessie flung herself onto the sofa. Fonda gathered her into her arms. She stroked Jessie's thick copper hair as the girl wept into her shoulder, soaking the black material of her dress with her tears. "*Why*, Fonda? Why did Michael have to die?"

"I don't know, love. It's something we can't understand. It doesn't feel like it right now, but we'll get through this. Michael would want us to be strong, you know."

Meaningless words, of course. But at the moment, it was the only comfort she could give. If she talked long enough, perhaps she could make *herself* understand why Michael had to die.

PART TWO

Devin

3

BRAM GRADEIGH stepped into the dingy mobile cabin that served as a dressing room and wiped a printed kerchief across his sweaty head. "Christ! It's so bloody crowded out there, there's not enough room for a louse to take a leak on a pinhead." Through the door he'd left ajar came the reverberating sound of Paul Young singing a duet with Alison Moyet on the Live Aid stage. "Bloody hot, too!"

Devin propped a booted foot onto a wobbly table and drummed his fingers nervously on his thigh. "Don't remind me about the crowd. I'm jittery enough as it is." He took a deep breath to calm his nerves, but all he inhaled was stale, stuffy air that reeked of human sweat, cigarette smoke, and the tepid piss the English called "beer."

Behind him, Caitlyn pressed reassuring fingers into his tense shoulders. "You'll do fine, love. This could be the break we've been waiting for. Once America catches sight of your live performance, they'll be under your spell just as all of Europe is."

A ripple of irritation ran through Devin. He loved Caitlyn dearly, but her constant preoccupation with the state of his career sometimes wore thin. "I don't friggin' *care* whether America sees me or not," he said. "What worries me is going on stage between the likes of Paul Young and Bryan Adams. Not to mention all the others. Phil Collins, Elton John. Christ! I saw Paul McCartney backstage having a chat with Pete Townshend. It scares the bejesus out of me to think O'Keefe is playing in the same league with bloody legends!"

"You're as good as any of them," Caitlyn said, her voice soothing. "Look at U2. I'll bet Bono isn't nervous about going up against the big wheels."

"For Christ's sake," Devin went on. "Even Prince Charles and Princess Di are out there. We'll be singing in front of bloody royalty!"

Her fingers bit into his flesh. "Who gives a shit about them?"

Seamus, O'Keefe's lead guitarist, stood up and began to pace the floor of the tiny room. "We're all jumpy, Dev. But just remember the cause. That's what's important. Some little Ethiopian child may live a few years longer because of what we're doing today."

Devin nodded, chastened for his pre-gig grousing. Seamus was right, of course. It didn't matter if O'Keefe went out there and fell on their collective faces. After all, the sound system during the Live Aid extravaganza was unpredictable; Bryan Ferry's vocals had been completely wiped out. What mattered in the end was the money that poured in for Ethiopian famine relief. For perhaps the hundredth time in this long, hot—by British standards—summer day, Devin felt his heart swell with pride at the realization that it was a fellow Irishman who'd organized this monster concert to help the starving. Bob Geldof, whom he'd met for the first time just this very morning, was truly a saint.

From the stage area, a roar drummed from the crowd. The entire stadium rocked with shouts, whoops, and whistles. Above the noise of the seventy-two thousand rock fans, a voice blared over the P.A. system, welcoming American audiences in Philadelphia via satellite transmittal. "Please, please give us as much money as we know you have!"

It was the Man. Geldof.

Bram stood up from where he'd perched on the edge of a worn sofa. "You're on next. Let's go."

Barry Pearse, who'd been calming his nerves by beating his drumsticks on the table, stood up with a thankful sigh and ran his hand through his long, silky blond hair. Liam, the bassist and least edgy of the four, gave an exaggerated yawn and grunted, "About fuckin' time!"

Devin glanced at his wristwatch and got to his feet. "Bram, what could be keeping Pat? He said he'd be here long before our set."

Bram shrugged. "Perhaps the flight from Dublin was delayed. Or for all we know, maybe something went wrong with Susan or the baby. God forbid, I hope that's not the case."

Just as their manager was due to join them in London the day before, his wife had gone into premature labor. Devin had received a frantic call from Pat at Rotunda Hospital, insisting that the band carry on with rehearsal; he'd catch up just as soon as he was reassured that Susan and the baby were okay. This morning, he'd called Wembley Stadium and after some delay, finally reached Devin to announce the arrival of Donald Lee Sullivan, all six pounds of him. Susan was fine, and so was the baby. Pat would be leaving on the next available flight to London. With any luck, he'd be there in time for their gig.

But now, it didn't look as if he'd make it. Foreboding filled Devin. It had been a long time since he'd performed without a manager around. And this was the biggest performance of his career. What if Pat's absence was a bad omen?

But there was no time to worry about that now. Devin and the other members of the band positioned themselves on one of the three revolving stages. Blood roared through his head. Or was that the sound of the crowd? Seventy-two thousand bodies out there! It was by far the largest crowd he'd ever played to, and face it, he was scared shitless. Every drop of saliva in his mouth had turned into Sahara sand. His skin was clammy, seesawing from hot to cold by the minute. Suddenly, he doubted his ability to deliver. *This is too soon,* Devin found himself thinking. *I'm not ready for this!*

But the stage was turning. The roar of the crowd grew louder. Seamus's guitar began the introductory riff of "Talk Is Cheap," the single just released from the new album, and there was no escape. For a millisecond, Devin stared out at the sea of faces, dumbstruck. He found himself thanking the Almighty that they'd chosen a song with a long intro. If he'd had to come out singing, he was sure the sight of the massive crowd would've blanked him right out.

Those few extra seconds were exactly what he needed. As his customary stage confidence took over, he unhooked the mike from the stand and jauntily moved to the end of the stage. "Hello! We're O'Keefe and we're here from Dublin!" The crowd roared. Devin whirled around to face the band and launched into the song, a scathing condemnation of politicians and their double-talk. He strutted back and forth on the stage and then joined Seamus for the harmony of the chorus.

Earlier, when Devin discovered each act had been allotted only fifteen minutes on stage, it had seemed like an eternity to him. Now, it hardly seemed enough. The muggy afternoon heat and the stage lights combined to draw the perspiration from his body. It streamed down his face and neck, soaking through his black sleeveless T-shirt within minutes. Out beyond the stadium, the sky had darkened and thunder rumbled ominously in the distance. But even the danger of electrocution didn't dampen Devin's enthusiasm. He grinned at Seamus as the song wound down. The guitarist smiled back cautiously.

They both knew they were in the middle of something special, something that may or may not ever happen to them again. But at the moment, it didn't matter if it was a once-in-a-lifetime thing. It was happening now, and it was enough.

Throughout the song, the crowd cheered boisterously, and Devin responded to it with everything he had. His heart brimmed with excitement, with love for these people who loved him. For the first time, he understood all the rock singers who stood on the stage and screamed into the mike those oh so pat exclamations of "You're beautiful! I love you!" He wanted to scream it out too, but couldn't, because they wouldn't believe he meant it. Wouldn't believe that he *felt* it through every pulsing artery in his body!

O'Keefe launched into "Hit and Run," the biggest hit from *Winter Rain*. The noise of the crowd intensified. At one point, Devin, at the end of the stage, held the mike toward the audience and stopped singing. Thousands of voices sang the chorus from beginning to end. A thrill of sheer intoxication went through him. At that moment, it struck him that there could be no greater measure of success than to have words he'd written himself sung by the crowd—especially a crowd such as this that had gathered to see some of the top names in the rock music business.

As "Hit and Run" ended, Bram rushed onto the stage with Devin's guitar. Devin nodded his thanks and adjusted the strap over his shoulder. Seamus went to the keyboard and began the intro of "Belfast Girl." Caitlyn's song. It was the title cut on the new album, and would be the first single released. Just the week before, O'Keefe had wrapped up the video filming for the song in front of Belfast's "peace wall." Pat was convinced this was the single that would break O'Keefe into the American Top Forty.

"Belfast girl, defiant and proud . . ." Devin's eyes searched the stage wings for Caitlyn, but he couldn't see her anywhere. He felt a pang of disappointment. With typical Irish superstition, he wondered if the song was bad luck. But then the intensity of the chorus took over, and he forgot everything except the crowd, the cause, and the beauty of the melody.

It was over too soon. Obviously, Devin wasn't alone in this thought. The crowd howled with disappointment as the stage began to revolve, but when they saw the next performer was Bryan Adams, a roar of approval reverberated throughout the stadium. Sweat poured off his face as Devin stepped off the platform backstage and handed his guitar to a grinning Bram.

"Man, ya outdid yourself out there, ya did!" His roadie gave him a one-arm hug and pulled away, his adam's apple bobbing with emotion. If Devin didn't know better, he'd swear the big man was going to start blubbering. "Just promise me one thing, Dev. When you become a big superstar, you'll take me along with you."

"It's a promise, Bram, lad. If it weren't for you, I would never have experienced that out there." Some of the exalted feeling he'd had out on stage was still with him. He wanted to share it with Caitlyn. Where was she?

"Uh—Dev?" Bram nodded to the shadows behind him. "There's someone here who's wanting to have a word with you."

A figure came toward him. She was vaguely familiar, but it wasn't until she spoke that he realized who she was. "Mother Mary! I'm so proud of you, Devin O'Keefe, I can barely see straight!"

Arms squeezed his waist and a brown head with sun-lightened blond streaks burrowed against his chest. The scent of a light citrus perfume surrounded him. Devin's jaw dropped. It took him a moment to find his voice. "Christ! Is that you, Bonnie? Stand back and let me look at you, lass." His eyes scanned her trim body from top to bottom. For sure, it was his sister, but then, again, it wasn't the sister he'd always known.

Bonnie was dressed in a fashionable short denim skirt and a red T-shirt. Her lank brown hair had been streaked and cut into a sleek bob that emphasized her clear hazel eyes. And wonder of wonders, she was wearing a bit of makeup! By no means had Bonnie blossomed into a beauty, but she was no longer plain. Not only that, she looked happy. That pinched, hopeless look, a trademark of life in the Bogside, was gone. Could Belfast be that much better?

He shook his head, amazed at the change. "Sure, but you look pretty, love. What ha . . ." He stopped himself in time. It wouldn't do to get her ire up.

But she laughed. "*Molly* happened to me, don't you know? For a thirteen-year-old, our wee sister is quite an expert on makeup and the like."

Devin looked from her to Bram. "You had something to do with this, didn't you? Her being here, I mean."

"Bloody right," Bonnie said, her eyes dancing. "This no-good, blarney-mouthed roadie of yours arranged it. Practically kidnapped me, he did!"

Devin stared at her. She was downright vivacious. What had happened to bring about this great change? Then it hit him. A beau. Bonnie had a beau. What else would bring the sparkle to her eyes or the color to her cheeks? It really *was* a day for surprises. Later, perhaps, he'd be able to find out who the poor slob was. Question was, did the young man know what he was in for?

Bram grinned at Devin. The color was high on his abashed face. "Well, I thought it was about bloody time your little sister saw what a big star you're going to be. Of course, she gave me some bullshit about having to study, but I convinced her to see my side of things."

Bonnie gave him a sharp elbow in the ribs. "Bloody liar! Why don't you tell him how you threatened to burn my books if I didn't come? It was coercion, it was. Pure and simple."

Devin couldn't stop gaping at the two of them. When had they become such mates? Sure, Bram went up to Belfast every so often, and come to think of it, had mentioned "running into your sis" now and then. Could it be that Bram was the reason for the sparkle in Bonnie's eyes? Jesus, he hoped not. Poor Bon didn't come close to being Bram's type. Sure, she'd end up with a broken heart for her trouble.

"Devin, love," Caitlyn appeared at his side and slipped an arm around his waist, eyeing Bonnie curiously. "You were wonderful out there."

Devin pulled her closer. "Ah, Caty! I was wondering where you'd got to. Meet my sister, Bonnie. Bram hauled her over from Belfast. She's a student at Queen's, too."

"Yes, I know. You've told me." She smiled at Bonnie. "I was wondering when we'd get to meet. You'd think living in the same city, we'd have done so before now, wouldn't you?"

Bonnie gave Caitlyn a direct appraisal. Her expression told Devin that although her appearance may have changed, her personality hadn't. She shook Caitlyn's outstretched hand, her hazel eyes cool. "I guess you could say we run in different circles. We haven't met, but I've heard about you."

Caitlyn stiffened. "Oh? And what is it you've heard?"

Bonnie didn't back down. "That you're an outspoken Fenian folk singer, for one thing. Your songs of insurrection seem to be quite popular in some sections of Belfast. And I don't mind telling you I believe it's old traditions like that that keep the Troubles alive in the North."

Devin placed a hand on Bonnie's arm. "Settle down, Bon. Just because Caitlyn sings Republican songs doesn't mean she's ready to take up arms, right, love?"

For a split second, Devin saw the flash of anger in Caitlyn's blue eyes, but she covered it so quickly with a smile that he thought he'd probably imagined it. "Yeh, can you see *me* with a AK-47? No, Bonnie, I'm not going to take up arms. But we all fight in our own way, you know? I don't deny that I want to see the Brits out of Ireland. And I see nothing wrong with singing songs of our heritage to get my point across. Surely, you're not saying I don't have that right?"

Bonnie's thrusting jaw and the steely look in her eyes made it clear exactly what she thought about Caitlyn and her question-able choice of folk songs. Just as Devin was about to suggest they go find a quiet spot so the two of them could get to know each other, Bram was summoned by a harried crewman to pick up the phone in the stadium office for an emergency phone call from Dublin.

Leaving the girls on their own, Bram and Devin waded through the backstage throng to get to the office. At the word "emer-gency," Devin's stomach had tightened with tension. Was it Susan, or the premature baby? The wee one, most likely. Had his health gone downhill, then? If so, how on earth were they going to get in touch with Pat? They'd have to try paging him at Heathrow. Poor man. He'd have to turn right around and head back to Dublin.

Devin stood in the doorway of the office and waited as Bram took the phone call. One of the young secretaries looked up from her desk and beamed at Devin. "I caught a glimpse of your performance. It was lovely!"

"Thanks." He managed to smile back at her. "It was quite an experience." Anxiously, his eyes moved back to Bram. His heart gave a jolt.

The man's face was sheet white as he listened to the voice on the other end of the line. Finally, he swallowed hard and mut-tered, "Christ! It's that bad?"

Devin moved across the room to him. "What is it, Bram?"

He shook his sandy head, his eyes wide with shock. "Yeh, right. You arrange the details and we'll get to the airport straight-away. Thanks for calling, Diane. Stop crying, love. It won't do to make yourself sick. Tell him"—his voice caught with emotion—"tell him to hang in there. Okay. We'll see you soon."

Slowly, he hung up the phone. Devin waited, his heart in his throat. Christ, why *now*, when everything was going so well? Poor Pat! He'd been so excited about the baby. Why did tragedy have to strike when you were so fucking unprepared?

"It's Pat," Bram said. "A drunk driver ran him off the highway on the way to Dublin Airport. He's been taken to Mater Hospital." His hand was trembling as it reached out to clasp Devin's. "Devin—he might not make it."

4

April 1986
Dublin

DEVIN HAD just taken a bite of the birthday cake Caitlyn had made for him when she asked him a question that nearly made him choke on it.

"Do you still want to marry me?"

The first time Devin had proposed to Caitlyn had been on Christmas Eve 1984, one year after they'd met. She'd refused. Why change things? she'd asked. He'd proposed again just after Live Aid, and again, she'd turned him down. He couldn't understand it. She loved him. He knew it. Her reason had been that their lives were too different. She was just beginning her last year of pre-med at Queen's. In the fall of '86, she would start medical school at George Washington University. It was a long way from Dublin to Washington, D.C. And she couldn't give up medical school, not even for him.

On one hand, Devin had understood her reasoning. Yes, medical school was important. But why did it have to be America? Why not Dublin, or even London? If she really loved him, how could she go so far away? He wanted a wife and wee ones. And he didn't want to wait another eight years. Christ, he'd be thirty-two. An old man, for God's sake!

Now he stared at her, wondering if he were hallucinating.

She smiled, her blue eyes glowing. "I mean it, Devin. I've been doing a lot of thinking lately about going to medical school here in Dublin. And"—her hand covered his as her smile widened—

"if we do it soon, I can go on your American tour with you. It'll be entirely proper then."

He grinned at her, unable to believe she really wanted to marry him. "Proper? Since when do you care about propriety? Come here, woman."

Laughing, she dropped onto his lap, her mouth opening invitingly for his lusty kiss. "Mmmm." She pulled away, licking her lips greedily. "That's not bad cake. And you thought I couldn't bake!"

Devin gazed into her eyes. "Do you mean it, lass? You're ready to make it official?"

"That I am." She smiled back at him. Her slightly crooked mouth gave her a smile that appeared a half-pout. It was a smile that drove him crazy.

"God, I love you." He bent to kiss her again.

"Wait!" She reached over to his birthday cake and ran her index finger across the top of the icing. Then, grinning, she smoothed the soft white cream over his lips. "Now."

Giggling, they shared a long slurping kiss as their sugared tongues mingled. Devin's fingers moved to undo the snaps on her skimpy tank top. He slid his hand into the opening to curl around the tip of a bare warm breast. It seemed to leap against his touch. For a heady moment, he visualized a wee *wain* nuzzling there. Christ! He could hardly wait to see Caty heavy with his child.

Deliberately, Devin reached toward the cake and scooped a mound of icing onto his finger. Caitlyn watched him, shaking her dark head and laughing. "Devin! Don't you dare, man."

With a wicked grin, he proceeded to draw a line of icing down Caitlyn's neck and onto the swell of her left breast. She squirmed on his lap, her firm bottom pressing intimately against his stiffening penis as his tongue trailed down the avenue of icing he'd traced upon her creamy skin. Mother Mary, the woman never failed to ignite him.

The phone rang. For a moment, he continued his slow, sweet journey to the crest of her nipple, ignoring the intrusion. After three rings, Caitlyn pulled away and scrambled off his lap.

"Make it fast," he rasped, uncomfortably aware of the tightness of his jeans in the crotch area.

Caitlyn answered the phone, and her smile vanished. She held the phone out to Devin. "It's Susan."

Devin got up from the table, wondering why Caitlyn seemed to dislike Pat's wife so much. She was a lovely woman. And little Donny was a delight. The last time Devin had stopped by their home in Dalkey, the *wain* had been crawling all over the place.

"Hullo, Susan. How's everything? That's grand. You *deserve* a rise, don't you? I hear working for old man Stuart isn't a bowl of Cheerios. And Donny?" He nodded his head and laughed. "Did he, now? Took his first step without his old uncle Devin around to see him?" His smile dimmed. "Pat? How's he doing? Yeh, I know it's hard for him being in that wheelchair. Such a ball of energy he was before . . ." His voice trailed off.

As always, the unfairness of Pat's situation made him want to howl with anger. But it hadn't done any good last summer. The drunk driver had never been caught. He'd gone on his merry way after destroying a man's life, perhaps not even aware he'd done it.

Devin dragged his attention back to Susan's cheerful voice. What a woman she was. It had been her strength that had brought Pat back to the land of the living when he'd wanted to give up.

"Yeh, so it is! I'm an old man of twenty-four today. You should see the cake Caty made me. Well, you *should* have seen it. We've quite destroyed it now." He smiled across the room at Caitlyn. She shrugged and began to clear the table. His eyes centered on the open flap of her top where he could just see her luscious cleavage. It reminded him that he'd wanted to keep the phone call short. But then, Susan brought up the money.

He listened as she went through her speech. It was one he'd heard before. Finally, her voice faltered. "Listen, love," Devin said. "We've discussed this before. It's something I want to do. It's the *least* I can do to repay Pat for everything he's done for me."

The rattle of pots and pans drew his eyes to Caitlyn. She was at the sink, filling it with water for the dirty dishes. "Don't you see, girl, I love Pat. I love you and Donny, too. I want to help take care of him. Let me do this, okay? Please?" He listened and finally smiled. "Okay. And let's not have this conversation again, you hear? Yeh, tell him I'll stop by in a day or so. Did he say what he thought about the new single? Yeh, we're all set for early June. Our first date is at the Meadowlands in New Jersey. Don't make me think about it. I'll piss me pants! Okay, Susan. 'Bye, love."

He hung up the phone and turned to Caitlyn. Her back was to him. He couldn't help but notice the inordinate amount of noise she was making as she washed the dishes.

"Okay, Caty. Let's get it over with."

Her jaw was clenched, her movements jerky. "You know how I feel. Susan is right. There's no need for you to send her a check every month. Don't you see, Devin, you're taking away from Pat's manliness?"

"I don't see it that way at all," Devin said shortly. "I owe him, Caitlyn. As long as I have the cash to help him and his family out, I will."

She methodically dried her hands on a dish towel and turned around, eyes glittering with anger. "Owe him? What did he do for you? Oh, sure, he got you started. But it's no thanks to him your second album is selling like ice cream in July in Britain. It's no thanks to him that 'Belfast Girl' is climbing the charts in America. Jesus, Devin! It's no thanks to him you're going on your first concert tour of America in two months!"

Devin stared at her, waiting for her to finish.

She gazed back defiantly. "All I can say is, it's a bloody good thing that when Pat had his accident, Ian Brinegar was waiting in the wings. Sure, it's him you should be thanking. He's going to make you a superstar, Devin. And I know it's a cruel thing to say, but if it weren't for Pat's tragic accident, you wouldn't be where you are today. You won't admit it, but deep down in your heart, you know that, don't you?"

When he didn't answer, she went on, a cool look of triumph on her beautiful face.

"Ah, you can't admit it out loud, can you? But you believe it. I know you do. Why else do you insist on sending that woman a big check every month? It's your guilt talking, Devin. You know

Pat Sullivan would've kept you in the backwaters forever." She paused, and then said the one thing Devin had been pushing to the back of his mind for the last year. "You feel guilty because you know his accident was the best thing that could've happened to you."

5

IAN BRINEGAR was as unlike Pat Sullivan as a man could be. Where Pat had been warm and emotional, Ian was reserved and undemonstrative. Pat, a born and bred Dubliner, was Irish to the core. Ian, although a Derryman, seemed more British than the Brits, most likely because of his education at Queen's and subsequent move to London, where he'd been living for the past twenty years.

When Devin made his decision to hire Ian to take Pat's place, he'd done so with more than a few reservations. Brinegar, despite what Caitlyn said about him being a good Irishman, was an inapproachable man, not one who inspired the kind of close relationship Devin envisioned should be between a musician and his manager. But he soon discovered that whatever Ian Brinegar lacked in charisma, he made up for with his canny business insight.

Within two months of his taking over, "Talk Is Cheap" hit number one, not only on the British charts but also in West Germany, Sweden, Norway, and Holland, thanks to Ian's heavy-handed promotion of O'Keefe through every major radio market in Europe. Then, while the song was still hot, he organized a whirlwind mini-tour of major European cities that resulted in record sales soaring into the stratosphere. The simultaneous release of "Belfast Girl" as a single and on video only reinforced the huge "overnight" success of O'Keefe.

Europe was conquered. Instead of basking in the glow of success, Ian set his sights on making Devin and O'Keefe a superstar. There was only one way to do that: America.

THE WEDDING date was set for June 18, just a week after Caitlyn graduated from Queen's. She and Devin would honeymoon for four days on the coast of Brittany before flying back to Dublin to meet Ian and the band for the long flight to New York.

The plans were finalized. To the delight of Caitlyn's ailing mother, they'd decided on a quiet mass in her Falls Road parish. Of course, Molly and Bonnie would be there as well. So would Auntie Sinead. Devin had asked Bram to be his best man, and although he'd accepted, it had not been with the degree of enthusiasm Devin had expected. Devin just couldn't figure it. It was as if Bram had developed a sudden dislike for Caitlyn in the past months. But why? Sure, since her arrival into Devin's life there had been less time for him and Bram to get together like they used to, but that was nothing new. Could it be that the whole thing was his imagination?

On a Friday night in late May, the first one in weeks that a gig hadn't been scheduled, the opportunity came for Devin to find out what was behind Bram's coolness.

Caitlyn had arrived from Belfast just before dinner. Exhausted from a full day of exams, she'd immediately fallen asleep on the sofa while watching the telly, too tired to eat the bit of tea Devin had prepared for her. He left the tray of food cooling on the coffee table and settled himself into a corner chair with the Belfast newspaper she'd brought down. He'd left the television on, afraid the sudden cessation of sound might wake her. Poor lass. She'd had a bloody tough week. Just as he was reading about the latest series of bombings in the North, a knock came at the front door.

"Surprise!" Bram leaned against the doorway, grinning. "Just who you were hoping to see tonight, right, mate?"

Devin scratched his head thoughtfully. "Well, as a matter of fact . . ."

"Don't worry," Bram stepped into the flat, "I won't stay long. But I promised to get you to autograph a couple of copies of 'Belfast Girl' for my nieces. I'm heading to Galway tomorrow to see the family."

"Well, if you'd give me a chance to get a word in edgewise, I was going to tell you I'd welcome a chat with you, Bram." With a nudge of his head, Devin headed toward the kitchen. "We haven't had too much time to do that lately, have we?" He hit the switch for the kitchen light. "Sit yourself down. I'll pour us a pint."

Devin pulled two bottles of Guinness from the refrigerator and sat down at the kitchen table across from Bram. Silently, they emptied the foamy dark liquid into glasses. From the living room, the drone of a crime drama came from the TV. "Caty's dead to the world in there. Taking exams all day, poor lass." Devin took a long draw from his beer, wondering how to put his worries into words.

After a thirsty gulp, Bram set his glass down and grinned. "Did I tell you Bonnie is coming down in the morning to take the drive to Galway with me?"

Devin stared at him. "No! You forgot to mention that."

"Yes, she mentioned she'd never seen the west coast. Can you believe that, man? What did you do, lock your sisters up in the closet or something?"

Devin's muscles tensed. "There wasn't much opportunity for holiday travel in Derry."

"Sorry. That was bloody stupid."

"Don't worry about it. It's hard for someone like yourself to understand what it was like living there." Devin grew silent. Bram's revelation about Bonnie brought new problems to mind. "Bram, I don't mean to play the part of the overprotective brother or anything, but—just what's going on between you and my sister?"

Bram met his eyes. "We're friends, that's all. We enjoy each other's company." He gave a short laugh, his eyes twinkling. "I know. We're like oil and water, but Christ, Devin, I'd rather spar with that woman than screw a whole dorm of blond beauties. Go figure!"

Devin smiled. He drummed his fingers on the tabletop, his face sobering. "Just don't hurt her, Bram. That's all I ask. If friendship is all there can ever be between the two of you, tell her that up front."

Bram's face was solemn. "She knows that, Devin. Sure, she does."

One Guinness turned into another. They were on their third before Devin brought up Caitlyn. Almost immediately, he sensed the lines of communication closing between them. Bram's facial muscles tensed and he drew back from the table slightly, as if ready to offer an excuse to leave.

"It's not that I'm unenthusiastic about your marrying Caitlyn, Devin." Bram glanced at his wristwatch, obviously feeling as if the conversation had taken a downside. "Sure, it's just that I hate to see any of my mates take the irreparable step into matrimony." He gave an easy grin. "It's against me religion."

Devin laughed. "Another one bites the dust, huh?"

A crash came from the living room. Devin felt the blood drain from his face. Visions of Derry swept through his mind. Of firebombs thrown through the front window of Catholic homes in Protestant neighborhoods, families screaming in horror as their dwellings became infernos. He'd seen it all before. Was it now happening in Dublin?

He reached the living room first, with Bram just behind him. Caitlyn stood in front of the sofa, her face the color of gray putty as she stared at the TV. In front of her on the parquet floor lay the fragments of a shattered tumbler.

Devin took a step toward her. "Caty, what is it?"

She didn't answer. Her eyes were glued to the TV screen. It showed a newscast of some kind, a burning building. An upperclass British voice narrated the newscast: "Sources state it is likely the IRA terrorists killed by the SAS today were responsible for the bombing of the UDR police barracks in Armagh last summer." Mug shots of two men appeared on the screen. "Bobby O'Casey, age forty-four, was a known IRA terrorist, having served more than fourteen years at Long Kesh. He was released only a few months before the Armagh bombing. His accomplice, twenty-three-year-old Sean MacManus, was skilled in bombing devices, and may have been responsible for as many as sixteen attacks against British facilities in the last three years. The two men were shot today in London as they prepared to engineer a terrorist attack in the vicinity of 10 Downing Street."

The newscast moved on to the weather. Slowly, Caitlyn sank to the sofa. She still hadn't regained her color. Devin sat down beside her and placed an arm about her trembling shoulders.

"Caty?"

She looked at him. Her eyes were old beyond years. It sent a chill through Devin. "Did you see what they've done now?" Her voice was dry and raspy.

Bram went to the bar and splashed a finger of whiskey into a tumbler. He handed it to Devin. Silently, Devin passed it over to Caitlyn; she swallowed it in a thirsty gulp. Then she held the tumbler in her hands loosely, staring down into the crystal.

"They were unarmed, and the Brits shot them dead like they were nothing!"

Bram, on the other side of Caitlyn, met Devin's eyes and jerked his head toward the bedroom. Devin nodded. "Come on, love. Let me put you to bed."

She yanked her elbow away and stood up. "No! I need another drink." She crossed to the bar and filled the tumbler half-full of whiskey.

Devin protested, "Caty, you haven't had any tea. You'll make yourself sick."

She took a sip of whiskey, her eyes glittering angrily over the top of the tumbler. "What now, man? Do you think because we're getting married, that gives you the right to regulate my drinking habits? This isn't the Dark Ages, you know. Irish women have equal rights now." Her eyes moved to the TV, where a weatherman warned about a squall of thunderstorms moving in from the west. "Equal rights for all Irishmen. That's the ticket! Unless, of course, you happen to be Catholic and you live in the North. There, the only equal rights you get is a 'fuck you' and a bullet in the back!"

Bram took a step toward her. "Caitlyn, why don't you just call it a night. You're tired and upset—"

"Bloody right, I'm upset!" She pointed a trembling finger at the TV screen. Her face crumbled. "You saw it. They *killed* him, Bram. They killed my baby brother!"

6

"DID YOU know, Bram?"

Dry-mouthed, Devin stared at his roadie, waiting for an answer to his question.

Caitlyn slammed the whiskey tumbler down on the bar. "Of course he didn't know! You don't exactly advertise it when your brother . . ." She choked on the words.

"Is a terrorist," Devin finished the sentence for her.

She began to sob. Bram threw him a fearsome look. "Jesus, Devin. Can't you see how upset the girl is?"

Devin saw. As soon as he'd uttered the words, he'd felt ashamed. What was he doing standing here feeling betrayed when the woman he loved was heartbroken? He moved to her and took her into his arms. She cried into his neck, her tears wetting his skin.

"He was just a baby, Devin," she sobbed. "A baby."

Yeah, a baby who built bombs to kill others. Devin shook his head, his hand stroking Caitlyn's silky black hair. He had to stop this. Over her head, his eyes sought Bram's.

He had been the one to bring Caitlyn into Devin's life. Had he known there was a younger brother involved with the IRA? And if Bram had told him, would that have stopped Devin from becoming involved with her? He'd wanted nothing of this world, this violence he'd escaped by sheer force of will. But dear God, he loved Caitlyn! Could she help it if her brother hadn't been strong enough to resist the hypnotizing pull of bitterness and hatred around him? And wasn't it impossible for her to stop loving him just because he'd followed that road of self-destruction?

"I'd best be going," Bram said. "Have an early day tomorrow." He walked over to Caitlyn and placed a hand on her trembling shoulder. "I'm truly sorry, Caty."

When she didn't respond, he looked at Devin. "Perhaps a cup of tea." He turned away. "I'll give Bonnie your love."

When Bram was gone, Devin led Caitlyn into the bedroom. "You're shivering, love. Let's get you into bed." She didn't protest as he pulled back the covers and guided her into bed. He pulled the blanket up around her shoulders. She stared up at him, her lovely blue eyes luminous with tears, but Devin knew it wasn't himself she was seeing.

"Sean," she whispered. "Oh, Sean. I knew this was going to happen to you. I knew it."

Devin gazed down at her, his heart breaking for her pain. It was almost as if he were reliving that horrible day in Derry when Glen had gone down in a hail of British bullets. He touched her shoulder gently. "I'm going to put on some tea. You should try and eat something. Can you think of anything I can make for you?"

Silently, she shook her head, the tears trickling out of the corner of her eyes and moistening her hair. Devin bent down and kissed her forehead lightly. "I won't be long, love. You rest. And after you drink your tea, we'll talk. You can tell me all about Sean."

THE ROOM was lit only by a flickering candle. It cast a soft light on Caitlyn's flawless oval face. Her eyes were like dark pools, haunted with sorrow and memories of an earlier time.

"It was a game to me at first." Her voice was soft and husky. "I was part of the 'Bin Can Brigade.' It was always more *craic* than serious. As soon as the barricades went up, we knew it meant a night of staying out harassing the peelers. Oh, how they loved to terrorize us, with their bloody armored pigs." She gave a short bitter laugh. "But the thing was, the RUC didn't terrorize us. *They* were afraid of *us!* Yeh, they had the protection, the tanks, the gas masks, the rifles and rubber bullets, but they were afraid of us because they knew they were the guilty party. They were the invaders, and they knew we'd fight to the death for what was ours." She paused, taking a sip of tea.

Devin lay on his side, his head propped up by a hand while the other lay on Caitlyn's thigh. He needed that touch, the physical connection with her, not only to let her know how much he cared but for himself as well. The night's events had awakened a sense of foreboding in him. Once again, the strife of Northern Ireland had invaded his life and his peace of mind.

"I didn't realize how serious our situation was until my older brother, Brendan, came home one afternoon, all bloody and bruised from a run-in he'd had with three Protestant boys. They'd been waiting for him along the route he took home from school. While they were busy beating him to a pulp, a UDR man arrived. To help, Brendan thought."

Ulster Defense Regiment. Volunteers made up from the toughest, anti-Catholic British soldiers. There it was again. Caitlyn's bitter laugh. Devin moved his hand from her thigh to reach for his teacup. He took a sip and waited for her to go on.

"Some help! The Prods ran off and the UDR man took over 'teaching the R.C. a lesson.' It was at that moment I realized we were truly alone. The Brits weren't here to protect us against the Prods' sectarian violence. They hated us every bit as much. Of course, I'd known that all along. It just hadn't really hit me until then. The next day, Brendan and I joined *Na Fianna*."

Devin's heart gave a lurch. Christ! The Junior IRA. He placed his teacup on the nightstand, a sour taste in his mouth. His hand dropped back to her smooth thigh as she continued her story.

"It was the usual thing, you know. Acid bombs and eventually, petrol bombs. I was consumed by *Na Fianna*. You see, it was the only way I could release my anger at our oppression, at the poverty we suffered every day on Falls Road." Her voice lowered, became huskier than usual. "When I was fifteen, I fell in love. His name was Skelly Houlihan and he'd just moved to Belfast from

County Down to live with his aunt. His parents had died when the UVF threw a firebomb into their house in a mixed neighborhood. Apparently, the Prod paramilitaries had been trying to get them out for the last year, but Skelly's da wasn't about to be intimidated." Her lips twisted in a sardonic smile; her eyes were cold. "Well, they finally succeeded. If Skelly hadn't gotten sloshed and spent the night with a mate, he would've died, too." She closed her eyes, expelling her breath in a long shuddering sigh. "I'd never met a boy like Skelly before. He was so—dedicated. Strong and fearful of nothing. He was the youngest man in the Provo ranks, only twenty-one."

Devin's hand left Caitlyn's thigh and fell to the bed between them. His eyes fastened onto the crucifix on the wall next to the bed. Outside the curtained window, a hard rain beat against the glass. Tomorrow would be an ugly, dark day.

"I lost my virginity to Skelly." Her hands were curled around the cold teacup, her eyes miles away. "I would've died for him. We'd been together only a few months when he was captured during an operation and sent to Long Kesh. It wasn't a good time to be there. You remember why." She paused, as if waiting for a response, but when he remained silent, she went on. "It was just after the Brits changed the rules on us. We were no longer considered political prisoners. No, we were simply criminals. And treated as such. You know what's coming, don't you, Devin? The Hunger Strike. Bobby Sands. Yes, Skelly died just a few days after Bobby. Insiders told me later that he looked like a living skeleton in the days before he died." She heaved a deep sigh and then said quietly, "After I heard about Skelly, I went active. I was sixteen."

Devin rolled over onto his back and closed his eyes. A brief flash of lightning lit the shadowed room. Thunder rumbled. Her voice flowed over him, at times coming to him from a great distance, or so it seemed. Still, he heard every nightmarish word. He couldn't escape hearing, much as he wanted to. Even the harsh drum of rain on the roof couldn't drown out her voice.

"At first, it was simple stuff. Courier service, arranging safehouses, dropping off supplies. The summer before I started at

Queen's, my responsibilities became more important. There's no need to go into it. Let's just say the organization's leaders were gaining respect for me. It was just as I started my first semester at Queen's that Brendan was murdered. Shot dead outside our home by two UVF members. There were twelve bullet holes in his body. Because of that, Sean went active. He was only fifteen." Her voice broke. She began to cry softly.

Devin lay stiffly. He couldn't have moved even if the bed had suddenly burst into flames. He felt empty, a hollowed-out gourd. After a few moments, Caitlyn's weeping softened. Devin could feel her eyes upon him. Still, he couldn't move. There was no way on God's green earth he could look at her. Not now. Maybe not ever again.

"Devin?"

There was a rustle of the bed sheets and he felt her roll toward him. The sweet womanly scent of her invaded his nostrils. His flesh crawled. If she touched him, he was afraid of what he might do. *Don't do it, Caitlyn, if you know me at all, don't touch me.*

She didn't, but he could sense her need to be held. The realization moved nothing in him. "Say something, Devin. Tell me you understand."

"You lied to me." His voice was soft, hollow.

She didn't answer immediately. Then, "What do you mean?"

"In the beginning. After Bonnie confronted you about your political leanings. You said you weren't involved with the IRA. Because you knew how I felt about it."

"You didn't ask, did you?" Her tone was lightly mocking. "You didn't want to know, so I didn't tell you. But Devin, surely you understand what's at stake here. Don't you see? We have to fight. It's the only way we'll get back our country. We have to hit them hard, kill if we have to. The Brits *and* Prods who oppose us." A crash of furious thunder emphasized her words.

Devin rolled off the side of the bed and stood up. He'd reached the bedroom door before she spoke again, stopping him cold.

"We could use someone like you in the Cause, Devin. You grew up in Derry. You know what it's like. Now that you've made it out, you *owe* it to the ones left behind. You're in a position not only to supply the capital, but to recruit others. You're a natural leader." When he still didn't speak, she went on quietly, "You've waited a long time to take your revenge for Glen's murder, haven't you?"

Slowly, Devin turned and forced himself to look at her. She sat cross-legged on the bed, the candlelight spilling around her, illuminating her porcelain skin. Her shiny black hair fell to her creamy shoulders and onto the eyelet trim of her cotton nightgown. She was more beautiful than he'd ever seen her. Even the tears she'd shed in the last hours had done nothing to mar her lovely face. But it wasn't Caitlyn sitting there. It was a stranger.

"How did you know about my brother?"

Her eyes lowered and one long slender finger began to trace the flower design on the sheet. "Bram told me how he was shot down on Bloody Sunday." She looked up at him. "We'll help you do it, Devin. Pay them back for Glen's death. Help us, love. Do it for Glen, and for Ireland."

Lightning flickered and thunder rumbled from a distance. The storm was moving on. It took a long time for Devin to find his voice. When he did, it was low and hoarse, strangled with horror and pain. "It's late and stormy out, so I won't be asking you to go now. *I'll* go. But when I come back in the morning, Caitlyn, I want you to be out of my flat."

There was no need to add anything else. From the look on her face, he saw that she understood.

7

June 1986
Dublin

THE PHONE call came in the middle of the night. Devin knew immediately that Bram was drunk because his voice was warbled and thick. That alone told him something was bitterly wrong. Bram was a drinker, but only once in the five years Devin had known him had he seen him sloshed. That was the night of Pat Sullivan's accident.

"It's Caitlyn," Bram rasped. "Ye've got ta go ta her."

Devin almost hung up on his best friend. In the three weeks since he sent Caitlyn away, Bram, oddly enough in the face of his previous coolness, had been her staunchest defender. Even after hearing of her admission of being an IRA volunteer, Bram had downplayed it, insisting that most of her "responsibilities" were probably exaggerated, a product of her feminine imagination more than anything else. It infuriated Devin. He knew Caitlyn. Nothing she'd admitted had been in her head. But he couldn't make Bram believe it. Bram's sheltered Republic of Ireland upbringing made it impossible for him to accept that ordinary people could kill as easily as Devin could swat a wasp in the summertime.

"Man, why don't you go to bed and sleep it off?" Devin said now. "I don't need this bullshit."

"No! Ya don't unnerstan—Dev, she's in hospital. She tried to kill herself!"

"How did you find out?"

Bram held his head between his hands as if to make sure it wouldn't roll right off his neck. A cup of black coffee steamed in front of him, his sixth. Its aroma filled the tiny kitchen with a sense of homeliness that was at direct odds with their conversation. Gingerly, Bram lifted his head and reached for the cup. His hand shook slightly as he brought it to his lips.

"Her dorm roommate found her. Apparently, Caty had downed an entire bottle of Seconal. Tara, the roommate, called me because she knew I'd get in touch with you."

"Jesus!" Devin stood up and began to pace Bram's kitchen. He ran his hand over his stubbled chin and gazed out the window into the dark street. It was two in the morning; nothing stirred outside. "*Why* for God's sake?"

"Ah, come on, Devin. You know fucking well *why!* The girl has lost you. And it took that to make her realize that you mean more to her than the Cause."

"The Cause," Devin muttered. One fist crashed into the other. Christ, if it weren't for the Cause, his life wouldn't be so fucked up now.

"They pumped her stomach, and the doctor says she's out of danger. But they're worried about her mental health." His eyes met Devin's. "All she does is cry and call out for you." He waited, but when there was no response from Devin, he burst out, "You have to go to her, man!"

"Why?" Devin lashed back. "What good will it do? Nothing has changed. Don't you see, Bram, the woman is involved with the fucking I-R-A." He paused to let the significance sink into Bram's thick skull. "That is the one thing in this world I can't accept. I *won't* accept it! No matter how much I love her."

"So, you do still love her?"

"Christ! How can you love someone you don't even know? She kept this from me for three fucking years! It's like waking up one morning and finding out the woman you've been married to for the last twenty years sells her body down on the wharf at night." Devin fell into a chair and drummed his fingers on the table. "Do you have any fags? I'd *kill* for a smoke right now."

Bram gave him a sour look. "Remember who you're talking to. Devin, they're afraid she'll try it again. Tara said Caty wants to die. She as much as told her roomie she'd do it right next time. Tara said she kept talking about this woman in Derry who cut her own throat with an electric carving knife."

Devin's gut twisted. He thought of Caitlyn's long, creamy neck, the mole in the V-shaped hollow, a spot he'd never tired of kissing. Then he thought of that beautiful white neck splashed with blood, jagged and gruesome. He pushed away from the table, his stomach heaving.

"We can leave at first light," Bram said.

Devin made it to the bathroom just in time. He retched into the toilet bowl, but nothing came up. After a few moments, he dropped to the floor as beads of sweat popped out over his clammy body. Glassily, he stared at the wall as the truth hit him.

Physically, he was empty. But emotionally, he was still full of Caitlyn.

DEVIN STOOD just inside the door of the hospital room. Although an average-sized woman, Caitlyn was dwarfed by the hospital bed and its white coverings. She lay stiffly, her face turned away from him. His eyes fastened upon her tangled black hair; he'd never seen it so matted and scrungy.

He felt a pang in his chest. Had she really given up on life, then? He moved toward the bed. When she heard his footsteps, her head turned. Dully, her blue eyes stared at him. Deep purple shadows traced her lower lids. Her ordinarily luminous skin was sallow and unhealthy. Weight loss had given her high cheekbones a skeletal appearance. When had she last taken a meal?

She peered at Devin blankly, almost as if she weren't seeing him at all. He stopped a few feet from the bed and waited. A war waged inside him, one between his heart and his mind. Christ!

He wanted nothing more than to gather his frail darling up in his arms and kiss the shadows away from her pinched face. Even now, knowing what she was, he loved her. How was that possible when she was a symbol for everything in Ireland that he hated?

Suddenly, Caitlyn's face crumbled and her eyes filled with tears. "You came." Her voice was a husky whisper. She raised a weak hand out to him.

He moved to the bed, automatically reaching out to grasp her hand. At the last second, he realized what he was about to do and thrust it back into his jacket pocket. He searched for something to say. "Bram told me."

She closed her eyes. "I've had some black periods in my life, but I never wanted to stop living before. Not until I lost you."

Her statement unleashed the anger boiling beneath his surface calm. "It was a bloody stupid thing you did, Caitlyn."

She nodded. "It was that! I've always hated people who play it halfway. I should've used a gun. Next time . . ."

Devin grabbed her shoulders and gave her a good hard shake. "Stop that, woman! One more threat out of you and I'll be out that door. I didn't come here to listen to that!"

Her hand touched his stubbled face. "So, why did you come, Devin?"

He stared at her silently. Outside, in the early morning gloom, a siren moaned at the emergency entrance. It cut off abruptly just as Caitlyn spoke, her voice louder than necessary. "Because in spite of everything, you still love me, don't you?"

He started to pull away from her, but her hand, surprisingly strong, latched onto his denim jacket. "Devin! I'll give it up for you. I swear! It goes against everything I've believed in all my life, but God forgive me, I love you more than I love Ireland. I'll let it all go for you, Devin. I swear on the Holy Mother herself, I will!"

Devin gazed down at her. It occurred to him that in all the years they'd lived together, she'd never actually told him she loved him before. Until now. But could he believe her? Jesus, he wanted to. It wasn't easy to throw away almost three years of a relationship, even if the relationship *had* been a lie.

Could she give up the IRA for him? And could he trust her to give it up? Would there always be a doubt that she was involved?

"Take me back, Devin." The tears flowed down her gaunt cheeks. "I love you. I want to have your children."

He closed his eyes, struggling with the warring factions inside him. For some reason, the thought of Mary Marie went through his mind. He'd loved her with all the exuberance of youth, and after she'd died, he'd been convinced he'd never love again. Yet Caitlyn had come along. Wasn't their love meant to be?

Her hand entwined in his. She watched him silently, waiting for his answer. He looked away from her. It had started to rain. Sheets of it beat against the window, washing the gray city of Belfast a darker shade of grim. At the moment, Devin felt that his heart was more or less the same color. His eyes moved back to Caitlyn.

"You know what happened to my brother," he said quietly. "Shot down on Bloody Sunday when he was only sixteen. And my da! On his death certificate, it said he died of a heart attack. But it was the Troubles that killed him as surely as if the Brits had put a bullet through him themselves. His spirit died in Long Kesh years before he was released." He paused and bit his lip, his mind lost in the past. "I never told you about Mary Marie. She was my first girl. Sure, I would've married her, but the IRA blew up the bus she was on just a few days before Christmas 1978." His hand clenched hers as his voice grew husky with intensity. "I *won't* go through that again, Caty! Your cause has taken too much from me."

Her blue eyes showed a spark of the old Caitlyn. "You won't have to, Devin. I'll leave Belfast forever." She spoke quickly, almost breathlessly. "We can make our home in America. In London, even, if that's what you want. If it will make you take me back, I'll never step foot in Ireland again." Her hand slid up to his face and traced the line of his lips. "Oh, Devin, I love you so, man. You're all I want in the world."

"I want to believe that."

"You *have* to believe it," she pleaded, her eyes shimmering with tears. "Devin, there's been no one but you for three years. Doesn't that tell you something? You are my life."

He stared at her for a long moment, desperately wanting to believe she was sincere. Her eyes melded with his, shining with tremulous hope. He felt his heart thawing. "I can't set the world right," he said. He pressed her fingers against his lips, kissing them softly. "I can't heal the scars of your past or mine. But together, we can work toward changing things in a peaceful way. I can do that through my music, and you. . . ."

"Through my medicine," Caitlyn completed his sentence. Her eyes searched his face. "If only I'd met you sooner, Devin. Perhaps it would never have come to this. How did you become so wise?" Her hand tightened on his. "I know I'm dreadfully ugly today, but darling, I need you to kiss me in the most terrible way."

Leaning toward her, he gently touched his lips to hers. But when he started to draw away, her hands clenched against his shoulders.

"A proper kiss," she said huskily, pulling him back. His mouth opened under the pressure of her lips, her tongue stealing in to taste the texture of his. "Oh, Christ! I want you, man. It's been too long since I've felt you inside me."

Her words brought an instantaneous physical reaction to his body. It *had* been too long. He drew away from her. "When do you get out of here?"

She shook her head. "I don't know. They've been worried about my mental state. When do you leave for America?"

"Day after tomorrow. Christ!" He ran his hand through his hair. "We've got to get you out of here."

Her hands tightened on his. "Marry me, Devin. Now. Right here."

He stared at her, wondering if she were on medicine that caused her mind to wander. Her eyes began to sparkle.

"No, I mean it. Don't you see? If we can get a priest in to marry us before you leave, I'll join you in America as soon as the doctors will let me travel." A tremulous smile touched her lips. "Oh, Devin, think of it. With any luck, by the time we come back to Ireland, I'll be pregnant. I'll give you what you've always wanted."

"But medical school?"

She shook her head. "It can wait for a year. I want to have your baby. Marry me, Devin. Let's do it before you leave."

"But how? The wedding was supposed to be a week ago. How will we arrange it at such short notice?"

Her eyes danced. "Bram! He knows Father Kelleher in my neighborhood. He'll bring him here to marry us. Tomorrow. Let's do it tomorrow. I'll spend the rest of today getting ready for you. I want to be pretty on our wedding day."

Slowly, Devin released her hand and stood up. "Are you sure this is what you want, Caty? There can be no going back once we're married."

Her jaw tightened. He'd seen that expression before during the few spats they'd had. It was one of iron determination. "I've never been more sure of anything in my life, Devin O'Keefe. You're going to be mine forever."

As he drove back to the hotel where Bram was waiting, her words played in his mind in rhythm to the windscreen wipers. *You're going to be mine forever.* It was like a mantra. On the tail of this thought came another, a more disturbing one. *You're going to be mine forever.* It wasn't a mantra but a threat!

Fourth of July, 1986
Washington, D.C.

THE MUFFLED voice from the TV in the hotel room provided the only background noise to the melody Devin hummed to himself as he strummed the guitar resting on his thighs. He dropped the guitar to the bed and reached for the pen and pad of paper on the end table. He scribbled a phrase that had popped into his head and then chewed thoughtfully on the end of the pen. Christ! He missed Caitlyn so desperately he literally ached from it. But how on earth was he supposed to translate that hungry feeling onto paper?

"Bloody hell!" He tossed the tablet to the bed and flopped down on his back, his hands folded beneath his head. Men had been trying to write down those feelings for ages, for *centuries,* for

Christ's sake, yet how many had succeeded? McCartney and Lennon, maybe, but who else?

One more week, then Caitlyn would be arriving for the concert in Miami. It seemed far longer than just over two weeks since he'd seen her. They'd had only one hurried night together as man and wife before he'd had to leave for the airport and the flight to New York. And that had been less than satisfactory, as they'd had to spend it in her hospital room.

Outside the windows of the hotel, the night sky lit up in Technicolor. Devin went to the window and gazed out at the Washington Monument back-lit by the exploding fireworks. It was the anniversary of America's Independence Day. The next night, O'Keefe would be playing at Constitution Hall. He hoped the response would be as great as it had been in Boston, New York, and the other venues they'd played since their arrival in the United States. No reason why it wouldn't be. Word of mouth had O'Keefe drawing in new fans with every concert.

A final simultaneous burst of color and noise outside brought the fireworks show to an end. Just as Devin resolved to tackle the new song again, he felt the hairs on his arms raise at the mention of Belfast on the TV.

With a sense of dread, he turned to watch the newscast footage of bomb rubble in a Belfast shopping center. His immediate thought was for Caitlyn. A moment later, he breathed easier, knowing that she was in Dublin closing up the flat for the summer. On the screen, medical personnel were carrying out the wounded from the destroyed building.

"The IRA has claimed responsibility for today's bombing of a department store in Cave Hill, a predominately Protestant area of Belfast. At last count, there were three dead, one of whom is thought to be a suspect in the bombing. Eight people were injured in today's incident, one critically. Another suspect is in custody."

Grimly, Devin strode across the room and switched off the TV. Christ! Even crossing the Atlantic couldn't get him away from the savagery of his accursed country. What he needed now was a drink. He wished he'd gone out with Bram when he'd been invited earlier. The hotel room was closing in on him.

As if in cue with his thoughts, a knock came at the door. Devin grinned. Bram. What a mate! He'd come back to drag him out. He opened the door.

It wasn't Bram who stood there, but Ian. Devin's smile faded. His manager's face was grimmer than usual. Ian stepped in and glanced around the room. His eyes returned to Devin, resting on him almost warmly, yet Devin saw something else in them. Something that sent icy shivers down his back.

"You'd better pour us a couple of strong ones, Devin," Ian said slowly. "And sit yourself down. I'm afraid I have bad news."

Devin made no move toward the liquor cabinet. The icy feeling had reached his heart, encasing it; yet, at the same time, his body felt hot and flushed. He struggled to find his voice, and when it came, it was almost a croak.

"Caitlyn?"

Ian gave a terse nod. "She won't be coming to America, Devin. Not ever."

A firecracker exploded outside as Devin and Ian stared at each other. It was a sound Devin would never hear again without thinking of the night his world shattered.

PART THREE

The Eclipse Tour

8

THE ULSTER countryside teemed with the ripeness of spring. Daily showers brought a vivid color of green to the rich landscape—a hue that surpassed even the most emerald of photos in the tourist brochures. Apple trees dotted the rolling hills of County Armagh, bursting forth with peachy-pink blossoms and providing a canopy of shade for a moment's respite from the brilliant but fickle sunshine of the morning. The stillness was broken only by the sound of birdsong and the rush of the brook that separated the North from the Republic of Ireland. The man in black squinted as he gazed southeast toward the empty road that paralleled the border.

'Twas a bloody bit of bad luck that the Brit patrol had chosen daybreak to roust out the Crossmaglen neighborhood where their safehouse was located. Damned inconvenient, it was. No surprise to him, though. Typical Brits! For centuries, they'd been nothing but an inconvenience to the natives of Eire.

He glanced over his right shoulder at the figure huddled in the brambles behind him and signaled for her to stay put. A comely lass, she was, this Caitlyn MacManus, but colder than an outside privy seat in January. For almost a week now, they'd been together, cautiously making their way from one safehouse to another en route to the border—and freedom. Even so, she'd yet to say one kind word to him or crack the slightest of smiles. In fact, she was downright churlish! Even refused to share a pint with him after the good meals prepared for them by kind country folk who ran the safehouses. Never gave *them* a by-your-leave, as well.

But then, perhaps prison had hardened the poor wee girl. He himself had been a guest of the Brits' H-Block from time to time. Jury's Hotel it was not. His back and legs still bore scars from the torture tactics used by the "civilized" British.

Fact was, his job was to get the woman across the border safely. Whether or not she appreciated it was beside the point.

One more glance down the empty road assured him it was time to go. He gestured for Caitlyn to move up to join him. She did so in complete silence. He gave her an appreciative grin. It was obvious the girl had been trained by the best. But as usual, she didn't respond to his overture of friendliness. He sighed inwardly. It was a serious business they were involved in, true, but did that mean she had to act like a fucking robot?

He pointed to the west. "There's a border checkpoint about half a kilometer down the road. A bit too close for comfort, perhaps, but the creek here is as shallow as it gets this time of year."

Caitlyn gave a terse nod. "Let's get on with it, then."

"Okay. Just remember, we're going to be in a bit of clearing on both sides of the road. With that bend in the road up there, we can't be certain a farmer or such isn't out and about. Likely, if there is, he'll be a friendly sort, this far south."

"I'm not blind, Sheedy. Let's go!"

"Right. But should anyone come along, just say, 'Top 'o the mornin',' like you're out for a stroll. The people in these parts generally mind their own business."

Her black brows knitted together. "For Christ's sake, let's get the bloody hell out of here!"

Sheedy shrugged, and after another quick glance up and down the road, stood up. He stretched his cramped muscles and began to amble toward the road. Should a patrol come along, it was best to act natural, as if he had no more in mind than an early morning stroll. However, a glance at Caitlyn told him she wasn't of the same mind. Furtiveness was written all over her shapely body. Anyone whose brain wasn't pickled would know she was a fugitive. Bloody hell! Perhaps her training wasn't so flawless, after all.

"Relax," he said out the corner of his mouth. "You're too fuckin' stiff."

She threw him an ugly look and opened her mouth to speak.

Suddenly, a bicycle rounded the curve and careened toward them. Sheedy froze in the middle of the road, the woman beside him. The boy on the bicycle slammed on his brakes, his freckled face alight with astonishment. The front wheel of the bike skidded on loose gravel, but somehow, the boy managed to maintain his balance as he brought it to a stop.

"Jaysus, mister! I'm sorry. Wasn't expectin' ta see anyone out here this early." His blue eyes went to the woman. "Sorry, miss."

Sheedy placed a hand over his pumping heart, his throat dry. With an effort, he forced a smile upon his face. "No harm, lad. Gave me a bit of fright, that's all. Where are ya off to this fine mornin'?"

The boy grinned and placed a hand on a crate in the basket behind him. "Deliverin' eggs to the general store in Forkhill. Likely, a few of them will be broken after a stop like that. Not your fault, of course," he added quickly. "Me ma tells me not to ride like a banshee from hell."

"And she's right." Sheedy felt Caitlyn's impatience to move on, but ignored it. Better to ease the boy's suspicions, should he have any. It was obvious, though, he was a poor Catholic lad from a local farm. Still, it wouldn't hurt to buy themselves some insurance. He reached into the pocket of his jacket and pulled out a fifty-pence coin. "But seeing as how I'm partly responsible if there's any damage, take this and buy yourself an ice cream in town."

The boy's face lit up. "Thanks, mister."

Sheedy grinned. He could almost read the lad's mind. Chocolate or vanilla? For a moment, he felt a pang inside him as he thought of his own boy, Sean, back in Carrickfergus. How long had it been since he'd seen the lad?

Caitlyn gave him a nudge. Her lips twisted in a frozen smile as her cornflower blue eyes blazed into his. "We should be going, James."

The boy on the bike doffed his grimy baseball cap. "Good mornin' to ya, mister . . . missus." He pushed off and began to ride down the road toward town.

"Mind, you watch your speed, now," Sheedy called after him. The boy flashed him a grin and waved. Sheedy chuckled. No sooner would he be out of sight before he'd be pedaling like, as his ma said, a banshee from hell. It was probably one of the few joys the poor lad had in his dismal life. A bike! That's what he'd get for Sean as soon as he made it back up north. Somehow, he'd scrape together the cash to do it.

He stepped off the road and into the ditch that ran beside it. "Ya see, I told you there'd be no problem with the locals."

It was a whisper of sound, almost as if the air in a balloon had been released. Sheedy's stomach took a plunge as he whipped around, recognizing it immediately for what it was. Like a film reel run in slow motion, he saw the bicycle topple and the boy rolling to the ground. His wiry body came to rest facedown on the side of the road. Even from the twenty yards that separated them, Sheedy could see the neat round hole in his back, dead-center of his spine.

For a moment, Sheedy fought for air, his diaphragm in shock. He turned to Caitlyn just in time to see her replace the gun in her shoulder holster. His gut twisted with nausea.

"Why for Christ's sake did ya *do* that, woman?" he said hoarsely. "He was but a wee lad! A Catholic, at that!"

Her beautiful face was expressionless. "He would be passing the border station in a minute. I couldn't take the chance he would say something."

Despite the warmth of the morning sun, a deathly chill seeped through Sheedy. He stared at her, shuddering. "Christ—oh, Jesus!"

"Put a lid on it, Sheedy. Let's go."

Sheedy felt as if he were choking. His stomach churned, and for a moment, he thought he was going to puke his guts out. His body began to shake. He'd seen death before. Many times. But an innocent wee lad! Jesus Christ! He'd come across some ruthless people in his day, but this woman—she was the spawn of Satan himself!

Her hand moved back to the automatic resting inside its holster. "Perhaps you'd like to meet your maker along with the lad, Sheedy?"

Sheedy swallowed the bile that had risen in his throat. He turned and slowly began to wade through the high grass that led down to the creek bank. His shoulder blades burned where he felt the woman's steely gaze. In his mind, he saw the boy's lifeless body huddled upon the roadside, his shattered eggs seeping their yolky innards around him. No doubt, his last thought had been about the ice cream he was going to buy with the fifty pence.

For the first time in years, Sheedy wanted to bawl like a wee babe.

9

FONDA GAZED at the stenciled gold letters on the door in front of her: COREY NEWTON, EDITOR-IN-CHIEF. Even now, five years after Corey had attained the position, his name on the editor's door still rankled. Working with Corey had been even more difficult than she'd ever expected. And although she'd advanced to the position of senior editor, she still had to fight with him over every little decision as if he were the father and she the errant child.

Still, despite everything, she had to admit Corey was a good editor. Not that she'd ever tell him that to his face. The pompous ass was egotistical enough as it was. She knocked and the door immediately opened.

"It's about time," Corey said, stepping back for her to enter. One square hand swept through his spiky blond hair in a nervous gesture as he eyed her up and down. "Where the hell you been?"

Fonda's lips quirked. "Interviewing the overinflated ego of Zerkel Wynstram, as you instructed, remember?" As she spoke, she became aware that Corey wasn't alone.

His eyes glittered a warning as if afraid she would go off on a vocal tangent about one of his precious rock stars. Fonda grinned, enjoying his discomfort. He took her arm and guided her over to a tall, gaunt man in the plush leather chair across from his desk. "Fonda, this is Ian Brinegar, Devin O'Keefe's manager."

Her eyes assessed the stranger. He looked like anything but a rock star's manager, more like a professor or a corporate attorney with his steel gray eyes and salt and pepper hair. His mouth was a thin grim slash in a face pitted with pockmarks and creased with deep grooves from temple to jaw.

He stood up and extended a hand to Fonda. The stern expression on his face didn't soften. "Pleased to meet you," he said in a strong accent she couldn't immediately identify.

"Have a seat, Fon. Mr. Brinegar has a proposition for you."

"Great." Fonda said dryly, plopping down in the other chair across from the desk. "I hope it's better than the one Zerkel offered me." She ignored Corey's glower and smiled at Ian Brinegar. "So, what do you have in mind, Mr. Brinegar?"

If possible, he looked even grimmer than before. "You've heard, I suppose, that Devin is planning an American tour this summer to support his new album. His publicist and I have decided it would be a grand opportunity to publish a pictorial of the Eclipse Tour. And Devin has agreed, provided you write it. And do the photos, of course."

Fonda stared at him. "Are you serious? You're commissioning me to do a pictorial on Devin O'Keefe?"

"Devin wants you. He's seen your work in *Spotlight,* and God knows why, it's you or no one." His tone plainly stated he had no such preference.

Northern Ireland. That was the accent. Years ago, Fonda's father had brought a fellow policeman home for dinner, a man who'd emigrated from Belfast. Brinegar's accent was just like his. And of course, Devin O'Keefe was Irish. It fit.

Fonda swung a sneakered foot nervously and clasped two damp palms around the knee of her stonewashed denim jeans. "Why me?"

"You'll have to ask Devin about that, miss. If you decide to do it." His gray eyes scanned her disdainfully. "The tour starts in Philadelphia on May 17. Of course, your expenses will be paid. Not to mention the quite large advance the London publisher will be offering you. But perhaps you'd like some time to think about it. It would mean a leave of absence from your magazine here." He leaned forward and handed her a folded slip of paper. "The compensation Mr. O'Keefe is offering."

Fonda opened the paper and tried to keep her face bland as she took in the figure written there. After a moment, she uncrossed her legs and hunched forward in her chair, casually tossing her braid off her shoulder. "When would I have to let you know?"

Corey's jaw dropped and a thumb and finger began to work the diamond stud in his left earlobe. "You mean you have to *think* about it?"

Fonda ignored him.

"Tomorrow," Ian Brinegar said.

Restlessly, Fonda stood and moved to gaze out the window behind Corey's desk. Across the Hudson River, brooding gray clouds hovered over the New York skyline, threatening a snowstorm. It was rather amazing, she thought. Years ago, she'd begged Corey to let her do an interview with the unknown Irish singer, but he'd adamantly refused. Now, she was being offered a chance to do an entire book about him. A smile came to her lips. When O'Keefe had made their first appearance in America back in 1986, they'd become an instant sensation. Fonda had gleefully screwed the knife into Corey, reminding him that *she* had been the one to predict their success. In retaliation, he'd sent another writer off to O'Keefe's New York concert to get the interview, but he'd come back empty-handed. Devin had stopped doing interviews.

There was no question whether or not she'd accept the proposition. Brinegar was talking big money. That was something she needed if her dream of starting her own magazine was to come true. She grinned out the window. What she wouldn't give to be able to see Corey Newton's face when she told him her new magazine was edging his right out of the market. Oh no, she didn't have to think about this assignment. It was the answer to her prayers. But Mr. Bigwig Ian Brinegar didn't have to know that, did he? She turned around to face him, her face blank.

"I'll let you know."

February 1990
Dublin

IT WAS raining when Ian Brinegar stepped out of Dublin Airport. The black Mercedes was waiting for him at the curbside. Quickly, he slid into the passenger seat and threw his umbrella into the back. Caitlyn, at the wheel, didn't glance at him as she shifted into first and slipped into the traffic leaving the airport.

"Bloody weather!" Ian murmured, brushing at the beadlets of rain on his cashmere coat. He pushed a button to lower his window a few inches, hoping the cool misty air would help clear out the musky scent of Caitlyn's perfume. He found it repugnant.

There was no response from the woman. She drove expertly, her blue eyes expressionless but alert. More beautiful than ever, Ian thought. Her sheen of black hair was cut short, hugging her perfectly shaped head. Arched eyebrows perched over those magnificent eyes, giving her a constant appearance of surprise. Yes, Caitlyn was a beauty, indeed. Too bad she left him cold. As all women did.

"Well?" Her voice was low and smoky, unconsciously seductive. The sound of it made his skin crawl.

"The girl has agreed to do it. I think it may be just the thing to keep Devin occupied during the tour."

"I hope you're not underestimating him. Sure, Devin is no fool."

Ian stared out the window as they crossed North Circular Road and headed into the heart of Dublin. It was dank and depressing under the soggy skies, yet he was happy to be back home. His lips twisted in a grimace. "Good heavens, no. Devin is a bleeding saint, isn't he now?"

Caitlyn turned icy eyes upon him. "There's no room in this operation for personal vendettas, Brinegar. Tell me now if that's the case, and we'll come up with another plan."

"Don't be daft. You know I'd never let my personal feelings interfere with the Cause."

Her lips thinned in a cruel sneer. "That's what I'm depending upon, love." She looked at him, her eyes cold. Ian felt a shiver run through him. "Because you wouldn't want to be letting me down, now, would you?"

Staring at her, Ian thought perhaps she wasn't so beautiful, after all.

10

THE DOOR opened immediately after Fonda's tap, and a big, sandy-haired man with an amiable face stuck his head out of the tuning room at Independence Hall. His blue eyes looked her up and down.

"And who might *you* be?" he asked in a pleasant Irish brogue.

"Fonda Blayne." When it was obvious her name meant nothing to him, she went on, "I'm the one doing the book on Devin."

His face cleared. "Ah, so you are!" He opened the door and motioned her into the tuning room. "Devin's been looking forward to meeting you. I'll introduce you in a sec." Behind him, Fonda could see two men singing in harmony to the accompaniment of an acoustic guitar. "He and Seamus are working on the lyrics to a new song. By the by, I'm Bram Gradeigh, Devin's roadie." He thrust out a hand and grinned. Fonda couldn't help but smile back as her free hand clasped his. The man oozed charm from every pore. He nodded his head to the singers. "They're trying to iron this out for tonight."

From the ragged sound of it, Fonda thought it would take more than "ironing out" to get it ready for the night's concert. The Philadelphia venue had been sold out for months, a good indication that the Irishman's Eclipse Tour would be a great success.

Fonda's eyes moved back to the two men behind Bram. She'd recognized Devin right away. Casually dressed in an open-necked gray shirt with black jeans, he looked just like the photos she'd seen in *Rolling Stone* and *Spotlight*. He was sitting on a sofa, tapping his hands against his thighs to keep the rhythm of the beat as the other man strummed an acoustic guitar. Whereas the guitarist was nondescript, Devin was arresting. His straight nose combined with high cheekbones and thin lips gave him a hawk-like appearance, yet was balanced by the unexpected gentleness in his brown eyes.

Suddenly, Devin's voice went noticeably off-key. He stopped abruptly, ran a hand through his rumpled black hair, and laughed. "Sure, that one is for the birds!" His voice was a softer version of Bram's lilting accent. "Needs just a wee bit more work, doesn't it, Seamus?"

The other man gave a slight smile and put his guitar aside. "Wouldn't hurt."

Bram grabbed Fonda's hand and pulled her forward. "Devin, look what we have here. It's the writer from *Spotlight*."

Devin looked up. Gradually, the warm light in his eyes disappeared to be replaced by a wintry wariness. He stood up. "Bram, why don't you relieve her of that bag. It looks a wee bit heavy."

Bram hit his head with the heel of his hand. "Jaysus, I'm sorry! I've been hanging around this lot so long I've forgotten me manners."

He moved to take the camera bag from her, but in the process, grabbed a lock of her hair along with it. Fonda grimaced and moved to rescue it. "Oh, bloody hell! I'm sorry." Bram helped to untangle the strand from the camera bag strap. "Lord, Devin! Look at this girl's hair. Have you ever seen anything so lovely?" His "lovely" came out like "loovvly."

Fonda smiled at him and smoothed her unruly hair into place. "Thanks. I guess it's true what they say about the charm of an Irishman." She turned back to see Devin studying her carefully. His eyes moved down the length of her hair where it brushed the top of her hips. She'd been in such a hurry to catch her flight this morning, she hadn't taken the time to braid it as usual. She felt herself coloring at his intent appraisal. What was he thinking? Frizz-Face—that hated nickname the kids at school had given her? Even now, she felt self-conscious about wearing her mane loose.

Fonda took a step toward Devin and thrust out a hand. "I'm Fonda Blayne. But then, you know that, don't you?"

Although he had resumed his remote expression of a moment before, he reached out and enclosed her hand in his for a brief moment. "Take a seat, Fonda. Before we start, there are a few things we have to get clear between us." He turned to the others. "Would you mind giving us a few moments alone, lads?"

Fonda felt mildly uneasy as she settled onto the sofa. What did O'Keefe have to say to her he couldn't discuss in front of his band?

He waited until the door closed behind the last man and then without speaking, perched upon the arm of the sofa opposite her. Still, he made no move to open the conversation. Instead, he peered down at the seam of his leather boot. One hand stroked the grain of the leather, over and over, as if searching for a defect. The silence grew between them and Fonda became more ill at ease. Still, her pride wouldn't allow her to speak first. Suddenly, without warning, he looked up.

Devin's brown eyes bore into her as if trying to dissect her. The expression on his face gave nothing away. Fonda sensed a tightness about him, an almost primitive power that, unleashed, could have devastating effects upon everyone around him. She could only guess what channel that power could take. Instinctively, she knew this was a man who did nothing halfway. A perfectionist.

She crossed her legs nervously and ran a hand down the denim of her jeans as she waited for him to speak. He took his time. Just when Fonda thought they'd spend the rest of the day locked in silence, he cleared his throat and said, "I don't want to do this book, you know."

Fonda stared at him. Then she made a move to get up. "In that case, I won't waste any more of your time."

Devin reached out and grabbed her arm. "I didn't say I *wouldn't* do it. I said I didn't want to."

Fonda looked down at his hand still clasped around her forearm. It was nicely shaped. Artistic. Slowly, he released her. Their eyes met. "Isn't that the same thing?"

"No, I'm afraid not. You see, my manager thinks it's essential to my career. I think it's a bloody waste of time. But I'm doing it for him because he hasn't been wrong yet." His eyes darkened, as if a painful memory had occurred to him. "So, there it is. I didn't want any hypocrisy between us. And I didn't want you to take it personally if I sometimes get . . . difficult."

Difficult? She knew about "difficult" when it came to rock singers. She'd handled most of them with no problems. The few she couldn't handle, she'd washed her hands of with no regrets.

Unconsciously, Fonda twirled a long strand of hair around her index finger as she pondered her response to Devin's confession. He sat back and watched her.

Sweet Mary, she was a delight to the eyes. Her pale oval face under that cloud of golden brown hair looked as if it had been molded by Raphael himself. And her eyes! He couldn't quite tell their color, somewhere between blue and green, with delicate arched brows etched upon a porcelain forehead. Devin felt the danger signals emanating from every pore in his being. This woman spelled trouble. He knew it. It had been the same way with Caitlyn from the very first moment he'd met her. And God knows how *that* ended. Caitlyn had not only taken his heart, but his soul too. It had all started with danger signals like he was feeling now.

"Your manager said you asked for me," she said.

Abruptly, Devin stood up. "That I did. I've seen your work. Read your articles. You strike me as a dependable sort. Well, as dependable as you people can be."

Fonda stiffened. She didn't like the tone in his voice. "Exactly what do you mean by 'you people'?"

Devin ran a hand through his glossy black hair. "Ah, you know. The press. The media." He spoke as if he were uttering obscenities. "I'll be honest with you. I don't like all this hype. I realize it's necessary, but that doesn't mean I have to like it." He paused and peered at her intently. "That's why we have to have some rules. For one thing, my music comes first. Nothing, and I mean, *nothing*, will interfere with it. That means you shoot *around* me. You will be invisible. Just do your job. Write about the tour, get your photos. That's it. I won't have this book interfering with the tour."

By the time he'd finished speaking, Fonda's temper was at a simmer. Still, she struggled to remain composed. "I think I understand what you're getting at. In other words, stay out of your way, right?"

Devin stared at her broodingly. Then he nodded. "That's about it."

Fonda stood up. "That should be no problem at all, Mr. O'Keefe. And just so we understand each other, I'm going to be honest with *you*. I signed a contract and I'm going to keep my end of the bargain. But remember, you signed the contract, too. You sanctioned this book, but you did *not* get the right to approve what I write. And whether you come out flattering in this or not is entirely up to you. Right now, I'd say you're not getting off to a good start." Fonda scanned the room for her camera bag and found it on a chair near the door. "Are there any more rules before I go? I'd like to get to my hotel and take a nap before the concert tonight."

Yeh, don't look at me with those eyes sparking fire like that.

Devin shook his head. "No more rules. I think we understand each other."

11

AFTER SHE'D gone, Devin sat on the edge of the sofa and stared pensively at the door. He knew he'd sent false signals to the American woman. It wasn't often he came on like a star. God, how he hated that trite word! But that's exactly how he'd come across to Fonda Blayne. *Just stay out of my way, girl, and we'll get along just fine.*

What had made him get so high-handed with her? Deep inside, he knew. It was his totally uncharacteristic reaction to the woman. Even now, thinking of her, he felt the first stirrings of desire, a feeling he'd believed had been buried forever after Caitlyn.

The door opened and Bram came in, grinning widely.

"Quite a lass, isn't she, Dev?"

Devin's eyes focused blankly on his friend while his brain clung stubbornly to the woman he'd just met. Finally, Bram's words sunk in. "Yeh, quite."

Bram took the Fender guitar out of its case and began to tune it. "Maybe she's just what you need."

Abruptly, Devin stood up. "Don't be getting any daft ideas, now."

"It's going to be a long tour," Bram went on. "Plenty of time to get to know her. You need a woman in your life, Dev. It's been too long."

Devin found himself growing irritated with his friend's nagging. He sounded like his mother, for Christ's sake! "Put it out of your mind, Bram."

Bram looked at him. "Bloody hell! It's been almost four years. Are you going to let Caitlyn ruin you for other women?"

Devin's face grew grim. "Perhaps she already did."

"Oh, Christ!" Bram couldn't hide his disgust. He slammed the guitar back into its case. "Perhaps I'll ask her out myself."

Devin forced himself to grin, although the thought of Fonda Blayne with Bram didn't sit well with him at all. "Ah, go on. You know you go for the tall leggy blondes, not a petite flower like her."

Bram cocked a humorous eyebrow at him. "Hell, you make it sound like I have a different blonde every week. You know I've settled down some in the last few years."

Devin's eyebrows rose. "That wouldn't have anything to do with my sister, would it?"

Bram's face reddened. "Now who's daft? Sure, we're just friends." He looked at his wristwatch. "Come on. Let's go rock that sound check."

Devin grabbed his guitar and hurried after Bram. As he left the room, he caught a whiff of a subtle perfume. It was gone almost immediately, but somehow, he knew it was the scent of Fonda.

IT WAS the afternoon of the RFK Stadium concert. In the tuning room of the venue, Fonda scribbled onto a sheet of notebook paper and then angrily ripped the page out and crumbled it into a ball. It fell against the ugly gray wastepaper basket in the corner to join several others at its base. It was no use. She couldn't write worth a damn today. For an hour, she'd been trying to bring last night's Boston concert alive on paper, but it wasn't working. The photos she'd taken at the gig had been beyond belief—capturing the essence of Devin's passion on stage. She'd known that even before she'd turned her hotel bathroom into a darkroom. Now came the hard part. Finding the prose to go along with the photos.

It wasn't easy to write about someone who didn't want to be written about. Not that Devin O'Keefe was being evasive or anything. Quite the opposite, actually. The Irishman was everywhere. Early on concert days, he appeared at the venue where he'd pace the stage, check out the sound equipment, and generally make sure everything was to his satisfaction. Then he'd climb to the highest seats to make sure there were no visual obstructions for the unlucky fans who'd been relegated there.

Bram, who'd turned out to be a great source of information about the reluctant subject of her book, explained that these rituals had begun at the very start of his career. It was of the utmost importance to Devin that his fans got their money's worth. In spite of her anger at his arrogant attitude when they'd met, Fonda couldn't help but feel a grudging respect for him. So many rock stars only cared about the green rolling in.

As Fonda went about snapping black and whites of the backstage concert life, she'd tried to make herself as inconspicuous as possible. At the New York concert after she'd just snapped a shot of Devin toweling off before returning to the stage for an encore, he'd turned and stared straight at her. When his piercing eyes met hers, a quizzical expression appeared on his lean face. Then, before Fonda could guess what it meant, he threw her a crooked smile. Disconcerted, she'd turned away, feeling the color rise on her cheeks. Devin O'Keefe was beginning to confuse her.

"Oh, there you are. I've been looking for you."

Startled, she looked up at the sound of Devin's melodic brogue. He was dressed in faded jeans and a sleeveless black T-shirt that emphasized his hard biceps. How did he manage to keep in such great shape with his grueling concert schedule? Fonda wondered. Most recording artists she knew had muscles about as firm as overcooked linguine.

"You've been looking for *me?*" Why? Had she somehow violated his sacred rules?

Devin leaned against the wall and eyed her. "Look, I think I got us off to a bad start with each other. I know I come across too strong at times. It's just that I didn't want there to be any misunderstanding between us. I wanted you to know how I stand on the book."

"You made that pretty clear."

"That's just it. Perhaps I was too abrupt. You're free to do your job and I'm free to do mine. I just don't want your job to get in the *way* of mine."

"And have I done that?" she asked lightly.

"No, of course not. I've hardly noticed you." That was a blatant lie. He'd been aware of every move she'd made. "Actually, it occurred to me that we should talk."

"About what?"

His lips twitched in amusement. "Me."

Fonda didn't know what to say.

"You know, background for the book. I don't know how much you've read about me, but I want to make sure you get the straight story. There's a lot of bogus information floating about."

"Actually, there's not too much information on you at all. How long have you had this aversion to the press?"

"From the beginning." The amusement had gone from his eyes. He straightened up and glanced down at his leather-banded wristwatch. "I've got a sound check to get to now. But I should have some free time after the sound check in Chicago. Shall we say Thursday at three o'clock? In my dressing room?"

"Okay," Fonda said. She wondered if she looked as surprised as she felt. What had happened to change his mind about the book? She thought about it for a few moments, but when no answer came to mind, she shrugged and turned back to her notebook. She looked down to where she'd started yet another paragraph about last night's concert. Decisively, she marked a large X through it and then below it, in block letters, she wrote: WHO IS THE REAL DEVIN O'KEEFE? Perhaps on Thursday, she'd begin to find out.

12

THAT NIGHT, as Fonda watched the concert from the wings of the stage, she saw again that quality she'd noticed during Devin's Live Aid performance. It was his ability to reach out and embrace the audience, figuratively and literally, at the expense of his clothing and sometimes his body. She recalled reading that at past concerts, he'd actually been injured because of his unprotected jaunts into the crowd. But apparently, experience hadn't taught him any lessons. His need to form a physical connection with his fans appeared to be greater than his need for protection.

Just before intermission, Devin began a song Fonda didn't recognize. Accompanied by the acoustic guitar, it was a hard-edged ballad about the bombings in Northern Ireland. In his wrenching, almost gravelly voice, he sang about a little boy who'd died in the streets of Belfast, an innocent victim of sectarian strife. When the song ended, there was dead silence for a minuscule second, and then the thunder of applause began. The stadium went wild, begging for more from their idol. But Devin turned to make his way offstage. Fonda positioned the camera for a shot of him, but as he grew near, her finger hesitated on the shutter button. Slowly, she let the camera drop. He moved past her and went on backstage.

She stared after him, knowing she'd perhaps missed taking the photo of her life, but she'd simply had no choice. Even if she'd imagined the track of his tears in the dim light of the wings, the naked pain on his face had been unmistakable. It would've been a crime to intrude upon him at that moment. As it was, even now she felt like a voyeur.

The concert tour reached the Midwest and the cities began to bleed into one another. Cleveland, Cincinnati, Chicago. How did Devin remember which one he was in as he greeted the fans from the stage? In a little over a week, the tour would reach Indianapolis.

As always, when she hadn't been home in a while, Fonda found herself looking forward to seeing her family again. It never changed. Months would go by, dimming the memory of the bad times and leaving only the nostalgia for the good moments. But as soon as she arrived back home, the reality would surround her, making her count the moments until she could leave.

It was Dad, of course. He still hadn't resigned himself to her career choice. His disapproval had begun after Michael's death. Before, while he'd had his son to mold and shape into his likeness, he hadn't cared what Fonda did with her life. Now, the music business was wrong for his precious daughter. His hypocrisy infuriated her.

Better not to think of it now. There would be time enough to deal with that when she got home. Besides, it was time to prepare herself for the interview with Devin. A wave of nervousness twisted in her stomach. This was incredible! She hadn't felt so apprehensive about an interview since her first one three years ago with Bruce Springsteen.

At precisely three o'clock, she knocked at Devin's dressing-room door. From inside, she could hear the Waterboys singing "The Stolen Child."

"Come in."

When she opened the door, he was standing with his bare back to her, rubbing a towel briskly over his head. Apparently, he'd just come out of the shower. In the corner of the room, a set of barbells rested on the floor. So! That explained his great biceps.

Fonda waited a moment, but when he didn't turn around, she spoke, "I'm not early, am I?"

He dropped the towel around his neck and turned, his face

pensive. "Oh, sorry. I was lost in thought." The Waterboy's CD ended and there was silence in the room.

Fonda's lips quirked at the sight of his black hair sticking up in spikes around his face. Did he realize how impish it made him look? Her eyes were caught by a glitter of silver against the thick covering of black hair on his chest. It was a Celtic cross. So, he was a Catholic. Another difference between them. Not that religion was a big deal with her. Christians were Christians as far as she was concerned, but of course, in Ireland, religion was everything.

Devin gave her a tentative smile. "Here, sit yourself down. Just let me"—his head disappeared as he pulled on a black T-shirt emblazoned HUMAN RIGHTS NOW!—"get a shirt on." He ran his hands through his hair to flatten the unruly spikes. "I'm ready if you are." He swung himself onto the top of a portable wardrobe and leaned back against the wall.

Fonda cleared her throat and looked down at her notebook. "You mind if I tape this?" When he shook his head, she switched on the mini-recorder and positioned it on the sofa arm. "Okay. I'd like to get some background information. After I first agreed to do this book, I started researching you, but frankly, there isn't much to find. You've never given many interviews, have you?"

"Only when I was forced to," Devin said. "Look, it's not that I play hard to get. It's just I don't like talking about myself. It's the music that's important, isn't it? Not whether I grew up in Istanbul or Timbuktu."

Fonda smiled. "Well, if you get me started, we could debate about the merits of publicity all night, but right now, I'd rather get to know you. The people who buy this book will want to know who you are. What made Devin O'Keefe the superstar he is today."

He shrugged. "Fire away."

"You grew up in Derry at the height of the Troubles. Can you tell me what it was like to live in such a violent society? How did it affect you personally?"

A shadow appeared in his eyes, but he answered without hesitation. "Sure, it wasn't all violence and bombs. When I was a young boy, my life mainly revolved around school and the church. When I grew out of short trousers, there was the occasional trip to Belfast. And sometimes, I'd catch a ride to the Giant's Causeway for a bit of *craic*." He laughed at the stunned look on her face. "Not *that* kind of crack. It's Irish slang for fun."

Fonda nodded and then steered the conversation back to the strife in Northern Ireland. "But surely the events in Ulster, the political situation, had to have some ill effect upon you? Left scars, you know."

Devin's face grew somber. "No doubt about it. My brother . . ." His voice trailed off. He hesitated a moment as if he were about to elaborate, then an unbearable look of sadness crossed his face. "Look, Fonda. All of this doesn't matter anymore. Let's start with Dublin. That's where it all began for me. And this *is* about music, is it not?"

Inwardly, she sighed. He'd politely built a brick wall in front of her. This time, she decided, she'd let him get away with it. But before this tour was over, she vowed to get him to open up about his mysterious past.

"Fair enough. Let's talk about this tour. You seem to have a love-hate relationship with my country. A preoccupation with it, you might say. Your lyrics often criticize America's 'excesses' and its foreign policy. Aren't you, to use a cliché, biting the hand that feeds you by doing that?"

"I love the American people," Devin said, his face serious. "And I love the symbol of freedom America stands for. But when I see injustice, I can't be silent. Don't you see, America is still the promised land for us, not just the Irish, but for the whole world. You must set an example. You must have higher standards than the rest of the world. So, when I see your politicians screwing over the working-class people, it makes me livid." Devin propped one booted foot onto the wardrobe and leaned toward her, his eyebrows knitted in concentration. "The hierarchy in Washington dine on $500-a-plate dinners while just down the street, the homeless huddle over heating grates to keep warm. It's a crying shame, it is!"

"And the problem is not limited to America," he continued.

"Look at the state England is in. The crime rate is at an all-time high. Unemployment is rampant. Ireland, too. No wonder our youth are constantly in trouble, when they have nothing to do but stand about on street corners looking for a way to make an easy buck. The Western world needs to make some changes, and if my lyrics serve to make even *one* person aware of the injustices, then I feel I've accomplished something."

Fonda nodded. "So, you really believe rock 'n' roll can change the world?"

The spark of excitement in his eyes flickered out. "I'm not so much of an idealistic fool as to believe that. But I truly believe each person can work toward change with the unique gift God has given him. For me, that's my music."

Fonda cleared her throat uncomfortably. She'd turned away from religion when Michael died. Why, now, did she feel vaguely envious of Devin's faith? It obviously ran very deep.

"And sometimes, it *does* change things." Devin said, his eyes impassioned. "Look at Live Aid. What was it? A hundred and twenty million dollars that Geldof raised for the Ethiopian famine relief? That's a perfect example of how rock can change things!"

"Yes, but isn't it sad that it took a rock concert to get people to donate?" Fonda asked. "Where were all those concerned people before that?"

Devin shrugged. "That's the world we live in, isn't it? Awareness is the key. Live Aid was just the beginning. After that, there was your Farm Aid, Amnesty International, Artists Against Apartheid. . . ."

"Oh, yes. It was quite the fashionable thing to do, wasn't it?" Fonda said, unable to keep the mocking edge from her voice. "Suddenly everyone was singing for a cause. I'm surprised some of you guys haven't put together a benefit for Tammy and Jim Bakker. A Save the Heritage USA concert."

Devin studied her. "You're very young to be so cynical."

"I'm sorry." Fonda felt her face redden. "That came out too strong. It's just that I know a lot of musicians who participated in those benefit concerts who don't give a damn about causes. They dash out a record or make a fifteen-minute appearance in an all-star concert just because it's the thing to do. Then they go back to their security-guarded villas in Rio or wherever the hell, until the next big cause comes up. It's hypocritical."

Devin was silent for a long moment. When he finally spoke, his voice was low. "I can only speak for myself. When I was up on that stage at Wembley during Live Aid, it was the most moving moment of my life. The oneness with the crowd, the desire to reach out and make the world a better place. I felt it in here." He tapped his chest over his heart. "We may not have saved the world that day, but for a little while, we made it a better place to live in. And in the end, does it really matter *why* we do it? Whether we're sincere or not? If that five-minute set on the stage puts food into a young child's mouth, that's enough for me."

Fonda nodded. "You're right, of course. I sometimes let my prejudices get in the way of common sense."

He leaned toward her. "I get the feeling you've seen a lot of the unsavory side of this business. Why do you stay in it?"

She started to give him a pat answer, one like, "It's my job," but something in his eyes stopped her. Finally, she said, "Because every so often, I meet someone who renews my faith in the business. Someone whose soul belongs to the music, and it makes it all worthwhile."

Devin didn't respond. For a long moment, he stared at her. Fonda wanted to add that she believed he was one of those people, but somehow, she knew she didn't have to. He knew.

"Anything else?" Devin asked.

"Yeah. Why rock 'n' roll? Why not politics?"

Abruptly, Devin jumped down from the wardrobe and began to pace the small dressing room. After a moment, he turned around to face her. "Two reasons. And I know this will sound inane, but music is in my soul. I can't help but release it. And rock is the forum I identify with. Why not politics? Because the young don't listen to politicians. They listen to music. And, this I believe with all my heart, it's the younger generation who will change things. Make it a better world. That's why I'm a rock singer, not a politician."

Fonda glanced down at her notebook. "I know you went

through some lean times in the early years with the band. What gave you your big break?"

Devin grinned. "Well, all Irish bands have U2 to thank for paving the way. Things got easier when they made it big. Of course, we had our second album out by that time. Selling decently in Europe, anyway. Then U2 started Mother Records for up and coming Irish groups and all hell broke loose. The Hothouse Flowers, Sinead O'Connor—from what I hear, now, if you're Irish and have a halfway decent sound, you have a record contract. Which reminds me, have you heard Energy Orchard? Here, let me play you a track. They're from Belfast."

For the next half-hour, Fonda listened to some of Devin's favorite music as they discussed each other's likes and dislikes. She found they had quite similar tastes. Finally, when Fonda glanced down at her watch, she saw she'd been interviewing Devin for over two hours.

"Oh, Jeez! I didn't realize how late it's getting. I'd better go. If I should think of something later, can I ring you up?"

Something like disappointment crossed his face. Because the interview was over? Or because she wanted to talk to him again? His face brightened. "Any time. And I mean that, Fonda. Even though I was against the idea of this book, now that we're doing it, I want to help wherever I can."

Fonda stood up and reached for the tape recorder. "I appreciate that. I think we'll both be happier with it if we get your input." As he opened the door to let her out, she paused and looked up at him. "You know, I remember your performance at Live Aid. I saw it on TV. It was the first time I'd ever heard of you."

"There were so many artists performing that day, in London and here in America. What made you remember me?"

"Your intensity," Fonda said without hesitation. "I remember thinking, 'This Irishman is going to be a star.' I suggested to the editor at *Spotlight* that we do an interview with you. But I was at the bottom of the staff echelon at that time. And he wasn't interested. The next year, when you made your first American tour, he was kicking himself about it. By then, it was too late. You weren't doing interviews."

"Yes. I'd already been burned by the British press. I wasn't about to let the Americans start in on me."

Fonda grinned. "Well, you have now." At the look of surprise in his eyes, she added, "But I promise, I'll be gentle with you."

Having realized she was teasing, he smiled back at her. "That you will. I'm a very sensitive soul, you know." He paused. "Will you be at the concert tonight?"

"You'd better believe it. Thanks for the interview, Devin."

"Thank *you* for going easy on me."

Just as Fonda turned to step out of his dressing room, he spoke again, "Fonda?"

"Yes?"

"Where did you get a name like that? You have to admit it's a bit unusual."

Fonda grinned. "My mother was obsessed with Henry Fonda. And since Dad didn't consider him a threat, he went along with her naming me after him. That was before Jane Fonda starting visiting North Vietnam, you understand. He almost had a coronary then, being such a right-winger. There was even talk of dropping Fonda for my middle name." Fonda's smile widened. "But that didn't work either. My middle name is Jane."

Devin laughed, and with an answering smile, Fonda left his dressing room. He closed the door behind her, his smile disappearing. Christ! What was he going to do? For days, he'd been unable to get Fonda out of his mind. And now, after learning a little more about her, it would be even more difficult. She tried to appear tough, even jaded about this business, but her vulnerability clearly showed through. She was an idealist, just like him. A kindred spirit.

For the first time in years—in his life, perhaps—he'd felt like confiding in someone. When she'd asked about his childhood in Northern Ireland, he'd felt something break loose inside him. The memories had flooded back. The search for arms by hardened British soldiers, the Bin-Can Brigades formed by neighborhood women and children to warn of coming raids. The petrol bombs thrown by every self-respecting youth. Glen and Bloody Sunday. Mary Marie. Sweet, innocent Mary Marie and the horrible night of her death.

But in the end, he'd stopped himself from telling her about that life. What good would it do to bring it all back? After Da's release from prison and his death a few years later, Devin had left Derry for a new life. And that he'd found.

Besides, confiding in Fonda would only bring them closer. That he couldn't risk. Her perfume lingered in the air of his dressing room. In his mind's eye, he saw her perfect oval face and rippling golden brown hair. Fonda . . . a woman who could make a man forget his own name.

13

UNDER THE dashboard of the rented Mazda, Ian Brinegar struck a match and read the face of his gold Baume & Mercier watch. Nine-forty. Where the fuck were they? He blew out the match and stared gloomily into the darkness outside. Somewhere out there was the polluted White River, but in this bleeding fog, who could tell? Except for the stench, of course. Jesus, but this Indianapolis was a hellhole. Down here by the river, there was nothing but abandoned warehouses and railroad tracks. An appropriate place for business such as he had in mind. If the bloody help would show up.

He switched on the radio to distract himself. Simon & Garfunkle were singing "The Boxer." Music had been good back then, not the boring mumbo-jumbo they played on the radio these days. Ian hummed along with the song, recalling his days in London when he'd worked at the BBC. It had been a happy time for him. London's nightlife had suited him fine, offering plenty of opportunities to meet sensual young men. During the fade-out of "The Boxer," another tune began to play. Devin's "Ghosts."

Christ, he couldn't get away from the man for a bloody hour! As his finger jabbed at the button to change the station, a sharp rap sounded on the window. Ian jumped and turned to the dark shape staring in at him. He touched a button and the window lowered.

"Mulligan?"

It was the name Caitlyn had given him. Her reason had been simple. "You can't trust the Americans. They don't really understand our aims. The only green they believe in is the color of their paper money."

Ian peered at the man, but it was so dark, he couldn't make him out clearly. "Yeah, I'm Mulligan. Where's everyone else?"

The man jerked his head toward the warehouse behind him. "Man, we've been waiting in there for a half-hour. You coming?"

Ian leaned down to grab the cheap briefcase on the floorboard. Then he climbed out of the car and followed the dark shape through the fog. The man was short and stocky and walked with a swagger. A punk, thought Ian. They were all nothing but smartass punks. Trouble was, he needed them.

The warehouse was dark and appeared to be deserted. After Ian stepped in, the man shoved the sliding door shut and then spoke quietly, "Boys, this here is Mulligan."

A light flickered in front of him. Ian found himself staring into a pair of cold brown eyes. Lips twisted in a long, horselike face, revealing the rotten stumps of blackened teeth. Ian resisted an urge to step backward from the homely caricature facing him. Behind the man, four other figures lurked in the shadows.

Rotten Teeth spoke in a nasal twang. "So you're Mulligan." Hillbilly accent, Ian figured. He'd heard about these American hillbillies. A dangerous lot, they were. "Been looking forward to meeting you. I'm Harlen." He took out a pack of Camels. "Care for a smoke?"

"No, thank you," Ian said. "Shall we get down to business?" It came out with a pompous air. Immediately, he knew he'd made a mistake.

The man's eyes narrowed. "Why, you ain't particularly neighborly, now, are you? I always heard you Irishmen were a real friendly sort, but I guess we got us a cold fish on our hands. That right, Mulligan?"

Ian shifted uncomfortably. He tried to summon a smile. "I didn't mean to insult you. It's just that I can't stay gone for long. I'll be missed, you see. I have the money. You're welcome to count it to make sure it's all here."

Harlen grinned and his eyes began to gleam. "Why, I'll surely do that. Why don't you just put it down on this here table. Hey, Sam. You count it and make sure Mulligan here did his arithmetic right."

Ian snapped open the locks on the briefcase and stood back while a thin man with lank blond hair began to count the stacks of greenbacks. Harlen continued to stare at Ian and grin.

The room was thick with tension as the thin man counted the money. No one spoke. Harlen kept his cold eyes fixed upon Ian. Sweat popped out onto the Irishman's forehead. Outside, the wind began to blow and a moment later, raindrops rattled against the warehouse walls. The lonesome howl of a freight train echoed in the distance.

Ian's crotch itched, but he didn't dare move to scratch it. Jesus, these guys were nothing but hoodlums. He hoped to God Caitlyn knew what she was doing dealing with such trash. How easy it would be for them to take the money and simply disappear.

"It all there, Sam?"

"'Pears to be. Two hundred and fifty thousand."

"And you'll get the other half on delivery in St. Louis," Ian said, trying to stare Harlen down. "One week. Can you do it?"

A giggle escaped his thin lips "Well, I don't rightly know. How bad do you want me to?"

"Now, look here—"

"Hold on, now, Mulligan. Don't be getting your Jockeys in a wad. I'm just toying with you." He took a long hit from his cigarette and blew the smoke in Ian's direction. "We'll have them crates for you. There's this old abandoned building down by the Mississippi. Out past where the old riverboats are moored. Used to be a bait and tackle place. You just come down there on, say, the fourteenth at twelve-thirty in the morning. All them dinner boats will have closed up and there shouldn't be nobody around." Another giggle. "Excepting for people up to no good. You gotta watch out for some of them river folks. You can find yourself floating facedown in that old Mississippi if you ain't careful. Know what I mean, Mulligan?"

Ian suppressed a shudder. This hillbilly gave him the willies.

"Thank you for the warning, Mr. Harlen. And I'm sure you'll be equally cautious.

That seemed to delight him. He laughed, loud and ugly. "You know, Mulligan. I think maybe I was wrong about you. Hey, maybe in St. Louie, you and me can get together for a drink of whiskey. We Irishmen have to stick together, you know. My great-grandpappy came from the old sod. That's why I'm so happy to be helping you out. I'm a true-blue American, but there's still a soft spot in the old heart for the Emerald Isle."

And a soft spot for the emerald paperbacks emblazoned with presidents. Ian turned to go. "The fourteenth at half-twelve. I'll be there."

Harlen let out an obnoxious chortle. "Half-twelve," he mimicked. "Ain't we hoity-toity?" Even after he got his glee under control, he kept grinning. "You do that, Mulligan. You be there at *half-twelve*. I'll bring the whiskey. You bring the bucks." As if to add emphasis to his words, Harlen released a loud, vulgar belch.

Ian tried to keep his face expressionless. The hillbilly's ugly laughter followed him out the door. Only the hard patter of the rain blocked out the mad sound of it as he made his way to the car.

⊛

WITH A strained smile, Fonda kissed her mother good-bye and gave Jessie a warm hug. The copper-haired fifteen-year-old pulled away, her freckled face alight with excitement.

"Fon, I can't wait for tonight. All the kids at school are going to have a cow when they find out April and I have front-row seats at Devin's concert. That's so cool!"

"You'd better make sure she'll be safe there," Ed Blayne said. "I'm not crazy about the idea of her in the middle of that rabble-rousing crowd. God knows what kind of scum will be there."

Fonda bit her lip and turned to her father. "Jessie will be fine, Dad. I told you I've arranged for a limo to pick her up and bring her back home. Look, I really have to go." She gave him a quick impersonal kiss and got into her rented Lumina. With a final wave, she was out of the driveway and heading toward the interstate. But even as she put the miles between herself and her family home, the tension in her stomach didn't diminish.

Another stressful visit with the family to be catalogued with all the rest. But perhaps things were getting better. This time, there had only been one moment of real animosity when Dad had started in about her career. He'd suggested she give up the music business and apply for a job as a police photographer.

"Don't you want to make something of your life, Fonda? Something that means something?" he'd asked.

Her reply had been short and to the point. "You mean like Michael did?"

That had put an end to that conversation.

As she pulled onto the interstate, one of Devin's old songs came on the radio. It reminded her of the video she'd seen just that afternoon with Jessie. It had been filmed several years ago, an on-stage performance in Australia. Fonda had seen it before, but not since she'd met Devin. In the video, he'd looked younger, less careworn than he did today. But the fire and passion had been there even then. The song was one of strife and angst, typical Devin material. At one point near the end, he'd whirled around, sending a shower of sweat droplets across the stage, and the camera had caught an expression on his face that was startling in its intensity.

Fonda remembered how her heart had leapt at that point. Jessie had mentioned earlier in the day that she thought Devin was sexy. Fonda understood what she meant, but as she watched the video, another word had come to mind. Devin O'Keefe was sensual, like a prowling lion stalking his prey, and that she found even more exciting than if he did exude sexuality. Those thin lips, so smooth and somehow vulnerable. The piercing brown eyes, blazing with fervor.

Just as Devin's song reached its climax, it was interrupted by a warning blare, one that was sickeningly familiar to Fonda. A deejay began to speak, and she realized why her stomach was still churning. It was the ugly black clouds in the western sky she'd started to notice as she drove toward Indianapolis. For a little while, she'd almost forgotten what it was like to live in Indiana in the early summer.

"The National Weather Service has issued a tornado watch for the counties of Hendricks, Marion, and Franklin. Radar reports a line of severe thunderstorms. . . ."

Fonda switched off the radio, her heart racing with dread. The years melted away, and for a moment, she was an eleven-year-old girl again, clinging to Michael and her mother in a dark basement as the wind shrieked havoc outside. Oh, God! Would she ever be able to sit through a thunderstorm again without thinking of the tornado that had swept away the entire Smith family? She gritted her teeth, hating her weakness, the paralyzing fear of tornadoes that had become her only true phobia.

"Why do I come back to this state?" she muttered, as she pulled into the arena parking lot. She jumped out of the car, casting an apprehensive glance over her shoulder toward the southwest. A sickening jolt shot through her stomach at the sight of the menacing line of inky clouds on the horizon. The air was close and muggy, without the slightest hint of a breeze. Beads of sweat popped out on Fonda's face, yet she shivered as she glanced around. The afternoon light was suffused with a greenish tinge. It was almost as if she'd taken a step back in time to that terrifying afternoon in 1974.

Her only thought was to get into the building and find someone to be near. The one thing she couldn't bear was to be alone during a violent thunderstorm. With hurried steps, she maneuvered through the maze of backstage equipment, rounded a huge crate, and ran smack into Devin. His hands reached out to steady her.

"Where's the fire?" he asked. Then his eyes sharpened. "Hey, what is it? You look like you've seen a ghost."

"There's a tornado warning!" She bit her lip, trying to control her fear. "It's really ugly out there."

Devin's serene expression didn't fade. He reached down and grasped both of her hands between his. "And why are you so terrified?" His brown eyes peered into hers warmly as he waited for an answer.

Fonda stared at him. "I just *told* you. A tornado! They *kill* people!"

There was a sudden rumble of thunder outside and she flinched. Devin reached out and drew her into his arms; the movement was so natural that Fonda immediately relaxed against him. With her cheek plastered against his chest, she could hear the steady thud of his heartbeat. His hands moved reassuringly on her back.

Over the sound of the rolling thunder, she heard his voice. "When I was a wee boy, I was afraid of storms. Especially thunder. But Da told me it was the gods having at a game of road bowls. Once I thought about that, it wasn't so frightening." His hands slid down her arms and grasped hers. "Come on. Let's go have a bit of tea."

She didn't protest as he drew her down the hallway toward the tuning room. Inside, it was dark except for the brilliant flashes of lightning that pierced through the windows. Blindly, Devin felt for the switch. The overhead fluorescent lights flickered to life.

"Sit yourself down on the sofa there while I get the blinds." He crossed the large room in a fluid movement that brought to mind the video she'd seen this afternoon, and a moment later, he'd closed the blinds against the blue-white flashes outside. "Now for the tea." Just as he reached the pot of water simmering on a hot plate, the heavens opened up and the rain began to beat down in a raging torrent.

Fonda shivered and drew her legs up on the sofa, hugging her arms around them for warmth. The shorts and sleeveless top she'd worn in the heat of the morning were now hopelessly inadequate.

Devin looked up from the steeping tea. "Cold, love? I'll fix that in a moment." A few seconds later, he handed her a hot mug of tea. "Be right back."

Fonda took a sip of the fragrant beverage and watched as he went to a closet and grabbed a pea green woolen coat. "Give me your tea and slip into this. It's made for Ireland's blustery weather."

It was big on her, reaching down past her knees, but the warm wool was pleasant against her skin and smelled of Devin's woodsy scent. He sat down on the other end of the sofa, his mug of tea between his hands.

"Better?" he asked.

Fonda nodded. The rain beat against the windows, punctuated by occasional rumbles of thunder. Funny, her fear had left her. Somehow, with Devin here, a tornado didn't seem quite so likely.

His eyes roved over her. "I like your hair down like that. It makes you look more . . . approachable."

Approachable? What did that mean? A deafening crash of thunder shook the building and she flinched, spilling a drop of tea over her fingers. "Ouch!"

Devin put down his mug and drew a handkerchief from his pocket. He slid over next to her and dabbed at her hand. "There, now. Drink your tea, Sweet Thing." He grinned and lapsed into a heavy brogue. "It'll warm up yer insides, as me mum always said." He gazed at her a moment, a perplexed look on his face. "Why is it every time I look at you, I hear that old Van Morrison song in my head?"

Fonda had no idea what song he was talking about, but before she could speak, he reached over the side of the sofa and grabbed his guitar. He strummed a chord. "You may recognize it." Softly, he began to sing, but the tune wasn't familiar to Fonda. He sang with only a hint of an Irish accent, his head bent over his guitar. It was strange to be listening to his world-famous voice in the intimacy of the tuning room. For a moment, Fonda had the feeling he was actually shy about singing to her. But on the chorus, he looked up and his penetrating brown eyes connected with hers. "Sweet thing . . ."

Fonda felt the color rise on her cheeks. When the song was over, he went right into another, this time, a lively Irish ballad in an exaggerated brogue. She couldn't help but grin. Never in her wildest dreams would she have believed Devin O'Keefe could be so relaxed and easygoing. She applauded when he finished.

Devin smiled and cocked his head toward the windows. "Sounds as if the rain is slowing down."

He was right. The downpour had changed to a light drizzle. Why, she'd forgotten about being frightened. And it was all because of the calming effect Devin had upon her. But was his mention of the rain his way of hinting for her to leave? Without looking up, he began to strum the guitar again. Relief flooded through her.

Why, suddenly, did she feel as if this were the only place in the world she wanted to be? He began to sing a folk song in Gaelic. As she watched him play, she became fascinated with his hands. They were strong and well shaped, not too large, but not small either. Dexterous. Yes! That was the word. For a fleeting moment, she imagined them moving over her bare skin, bringing her body alive. She felt warm inside Devin's coat, and with an effort, forced her mind to veer away from such dangerous thoughts.

Gradually, as Devin continued to sing, Fonda's eyes drooped. It had been a long day. Somehow, the hot tea and Devin's soft Irish voice had combined to bring on a delicious sense of relaxation, one she'd never really known before. It was as if she were wrapped in a warm cocoon, safe and snug from not only the storm outside but everything threatening. With the sound of the light rain falling and Devin's lilting Gaelic in her ears, Fonda allowed her mind to drift into sleep.

Later, she wondered if it was a dream. The touch of Devin's hand on her face, his voice full of sadness and longing as he whispered, "Sweet Thing . . why couldn't I have met you sooner?"

14

FONDA MET Jessie and her wide-eyed friend, April, in the arena foyer and gave them the backstage passes she'd managed to finagle from Bram. "Now, this doesn't mean you can go hog-wild back here," she said, as she took them on a brief tour of the backstage area. "It just means you can come with me backstage after the concert."

Jessie's voice was a breathless gasp. "Where's Devin? Can we meet him now?"

"In the tuning room, probably. Getting ready for the concert."

"Well, take us to him." Jessie's smile faded at the look on Fonda's face. "You're not going to do it, are you? Fonda! You promised!"

Fonda sighed. "It's just that I don't think it would be a good time to disturb him. After the concert, okay?"

Both girls suddenly looked as if they were in mourning.

"And who says you'd be disturbing me?"

At the sound of the soft Irish voice, the teenagers' faces paled, and in hushed reverence, they turned to see Devin standing in the shadows, a smile playing about his lips.

His eyes moved to Fonda. "Who might these lovely ladies be?"

"My sister Jessie, and her friend April. Bram got them concert tickets."

Neither girl had uttered a word. They were frozen where they stood, their eyes glued to their idol. Devin pretended not to notice. He walked to them and held out a hand to Jessie. "Sure, you're as darlin' as your big sister."

Jessie gazed up at him in adoration and smiled dreamily. His eyes went to April. "And you, love, you have a smile that would enchant the faeries. Careful they won't steal you away."

April giggled. Devin put an arm around each of them and turned to Fonda. "Your sister doesn't know me well enough to know my fans can *never* disturb me. But she's learning . . ."

Fonda felt her face grow warm. His eyes were boring a hole through her. And doing strange things to her insides.

"Would you girls like to come with me to the tuning room to meet the band?"

"Oh, yes!" they chorused, eyes shining.

"Fonda? Will you join us?"

"I really can't, Devin," she said. "I have some last-minute things to do before the concert. Can you give me fifteen minutes and I'll come and get them settled in their seats?"

He nodded. "Come on, girls." He waited until they stepped out in front of him, then turned and gave a small salute to Fonda. "I'll see *you* later."

And he was gone.

Fonda felt like kicking herself. Why hadn't she gone with them? There was nothing she had to do. During that moment this afternoon when he'd held her in his arms, she'd made a discovery. She liked being there. But maybe that was why she'd turned down his invitation. She was confused by the emotions Devin was arousing in her. Confused and frightened. The last thing in the world she needed was to become involved with a rock star. Her years in the entertainment business had taught her how fickle and jaded most of them were. In fact, the ones she'd met, with few exceptions, had been so insufferably egotistical, she'd never been tempted to break her personal rule of not dating artists.

But then, none of them had been Devin.

When the concert began, she was standing in the wings at her usual spot. Countless times, she found herself missing a photo opportunity because she was so caught up in watching Devin. It was amazing how he held his fans captive. Ruefully, she realized he had a pretty tight hold on her, too, as he finished one of the hits from his first album.

After the frenzied applause died away, Bram strode on stage with Devin's acoustic guitar. Devin slid the strap over his head, strummed a chord, and in his rich accent spoke into the microphone. "Sometimes, fear and lack of faith are emotions that go hand-in-hand. Here's a song I wrote about the importance of faith. It's called 'Storms.'"

> *"Reach for me*
> *When the storm is near*
> *I'll be your anchor*
> *Your flight from fear.*
> *Believe in me*
> *Put your hand in mine.*
> *The storm's grand fury will disappear.*
> *There'll be no more fear.*
> *No more fear."*

When the last lingering note faded away in the near silence of the auditorium, Devin sat unmoving on one of the platforms, his head bowed over his guitar. The applause spread through the audience like a rumbling earthquake. Finally, his head came up. Fonda's heart skipped a beat as his eyes centered on her. For a long moment, he gazed at her solemnly, then one eye closed in a wink and he smiled.

She felt as if she'd never been smiled at before. He jumped to his feet and launched into one of his well-known rock songs. The crowd roared. It was a bluesy rocker, one of the few lighthearted songs he did. Throughout it, he grinned, obviously enjoying the change of pace.

There was a nudge on Fonda's arm. Bram held out a can of Coke. "You look a wee bit thirsty."

Fonda grinned. "Thanks. I am." She took the soda and popped the top, her eyes still on Devin. "He's really full of fire tonight, isn't he?" When there was no response, she turned, only to find that Bram had already disappeared.

The first half of the concert came to an end. Devin gave his guitar to one of the stagehands and turned to look at her. Fonda caught her breath as abruptly, he began to stride toward the wings. She didn't move. If she'd wanted to, it would've been impossible, because suddenly, she felt like a butterfly pinned to a board. He stopped directly in front of her, only inches away. With her heart beating in overdrive, she looked into his sweat-streaked face and felt an almost irresistible urge to run her fingers through his damp hair. Still gazing at her, he reached out and slowly took the can of soda from her. He took one long draw from it and gave it back. In almost the same motion, he lifted his hand and brushed his thumb lightly along the line of her cheekbone.

"Later," he said. "I want to talk to you."

Then he strode on backstage to grab the towel the wardrobe woman held out for him. Fonda looked down at the can in her hand. Then almost caressingly, she brought it to her lips and drank.

FONDA WAS waiting for him as he came backstage after his last encore. Wiping his face with a towel, he walked toward her, his white lawn shirt wet with sweat and plastered against his chest. He reached her and without hesitation, dropped the towel and took her hands in his. "How are you?"

She nodded. "Okay."

"Shakes are over?"

"Yeah. Thanks." For some reason, she found it difficult to meet his gaze. Instead, her eyes focused upon the glistening patch of black chest hair exposed by his half-opened shirt.

"So, you see, you were worrying for nothing. Your windstorm didn't come."

"Yeah, it's silly of me, I guess. A tornado wrecked my town when I was a child." Finally, she met his eyes. "I guess I just can't forget the horror of it."

His face was solemn as he stared down at her. "You're not supposed to forget." He reached out and touched a strand of her hair; because of what he'd said that afternoon, she'd left it unbraided for the night. "Tragedy is senseless, of course. But for those of us left behind, we have to learn from it. Go on, and make some sense out of our lives."

It was as if he were talking about Michael. "But sometimes it's so frightening," she whispered. "And even though I try, I get scared."

"We all do. But that's where faith comes in. I wrote 'Storms' for you this afternoon, you know. While you were asleep. Did you guess that?"

She shook her head. They stared at each other for a long moment, not speaking. Then Devin made a barely perceptible move to go. Fonda didn't think. She simply reached out and touched his chest in a silent plea to stay. He hesitated, staring at her. His hand moved to cover hers. Afterwards, Fonda wasn't sure who moved first. But once again, she found herself in his arms, her face against his chest. Like a soft whisper, she turned her mouth against his skin and tasted the salt of his sweat. He expelled his breath in a long sigh and murmured some words in Gaelic, then with his hands under her ripples of hair, he bent his head to kiss her. Fonda's hands slid up his damp shirt to where his hair swept his collar. His mouth moved across hers tentatively, tasting, testing, almost questioning. Then suddenly, the kiss deepened—became urgent. A white-hot heat radiated through her body. Her hands tightened onto the damp fabric of his shirt and a soft moan escaped her lips even though they were locked against his.

Suddenly he wrenched his mouth away, breathing heavily. His eyes were stormy as he stared down at her. Then he spoke a few words in Gaelic.

"What does that mean?" she asked, breathless from his kiss. Her hand was still clutched against his shirt front and beneath it, she could feel the rapid thud of his heartbeat.

"It doesn't matter," he said finally. "Fonda, do yourself a favor, and go find a nice American man." He turned away and disappeared into the backstage shadows.

WITH A vengeance, Devin slammed the door of his dressing room. He sat down on the edge of the sofa and raked his hands through his damp hair. His heart thudded hard against his sweat-soaked shirt. He groaned aloud and held his hands out in front of him. They were shaking.

What was he doing? Had he lost his mind? He'd known, even as he was writing the damn song, that he was playing with fire. And as if that was not enough, he'd shared it with her, letting her know it had been written for her. Had he, for one insane moment, thought he could get away with a harmless flirtation? One stolen kiss in the wings of the stage and then walk away? That's exactly what he'd done, wasn't it? But his heart knew there was no going back.

Damn! He had no right to get involved with another woman. Not after Caitlyn. She'd turned him inside out, shredded his heart and patched it up again. He slammed his hand into the sofa. No! He wouldn't think of her now. Not now. Like a magnet, his mind swept back to Fonda.

God, what *was* it about the woman? Her perfect oval face swam in front of him. So ethereal, with her ivory skin and the light dusting of freckles across her delicately molded nose. Petite and small-boned, her long, slender neck appeared almost too fragile to hold the weight of her waist-length, rippling hair. Her hair! Jesus, he loved the soft silk of it against his hands. And those clear hazel eyes that seemed to peer directly into his heart. He remembered the moment just before he'd pulled her into his arms for that searing kiss, how they had darkened to a deep shade of green. It had been that and the soft touch of her mouth against his skin that had caused him to lose control of his tightly reined emotions.

He stood up and paced his dressing room. One thing was for sure. He had to push Fonda away from him. She was a sweet woman. Special. He wouldn't risk hurting her. And that he knew he would do, sooner or later, if he didn't stop things right now. He would simply have to be stronger. Would have to resist her.

There was only one way to do that. He had to stay away from her.

BRAM STARED at Devin's dressing-room door. He could hear him inside, pacing like a caged beast. It was obvious the girl, Fonda, was playing havoc with his emotions. And that, he thought, was good. It had been way too long since any woman had gotten close enough to get any kind of reaction out of Devin. But Bram didn't like the way he was handling it. The man was wound up tighter than a time bomb. He could almost imagine the ticking of it. If some of the pressure weren't released . . . sweet Jesus, who *knew* what would happen?

When he'd seen them kissing backstage, he'd been elated. Fonda would be good for Devin. She was different from all the besotted groupies who'd been after him for years. Somehow, Bram knew that what Fonda wanted from Devin went much deeper than sex with a rock god. And what she wanted was exactly what he needed. Love, pure and simple. He just hoped his friend would have the good sense to accept it. If he didn't, he was a bloody fool, and Bram would tell him so to his face.

But then, Devin was a man of honor. Unlike himself. Bram wished he could be more like Devin, a man who could see a clear difference between right and wrong, and who would unerringly choose the former. Or if he did choose the wrong way, he'd have the guts to come forward and admit it. Cleanse himself. Instead of wallowing in the dirt and deceit.

He heard a footfall and turned to see Ian coming down the hall. "Devin in there, Bram?"

"Yeh, but I don't think he's in the mood to talk business."

Ian brushed past him. "We talk business whenever I say so." He rapped hard on the door and opened it.

It slammed behind him. Bram couldn't control the disgusted look on his face. Try as he might, he just couldn't stomach that man. He was a sly son-of-a-bitch, he was. He and his cover stories, his web of lies after what had happened with Caitlyn. To protect Devin's image, he'd said. Bullshit! It was his own ass he was protecting. All those business deals in England would've blown up in his face if the taint of the IRA touched him. Brinegar was no fool.

If Brinegar had come clean with the press, if instead of covering up Caitlyn's IRA connections, he'd admitted she was wallowing in a Brit prison for life, perhaps Devin could've weathered the bad press and been able to put Caitlyn behind him forever. But then—there was the other thing. Bram's own deceit. He didn't kid himself in thinking Brinegar was alone in the muck. By harboring his own secret, Bram was doing *his* part in keeping the woman alive in Devin's heart. Even so, he knew he couldn't tell him.

Not now. Maybe never. He was simply too weak.

THE HUMILIATION was too much to bear. Fonda had thrown herself at Devin, and he'd flatly rejected her. Just like that. Every time she thought of it, her face burned with chagrin. What a fool she'd been. Thinking she could make a difference in his life. The man probably had to fight off women every day. How could she have done it? Her? Someone in the business who *knew* how impossible a lasting relationship with an entertainer would be. And yet, like a besotted groupie, she'd returned his kiss. Idiot!

There had been no words exchanged between them since the night in Indianapolis, almost a week ago. But the smoldering glances he'd been directing at her hadn't gone unnoticed. What was he thinking? That she was easy? Just another groupie? How galling!

And here they were in St. Louis for a two-night gig. There was no way she could avoid the man. Not when she was writing a damn book about him.

Fonda was in her room at the Clarion Hotel, fleshing out a chapter on the Indianapolis concert, when the phone beeped. Distracted, she picked it up. "Yes?"

"Fon! It's me, Jessie!"

Her heart skipped a beat. "Jessie! What's wrong?"

There was a pause at the other end of the line. Then, "Nothing. Well, nothing much. I'm at the bus station."

"Here? In St. Louis?"

"Yeah." Her voice was exhilarated. "I've run away!"

FONDA GRITTED her teeth and maneuvered through the heavy rush-hour traffic of St. Louis. Jessie's eyes grew wide as they passed the Gateway Arch, glowing amber in the last light of the setting sun.

"Wow! Can we go up in it tomorrow, Fon? I bet the city is gorgeous from up there."

"Ha!" Fonda said grimly. "You can see it just as well from the airplane."

Jessie's mouth dropped open. "You're not *really* sending me home?"

"Well, what am I supposed to do? Allow you to tag along with me all over the country?"

"Well, yeah. That's why I came to St. Louis. I knew you'd be here."

"Jessie, this is impossible! The rock scene is not what I'd call a healthy atmosphere for a fifteen-year-old girl."

"Sixteen," Jessie corrected. "I had a birthday last week, remember? Just for the summer, Fon. Please! I just couldn't take another day in that house with Dad. He's always on my back about something." Her hazel eyes widened in mock horror. "Fon! They were going to send me to a Girl Scout camp. Can you imagine? Me, sitting around a campfire, reciting 'Hiawatha'?"

Fonda laughed and then immediately sobered. "Damn it, Jessie. Don't do this to me." She turned into the underground parking lot of the hotel.

"Fon, you can talk them into letting me stay. You know you can. Just tell them you'll take care of me. You won't let me go to any wild parties, and you won't let me even *talk* to any boys, and when you have to work, you'll tie me up in your hotel room and gag me and . . ."

"Dad will never go for it."

"But he doesn't have to! He left yesterday for a two-week conference in Chicago. Once you convince Mom, it'll be too late for him to object."

"Jessie!" Fonda slid into an empty parking space and turned off the ignition. She looked at her sister. "She won't defy Dad."

"Yes, she will," Jessie said, her eyes shining in the gloom of the parking lot. "If *you* convince her. Look, you can tell her I'm your apprentice for the summer. I'll run errands for you, learn the business. It'll be good experience for a career. It's better than being a candy-striper or a camp counselor. Please, Fon, *try!*"

Fonda stared at her sister's earnest face, knowing her will had already weakened beyond the point of refusal. "I'll *talk* to her," she said. "But remember, the final word is hers. If she says you have to come home, I'm taking you straight to the airport tomorrow."

Jessie flashed a triumphant grin. "You'll do it, Fonda. I have complete faith in you."

As soon as they reached her room, Jessie disappeared into the bathroom to soak in the tub while Fonda made herself comfortable on the bed and reached for the phone.

As the phone rang in Indiana, Fonda thought of her father's reaction to his baby daughter serving an apprenticeship on the rock concert circuit for the summer. An ironic smile crossed her face. Wouldn't he be livid if Jessie decided to make it a career?

"Hello, Mom?"

15

"JESSIE, YOU'RE in luck." Fonda flashed her crew badge at the guard standing at the stage door. "She's with me." She gave Jessie a gentle push. "We'll have to get you a badge tomorrow. As I was saying, one of the Irish sound technicians has a daughter about your age touring with him this summer. He's supposed to meet us backstage to introduce you."

Much to Jessie's delight, she'd been allowed to stay with Fonda until mid-August. Of course, Fonda made sure Jessie realized that had come about after she'd endured twenty minutes of warnings from her mother interspersed with dire predictions of how her father would take the news. Something about how it would be Fonda's ass on the chopping block if anything bad came of the arrangement. She didn't exactly use those words, but the meaning had come through loud and clear.

"So, what if I don't like this girl?" Jessie asked, as Fonda led the way backstage.

"Oh, you'll like her. She's Irish."

Jessie rolled her eyes. As if *that* meant anything.

But Fonda was right. Jessie liked Laoise Meehan immediately, even though her lilting brogue made her rather hard to understand. The first half-hour of their acquaintance found the vivacious dark-eyed Laoise talking non-stop, and Jessie responding with, "What?" "Excuse me?" "I'm sorry, what did you say?" But after a while, her ears adjusted and she found she was understanding more and asking her to repeat less.

The two girls made themselves comfortable in a cubbyhole backstage where Laoise, who'd been with the tour all of two weeks, began to educate Jessie on the idiosyncrasies of the various members of the crew. She was in the middle of telling her about one of the sound crewmen, Jacky-something, who had a thing going with a "jealous bitch" named Mairead, when a shadow fell over them.

"What have you got here, Laoise? The prettiest girl in America and you keeping her all to yourself?"

His voice was like a lilting Irish pipe. His looks were even better. Mouth open, Jessie gaped at the vision of perfection standing only a few feet away from them. He was young, not more than seventeen, she was sure. Blond hair, cut short and spiked, and in one perfect earlobe, a diamond stud. His eyes were deep, deep blue and intense. Eyes a girl could swim in. He smiled, and when he did, a dimple flashed in his left cheek. His perfect adolescent body was clad in tight stonewashed jeans and a black leather motorcycle jacket emblazoned with *Motley Crue* in glittery scrip.

His name was Ryan and he was Laoise's brother. He was working as an assistant roadie to Barry Pearse, the drummer.

It took all of five seconds for Jessie to fall in love.

IAN TOOK a quick glance up and down the street as he paused at the door of a telephone booth. The only living creature in sight was a seedy black man hunched up against the brick wall of a pawn shop, nursing a brown-bagged bottle of liquor. He paid no attention to Ian. He was too busy cowering from the biting wind blowing in from the Mississippi River. A cold front had passed through the day before and it was unseasonably cool in the midwestern city.

More's the pity for America's homeless, Ian thought. A shame, it was, the government didn't do something about the problem. No one saw that shameless sort of thing in Northern Ireland. No drug addicts hanging around the streets, either. Ian cracked a wry grin as he stepped into the telephone booth and deposited a quarter. Then, again, the IRA ran a quite successful rehabilitation program. They shot the druggies.

"Yes, Operator. I'd like to make a collect call to Dublin, Ireland. Name is Mulligan."

As he waited for the call to go through, his eyes fell again on the derelict. Jesus, if Devin were here, he'd be outraged. It would've taken him about half a second to go over there and offer the bum a hundred or two. Ian felt no such inclination. He was a realist, not a starry-eyed idealist like O'Keefe. That piece of human garbage was born a bum and would die one. And who cared?

Ian turned away from the street and gazed out over the buildings where the top of the Gateway Arch glimmered in the light of a full moon. A harsh laugh escaped his throat. Devin was a real good one for charity. At least, he *thought* he was. Wouldn't he shit a bleeding brick if he knew that most of his "charitable contributions" went to help the boyos up north?

"Your party is on the line, sir."

"Caitlyn?"

"What is it, Mulligan?"

"Just wanted to check in with you. We're here in St. Louis and everything is on schedule. The delivery of the goods will be made day after tomorrow, the fourteenth."

There was a pause at the other end of the line. Then, "Is that it?"

Ian hesitated. He decided to dive in. "I don't know about these Americans. They're an unsavory lot. Are you sure we can trust them?"

Her voice was calm. "They know what will happen if they cross us."

"But . . ."

"What?"

"I don't like the feel of this. They . . ." He stared out at the drunken man. He was staggering to his feet, leaning heavily against the building for support. "The leader doesn't seem right in the head. He threatened me back in Indianapolis. It was thinly veiled, but a threat all the same."

"Ian, you're whining. You wouldn't be losing your nerve on me now, would you?"

"Of course not, Caitlyn." The bum was unsteadily making his way toward the telephone booth. Ian turned his back on the man. "I just want you to be prepared should—anything happen to me."

Her laughter came across the telephone wire like a silver waterfall. Something clicked against the glass of the booth. Ian turned around to see the drunk grinning in at him. The empty liquor bottle tapped against the window.

"Don't be daft, Mulligan. You've been watching too many James Bond movies. How is Devin?"

Scowling, Ian gestured for the man to go away. Instead, the drunk grinned and waved back, his hand wrapped in what looked like a moth-eaten sock. "He's just the same. Oblivious to everything except his bloody tour."

"Let's hope he stays that way. How's this book thing working out? Is this woman keeping him busy?"

"I suppose so. She's always in the way. Hanging about the stage, taking her bleeding pictures. I seem to be tripping over her all the time."

"No matter. The important thing is she distracts Devin from paying too much attention to the business end of things. Let me know how it goes on Monday."

The phone went dead. "Bloody hell," Ian muttered. He slammed down the phone and opened the door of the booth. The drunk blocked his way.

"You gotta spare dollar, mister?" His breath was fetid with sour whiskey.

"Get the fuck out of my way!" Ian shoved past him and walked down the street toward a busy intersection. Just as he reached it, an unoccupied cab drew up at the traffic light. Ian grinned and flagged him down. It was his lucky night.

"The Clarion," he told the cabbie as he slipped into the backseat. "Oh, and would you mind turning the heat up a wee bit? It's bloody cold out here tonight."

He settled back to enjoy the ride.

DURING THE stop in St. Louis, Ian had arranged for Devin to shoot a music video at a restored pre–Civil War mansion on the banks of the Mississippi. It was for a soon-to-be-released single off the *Eclipse* album, a song called "Déjà Vu." The next concert wouldn't be until June 18, four days away, at Red Rocks outside Denver, and if the video could be finished in two days of shooting, everyone would have a free day in Colorado.

Since most of the crew were off for the day of the video shoot, Fonda arranged for Jessie to spend it with Laoise and her parents. Laoise's mother, Darcy, had volunteered to take the two girls to an amusement park outside St. Louis while Fonda covered the video filming.

Fonda found the riverside mansion without any trouble. Just as she parked her rented Toyota Celica beside the equipment trucks and other vehicles, she saw Bram coming down the winding stone walkway toward her, a big grin on his face.

"About time you made it. You're needed up at the house."

"Okay. Let me get my equipment."

He grabbed her hand and began to draw her toward the imposing mansion. "You won't be needing it just now. Come on."

"Bram! My cameras!"

But he refused to release her hand. What was his all-fire hurry? She suppressed a sigh of exasperation and allowed him to lead her up the morning glory–embroidered path to the house.

The Southern plantation home perched on a small hill overlooking the banks of the Mississippi, its classical Grecian columns facing the water. Bordering the huge mansion were lush bushes of fragrant lilac and delicate yellow roses, alive with the sound of buzzing honeybees. Fonda gazed up in admiration at the estate's splendor. Why, it was Tara! She could almost imagine Scarlett O'Hara wearing a pink ruffled hoop-skirt and holding a mint julep in her hand as she stepped daintily out onto the wide veranda.

Fonda followed Bram up the wide steps that led to the veranda, but at the top, she had to stop to take in the magnificent view of the huge Mississippi as it rolled lazily past on its endless journey to the Gulf of Mexico. For a moment, the atmosphere was so timeless it wouldn't have surprised her to see Mark Twain come around the bend in an old paddleboat.

"Darlin, I'm sorry to intrude on your reverie, but everyone's waiting."

Fonda turned to see an amused look on Bram's face. Abruptly, she was thrust back into the present. "Waiting for *what?*"

"I keep telling you. You'll know soon enough." He grabbed her hand again and led her into the imposing foyer. Immediately, the sensation of being back in the past dissolved for good as Fonda gazed at the bustling crewmen, the cables strewn across the floor, and the harsh lights glaring down onto a plushly decorated nineteenth-century parlor set. Bram didn't give her much time to look around. He was on the move again, leading her through the busy crewmen and over to a woman dressed in leather pants and a skimpy knit top. Her clothes were considerably less eccentric than her hairstyle. One side of her head was shaved and the other sported spikes of hot pink.

"Here she is," Bram said and pushed Fonda forward, as if offering a sacrifice to the gods.

The woman's brown eyes inspected her. Then she grinned, revealing a large gap between her front teeth. "Oh, me God! She's *perfect!*" Her accent was a slurring Cockney. She turned and without preamble, planted a huge wet kiss on Bram's mouth. "Ya a lifesaver, ya are!" Then she looked back at Fonda. "Come on, honey. Let's go. By a way, I'm Rocki. What's your name?" As she spoke, her scarlet spear-tipped fingers grasped Fonda's upper arm and she began to lead her out of the room. Fonda looked back over her shoulder at Bram, who gave her the thumbs-up signal and grinned. "Leave it to an Irishman to come to the rescue," Rocki was saying. "He said you were perfect, and boy was he ever right! That hair! Me God, the hair is fabulous! Is it natural?"

Fonda opened her mouth to speak, but Rocki went on talking. "What did ya say your name was, luvvie?"

They'd reached a small room that looked as if it had been converted from a maid's quarters. It was full of wheeled racks of clothing and other gaudy paraphernalia.

"It's Fonda."

Rocki had let go of her arm and was rummaging through a rack of ball gowns, mumbling to herself. "No, not yellow. Skin would look sallow. Maybe a rose or lavender . . ."

"What *exactly* am I perfect for?" Fonda managed to ask.

Rocki's huge brown eyes stared at her. "Ya mean he didn't tell ya?"

"No one has told me *anything!*"

Rocki shook her head and turned back to the clothing rack. "Men! They leave out the most obvious things. Honey, you're going to be in Devin O'Keefe's video. Ah, this is it! Is this you, or what?" She drew out a pale lilac ball gown. "What was I saying? Oh, yeh. You're going to play Devin's leading lady."

"But I'm a photographer, not an actress!"

Flustered, Fonda paced in front of Lindsay Hamilton, the video's director, but it wasn't easy in the lilac ball gown with the swaying hoop-skirt underneath. Rocki had paid no attention to Fonda's sputtering protests as she'd unceremoniously stripped her of her clothes and somehow got her into the nineteenth-century gown. So far, Fonda was having an equal amount of success in reasoning with the director.

Hamilton was an Englishman, but as far as Fonda was concerned, he was having a lot of trouble understanding the Queen's English. For five minutes, she'd been arguing with him about appearing in the video. Now, he ran his large bony hand through his disheveled graying hair and scowled.

"I'm quite aware of that. Believe me—you've told me so four times now. However, you're all I have at the moment. Be assured, I'm as unhappy as you are that Carroll had strawberries with her Cheerios this morning and broke out in hives all over her lush body. *Rocki!*" he screamed out, and a second later, the garrulous wardrobe mistress appeared at his elbow. "You must do something about *that!*"

In horror, Fonda realized he was pointing at her breasts.

"We must have *cleavage*, Rocki. Lots and lots of cleavage! Everyone knows plantation belles have"—he grappled for the right word and cupped his hands in front of his chest—"you know, big boobs."

Rocki bobbed her head like a baseball doll in the back window of a car. She grabbed Fonda's arm. "I can take care of that. I 'ave an underwire corset that . . ."

Lindsay rolled his eyes, his booted toe tapping the floor impatiently. "Spare me the details. Just do it. Oh, and put her hair up. Leave some tendrils hanging down onto her shoulder, though. Just enough to make her sexy."

A half hour later, Fonda stared at a stranger in the mirror. *This was not her.* Not the Fonda she'd become used to in the last twenty-six years.

"There, now!" Hands on hips, Rocki stood back and grinned. "Why, you're a bleedin' beauty! Just like Bram said."

The British wardrobe woman was right. Rocki's magic fingers had transformed her face into cover-girl glamour, yet with such expertise that the glow of her fresh peaches and cream complexion shined through. Her mass of golden brown hair was pulled back from her face and styled into a cascade of curls that fell onto her creamy shoulders, revealed to seductive advantage by the low-cut bodice of the lilac gown. As the director had requested, the uplift corset had helped to give her a cleavage she'd never dreamed of possessing. Fascinated, Fonda watched as her breasts rose and fell with her breathing, the soft swells above the silky material enticing, alluring.

Her pulse quickened. Suddenly, she felt heady with power. For the first time in her life, she saw herself as captivating. She was no longer "Frizz-Face," but a seductress.

Bram's head appeared through the doorway. "We're ready to roll." His eyes widened at his first sight of Fonda. A low whistle escaped his lips. "Jaysus, Mary, and Joseph! It that really you, Fon?

I knew you were pretty, but Lordy!" He turned back to Rocki. "We're all set up out by the summerhouse. You ready?"

Rocki grinned. "Oh, yeh! Ya are, aren't ya, Fon?"

"I don't know if I'll ever be ready for this."

Bram and Rocki laughed. They thought she was kidding.

The first thing Fonda saw when they reached the back lawn was the horse. A huge black stallion, saddled and ready to go. Next to the horse stood a figure dressed in a Confederate officer's uniform. Devin. He was engrossed in stroking the stallion's forelock. They were halfway across the lawn before he looked up and saw them. Fonda was busy trying to walk in the awkward hoop-skirt without tripping and breaking her neck. It felt like she was carrying the entire clothes rack with her. When she finally glanced up again, it was to see Devin's gaze upon her. His face was pale, his eyes smoldering. The three of them came to a stop in front of him.

Bram gave a dramatic bow. "Presenting your leading lady!"

Neither Devin nor Fonda acknowledged his announcement. For a moment, it was as if the two of them were alone in the world. Fonda stood still as Devin's eyes burned into her.

Slowly, his gaze raked down from the top of her head to center for a moment on her lips, and then still lower to the soft swells that peeked above the thin bodice of her dress.

Fonda's breathing quickened. Devin's gaze finally dragged away from her breasts and moved back up to her eyes. She felt the way she had the night he'd kissed her. But now, they weren't even touching!

A loud clap broke Fonda from the magic spell Devin's searing appraisal had woven around her. Lindsay Hamilton had appeared at their side.

"All right. Let's get going. Devin, you're going to mount Montague here and come riding in from that direction." He pointed away from the river. "You . . . uh, sorry, what was your name, love?"

"Fonda." Her voice was low, husky.

"Right. Fonda. You'll be sitting here in the summerhouse waiting for your lover to return from battle."

With a nod, Fonda nervously licked her dry lips and looked back at Devin. It was all she could do to hold in a gasp. The expression he'd worn a moment ago, the look of longing and repressed desire, was gone. In its place was a cold mask. As if a switch had been turned off. Devin turned away. Then, just as suddenly, he whirled back and glared at the director.

"No!" he said quite clearly. "I can't fucking *do* it! I can't do a love scene with this woman!"

16

"Can you tell me just exactly what the problem is?"

Scowling, Lindsay Hamilton paced in front of the crowd of technicians who'd gathered after Devin's indignant protest. He stopped in front of the Irishman and snarled. "Well?"

Devin pulled the Confederate cap off his head and ran a hand through his sweat-dampened hair. "It's just not for me, Lindsay. Christ! You know how I detest these concept videos. I wish to God I'd never let Ian talk me into it."

"But you did approve it, Devin." Lindsay took a deep breath and then went on, making an effort to keep his voice calm. "And thousands of dollars have already been spent. We can't very well chuck it now, can we?"

When Devin remained broodingly silent, Lindsay heaved a deep sigh. "Damn it to hell! Will somebody *please* talk to this man? Take fifteen minutes!"

Bram threw his arm around Devin's shoulders and together, they walked off toward the river, leaving Fonda standing with Rocki. When they reached the river's edge, Bram turned to his friend. "Okay, Dev, what's the problem?"

Devin threw him an angry look. "You bleeding well know what's the problem. You probably engineered it!"

Bram shrugged. "Lindsay was in a bind. The actress got sick and I suggested Fonda. Christ, you have to admit, she makes a fetching Southern belle."

Devin stared down at the soggy ground beneath his boots.

"You know what she does to me," he said softly. "Why are you encouraging it?"

"She's good for you, Devin. Can't you see that, man?"

Devin looked at Bram, his eyes dark with pain. "But I'm not good for *her*. You know that. I can never be."

Bram wrestled with his conscience. It would be so easy to put Devin's mind to rest. But Jesus! If he did, the whole world would blow up in his face. He threw his arm around Devin's shoulder. "Devin, Caitlyn is in prison, but to the world, she's dead. For Christ's sake, bury her and get on with your life."

Devin didn't respond for a moment. Then, as if reaching a decision, he shook off Bram's arm and turned back to the summerhouse. "Let's get on with it."

"OKAY, FONDA. Here's the deal. Devin will ride up and dismount. He has returned for a few days from the war. You run down the steps of the summerhouse toward him. I want the expression on your face to show how thrilled you are. When you reach him, you kiss passionately. Got that?" Lindsay waited for her answer.

When she nodded, he turned to Devin. "Okay, got it? Let's go for it."

Heart pounding, Fonda went to take her place in the summerhouse. This was crazy! What was she doing here? She knew absolutely nothing about acting. How would she ever be able to carry it off?

Lindsay raised a speaker to his lips and shouted, "Take one. Roll tape. Action!"

When Fonda saw Devin crest the hill astride the black stallion, a gasp caught in her throat. As he rode closer, she moved to the entrance of the summerhouse. He jumped off the horse. She hesitated a second, and just for that moment, she visualized him as a soldier returning from war, and she his adoring sweetheart. Behind him, she saw the director motioning her forward. She lifted her skirts and gingerly walked down the steps. Her hoopskirt swayed gracefully as she crossed the lawn toward him.

A few feet away from Devin, she stopped. He, too, was motionless. Seconds passed as she stared into his brown eyes. She took a step toward him, and at the same moment, he closed the distance between them. His expression was sober as his arms closed around her, and then, his mouth was warm and sure upon hers. Fonda sagged against him, helpless against the onslaught of his sweet searching tongue. Her hands moved up the rough fabric of his gray uniform, up to where his hair brushed his collar. A soft moan vibrated from her throat. With an answering groan, Devin dragged his mouth away from hers and began raining kisses upon her face and throat.

"Cut! Okay! That was bloody marvelous!"

Devin released her. Fonda, her head spinning from his kiss, became aware of applause coming from all around them. Dazed, she stepped back and stared at the smiling faces. A wave of color stained her cheeks. She'd forgotten they were there. Devin too appeared disoriented.

"I can't believe we got that with one take," Lindsay said. He looked at Fonda. "And you deny you're an actress. And you, you bloody Irishman! For a reluctant lover, you come across quite well. This is going to be one hot video. Okay, let's go on to the next scene. Take your places up in the summerhouse."

"CUT! OKAY, that's a wrap. Thanks, kids. You were great."

Fonda wearily turned to look at Devin, but he'd already moved away and was talking to Bram. It had been like that throughout the long afternoon. Fonda was tired, more than a little hurt, and growing angrier by the moment. What *was* it with the man? Every time he touched her, she could see the fire in his eyes. But the minute the director called out, "Cut!" he would freeze up and the cold mask would drop into place. Fonda couldn't understand it. He wanted her. She knew it! Then why this hot and cold act? Why these games?

She was determined to find out. After all, they weren't children. And it was time he quit acting like one.

"Here, luvvie, slip into this." It was Rocki with a robe. Gratefully, Fonda shrugged into it and smiled her thanks. The parlor scenes had called for her to be clad in a long, white muslin nightdress. If it weren't for her heavy hair rippling free around her shoulders and the bright lights bearing down on them, she was sure she would've been unbearably cold as the late afternoon breeze from the river drifted in through the opened windows.

She tied the belt of the robe and walked over to Devin and Bram. "Devin, I think we should talk."

In mid-conversation, they stopped and looked at her. She blushed, but went on, "I'm sorry, Bram, but I think Devin and I need a few moments alone."

Bram grinned. "Why, surely, darlin'." He started to back away.

"Bram, don't go." Devin's voice was husky. His eyes fastened on hers. "Fonda, don't do this. Look there's something between us. That's true. But it can't work, so it's best if we just leave it be. Will you try and do that?"

Fonda stared at him. And suddenly, she was furious. How *dare* he play games with her emotions like this. "I don't know what you're talking about," she said. "I was *acting*, Devin. Pretending. I should've known a man with an ego like yours would take it seriously." She whirled around and walked away, her feet echoing across the hardwood floors in angry staccato taps.

"Fonda!" he called after her.

But she kept going. *Who needs him?* He was nothing but a moody self-preoccupied prima donna! She'd been a fool to think differently.

DEVIN WATCHED her go and then turned to Bram. "Don't give me that disgusted look. I have to do it like this." When Bram made no response, he went on, "It's better than leading her on, isn't it? Make her think we have a chance together when we don't?"

"Isn't that exactly what you were doing?" Bram asked, blue eyes amused. "For a man who claims he doesn't have any acting ability, you were doing a bloody fine job with those love scenes."

Devin muttered an obscenity, feeling the heat rush to his face. Then Fonda's angry words came back to him and he looked up at Bram. "Do you think she meant it? That she was acting?"

Bram stared at him, then shook his head sadly. "You're a thick-headed numbskull, you know that?"

Devin turned away. "Let's go get a pint. Why don't we try out some of those blues clubs downtown? I don't think I'll be recognized there."

Later, in a dark bar, Devin sat with Bram at a grimy table covered with empty beer bottles and listened to a skinny black man make slow sad love to a sax. Moodily, he toyed with a cardboard coaster and thought again of the video shoot. The love scenes with Fonda had been excruciating for him. It was a bit like being offered a wee taste of a rich, satisfying dessert when he craved the whole dish. Even now, he could remember the taste of her smooth warm neck against his lips. Acting? Of course not. No more than he'd been.

How much better off they'd both be if they were. If their feelings for each other could be disregarded as make-believe. Because the only future they could have together would be just that.

A fantasy.

IAN GOT out of his rented sedan and carefully locked the doors. He gave a quick glance around and began to walk along the wharf. It was quiet, with only the sound of the river lapping softly against its banks and the occasional mournful call of a boat whistle downstream. He glanced up at the sky and grimaced. Damn that full moon beaming down like there was no tomorrow. How come Harlen and his cronies hadn't thought of that? Or did they bloody well *want* the world to know what they were up to?

Where *was* the gruesome hillbilly, anyway? Ian looked around nervously, his steps slowing. Why hadn't the man been more specific about the old bait and tackle building, for God's sake? There was nothing *but* fucking abandoned buildings down here. He shifted his briefcase to his left hand and continued to walk parallel to the river.

A low whistle broke the silence. Ian stopped and peered around, his heart accelerating.

"That you, Mulligan?"

It was Harlen's nasal whine. Ian tried to dismiss the quiver of anxiety it sent through him. "Yeh, it's me."

The man appeared from the corner of a warehouse, blackened stumps of teeth gleaming in the moonlight. "You brought the money, sweetheart?"

Ian's face blanched at the endearment. *Jesus, he isn't . . . does he know I'm . . .* his mind banished the thought. It was just too sickening.

"In here." Harlen nodded his head toward the warehouse and indicated for him to follow.

Inside, it was dark, just like it had been before. Then a flashlight speared a tunnel of light into Ian's face and he blinked, turning away.

"Turn that blasted thing away!" Harlen demanded. "Jesus! You trying to blind my man, Mulligan, here? He's got our money, boys."

Ian's eyes had adjusted now and he could just make out the four shadowy figures standing before him. His hand tightened on the briefcase. "You've brought the crates?"

"Eddie, show him the crates."

The flashlight swept to a spot to Ian's left. The crates were stacked five feet high along one wall. Ian judged there to be about twenty of them. He knew they contained different instruments of death. Rifles, machine guns, grenades, and probably other things Ian had never heard of. He didn't know where the Americans had acquired them. He didn't care. All he knew was that very soon, they'd be on their way to Ireland. That was enough for him.

"Where's your truck?" Harlen asked with a smirk. "Or you gonna haul them crates in the back of that pussy car you're driving?"

Ian bit his tongue to keep from telling the sleazy little man to get fucked. "Down the street. He's waiting for my signal."

"Hokey-dokey. But before we do anything, we're gonna count the money you brought us, ain't we, boys? Not that we don't trust you, sweetheart. Hey, Sam! Take the money over to this here table and count it." He looked back at Ian, grinning. "Sam here is my best man. Upstanding young feller, he is. Talk about trustworthy! Why, he'd drop over dead for me, wouldn't you, Sam?"

Sam, the greasy blond man who'd counted the money back in Indiana, shrugged his shoulders and grinned as he opened the briefcase and began to methodically count the contents. Harlen watched him, his eyes cold.

Ian stared past them to the crates of weapons. If Harlen was going to be so bloody suspicious, he would be, too. He'd make them open at least one crate, of his choosing, of course, to make sure he was getting what he was paying for.

"All there, Sam?"

The man slammed the briefcase shut. "Every penny."

"Good."

Harlen reached into his jacket and drew out a .357 Magnum. He casually screwed a silencer onto it, his eyes gleaming at Ian. As he realized what was happening, the blood pumped through Ian's arteries at a maddened pace. His legs began to shake; his chest constricted. One hand clutched at his throat. It was so tight, he felt as if he'd swallowed a baseball.

Smiling, Harlen lowered the gun so it was even with Ian's heart. Jesus Christ, the maniac was going to kill him! Ian's legs gave out and he sank to the uneven wooden floor.

"Please . . . no . . ." he whispered. His stomach gurgled. A damp warmth spread across the front of his trousers. God . . . God . . . they would find him soaked in his own piss. Ian's eyes dropped from his killer. Dear God, let it be fast!

"Mulligan, look at me."

Ian obeyed. Harlen turned, and arms outstretched, leveled the gun at Sam. For just a second, the blond man's eyes grew wide with doomed realization, and then the gun whispered. A neat black hole appeared between Sam's blue eyes, still wearing an expression of horrified surprise. He thumped to the floor.

Ian couldn't draw his eyes away from the dead Sam.

"Mulligan?"

Harlen's voice was soft, insistent. Finally, Ian looked back at him.

"Want to know why I killed him?"

The man was grinning pleasantly. Ian couldn't speak, couldn't do anything but stare.

Harlen shrugged. "Got word he was dealing on the side. Now, that wasn't a nice thing for him to do. That boy has been with me for years. Hell, we served time together in the Oklahoma state pen. We been through a lot together. And he done me that way? Double-crossing his old friend. Tell me, Mulligan, what's the world coming to when you can't even trust an old friend?"

Ian finally found his voice. "You killed the man!"

"Yep." Harlen stared down at Sam's body. "I guess I did, didn't I? Well, he ain't been the first." His eyes connected with Ian's "and he won't be the last." His gaze fell to Ian's crotch and he grinned. "Say, you better give your truck driver that signal, Mulligan. You'll be wanting to get back to that fancy hotel to change your pants." His words were accompanied by an ugly giggle.

An hour later, Ian watched the lorry pull away and round the corner to disappear onto the interstate heading west. It was off to the rendezvous in Tempe, Arizona. The two drivers were burly Irishmen hired by Caitlyn. As they'd loaded the crates onto the lorry, they'd barely spared a glance at Sam's corpse lying in the abandoned bait and tackle shop, and no questions were asked.

Ian wished he could feel the same indifference, but the murder had shaken him. Although he'd been involved with terrorism since his college days, he'd never actually come into such close proximity to violence. And for the first time since the start of the operation, he realized how very high the stakes were. And how very dangerous. He didn't like it. Not one bit.

After the lorry was gone, he stood for a moment next to his car, listening to the silence. He touched his crotch and grimaced.

He couldn't go back to the Clarion yet. His trousers were still damp from where he'd wet himself.

JESSIE STARED out at the rain falling from a slate gray Colorado sky. She sighed elaborately. "If it doesn't stop soon, the concert will be ruined."

With a loud crunch, Laoise bit into a crisp Granny Smith apple and followed Jessie's gaze up to the sky. "No, it won't. Devin has performed in all kinds of weather and it doesn't bother him a wee bit. And the fans don't care, do they now?"

The two girls were crouched under a tarpaulin the crew had rigged up to protect them from the rain, watching the setup for the night's concert at Red Rocks. Until a few moments before, they'd been playing Black Jack. Jessie had taught the game to Laoise, who'd been winning steadily all afternoon.

Jessie yawned and eyed the jeans-clad figure of a crewman outside in the rain, wondering if he was a babe. With that school bus yellow slicker on, she couldn't tell, but he had nice legs.

Laoise caught her yawn. "Yeh, who would ever think it would be so boring on a concert tour? We need to do something to liven this place up."

"Like what?"

Suddenly, there was a flurry of activity on the stage nearby. The sound man, Jacky O'Brien, strode by, followed closely by his rabbitty-faced girlfriend, Mairead. She was clutching his arm as if he were the only object that stood between her and certain death.

"I said, where the fuck do you think you're going?"

He wrenched his arm away and threw her a glare that would've frozen lava. "What's it to ya? I don't have to explain myself to the likes o' you!"

Her lips curled away from her teeth in a furious snarl. "It's to pick up some little dolly, isn't it? What is it, I'm not good enough for you?"

"Christ, Mairead! You got to let me *breathe* now and then. I just want some time with the boyos. Throw back a pint or two. Can you not understand that, woman?"

She grabbed his arm again. "I understand you think I'm some kind of bimbo. You don't really expect me to believe that load of crap, do you?"

Carefully, he loosened her fingers from the arm of his jacket. "I don't care what you think. Now, leave go of me jacket. You're wrinkling the material."

"That's *my* jacket, you son-of-a-bitch! I bought it for your birthday, remember? And I'll be damned if you're going to wear it when you go tomcatting around!"

In a flash, Jacky had the jacket off. He tossed it in her face. "There, now! There's your bloody jacket. Now, fuck off!" He bounded off the stage.

Mairead stood there in the rain and stared down at the soggy black material at her feet. Suddenly, she took one muddy booted foot and ground it onto the jacket. A moment later, she was gone, leaving the jacket lying forlornly on the stage floor.

Laoise turned to Jessie and grinned. "I think I just discovered how to liven this place up."

LAOISE GIGGLED and wiped her mouth with the collar of Jacky's jacket. "There, now!" She peered at the streaks of Avon's "Rose Lustre" lipstick and grinned. "Okay, now for the cologne. Hand it to me."

"Let me do it," Jessie said, grabbing the jacket. She took the top off a bottle of "Electric Youth" and squirted it generously over the fabric. "I don't know," she said, staring at her handiwork with a worried frown. "Maybe we should've used something for older women. Would Jacky mess around with a girl who wears 'Electric Youth'?"

Laoise snorted. "That sleazebag? He came on to *me* just a few days ago. And look." She thrust out her chest. "I barely have boobs yet!" She looked enviously at Jessie's budding breasts. "You better watch out. It'll be you he'll come after next."

"Jaysus! What's that stench?"

At the voice from outside, Laoise grabbed Jacky's jacket and thrust it behind her as Jessie's head whipped around to see Ryan grinning down at her. He was hunched in his motorcycle jacket with his hands in his black cord pockets, heedless of the rain beading in his cropped blond hair.

Jessie smiled brightly, wondering if Laoise had managed to get the jacket out of sight in time. "Hi! Oh, we're just trying out some new perfume. Do you like it?"

He wrinkled his nose. "I've smelled better things in a cow pasture."

Jessie immediately vowed to throw away what was left of her cologne.

Ryan's eyes went to Laoise. "Mum is looking for you. She's ready to head back to town."

"What about Fonda?" Jessie asked. "Is she leaving, too?"

He shook his head. "I heard her say she was sticking around until after the concert. They're sending out for coffee and sandwiches."

Laoise's jaw clenched stubbornly. "I don't want to go. Did she say I had to?"

"Yes, she said you had to," Ryan mocked, blue eyes gleaming. "Get along now. I'll keep Jessica company until you come back."

Jessie's heart jumped at his words. Laoise scrunched the jacket up against her stomach and scrambled out of their shelter. "You bloody well *better* be telling me the truth, Ryan Finlay Meehan. If you're not, I'm going to come back and let you have it!"

"You'll have to catch me first, little girl." Ryan laughed as he took her place next to Jessie.

"See you tonight, Laoise," Jessie called out after her fleeing figure. Laoise's answer was lost in the rain. Jessie turned to look at Ryan, her heart drumming. It accelerated even more when she saw his blue eyes studying her closely.

With a wry grin, he ran his hand through his wet hair. "It's a wee bit damp out there today, isn't it?" He looked at her again. "But nice and cozy in here." He leaned forward, his eyes on her lips. "Hey, nice color! I don't think I've ever seen you in lipstick before."

Jessie felt the heat rush to her face. "Oh! Well, Laoise found it in"—*your mother's purse*—"oh, somewhere! And we were trying it out."

"It looks nice." His eyes hadn't veered from her lips. "Makes them look very kissable indeed." He looked back into her eyes. "Have you ever been kissed, Jessie-girl?"

Jessie almost stopped breathing. She knew her face looked like a ripe tomato. "Well . . . uh . . ." She struggled to find words. "When I was twelve, Bobby Randolph kissed me in our garage. But I didn't like it."

He grinned. "And now, you're what? Fourteen? Fifteen?"

"Seventeen."

He gave her a who-do-you-think-you're-kidding? look.

She sighed. "Okay. Sixteen."

"Sixteen, and only been kissed once? You're a late starter, aren't you? For an American girl anyway."

"Well, you don't know my parents. They watch me like a hawk. My dad's a cop. That tends to make the boys stay away."

"For real?"

"Uh-huh. My brother was one, too."

"Was? Did he quit?"

"No." Her eyes dropped. "He was killed in the line of duty."

"Oh." Ryan was silent for a moment, then he said softly, "Sorry, love."

Jessie looked back at him and saw the genuine sympathy in his gold-flecked blue eyes. If she hadn't fallen in love with him before, this would've done it for sure. "Anyway," she said, getting back to the subject at hand, "it was disgusting kissing Bobby Randolph. He stuck his tongue in so hard I thought I was going to gag. And he slobbered on me!"

"You haven't been kissed properly then." Ryan's finger touched her chin. "Would you like me to show you?"

"Uh . . . okay . . ." Jessie said, hoping she wasn't looking too eager.

He slid closer to her. "Okay. First, close your eyes." When she did so, she felt his fingers stroke the side of her jaw. She shivered. "Now . . ." His voice was soft. He was so close, she could feel his breath against her face. "Relax your mouth. That's it. Just so it's parted a wee bit. Ready?"

She nodded, not trusting herself to speak. Something warm touched her parted mouth. It was a soft caress, almost a feather touch, and then it was gone. Her eyes fluttered and just as she started to open them, the warmth was back, but this time, it was different. His mouth moved against hers with a slow, subtle pressure. Jessie's heart slammed in her chest as a curious lethargy stole through her body. Then, she felt the tip of his tongue exploring her parted lips. It inched its way just inside, not thrusting like Bobby's had been, but delicately, almost tentative. She felt her jaws relax as she began to enjoy the kiss, and finally, she found the nerve to use her own tongue to touch his. For a moment, their tongues touched, withdrew, touched again in a dance of exploration.

At last, Ryan pulled away, his breath uneven. "Well?" he asked. "Was that better than Bobby Randolph's kiss?"

Jessie grinned at him. "I'm not sure. Could we try it again?"

He didn't answer. Instead, he put his arms around her and drew her against him. When his mouth lowered to hers, Jessie's lips were already parted, anticipating more of the pleasurable sensation his kiss had sent rushing through her.

They kissed for a long time, growing more practiced with every moment. When Ryan's hands found their way inside Jessie's jacket to rest lightly against her rib cage, she didn't think anything about it. She sighed softly and moved her mouth against his for another kiss. His hand moved to caress the tiny nub of nipple that had hardened against her T-shirt.

"Ryan!" She pulled back, shocked.

His hand dropped. He gazed at her, an innocent expression on his face. "You don't like that?"

She stared at him, and then answered truthfully. "Well, I'm not sure. But we hardly know each other."

He nodded solemnly and then withdrew his hands from inside her jacket and drew the zippered halves together. "Yes, I suppose you're right. But I really like you, Jessie. And I know you're kind of innocent and everything. I promise I won't go too fast."

"Too fast for what?"

He gave her a strange look. "Come on, Jessie! You're not that naïve. You're looking to lose your virginity, aren't you?"

Jessie's mouth dropped open. A thousand different replies zipped through her mind, but she couldn't formulate even one of them into words.

"It's not the sort of thing to be embarrassed about," Ryan went on. "It's always a bit awkward the first time. But you catch on quickly. A bit like riding a bicycle, you know."

Jessie stared at him. "You sound like you've had a lot of experience."

His face reddened. "Well, not so much. There's only been one girl—well—woman. And that was a long time ago."

A long time ago? How old *was* he, anyway? She decided to ask.

"Sixteen." He leaned forward and planted a quick kiss on her surprised lips. "Don't worry. We'll do it whenever you're ready. I have to go now." He scrambled out of the shelter into the rain and flashed her a smile. "See you later, Jess."

Still reeling from his words, Jessie stared after him until he disappeared into the rain. Then, slowly, she touched her mouth. It still tingled from his kisses. Sex? Going all the way? With Ryan?

Actually, she'd be happy just to settle for the kisses. But she knew guys were different. She'd learned that in sex education class. Men got excited at the drop of a hat. That's what Sandy said about Brian, anyway. Maybe that explained why their older sister was always pregnant. Even kissing got guys excited. Made them real hard, and the only way they could get soft again was to . . . what was the word? Evacuate? Well, that didn't sound right, but whatever, it was some messy process she really didn't want to think about. She'd rather think about how good Ryan kissed.

Hmmm . . . maybe if he was such a good kisser, maybe the rest of it wouldn't be so bad either. She'd lied to him about not being sure whether she liked his hand touching her breast. Actually, it had sent a strange wave of heat down there between her legs — especially when his thumb had brushed against her nipple.

She'd just have to give some thought to this sex thing. After all, she had to lose her virginity some day. Why not with gorgeous Ryan? She wondered if kissing her had made him hard. The thought gave her a curious sense of satisfaction.

FONDA SQUINTED up at the broiling Arizona sun. "I wonder why Laoise and Jessie aren't out here sunning with us?" she asked Darcy. "It's such a gorgeous day."

The pale blond woman was busy smearing sunscreen on her fleshy winter-white arms. She didn't glance up from where she was stretched on a lounge chair next to the pool. "I don't know. It's the strangest thing. This morning, Laoise insisted I take her and Jessie to the mall. They spent over an hour in a bookstore!" She peered at Fonda through round gray-tinted sunglasses. "Laoise has never been much of a reader. Perhaps your Jessie is broadening her mind."

Fonda gave a short laugh and took a sip of iced tea. "Have you checked out their reading material? For all I know, they could be buying Jackie Collins or Pat Booth, God forbid!"

Darcy grinned. "I dare say we have nothing to worry about. They were probably stocking up on those heavy metal magazines they're so fond of."

"Yeah, I guess so." Fonda fell silent and gazed out into the sparkling blue depths of the pool.

They'd arrived in Tempe the day before. Two concerts were scheduled at Sun Devil Stadium, the first of which would be the next day. Today, they were free to relax, and Fonda was making the most of it. She was glad she had Darcy to share it with.

In the last few weeks, they'd become close, thanks to Laoise and Jessie. Although the plump, blond Darcy didn't look at all like her dark-haired strapping daughter, they shared the same ebullient personality. Outspoken, with a maddeningly dry sense of humor, Darcy had a habit of saying exactly what was on her mind.

The sun beat down out of a cloudless azure sky, producing a film of perspiration over Fonda's skin. Her eyes closed drowsily and her thoughts began to drift.

"What's with you and Devin?" Darcy asked suddenly. "Both of you seem to be going to great extremes to avoid each other."

Fonda's eyes flashed open and she groaned inwardly. Was it so obvious to everyone? She sat up and reached for her sunscreen. "I hadn't noticed," she said lightly.

"Bullshit."

Even through her dark sunglasses, Fonda could feel Darcy's eyes drilling into her. "Come on, Fonda. I'm not blind. Things were heating up between the two of you. Something's changed now. And I think it's a bloody shame!"

Fonda sighed and slowly began to stoke the sunscreen onto her legs. "Why is it when someone has a happy marriage, they can't stand it unless they play matchmaker for everyone around them?"

"Because marriage does something to our brain cells," Darcy said with a straight face. "Really, though. I was hoping Devin had found someone to replace Caitlyn."

"Who's that?"

"You don't know? That was Devin's wife. She was killed by an IRA bomb in a Belfast department store. From what I've heard, he's steered clear of women since then. They say he's never gotten over her death. Blames himself." Darcy took a sip of her iced tea. "Bloody stupid, isn't it? How people hold themselves responsible for things they have no control over. Devin is a classic case. If he were living back in the Middle Ages, he'd be wearing a hair shirt. Today, he just gives most of his money to charity."

"I didn't know that."

"Oh, yes, love. Back in Ireland, he drives an old beat-up Volkswagen van and lives in a little thatched cottage in County Wicklow. No fancy rock star life for him. Ian gives him a living allowance and uses what he needs for his career, and the rest goes to charity."

Fonda was staring blankly into the pool, remembering the night Devin had talked about tragedy. The same night he'd kissed her backstage. She'd never dreamed he was speaking from personal experience. But surely it wasn't true about there being no other women in his life. Devin was a virile man, a rock star with women chasing him all the time. How could he have resisted all of them?

But he'd sure resisted her, hadn't he?

Could it be he was afraid to love again? This knowledge about a dead Irish wife changed things. Before, she'd convinced herself that Devin simply didn't want her. Now, she knew it was more than that. Perhaps if she had another chance with him—but how? Lately, Devin had been so distant, encased in the aloof armor he donned for the press. How could she get past defenses like that?

Maybe it was impossible. Maybe Devin's armor was so strong and indefensible that no one could get through it. Ever.

"I'M TELLING you, Caitlyn, the bloody lunatic shot the man dead right in front of me!"

Caitlyn's voice traveled clearly across the overseas line. "I've had a full report on it, Mulligan. There's no need to get into a dither."

"A dither?" Ian sputtered, his hand clutching the phone receiver. "I don't think you understand the seriousness of this. The man could've killed me, as well. In fact, I thought he was going to."

Caitlyn gave a short laugh. "I said, I heard all about it. Tell me, were the cleaners able to remove the stain?"

Ian felt a flush creep up from his neck. Anger coursed through his veins. Damn the woman! How she loved humiliating him. She was probably creaming in her undies right now. "I say, you've got me involved with a rather unsavory lot, and I bloody well don't like it!"

"Unsavory?" Caitlyn's laugh floated across the wire. "For Christ's sake, Mulligan, you sound more like a Brit every time I talk to you. Forget this business in St. Louis. It doesn't concern us."

Ian's mouth dropped open. "I beg to differ with you. It surely concerns me. I witnessed the carnage."

"Good. Perhaps now you'll know just how serious this business is. I think the Americans call it 'playing hardball.' You'll get used to it."

"I don't want to get used to it! When we started this, you didn't say I'd have to get involved in the dirty work. I was to handle the business end of it. I shouldn't have to skulk around in dark alleys like a common criminal."

"You know what I think, Mulligan? You've grown too soft working behind the lines. It's good for you to get out in the field. As for calling it the dirty work, your hands aren't exactly clean, now, are they? Remember the Mountbatten operation? If it weren't for you and the information you gathered, we could never have been so successful."

"That was different," Ian said, his voice rising. "I didn't have to watch the man die!"

Caitlyn's voice was cold. "Don't you fall apart on me, Mulligan. You know what happens to volunteers who don't follow orders. You wouldn't want to be without your kneecaps, now would you?"

Ian felt a cold knot of fear in the pit of his stomach. Jesus, he'd pushed her too far. He tried to keep the panic out of his voice. "Caitlyn, you know me better than that. I'm a loyal volunteer. I'll do whatever you order."

"Bloody right, you will."

The phone went dead.

18

ON THE afternoon of the second concert at Sun Devil Stadium, Fonda ran into Bram and accepted an invitation for Irish tea in the tuning room. He told her it was his grandmum's special recipe and claimed it was good for just about every ailment there was, including a broken heart. Fonda raised an eyebrow at that, but didn't respond. Instead, she took a sip. It *was* good, if just a little too alcoholic for her taste. No wonder it cured ailments!

"What was all that about Jacky O'Brien and Mairead?" Fonda asked. "I hear they had one hell of a screaming match last night before the concert."

Bram grinned. "Well, it seems my good lad, Jacky, was a wee bit indiscreet about some recent liaisons. And Mairead isn't taking it kindly. Fool, he is, Jacky left some fairly strong evidence in his jacket of another woman's presence. There was talk of cheap perfume and a note thanking him for 'last night.'" He laughed. "It was written in lipstick."

"Not too smart of him, was it?"

"The thing is, Jacky is daft enough to swear he doesn't know a thing about it. That's making her more pissed than ever! And believe me, there's nothing more fearsome in the world than a furious Irishwoman. Now"—his eyes grew intent as he stared at her—"what about you and Devin?"

Fonda's heart thumped. "What about us?"

"What happened between you? All of us were hoping you

would finally drive away Caitlyn's ghost. He's been living with the guilt of her death for going on four years now."

"But it wasn't his fault!"

"Yeh, but you can't tell *him* that. He was off on his first tour here in America when it happened. Had left her behind in Belfast. He blames himself for that."

Fonda stared into her tea. "He must've loved her very much."

Bram didn't reply. Fonda looked up and met his eyes. "And there hasn't been any other woman in his life since then?" When he didn't answer, she said quickly, "I'm sorry. That's none of my business."

Bram's blue eyes gazed into hers frankly. "I think it *should* be your business. He hasn't so much as looked at another woman since Caitlyn. Until you. The man has the iron will of a monk, if you ask me. As far as I know, he's never even been tempted to have a one-night stand."

"You expect me to believe that a twenty-eight-year-old rock star like Devin has never slept with any of his legion of groupies? Yeh, *right!*"

Bram's serious expression remained unchanged. "If you believe that, Fonda, you don't know Devin. If the man hadn't become a musician, he'd probably be in the priesthood today. He is the most devout, honest man I've ever met." He touched her arm. "No, love. I'm not suggesting a quick fling. What I'm saying is, I think Devin is ready for a real relationship. He may not know it yet, but I believe you're the one that can turn him around. Bring him back to the land of the living, so to speak."

"That's not going to be easy. Especially since he doesn't want anything to do with me."

"Ah, but that's where you're wrong. He's forcing himself to stay away from you. You know why? Because you've gotten under his skin. And no other woman has done that since Caitlyn. He's afraid."

Fonda got to her feet. "Well, he's not the only one. I don't know, Bram. Maybe we should just leave it alone. The timing isn't right for either one of us, anyway. Devin isn't looking for a relationship, and I certainly don't need more complications in my life."

Bram spoke again just as she reached the door. "Go to him, Fonda. He needs you more than you think."

Fonda looked back at him. "You really care about him, don't you?"

"Like a brother. Will you do it?"

She hesitated a moment. Then, with a confused shake of her head, she left the room.

FONDA DIDN'T really know what she was going to do. Yet her feet carried her unerringly to Devin's dressing-room door. She stood there for a moment, her mind whirling with thoughts of Devin and the ravaged pain he'd been living with in the years since Caitlyn died. One thing was for sure. She knew she couldn't stand to watch him that night from the wings, to see the pain on his face and hear it in his voice without trying to do something about it. And the time was now.

Her heart raced. She took a deep breath and knocked. Then, before she could change her mind, she pushed the door open.

She was stunned by what she saw.

Devin sat on the edge of a sofa, his head in his hands. At his feet, remnants of *The Irish Times* lay scattered on the floor. The tension in the tiny room told Fonda something was very wrong. Then she saw the glaring headlines: *Four British Soldiers die in IRA Ambush.*

"Devin?"

Slowly, he lifted his head and stared up at her. For the second time since she'd known him, his face was streaked with tears. It was instinct that made her go to him and take him into her arms. He held her tightly, as if she were his last link to survival. But then, suddenly, he pulled away and got to his feet.

"Christ! Do you see what they've done now?" he said, his voice rough with emotion. "My people. Catholics slaughtering young men!" Through reddened eyes, he stared at her grimly. "They were fresh recruits from England —barely been in the country three weeks. Off duty. Out for a night on the town. But the IRA had targeted them. They were *riddled* with bullets. My God, it makes me ashamed to be an Irish Catholic!" He turned away from her.

Fonda stood up and tentatively reached out to touch his back. He was trembling. "You don't mean that, Devin. *You* know, more than most people, that you can't condemn an entire group because of what a few do."

It was as if he hadn't heard her. "Last night I wrote a song about the American government's waste of money while their poor starve to death on the streets. But what right do I have to lecture Americans on their excesses when my own people are so depraved? Christ, I'm such an ass."

"No, you're not." Fonda slipped her hands about his waist and pressed her face against the warmth of his cotton shirt. "You're an idealist. And if more people were like you, the world would be a better place. That's why I love you, Devin." For a moment, she stood still against him, digesting the fact that she'd really uttered those words.

He stiffened. Then slowly, he turned around and gazed down at her, his eyes sad. "No," he whispered. "Don't love me. I'll only make you unhappy."

"I'll risk it." Fonda searched his face. She took a deep breath. "As long as I know you feel the same." She waited for him to speak, her heart hammering in her chest. Oh God, *why* had she said it? Why was she opening herself up to rejection again? Would she *never* learn?

He closed his eyes. His hands tightened upon her shoulders. "My feelings for you are so strong it frightens me."

Her heart began to sing. He *did* care for her. Her instincts hadn't been wrong. Fonda stared up at him earnestly. "That afternoon of the storm, you told me not to be afraid. And now, you're telling me you're frightened of your feelings for me. Why?"

"Because . . . it's too painful to lose someone you love."

Fonda reached up and brushed her lips against his. "I'm not

Caitlyn," she whispered into his ear. "I won't go away, not as long as you want me with you." She began to plant shivery kisses from his ear back to his lips.

This time, she felt his mouth respond to her kiss. She drew away and looked into his eyes, still damp with tears. Her hands moved slowly down the front of his shirt, seeking the warmth of his skin. One by one, she undid the buttons, sliding her hands inside his shirt and around to his firm back. Leaning against him, she kissed the hollow of his throat. Felt the steady thud of his heartbeat under her lips. She pulled away and began to draw his shirt away from his shoulders. A tiny crescent-shaped scar on his arm caught her eye. Impulsively, she kissed it. He groaned and crushed her against him tightly, his face buried in her hair.

"What are you doing to me, girl?" His Irish accent had thickened with emotion. His hands gathered up rich ripples of her hair as he tugged her head back to stare into her eyes. "Do you have any idea what you're getting yourself into?"

She looked back at him steadily. "I just know I want to be with you. And nothing else in the world matters more than that right now."

"I don't want to hurt you," he whispered. "I seem to do that to everyone."

Fonda buried her face into his neck. "Hurt me," she murmured. "I don't care."

"I do," he said. But he bent down toward her, his lips searching for hers. His mouth moved over hers, hot, wild, branding her with his heat. Finally, Devin drew away to gaze at her. Then he gathered her up in his arms and carried her to the sofa. But after he placed her upon it, he stood looking down at her, indecision written in his expression.

She raised her arms to him in a silent plea, and finally, he moved. She drew him down and their mouths met in another fiery kiss.

After a long moment, he pulled back and with one hand, brushed the hair away from her face, and stared into her eyes. "Give me your hand. You must know something before we go further." Still half-dazed with hunger for him, she felt Devin take her hand and press it against the hard ridge straining against his jeans. "This is for you. Only you. There hasn't been anyone in my life for several years. You cannot be a casual affair to me. If we make love, I warn you, I won't be able to let you go."

Fonda moved her hand against him. He groaned. She unzipped his jeans so there were no barriers between her and the evidence of his arousal. Her mouth moved to his, her tongue teasingly tracing the outline of his lips. "That's exactly what I'm counting on," she murmured. "Now, hush. This isn't a time for talking."

"Aye, that it's not." He crushed her against him, his mouth pressing hot kisses down her neck toward the V of her thin cotton blouse. His fingers were like lightning as they undid each button and released the front closure of her bra. Fonda shuddered in anticipation at the electric touch of his hands on her breasts. Hungrily, his mouth closed over a peaked nipple.

"Oh, Devin," she sighed. Molten rivers of fire flowed through her veins as his tongue tantalized her tender flesh.

With a frustrated groan, Devin wrenched away. Frantically, simultaneously, they began to rid themselves of their clothes. Devin finished first, and feverishly, he tugged at the lace of her underclothes to help her escape them. Finally, the dainty wisps of cloth lay discarded on the floor. Like a zestful quench of cool water onto a parched throat, Fonda felt the heat of Devin's lean body against hers. She knew that later there would be time for a slow, sensuous exploration of his body, but now, now, there was only the fire of a white-hot need, one that had to be slaked immediately. As his mouth locked upon hers, she accepted the searing entry of him inside her. Sensuously, she thrust forward to receive all of him, but when he didn't move immediately, she opened her eyes and saw the wondrous, half-fearful expression on his face.

"Devin?"

"I've forgotten," he murmured. "I . . . don't know how long . . . I can . . ."

Slowly, Fonda moved against him, her fingers clenching into his back. "It's okay," she whispered. "Come home to me, Devin."

With a shuddering sigh, Devin closed his eyes, and a moment later, he relinquished all the tight-reined restraint that had been a way of life for him for so long. Fonda held him tightly. Although she was still far away from fulfillment, it didn't matter. There would be time for that later. Now, it was enough to hear the sound of his breathing and the soft thud of his heart against her damp skin.

"I'm sorry," he whispered.

She shook her head, her hands caressing the firm muscles of his back. "It's okay."

Slowly, Devin turned on his side, pulling her with him. His hands smoothed back her hair as he stared into her eyes. "Christ!" he whispered. "I do believe you're a wee faerie woman. You're magic!"

"No." Fonda snuggled against him, smiling. "The only thing magical is us, Devin."

FONDA'S HAND traced the sinewy muscle of Devin's arm, lingering over his rock-hard bicep and down across the wiry hairs of his forearm. Her face nestled against the hollow of his throat, and with every shallow breath, she inhaled the fragrance of his masculinity. All down the length of her body she could feel his warmth against her, and suddenly, she felt more complete than she'd ever been in her life. Why, he was the missing piece in the puzzle! That was how perfectly they fit together. How was it possible she'd lived twenty-seven years of her life without him beside her like this?

She felt a stirring against her leg and a soft laugh escaped her throat. "Again? Already?"

"Aye, love." With a quick movement, he rolled her over on her back and bent over her. His mouth nuzzled her neck. "Again. And again—and again—"

With a soft groan, Fonda drew his mouth down to hers.

This time, their lovemaking was different. They took the time to explore each other, all the soft sinews, the hard muscles, the skin textures, the curves and corners, the secret hidden places reserved only for lovers. Devin was eager, almost boyish, in the delight he found in Fonda's unreserved ardor. For her, it was the Fourth of July, New Year's Eve, and all twenty-seven of her birthdays at once. Along with the sound of Devin's ragged breathing against her ear, she heard joyous Christmas bells and Beethoven's Fifth Symphony. Then, finally, the music died away and the explosion of light dimmed.

They held each other for a long moment, shuddering in wondrous ecstasy. Finally, when Devin was able to speak, he slid his lips across her damp throat and said, "Christ Almighty, I love you, Fonda."

"I know," Fonda whispered. "Oh, yes. I know."

A long time later, he drew away to look at her. "You mentioned Caitlyn. You know about her?"

Fonda nodded. "Bram told me. I know you loved her. And I know she was killed during a terrorist bombing in Belfast."

He looked troubled. "There's more you should know. About us."

Fonda shook her head. "Not now. I don't want to talk about her now. Let's forget the past, Devin." She took a deep breath and then asked the question. "But what about the future? Do you think there can be one for us?"

For just a second, Devin appeared to hesitate, then he kissed her nose, her cheeks, and finally her mouth. He drew away. "After the tour is over, I have to go back to Ireland to work on my new album. Will you go with me? As my wife?"

PART FOUR

Into the Fire

19

FONDA SHIVERED in the chill of the desert night as she gazed out at the city lights of Tempe. Immediately, Devin's arm tightened around her. He bent to nuzzle the side of her neck under the rumpled fall of her hair. She smiled and leaned back against him, still finding it hard to believe this man loved her, *cherished* her, in fact, as archaic as it sounded. Devin was the kind of man who could do no less. In everything he cared about, he gave his all. His singing and song writing. His causes. And now, finally, with her, his loving.

Sighing with content, Fonda turned in his arms and kissed his jaw. It was bristly because he hadn't shaved since that morning. The hour was late, and creeping inevitably toward dawn.

Earlier, at the concert, she'd stood and watched Devin on stage, unable to quite believe that only hours before, he'd become her lover. It soon became clear something extraordinary had happened to him. For the first time in years, he didn't perform his bleakest songs, the ones about Belfast and pain and death. The new jaunty Devin ripped into some of his earlier rabble-rousing rock 'n' roll, some tender ballads, and then covered a Bob Dylan classic and a couple of Rolling Stone hits.

Near the end of the first set, Devin looked toward the wings and grinned at her. Her heart jumped. How was it possible that only a smile from him made her go weak in the knees? He lifted the mike to his mouth and turned back to the crowd.

"I have a great respect for my fellow countryman, Van Morrison." A cheer went up from the audience and Devin raised his hand, grinning. "No. I'm sorry to say he's not backstage." He looked around at his band members and laughed. "That I know of, anyway." He waited until the noise died a bit before going on. "A few years back, my good friend Van wrote a song called 'Sweet Thing.' I always liked it, but it wasn't until recently that it began to hold real meaning for me." He turned back to Fonda. "Fonda, this is for you."

Devin accompanied himself on the acoustic guitar while he sang the Van Morrison song. Fonda's heart sang along with him. She felt a nudge at her side and turned to see Bram's warm blue eyes staring intently at her. Suddenly, he leaned over and gave her a quick kiss on the cheek.

"You're a fine gem, Fonda."

It had been the most wonderful night of her life. After the concert, she and Devin returned to his hotel room, where they made love again. And talked about the future. And made love again. But now, it was time to go.

She smiled up at him. "You know, I'm not going to be able to do this again. I can't make Jessie spend *every* night with Laoise. She's sure to get suspicious."

Devin's hand moved her curtain of hair aside so he could brush his lips along her neck. She shivered with the ever present desire his mere touch aroused in her. "Tell her we're getting married. She'll understand." He pulled away and looked at her. "There it is again. That shadow in your eyes when I mention marriage. What is it, Fon? You said you wanted to marry me."

"Yes, I do, but . . ." Fonda couldn't wipe the worry from her face. Her hands clutched at his arms. "Oh, Devin, I do love you! And I want to marry you, but what about my career? I'm just starting to get somewhere. How can I give it up to go live in Ireland?"

Devin drew her closer, nestling her against his warm body. "Don't think that hasn't crossed my mind. I know how important your career is to you. But I also know now we've found each other, nothing will stand in the way of us being together. I'll think of something, love. In fact, I already have an idea, but I don't want to discuss it until I mull it over some more." His lips brushed hers. "As for your little sister, you must tell her about us. She's a big girl. I don't think she'll frown on you for wanting to be with me now and again."

Fonda pulled away from him and grinned. "Oh, that's not what I'm worried about. Jessie will think it's great. But I'm supposed to be setting a good example for her. I can't be sneaking off to your room every night."

"Come inside," Devin said, drawing her into the hotel room. Slowly, he kissed one eyelid and then the other. "What better example to set than to show your affection for the one true love of your life?"

Fonda kissed his chin. "Is that what I am?"

"That you are." His mouth settled on hers with a sure mastery, his tongue gently probing, tasting the sweetness inside her lips. Against the thin fabric of Devin's oversize T-shirt, she felt the evidence of his excitement rising against her stomach. With a little laugh, she drew her mouth away from his.

"Devin! I really *do* have to go."

"Why?" he whispered, one hand moving slowly up the swell of her breast. Immediately, her nipple hardened under his touch. His mouth went to the hollow of her neck, where he leisurely began to nibble.

Fonda threw back her head and sighed shakily. "Oh, Devin."

"Yes, love?" he mumbled as he continued the journey down the V of her shirt to explore the tender valley between her breasts. When the fabric would stretch no more, his hands went to the hem to pull it up.

"Devin . . . I . . ." Tiny flames of desire fanned through her. In a moment, she knew she would lose all train of thought.

The T-shirt was above her breasts now, and Devin took one nipple into his mouth and circled it with his tongue. Then, like a cat lapping cream, he flicked at it in a languorous way, one that told Fonda they had hours yet to explore their newfound love. Her fingers entwined in his silky black hair as she gave herself up to the delicious sensations he aroused in her. Slowly, he pulled away from her to lift the shirt over her head. He tossed it to the floor and stood looking at her, his eyes burning.

"You said something about leaving?" he asked.

Fonda took a step toward him and reaching out, slid her hands up the bare expanse of his chest, following the line of wiry black hair that grew up from his stomach. "I don't have the slightest idea what you're talking about," she said. She drew his head down to hers and waited breathlessly for the onslaught of his devouring kiss.

"OH, MY God! My girlfriends back in Indiana aren't going to believe this! Devin O'Keefe, my brother-in-law!"

Jessie was ecstatic about Fonda and Devin's engagement. They broke the news to her on their last night in Tempe. After letting out a shriek that probably had the hotel manager thinking a horrendous murder was being committed, she wrapped her arms around both of them in a frenzy of excitement.

"*When?* When are you getting married? Can I be in the wedding?"

Fonda didn't know how to answer her. She and Devin had been so wrapped up in each other, they hadn't discussed the logistics of the wedding. But after leaving Jessie, Fonda asked him, "Well, is it going to be Ireland or Indiana?"

His answer was totally unexpected.

"Las Vegas," he said, as he walked her to her room. It was late, and they had an early flight the next day. "Let's get married in Las Vegas after the San Francisco concert."

Fonda laughed. "You're kidding, right?"

But his face was perfectly serious. Fonda's grin disappeared. "Oh, Devin. You can't be serious. That has to be the most unromantic place in the world to be married. Why not Ireland? You know, in one of those gorgeous cathedrals."

Devin wouldn't meet her eyes. "Not Ireland," he said softly. "Anywhere but there."

Fonda stared at him. "But Devin, *why?*"

Abruptly, he turned and began to pace up and down the hall. "Trust me on this, Fonda. Just let it be. I know!" He stopped and whirled around to face her. "How about Monte Carlo?"

She opened her mouth to insist he tell her why he didn't want to get married in Ireland, but something in his eyes stopped her. With a sigh, she nodded. "Okay. Monte Carlo."

He grinned and held out his arms to her. "Come here, woman."

Once in his arms, she forgot about her disappointment. After all, did it really matter *where* they were married?

IAN WAS waiting for him outside his room. One look at his agitated face and Devin knew why he'd come. He straightened his shoulders and unlocked the door. There was nothing his manager could say to make him change his mind. Nothing.

"Would you care for a drink, Ian?" Devin asked, when they were inside the room.

"I would that. The strongest you have."

Devin went to the bar and opened his liquor cabinet. His eyes scanned the row of bottles. He didn't touch the stuff, but at this moment, a stiff one didn't sound half-bad. "Whiskey? Brandy? Wine?"

"Whiskey. Neat."

Devin poured it and handed the glass to him. Ian downed it quickly. The glass thudded down on the bar and still Ian didn't speak, but his eyes glittered accusingly at Devin.

"Okay, let's have it, Ian. Say what you came to say."

Ian's face contorted. "Are you daft, man? What do you mean by telling the world you're going to marry that girl?"

Devin stood rigidly, his body taut with tension. "I *am* going to marry her." His voice was firm, resolute.

Ian stared at him, unbelieving. "Mother of God, Devin! You can't do it. You'll be committing a mortal sin!"

"Ian, try to understand. I love her. In my heart, I don't believe it's a sin. The sin was in marrying Caitlyn, a woman who has devoted her life to violence. And I'm going to tell Fonda that."

"You're going to tell her *what?*"

Devin eyed him steadily. "The truth. All of it."

"Christ, man! Have you lost your mind? If this gets out to the public, you'll be putting your career in a coffin. You won't be able to sell your records to your own sister!"

The muscles in Devin's face tightened. "Fonda is more important to me than my career. If that's the way it has to be . . ."

Ian gaped at him, astonished. After a long moment, he turned and strode to the bar. He poured himself another whiskey and took a long gulp. His voice was deadly quiet when he spoke. "And do you think your 'light of love' will go ahead and blithely marry you, knowing you're a bigamist?"

Devin didn't speak. But at Ian's words, a cold feeling of dread began to spread through him.

"She's an American, Devin. They're Puritans at heart. Even worse than we Irish. Mark my words, if you tell that woman the truth, she'll be out of your life before you can utter a Hail Mary." With that, Ian placed his whiskey glass on the bar and left the room.

Devin dropped to the bed, his body trembling. His bravura was gone. What if Ian were right? Would Fonda leave him when she knew the truth?

He couldn't take that chance. Caitlyn would have to remain a secret.

AS SOON as they arrived in Salt Lake City, Fonda, with Devin at her side, made a long-distance phone call to Indiana. When she heard her mother's voice, she grinned. "Mom, I'm getting married!"

The only response was a sharp intake of breath.

"Mom? Are you there?"

"Yes." Her voice sounded strange. "Who are you marrying, Fonda?"

"Devin O'Keefe." Fonda smiled at Devin and squeezed his hand. "He's the musician I've been touring with. Mom, everyone in the world knows who Devin O'Keefe is! Why haven't you heard of him? Oh, never mind. Mom, I'm crazy about him."

At that, Devin leaned over, kissed her on the neck, and whispered, "And I'm crazy about her daughter. Tell her that."

"He said to tell you he's crazy about me, too. Mom, listen. He's finishing up his U.S. tour in mid-August. He wants to get married in Monte Carlo. And well, he wants to fly all of you there for the wedding. Mom, are you there?" Fonda listened, but all she could hear was an indistinguishable mumble.

"Let me talk to her," Devin said.

Fonda nodded. "Mom, Devin wants to say hello."

But it wasn't her mother's voice that came on the line.

"Fonda Jane, what the hell's going on?"

"Oh. Hi, Dad." Fonda's voice was suddenly subdued. "Did Mom tell you? I'm getting married."

"To a rock singer, she said. Girl, have you lost your mind?"

"Dad, don't bellow at me. Can I please talk to Mom again? Devin would like to say hello."

"If you have half a brain in your head, you'll get on a plane and fly home right now. And bring your little sister, too. My God, it's no telling what damage you've done to her! Cavorting with rock singers and God knows who else. Your mother should never have allowed Jessie to stay with you."

"Dad." Fonda's voice was like ice. Devin stared at her curiously. "Please put Mom back on the line. Or I'm going to hang up."

"Louise!" he yelled into her ear.

"Honey." It was her mother again. "Are you sure you know what you're doing?"

Fonda's eyes brimmed with tears. Devin held her close, his eyes concerned . "I'm sure, Mom. I love him."

"But you hardly know him."

"I feel like I've known him forever. That's enough for me. Mom, will you come to the wedding? Devin knows how difficult it would be for you financially, so he's offered to pay the entire expense."

There was a short pause. Fonda imagined her on the other end of the line, twisting the cord around her finger and staring anxiously out the kitchen window. "I'm sorry, Fonda. I just don't think Ed would ever agree to that. You know how proud he is."

"But Mom! We're talking about my wedding!"

"I know, honey. I wish it could be different. Will we see you before you leave? Maybe you can come home for a while before you make any firm decisions. Who knows? You may decide this is all a silly infatuation."

Fonda could only swallow hard and remain silent. *Silly infatuation?* Didn't her mother realize how hurtful those words were?

"Let me talk to her," Devin said.

"Mom, Devin wants to say hi, okay?"

"Oh, dear, Fonda, I really can't right now. I have something on the stove. Perhaps later. Is Jessie doing okay? I haven't heard from her in over a week."

Fonda blinked quickly and turned away from Devin. She knew if she met his eyes, she'd burst into tears. "Jessie's fine Mom. She says hello. Look, I know you're busy. I've got to go, too. I'll call again in a couple of weeks. 'Bye."

Fonda hung up the phone and then stood still a moment, her back to Devin. She felt his hands upon her shoulders. His lips brushed her cheek.

"It's okay, darlin'. They'll come around."

"Oh, Devin." She whirled around, and now the tears flowed freely down her face. "They won't come to the wedding!"

"Do you know what it's like growing up without a father?" Fonda rubbed a hand across her tear-stained eyes. She sat on the sofa in Devin's dressing room, a cup of steaming tea in one trembling hand.

"I think I do," Devin said quietly. He sat next to her, his hand resting gently on the back of her neck.

She took a sip of tea, her lower lip still trembling from the phone call with her parents. "It was me and Michael, you know.

He just never connected with us. But Sandy! Now, that's a different story. She was his little princess. Still is. God! If he's not
yelling at me and trying to make me change my life to fit his cri-
teria, he's as distant as—as Ian Brinegar! Oh, why can't I just accept it? He'll never change."

"Have you tried talking to him? Tell him how you feel?"

"I told you. I can't talk to the man! He's unreasonable. Nothing
I say makes a bit of difference to him."

They were both silent for a long moment.

"My father was in internment prison for four years," Devin
said finally. "I was fourteen when he got out. He was a different
man. The Brits had taken the fight out of him. He never talked
about what they'd done to him in prison. But I saw the scars. The
thing is, I guessed even then that the scars on his back weren't as
bad as the emotional ones. You see, he'd been arrested for writing an editorial in a Republican newspaper. Sure, he wanted to
see the British out, but he didn't advocate violence to do it. The
Brits didn't see it that way."

Fonda stared at Devin's tense face. Her heart ached at the
wounded look in his eyes. "They put him in prison because he
wrote an article?"

"Yeh. Not uncommon in those days. When he got out, Da
never wrote for the newspaper again. There were times I grew so
angry with him, I wanted to shake him. When the Brits raided
our house, over and over again, he took their abuse without saying a word. I couldn't understand it. One night after a British
commander insulted my sister Bonnie—called her a homely Irish
bitch—in a fit of rage, I asked my father why he wouldn't put up
a fight. And for the first time, he told me about the brutalities he
witnessed in the H-Blocks. Then he said something I've never
forgotten. 'Armed rebellion will never resolve this conflict. No
amount of Irish blood spilt on this land will make a wee bit of
difference.' Then, with tears in his eyes, he begged me to leave
Northern Ireland. He said he couldn't bear to lose another son by
a British bullet."

"Another son?"

Devin's eyes had gone dark with memory. He shook his head. "My older brother, Glen, was shot dead by the British."

Fonda drew in a shocked breath. "Oh, Devin! I'm so sorry!"

He didn't speak for a long moment. "Getting back to your father, Fon. You should talk to him. I'd thought my da was weak. That they'd broken him. And perhaps they had, in a way. But he'd kept his pride and his humanity in spite of everything he'd been through. And I trusted in his wisdom. He convinced me to leave the North. But if we hadn't talked, who knows where I'd be today?"

Fonda stared down at her fingernails. "Yeah, I know. I wish I could talk to my father. But unfortunately, he isn't interested in anything I have to say."

IAN DREADED making the call to Caitlyn, but it had to be done. As he waited for her to pick up the phone, he nervously twisted the cord around his index finger.

Hell! She was going to hit the bloody ceiling when she heard about this. She'd wanted the pretty photographer to keep Devin busy, but she hadn't planned on it turning into a permanent situation.

"78393." It was Caitlyn's smoky voice.

Ian's heart lurched. Even thousands of miles across land and ocean, it sent shivers of apprehension through him. Thank the Blessed Virgin he didn't have to tell her face-to-face.

"This is Mulligan."

"Is everything on schedule?"

"Quite so. With one or two minor hitches." He thought of Sam's corpse abandoned in the St. Louis bait and tackle shop.

"Fine. Is there anything else? I was just on my way out."

"Yes, as a matter of fact, there is." Ian paused, wondering exactly how to put it into words.

"Well, what is it?"

He decided to simply blurt it out. "Devin has asked the photographer to marry him. It seems our idea to use her to distract him has worked better than we'd planned."

There was a long silence on the other end of the line. When her voice finally came, it was icy. "There won't be a wedding. Devin isn't free to marry, is he? Not as long as I'm alive."

20

DEVIN KEPT waiting for Bram to come down on him like Ian had about his announced engagement. But when it didn't happen, Devin cornered him in the tuning room at the Salt Lake City venue. Bram was lounging on a sofa, flipping through a girlie magazine and drinking a beer.

He looked up and grinned when he saw Devin. "Man, take a look at Miss July. What a pair of ginger jars!"

Devin gazed at him steadily. "Why haven't you said it, Bram?"

The roadie's eyes went back to Miss July's ginger jars. "What's that?"

"Tell me how I can't marry Fonda. How I'll be committing a sin if I do."

Bram closed the magazine and tossed it onto the coffee table. Then he looked up. "That's between you and God. What do *you* think?"

Devin stared at his friend for a long moment. "I think Fonda and I were meant to be together." He sat down on the sofa and leaned earnestly toward Bram. "She's a gift to me, Bram. She's awakened me to life again. How can that be sinful?"

Bram gave a solemn nod. "It's not. You and Fonda love each other. That's plain to see."

"And Caitlyn?" Devin had to ask.

Bram stared at him, then shrugged. "Caitlyn was faithful to only one thing, Devin. The Cause. Why don't you just let it go? Get on with your life."

"I want to." Devin clenched his fists. "Jesus, I want to!"

"Then, do it." Bram leaned over and placed a hand on his shoulder. "Believe me, Dev. You have nothing to worry about. I'm all for your marriage to Fonda."

Still, Devin couldn't shake the apprehension he felt. As much as he and Fonda were right together, he knew he was doing wrong. But he loved her. Jesus, didn't that justify it? "And Ian?" he asked. "He doesn't feel the way you do."

Bram scowled. "Ah, hell! The man isn't going to do anything to jeopardize what he has with you. Remember, you're the boss. You forget that too often, my friend."

Devin nodded. Ian wouldn't stand in his way. He might not agree with what he did, but he wouldn't make any trouble.

Bram stretched out a hand. "Congratulations, Devin. You're getting a fine woman."

Devin's eyes met his, and slowly he reached out to clasp his hand. "You're a good friend, Bram. The best." He pulled Bram to him and gave him a fierce hug. "You're the best!"

❦

> *"'When will we be married, Molly?*
> *When will we be wed?*
> *When will we be bedded in the same bed?'"*

Fonda laughed. "Will you cut it out with that silly song?" They were relaxing in Devin's dressing room before the afternoon's sound check. She threw a pillow at him.

It glanced off his shoulder and Devin grinned. He went on with his song.

> *"'Ya had your eye on Jimmy, Long Jimmy Vee*
> *Ya had your eye on Jimmy and a fine man, he*
> *Ya had your eye on Jimmy, but ya better let him be*
> *'Cos when you go, Molly-O, you'll be goin' with me.'"*

"Devin!" With a bound, Fonda hurled herself at him.

The guitar slid to the floor as Devin's arms tightened around her. Playfully, she nipped his cheek with her teeth, growling hungrily.

"Jaysus!" Devin said, his hands moving firmly down her tight-fitting jeans. "You're an animal!"

Fonda giggled and pulled away to look at him. "Well, as Clint Eastwood would say," she lowered her voice to a masculine drawl, "'You have a way of bringing it out in me.'"

"What's the matter, love? Don't you fancy Irish folk tunes?"

"Of course I do. But you've been driving me crazy with that one all day. Don't you know any others?"

"Sure, but right now, I seem to have marriage on me mind. Can't understand why, can you?" Devin lifted his arm to peer around her neck at his leather-banded watch. "Almost time for the sound check. Fon, sit up a moment. I want to run an idea by you, love."

Fonda snuggled against him and kissed his bristly jaw. "Do we have to now? Won't it be more fun just to lie here and kiss for a while?"

Devin pretended to be insulted. "Is sex all you think about, woman? We have serious matters to discuss."

Reluctantly, she pulled away and sat up. "Can I help it if I'm weak? Besides, it's your fault. If you weren't so darn sexy . . ."

Devin grinned and drew himself up into a more comfortable position on the sofa. "If you weren't so darn blind . . ." He reached over and took her hands. "Remember before, I told you I had an idea about what you can do after we're married. Well, I've been doing a lot of thinking about this." His brown eyes danced with excitement. "You would be perfect for it, Fon."

Fonda squeezed his hands impatiently. "What?"

Devin had the typical Irishman's inability to get to the point. "Well, you see, I have a friend back in Dublin who owns an independent record label. He's always in need of good photographers for the cover layouts. Just a word from me and you'll find yourself his in-house photographer. That would keep you busy, wouldn't it, now?"

Fonda stared at him, trying not to let the disappointment show. "Well—it's an interesting thought."

His smile disappeared. "You don't like the idea."

"It's just that . . ." Fonda drew her hands away and leaned back on the sofa. "Oh, it's a stupid dream, I guess, but I've always wanted to run my own rock magazine. You know, like *Spotlight.* I've been working for them for almost six years now, and there's so many things I'd do differently if I were the publisher. You know, I wouldn't concentrate on all the big names like so many music magazines do. I'd devote a huge part of it to the bands just starting out. The ones that are beyond the mainstream, the innovators . . ." Her voice trailed off at the look on his face. "But hey! Don't look so disappointed." She leaned down to give him a quick kiss. "As long as I'm with you, it doesn't matter what I do."

Devin's downcast expression didn't change. "No one should ever have to give up on their dream."

Fonda snuggled against him and began nibbling at his chin. *"You're* my dream."

He chuckled. "And you're a devil!" His hands slid under her knit top to caress her back.

There was a sharp rap on the door. "Am I interrupting anything?"

"Come on in, Bram." Devin called out. "I'm just trying to get Fon down from the chandelier."

Fonda gave him a quick punch in the stomach just as Bram strolled into the room. "What is this? She's beating up on you already? And you're not even married yet!"

"It's not too late to change your mind," Fonda said with a mock glare as she scrambled off him and got to her feet.

"Not a chance, love. You've already committed yourself." He grinned over at Bram. "So, what's up, lad?"

Bram's grin disappeared. "A problem with the Fender Telecaster. You turn the amp up to max, it's gonna explode like the fart of a bean-eating elephant. There's just not enough juice, Dev."

Devin leisurely got up from the sofa and handed his guitar over to Bram. "Well, let's go see what we can do. Hey, I've been thinking about adding a new song to the show. Remember that old folk tune about Molly-O?" He began to sing, "'When will we be married, Molly . . .'"

"Devin!" With a breathless laugh, Fonda followed Devin and Bram out of the room.

BRAM WAS still laughing as he headed to the tuning room to get the other guitars. Those two were great together. It was grand seeing Devin with a bright smile on his face these days. In the last few years, they hadn't seen much of that. He pushed open the door of the tuning room and stopped short.

"What are you two doing here?"

Laoise and Jessie stared at him, eyes wide and guilty-looking.

Bram looked down at the guitar case near Laoise's right knee. His eyes slid to Jessie and he grinned. "Helping yourself to a nice electrical snack, Jess?"

He was referring to an incident that had happened earlier that day. During an engagement luncheon for Devin and Fonda at a posh Salt Lake City restaurant, Jessie had helped herself to crêpes Suzette at what she thought was the dessert buffet. Unfortunately, it had turned out to be a display—a pancake filled with edible-looking shortening. Her expression after taking her first bite had been the highlight of the day for everyone at the luncheon. From that moment on, Jessie had been the object of good-natured ribbing.

After a nudge from Laoise, Jessie laughed. "Yeah, right, Bram. You know how it is when you get a craving."

"Bram, you should be ashamed of yourself, you should," Laoise said in her best Irish-mother tone. "Teasing poor Jessie like that. And to think, we came to help you carry the guitars to the sound check."

"Oh, you did, did you? What kindly souls you are." He reached down and grabbed the Bison 335. "Well, come on, then. Get to it."

Ian was the only one on stage when Bram and the girls arrived.

Whistling a tuneless song, Bram stared at him curiously. Devin's manager was standing near an amp, the Yamaha P2201, contemplating it with an odd smile. It was a strange place to see Brinegar, Bram thought. He rarely came near the stage equipment.

"Something I can do for you, Ian?" Bram asked.

Ian jumped, obviously startled out of deep thought. "Jesus, Bram! You shouldn't sneak up on people that way."

Lord, the man was jumpier than a grasshopper on speed. "Beg your pardon," Bram said, as sarcastically as he could manage without being insolent. "I'll whistle louder next time. Is there something wrong with the amp?"

The question seemed to agitate him even more. "Of course not," he said brusquely. "Can't a man just check things out without being interrogated?"

"Hey!" Bram held his hands up in mock surrender. "Sorry, man. Just trying to help out."

"Then just do your job and let me do mine."

Ian stalked from the stage. Bram stared after him. The man was losing his fucking mind. Turning into a blithering idiot, he was.

He looked at the two girls, who were holding some kind of conference over near the guitar cart. "Hey, you two! Go round up the band so we can get this bleeding show on the road."

LAOISE NUDGED Jessie. "There they are."

They scrunched down in their seats at the back of the huge auditorium and watched as Devin's band came on stage. Seamus settled the lead guitar strap across his shoulder and Laoise grinned. "Any minute now," she whispered.

Devin came on stage. "Let's start with 'The Forgotten.'"

"Good choice," Laoise said. "Has a grand drum intro."

"So what?"

"Just watch! When the guitars come in, you'll see what I mean."

The drummer began his energetic intro. The girls' eyes centered on the lead guitarist. It was supposed to be a rippling slide, but what came out was more like the screech of an injured goose. Laoise and Jessie convulsed in giggles as the music came to an abrupt end.

"What the hell was *that?*" Devin demanded.

All eyes were on Seamus. He shrugged.

Devin gazed toward the wings. "Bram!"

"What the bleeding hell?" Bram hurried on stage. "Devin, I swear, I tuned that guitar only a half hour ago. Okay, okay. I'll do it again."

"Get him the Fender. We'll do 'Ghosts.'"

But it was the same with every guitar Bram brought on stage. All were hopelessly mistuned. Laoise and Jessie were practically rolling out of their seats with laughter as poor Bram was mercilessly flayed by Devin's sharp Celtic tongue.

Laoise began to dig in her purse for a tissue to wipe the tears from her cheeks. "Oh, this is the best ever!"

"You're a genius, Laoise. You must get these ideas from living with three brothers."

From the stage, the music started again, and this time the sound was normal. Jessie nudged Laoise. She raised her voice so it could be heard over the music. "Looks like the show's over."

But she was wrong there. Suddenly, there was a loud pop from the stage and the music again screeched to a halt. Laoise and Jessie looked toward the stage and saw a puff of smoke rise from behind the bass guitarist. It seemed to be coming from one of the amps. An acrid stench filled the air.

Jessie grinned at Laoise. "Cool! Great effect, don't you think?"

But Laoise's face was white. "That's no special effect, idjeet!"

On stage, the band gathered around the smoking amp, while Bram yelled for a fire extinguisher. A crewman rushed over with one, and immediately, the defective amp was smothered in white froth.

Over the excited babble, Devin's frustrated voice rang out. "What the fuck happened?"

Laoise grabbed Jessie's arm. "Come on! Let's get out of here."

And she began to run like the devil himself was after her.

Stunned, Jessie hesitated a moment and then followed her. They raced out of the auditorium and didn't stop until they reached the outer corridor. Huffing and puffing from their exertion, they fell against the wall and struggled to catch their breath.

Finally, Jessie was able to speak. "Laoise, *what* did you do to that amp?"

Laoise's dark eyes snapped. "I didn't touch it! You were with me. I didn't go near the bloody amp!"

"But we must've done something to make it blow up like that. You know, when we messed around with the guitars. It's possible, isn't it?"

"I don't know," Laoise admitted. "But I'll tell you what. I'll bloody well deny it if anyone asks me if I know anything about it. Do you know how expensive that equipment is?"

"Oh, shit," Jessie muttered. "Fonda will kill me if she finds out."

"Then we have to make sure she doesn't find out, right?" Her eyes were dark and huge in her pale face. "Swear you'll never tell!"

"I swear. Now you."

"I swear, on my mother's grave, I'll never tell we touched a bloody thing!"

"But your mother isn't—"

"Shhh! Here comes Ryan."

Quickly, Jessie whirled around, her heartbeat picking up. She threw him a wide smile. "Hi."

"Hey, you missed all the excitement!" Ryan hooked his thumbs in the belt-loops of his jeans and grinned at them. "One of the amps blew up. It's a miracle no one was killed."

"Oh, God!" Jessie's knees went weak. Laoise nudged her hard in the side. "I mean . . . no one was hurt, were they?"

Ryan shook his head. "But Ian is screaming about saboteurs. He thinks someone is playing pranks."

"Did he see anyone?" Laoise asked, a wary look on her face.

"No. You know how neurotic that old bugger is. Every time something goes wrong, he has to look for someone convenient to blame. He'll probably pick on me since I'm the youngest roadie on the tour."

"Oh, no." Jessie took a step toward him. "Not you."

Ryan seemed to appreciate her concern. He gave her one of his dazzling white smiles and looked at his sister. "Do you think perhaps you could make yourself scarce for a few moments? I have something personal to discuss with Jess, here."

Laoise threw him a scornful glare. "Yeah, and we all know what *that* is." She glanced at Jessie. "Remember what those books said. You don't want to be getting in trouble."

"Just go!" Ryan ordered.

"All right! If you insist . . ." Laoise gave Jessie another warning look. "Remember what we said about—you know."

"I will." She turned her full attention back to Ryan.

He held out his hand. "Let's take a walk." His hand closed on hers, sending a wave of warmth up her arm. They began to walk toward Section E.

"You know what the trouble is?" Ryan burst out. "There's no place for a bit of privacy on this tour. Someone is always around. I've been wanting to get you alone since Colorado."

Jessie felt her heart give a lurch. "Why? Do you want to kiss some more?"

He gave her a sly grin. "Actually, I was hoping to do a wee bit more than kiss."

Her face was getting red—she knew it.

"Have you given it some thought?" he went on. "To what we talked about in Colorado?"

"Sure," Jessie mumbled, trying to sound nonchalant. "I've thought about it."

"Look what I've got." He pulled a hand out of his jeans pocket and showed her a square package with a photo of some silly couple in front of a sunset.

Jessie took it. "What's this?"

Inside the foil, she could feel the outline of something circular. Suddenly she realized what it was, and felt a blush creep up from her neck. The sex education classes at school had preached safe sex ad nauseam. What Jessie remembered most about the course was that some of the Christian Coalition parents had made a big stink out of it, proclaiming that the sex ed. courses were promoting teen sexuality. To get back at them, a few psycho students had blown up condoms so they looked like balloons and placed them on the Christmas tree on the front lawn of the Baptist Church. The editorial pages of the local newspapers had been buried in furious editorials for weeks afterward.

"It's a condom," Ryan explained. "So you don't get pregnant, you know."

"Or diseases," Jessie added with mature authority.

Ryan looked insulted. "I don't have any diseases. I've never . . . I mean . . . that one woman I was with . . . she was very clean."

"Whatever." Jessie gazed down at the gushy-looking couple on the package. "Can I open it up and see what it looks like?"

He grabbed it from her. "Of course not. You'll see it soon enough." He looked at her, his blue eyes hopeful. "It *will* be soon, won't it, Jessie? I think about you all the time. About how good it was kissing you."

Jessie looked around. They were alone in the corridor. "Can we do it now? Kiss, I mean."

She didn't have to ask him twice. His blue eyes became cloudy-looking and he moved against her, pulling her into his arms. His mouth came down on hers, his tongue immediately searching the cavern of her mouth. Jessie reciprocated with a sensual tongue search of her own, and immediately, it sent Ryan growling under his breath.

A new excitement rushed through her. She felt powerful! As if she could make him do anything she wanted. He started to pull away, but Jessie decided she wanted more, so she hungrily thrust her tongue into his mouth and the kiss deepened once again. She wondered if he'd grown hard yet. Her hand slid down his firm chest and hesitated at his belt buckle. Should she or shouldn't she? With his tongue and upper teeth, Ryan began to gently nip at her lower lip. Quickly, her hand dropped to the crotch of his jeans. And there it was, hot and hard and thick! He groaned and moved his pelvis against her hand.

She pulled away, alarmed.

"No!" he said in a strangled voice. "Don't stop!"

But Jessie's bravura was gone. She stared at him, her face flaming.

His eyes were heavy-lidded as he gazed at her, breathing uneven. "Jesus, girl! What are you doing to me?"

"I was just curious."

"Jessie-girl, you can't be doing things like that to a lad. Not unless you're planning on going through with it."

Her eyes dropped. "Sorry. I didn't mean to get you upset."

"*Get me upset?* That's not what you got me, girl!" He stared at her for a moment, and then his face softened. "It's okay. I keep forgetting what an innocent you are. Look, you let me know when you're ready. I'll figure out where we can meet." He leaned over and gave her a quick hard kiss. "You better go find Laoise. She'll be looking for you."

Jessie turned slowly and walked away from him. Her hand throbbed where she'd touched him. What a mystery! What a wonderful, delightful, fantastic mystery. And she couldn't wait to explore it further.

21

DRESSED IN maintenance uniforms of Aer Lingus, Caitlyn's men arrived at the venue early the next morning to pick up the damaged amp. Ian was there to meet them. As he watched them load up the crate stamped DEFECTIVE MUSICAL EQUIPMENT, he leisurely lit his pipe and took a long, pleasant draw upon it. Things were going very well indeed.

He still couldn't get over how smoothly it had gone during the sound check. No one suspected a thing. When he'd planted the explosive device, he'd been petrified. After all, what did he know of things like that? But Caitlyn had insisted *he* be the one to do it. She didn't want any strangers being caught messing around the stage equipment.

The damaged amp would be flown to Ireland, along with the crated arms, a perfect decoy in case customs officials insisted upon a search. Of course, even that was doubtful. Devin was so respected in his home country that most often, as soon as they heard his name, everything was sent on through. But Caitlyn was taking no chances. IRA men had been planted in the customs area at Shannon to make sure that the right crate was opened and inspected, if it became necessary.

The men finished loading the crate, and with a wave, pulled out of the parking lot. Ian drew a long sigh of relief. He could relax now. His part in the operation was over except for the final meeting with the arms dealers in San Francisco. There should be no problem with that meeting. As long as the boyos in the North were satisfied with the goods, he'd make the final payment and be on his way.

Humming a tune, Ian jauntily walked over to his rental car. One last concert here in Salt Lake City. Tomorrow, they'd leave for Seattle. Thank God. Of late, he'd felt a craving for a little excitement, and with all the Mormons in this city, there was none to be found. Seattle would be different.

He'd heard about those boys from the Great Northwest. A lot of lumberjacks and the like. Real he-men.

Just thinking about them made him hard.

"DID YOU see her? God! I couldn't believe it! How can a woman be so—*sleazy?*"

Like an angry lioness, Fonda paced the floor of Devin's dressing room. Sprawled on the sofa, Bram watched her, his blue eyes dancing in amusement. From the bathroom that adjoined the room, Devin's voice belted out an Irish ballad, almost drowning out the sound of the shower. Fonda stood still. "Listen to him. How does he have a voice left after that show?" She resumed her pacing. "Bram! *Did you see her?* She lifted her blouse and showed her *breasts* to Devin. Her bare breasts! I was absolutely mortified."

Bram grinned. "And perhaps a wee bit jealous?"

"Well, sure. She was built like a—a living monument to Marilyn Monroe. Bram, it was disgusting!"

"Ah, yeah, absolutely nauseating. Thank the Lord I missed it!"

Fonda glared at him. "You're making fun of me."

He patted the sofa next to him. "Come and sit down, love. Before you blow a fuse or something." When she reluctantly sat down next to him, he put an arm around her shoulder and squeezed her affectionately. "You've been around this life for a few years, Fon. I know this isn't the first time you've seen some girl in the crowd do such a thing. They'll do anything to get Devin's attention. It's part of a rock star's life. Now, why are you getting yourself in such a tizzy about it?"

"Because I've never been in love with a rock star before. And he's *mine!* I don't want some other girl trying to . . . to blatantly seduce him like that. And in Salt Lake City, of all places! I thought they were really religious here."

"There's women like her everywhere. Fon, don't be telling me you feel threatened by a woman like that. Shame on ya, girl. Think on it a moment. Can you seriously see Devin being attracted to her—a woman who would bare her breasts in public like that?"

Fonda began to smile. Of course she couldn't picture such a ludicrous thing. "You're right. I overreacted, didn't I?"

"A bit." Bram squeezed her shoulder again. "But you're entitled. I wouldn't know from experience, mind you, but I believe being in love makes a person unreasonably jealous."

"You haven't been in love, Bram?"

"Christ! I don't even know what it is. There's been a lot of women in my life, but none of them were special—except . . . oh, hell. Bonnie is special, but she's just a friend. Doesn't take me seriously, at all. Besides, she's not my type."

Fonda stared at him, wondering who Bonnie was. He had a faraway look in his blue eyes. But suddenly it was gone. He leaned over and grabbed the remote control for the TV. "Let's see what's happening in the world tonight."

Yawning, Fonda sat through a recap of a speech by President Bush, some sobering footage of a devastating earthquake in northern Greece and a report of a foundering vessel off the coast of Norway. She was just about to excuse herself and go make sure Devin hadn't drowned in the shower when Bram suddenly tensed.

"What is it?" Fonda asked.

"Shhh!" His eyes were fastened on the TV.

It was a report from Northern Ireland. Fonda tuned in to the announcer's voice: ". . . according to the Royal Ulster Constabulary, the four gunmen were executed while trying to escape after the brutal murders of the three government officials. James Douglass, reporting from Belfast, Northern Ireland."

Bram's face had lost color. Fonda had never seen him so grim.

"Will they ever go away?" she asked softly. "The Troubles?"

His finger punched a button on the remote and the news program dissolved into a commercial for a Sealy Posture-Pedic mattress. "No," he said. "Never."

Fonda stared at the beautiful blond model lounging upon the mattress, but her mind was on Devin and his country. "Why is it Devin never talks about Derry and the Troubles?"

"It's too painful," Bram said, his face grim. "Believe me, I know that from personal experience."

Fonda gave him a curious look. "But you're from Galway. Surely you don't have any problems down there?"

His mouth was cynical. "Belfast's violence reaches all the provinces of Ireland, love. That you can be sure of."

"What happened?" There was something in his eyes. Something very personal.

He looked at her. "My parents were killed in Belfast. Blown up by a Protestant petrol bomb that exploded under their car on Falls Road." His voice was low, still full of pain.

"Oh, God, Bram, I'm sorry."

He stared at the TV, eyes glassy. "They'd gone there for the wake of my aunt Finella. It was a bad time to go. The week of the Twelfth, and the Protestants were full of more hatred than usual because of the Orange parades and the usual rabble-rousing. I'd tried to talk them out of it, but my mum—she was determined to see her sister put to rest." A bitter laugh escaped his lips. "A week later, there was a double wake in Galway."

The door to the bathroom opened and Devin stepped out, wearing nothing but a towel wrapped around his middle. Fonda looked up at him, still lost in the images of Bram's tragic tale.

Devin grinned. "What's this? I leave the room for a few minutes and come back to find my best friend ensconced on the sofa with my girl. What gives, Bram Gradeigh?"

Bram had lost his brooding expression and was now all grins. "Who can blame me? You go off and take a bloody eon in the shower while your woman pours out her troubles into my willing ears."

"What troubles?"

Fonda's mouth dropped open. "No troubles!"

"Oh, yeh?" Bram grinned. "What was that about some lady out in the crowd who was—shall we say, rather well endowed?"

"Yes!" Fonda's eyes flashed to Devin. "Did you see her? The girl with the boobs?"

Devin turned away and began to rummage through the wardrobe for his clothes. "What girl?"

Fonda jumped up. "Come on. You couldn't have missed her. She stood up on her seat and pulled her top up. Wasn't wearing a stitch of clothing under it!"

"I must have missed it," Devin mumbled as he drew out a pair of jeans.

"Devin! She had boobs that looked like the headlights of a semi-truck! And you're telling me you didn't see her?"

His voice was unconcerned. "I don't think so. Which shirt should I wear? The blue one or this western-look one?"

Bram laughed. "Jaysus, Fonda! Can't you see he's blushing? Of course, he saw her."

Fonda looked at him. "Devin! You are. She embarrassed you, didn't she? And here, I was worried you'd be turned on by her." In a second, she was upon him, smothering him in kisses. "I *do* love you, Devin. You really couldn't care less about women like her, could you? I knew it." She kissed the side of his bristly jaw as her fingers played over the damp skin of his back.

Bram stood up. "That's my cue to leave. It's getting just a bit too steamy in here for me."

Fonda drew away from Devin. "Oh, you don't have to go, Bram. I'm just fooling around."

With an iron grip, Devin pulled her back into his arms. "Oh yes he does."

Against her jeans and under the damp towel he was wearing, Fonda felt just how much he meant what he was saying. She thought it best not to argue.

A few moments later, Devin dragged his mouth away from hers. "Sweet Mary," he murmured. "This means another shower."

Her eyes danced wickedly. "No problem. We'll take it together."

IAN TOOK a sip of his Scotch and glanced around the dimly lit bar. It hadn't been easy finding this place, especially for a dapper Irishman who had a reputation to protect. He had to be careful where he asked questions. It was a good thing he'd run into the bellhop at the hotel who'd had the "look." A few tactfully put questions and a hundred-dollar bill had resulted in the name of the Blue Diamond, Seattle's most popular gay bar. However, finding it had been the difficulty.

Although he had the address, Ian drove up and down the street several times without seeing it, and had finally pulled into one of those American convenience stores to call the place for directions. Then, as he'd searched again, he'd had to put up with a bloody tailgater who'd refused to go around him. By the time he finally found the tiny mall area hidden between office buildings and searched out a flight of stairs leading up to a nondescript door, he was almost too pissed off to order a drink.

But now that he was on his second one, he was feeling better. The bar wasn't bad, actually, by American standards. Of course, they insisted on playing that disco stuff. Music, some people called it, by flash-in-the-pan artists like Madonna and Janet Jackson. Dreadful noise it was. He'd been here less than an hour, and Madonna was begging for her lover to open his heart to her for the *third* time already!

His eyes roved over the crowded interior. Despite the bad music, the prospects for a night of pleasure looked good. So far, however, no one had approached him. That was just the way he wanted it. If there was stalking to be done, he liked to do it.

His eyes stopped on the young man sitting a few stools down at the bar—a handsome chap, with dark curly hair and a pleasant face. Ian was surprised someone hadn't latched onto him yet. But maybe it was his lucky night. He took his drink and moved down to sit next to him. "Can I buy you a drink?"

The young man looked up, and Ian saw that his eyes were very blue. Lovely eyes, they were. "Vodka and seven," the man said to the barkeep. Then he turned back and smiled, revealing gleaming white teeth. Ian felt a quiver of excitement run through him. Yes, he was just the thing.

"You have an interesting accent," the young man said. "Where're you from?"

"Ireland."

By the time the drinks arrived, they were chatting easily. The young man was a violinist in the city orchestra. Ian smiled, wondering what he'd say if Ian told him he was the manager of one of the biggest rock acts in the world. They were on their second drink together when Ian glanced up to see another man staring at him from across the room.

Ian glanced at him once or twice, wondering why he looked so familiar. He was a good-looking man, blond, with an angular face and dark eyes. Perplexed, Ian stared at him as Roy, his new friend, chattered on about his life in Seattle. Then, suddenly, it hit Ian. The 7-Eleven only an hour or so ago. He clearly remembered staring across the store at the man as he'd waited for the phone to ring at the Blue Diamond. The blond man had been at the magazine rack, casually thumbing through a sports magazine. He'd looked up once and their eyes had met. Ian remembered because he'd felt a shock of attraction run through him. Now, the sudden tremors that rippled through his body were caused by apprehension.

It was just too much of a coincidence. The man was following him! He remembered the car that had tailgated him all the way downtown, and he was more sure than ever.

He reached out and grabbed Roy's wrist. In mid-sentence, the boy stopped talking and stared at him, a dreamy half-aroused look in his eyes.

"Why don't we get out of here?" Ian said.

Roy smiled, revealing his white rich man's teeth. "I know just the place. My apartment isn't far. I just bought Mendelsohn's Concerto for Violin and Orchestra in E minor performed by the Bamberg Symphony Orchestra. You'll love it."

"Yeah, grand." Ian nodded and stood up. Surely that bastard wouldn't follow him now. Who the hell was he? One of Caitlyn's men sent to keep an eye on him? Or—Jesus, could it be possible? Even here in America, he wouldn't be safe from Protestant extremists if they were to find out what he was involved in. Had there been a leak?

No. He wouldn't believe that. He was *sure* it was one of Caitlyn's men. And if it was, damn him to hell! And Caitlyn, as well. He didn't need a bloody baby-sitter.

Ian and Roy reached the door and stepped out into the cool Seattle night. They made their way down the flight of stairs, where Ian automatically turned in the direction of the street. Roy reached out and stopped him.

"It's this way," he said, nodding in the opposite direction. "I have a little apartment over a candy store a little ways down."

Nervously, Ian glanced up the stairs, wondering if the blond man would follow. But the door remained closed. A sliver of moon sent its pale beam down onto the cobbled street and glimmered softly on patches of water from a recent rain shower.

"You're going to love my apartment," Roy chattered. "It's all done in Versace."

Ian wished he'd shut up. Christ, he'd hoped for a strong silent type, and instead, he'd ended up with a male version of Joan Rivers. But perhaps if the lad was as enthusiastic in bed as he was in conversation, it would make up for it.

Roy had stopped talking and was grinning at him. For a moment, Ian thought he'd missed something. But then, Roy looked straight ahead and spoke. "Ian, I want you to meet some friends of mine."

Ian looked ahead through the gloom and saw the silhouettes of two beefy men. His mouth dropped open. "Hey! What's going on? I didn't say anything about having a foursome."

Roy stopped and turned to him, an easy smile on his handsome face. "The more the merrier, I always say, lover-boy."

His fist slammed into Ian's stomach. An explosion of pain burst from his midsection and radiated outward. Ian felt the cold wet cobblestones under him. Slowly, he sat up and tried to speak. "Why . . . wh . . ." He could see Roy staring down at him, his pretty-boy face disfigured by ugly hatred. Two shadows converged behind him, and for the first time, Ian felt an icy fear begin to eat through him.

The biggest one bent down and grabbed him by the lapels of his jacket. Ian found himself on his feet once again, but now, the man was behind him, holding his arms in a vise.

"Okay, Roy. He's all yours."

Roy sneered, his blue eyes like buttons of ice. "Yeah," he said, fists clenched, chest rising and falling in excitement. "You're all mine, Faggot." He came at him, his beautiful young face murderous.

The world exploded in a concert of agony.

22

THE FOURTH of July dawned a clear bright un-Seattle-like day. The forecast called for a high in the mid-seventies with breezes out of the southwest and a near-zero chance of rain. Fonda had decided to treat Devin to an old-fashioned American Fourth of July picnic. She'd put together a wicker basket full of deli meats and cheeses, crusty Italian bread, several different kinds of salads, and for dessert, an ice-cold watermelon. When Bram discovered she was going to borrow several blankets from the hotel, he'd offered her an equipment tarp to put on the ground for the picnic. "Just in case the weathermen are wrong about the chance of rain."

Laoise and Jessie were giggly and excited about Devin's incognito trip into the crowd of Independence Day celebrants, not to mention the prospect of meeting some nice Washington State boys to practice their newly discovered feminine wiles upon.

Devin's glossy black hair was hidden under a cowboy hat he'd bought in Arizona and his eyes were covered with dark shades. Wearing jeans, a Greenpeace T-shirt, and a denim jacket, he was confident he wouldn't draw a crowd in the Seattle park. Fonda wasn't quite so sure. She didn't think he realized just how recognizable his striking looks were. It would be just a matter of time before someone realized the dynamic Devin O'Keefe was among them.

It was almost four o'clock when Fonda pulled the rented Datsun into the park near the harbor. Devin had refused to take the wheel because he still wasn't used to driving on the right side of the road. Never *would* be, he swore. The girls were out of the car almost before she'd switched off the ignition.

"We'll go ahead and find a spot near the lake," Jessie shouted, as she and Laoise hurried off.

"Yeah," Fonda muttered. "And guess who has to carry everything?"

"Sure, but she's a smart one." Devin grinned. "We'll manage, won't we?

As promised, the girls had scouted out a place to spread the tarp. It was early enough that the park wasn't terribly crowded. That would change as it neared evening when the Seattle Symphony Orchestra would begin its program. As soon as Fonda and Devin stretched out upon the tarp, Laoise and Jessie announced they were going to "check out the landscape."

"You mean the boys, right? Okay. But be sure and remember where we are," Fonda said. "I want you back here by the time it gets dark, understand?"

Jessie rolled her eyes. "Jeez! She sounds more like a mother every day."

"Perhaps she's just practicing," Laoise said with a sly grin.

Devin gave the Irish girl a nudge with the toe of his boot. "Ah, get yourself going. Can't you see we have some serious loving to do here?"

Laoise's brown eyes lit up. "Oh, then maybe we should stay."

"Yeah, pick up some pointers," Jessie put in.

Fonda glared at them. "Go on, you two. We're not going to be doing anything out here."

"That's what *you* think," Devin said with a chuckle.

He waited only until they'd walked away before grabbing Fonda and wrestling her down to the tarp. Laughing, Fonda halfheartedly tried to get away, but almost immediately, she found herself returning his greedy kisses enthusiastically. Just as she was about to forget they were in the middle of a Fourth of July crowd, he turned his lips to the side of her throat and sighed deeply.

"Lord, I'm tired. Would it bother you greatly if I took a wee nap, Fon?"

Fonda pretended to be affronted. "You'd choose sleep over me?"

He pulled away to look at her, his lips twisting in a wry smile. "Appears to me I've been doing the opposite lately."

"You poor darling. I've been wearing you out, haven't I?" Fonda struggled out of his arms. "Put your head in my lap. I'll be your pillow."

But when he did, she couldn't let him go to sleep right away. Her fingertips caressed his eyebrows and stroked his nose and cheekbones as if his face were a road map she wanted to memorize. Eyes closed, he grinned at her feathery touch, revealing a dimple in his right cheek she'd never noticed before.

"You know something?" she whispered. His response, a low "mmmm?" revealed he wasn't quite asleep yet, so she went on, "When my brother died, I felt like I'd lost a part of my soul. They say twins have that special closeness, you know. And once he was gone, I didn't think I'd ever feel that again. That spiritual kinship. But here you are, and I *do* feel it. Do you feel it, Devin?"

His eyes opened, and he looked up at her with an expression of such tenderness, it brought a lump to her throat. "Aye, girl," he said softly. "I think I felt it the first day we met. And that's why I ran like hell from you. It scared the bejesus out of me."

"And does it still?"

His answer was to draw her head down to him. Their lips clung together in a sweet assurance of love, until finally, Fonda pulled away. "Go to sleep, love. I promise, I'll keep quiet."

"I could listen to your lovely voice until the day I die," he said, but his eyes closed, and a moment later, he was asleep.

WITH THE flat edge of an envelope, Jacky O'Brien pushed the white powder into an even line, and then, bending over, snorted it into his left nostril with the tiny straw. Snuffling noisily, the sound man dropped the mirror onto the bedside table and pulled the blonde back into his arms. On his other side, the pretty brunette sighed and turned over, pushing her perfect bare ass into his thigh before drifting back to sleep.

"Looks like we've worn poor Michelle out, Debbie." His hand slipped under her arm to toy with the puckered pink nipple of her right breast.

She snuggled against him, her blue eyes stoned from the hit of high-grade Peruvian flake she'd snorted. "Guess it's just you and me, baby." Her hand moved to his flaccid penis, intending, he supposed, to work it back into its earlier state.

"No way, love. You've just about got all you can get out of old Paddy here. For now, anyway."

Her bottom lip pursed. "Are you sure, honey? And we were just starting to have some fun."

"Jaysus! Do I look like Superman to you? Just give me a minute, will ya?" He closed his eyes and allowed the coke to take over. It had been a fucking great idea to send Mairead off with Darcy for the afternoon. They'd decided to take advantage of the American holiday and have a tour of the harbor. By boat. Leaving the entire afternoon free for him to enjoy some of the fruits of the rock star life. The leftover fruits, albeit, but it was nothing to sneeze at. It hadn't taken him any time at all to find these two lovelies and entice them back to his hotel room. They'd been all over him like flies on shit as soon as they'd heard he worked for Devin O'Keefe.

They were good. Damn good. Nubile teenagers, not more than sixteen, he'd wager. Just the way he liked them. The way Mairead had been at first. Damn, she was getting old. Turned twenty-one back in the winter. And still hanging on to him with no bloody intention of letting go. She thought he was going to marry her, one of these days.

Not fucking likely. The only reason he hadn't given her the old heave-ho yet was the fact that she'd practically grown up with him in Dublin and he'd taken her virginity when she was a thirteen-year-old schoolgirl. And hadn't she been holding it over his head ever since? If it weren't for her three huge brothers who were rumored to have connections to the IRA, she would be history. Yeah, he'd ship her back to Dublin so fast, her shadow would still be looking for her here in the good old U.S. of A.

For Christ's sake, it wasn't fair that the woman had to dog his footsteps every moment of the bloody day. Hell, whenever he did get the chance to sample the delights around him, he damn well *would!*

Yeah, Debbie and Michelle were some crumpet. They might be young, but they'd been around the block once or twice. That was for fuckin' sure. But despite their professional expertise, he couldn't get his mind off the sweet pastry he'd really like to sink his teeth into. The little redhead that had joined the tour back in St. Louis. Jessie something. At the thought of her budding girlish tits under one of those skimpy tank tops she was always wearing, he felt himself begin to harden.

"Oh, yeah, babe!" Debbie cooed, and immediately set to work on him with her mouth.

His eyes were half-closed as the blonde's practiced tongue began to send waves of pleasure rippling through his spent body. Vaguely, in the back of his mind, he heard the door to the suite open.

Debbie stopped what she was doing. "Who are you?" Her voice was girlish with surprise.

Half-dazed and breathless from the magic of Debbie's magical tongue, Jacky opened his eyes. Mairead stood at the foot of the bed, her face pinched and white.

It was the most dreadful sight he'd ever seen in his life.

Quickly, he reached across and dragged the sheet over his rapidly deflating penis. "What the fuck are you doing back here?"

Mairead's chest rose and fell with each agitated inhalation of breath. Jacky had seen her angry before. Seen her furious. But he'd never seen her with this icy calm. It scared the hell out of him.

Her voice was low as she enunciated her words with an exaggerated slowness. "Jacky O'Brien, you aren't fit to wipe my arse."

She whirled around and headed for the door, but before she went out, she turned back, her face a mask of hatred. "Don't you come back to Ireland, you son-of-a-bitch. If you do, you're a fucking dead man!"

The door slammed behind her. Jacky gazed at it for a moment, then looked back at the naked Debbie, who was sitting on her haunches, staring after Mairead in shock.

He whipped back the sheet. "Well, woman? Get on with what you were doing."

"WE'RE STARVED, Fon. What do we have to eat?"

Fonda jumped. "Oh, when did you two get back?"

Jessie grinned at her. "You were thinking about Devin again, weren't you?"

Devin moaned softly and lifted his head from her lap. "Did someone mention my name?" He sat up and blinked sleepily.

"Oh, we're just teasing Fonda for daydreaming about you." Jessie looked back at her. "Well, what about it? Can we eat now?"

Fonda waved a hand at the picnic basket. "Help yourself."

The two girls dived at the basket. Laoise pulled out a long roll of salami and sat back on her heels, frowning. "*What* is this?"

Jessie stared at it in equal distaste. "Fon! Didn't you bring anything but deli food?"

"Sure, there's potato salad and macaroni salad. And bread—" Her voice trailed away as she realized both girls were staring at her in horror.

"No hot dogs?" Jessie said, her hazel eyes round.

"Of course not. What do we have to cook them on?"

"What's the Fourth of July without hot dogs?"

"Jessie, give me a break!"

"Hey, sisters! Don't be getting your knickers in a snit." Devin reached into his pocket and pulled out his wallet. "Here, Jess. Go buy yourself and Laoise some hot dogs. I'm sure they're selling them here somewhere."

"All *right!*" Jessie took the twenty-dollar bill from his hand and the two of them took off.

Fonda shook her head. "I can see right now you're going to spoil our kids rotten."

"Not *our* kids, love. I'll be an iron master. That was just a ploy to get us a few moments alone together. Here, give me the knife and I'll slice up the salami."

Fonda unwrapped the bread and began to slice it with the extra knife. "Mmmm . . . this looks terrific. I don't know what the girls were griping about." Suddenly she paused in slicing the bread, uneasily aware of being watched.

She glanced up to see a couple of college-age students sprawled on a blanket nearby and eyeing them curiously.

"Uh-oh," Fonda said quietly. "I think they've caught on to us."

"Who?" Devin made the mistake of looking straight up at them.

Fonda saw the expression change on the girl's face. Her eyes widened with recognition. "My God! That's Devin O'Keefe!"

Her boyfriend's jaw dropped. "It sure the hell is! Come on, let's go say hello."

There was absolutely nothing they could do but smile up at their visitors and try to be nice about the intrusion. For Devin, it wasn't difficult. He was accustomed to being on display everywhere he went. Privacy was more or less a thing of the past for him. But for Fonda, this was an entirely new situation, and she didn't like it at all. What right did these people have to intrude upon their time together? As Devin obligingly autographed scraps of paper and chatted with the couple, Fonda quietly munched on a slice of salami and tried to control the irritation she felt. Why did he have to be so darn *nice* to everyone? Perhaps if he were a little more aloof, his fans would keep their distance. She knew she was being selfish, but damn it, this was their day.

Others had gathered around now, their curiosity piqued by the familiar-looking man in the Stetson. Fonda worried that the crowd might get out of hand if word got around. The thought must've been in Devin's mind, too, because he politely suggested they keep his presence quiet.

"I'm just trying to enjoy a day away from the business. A man's got to do that sometimes, wouldn't you say?"

They all nodded and assured him they wouldn't spread it around. But at least one of them didn't keep their promise. Everyone had finally drifted away, and Fonda was just starting to draw a breath of relief when a skinny young man approached them. He was an unsavory-looking character with scraggly blond hair and bloodshot blue eyes. The threadbare jeans he wore looked as if they might have been worn at Woodstock.

"Hey, man," he said. "Nice to meet you."

Fonda didn't like his smile; there was something creepy about it. Devin shook his hand and threw her an apologetic glance.

"Look, brother." The young man clasped Devin's hand tightly. "I just want you to know, from one Irishman to another, I'm doing all I can here in America to help 'em kick some Brit ass over there in the North. I send our patriots money every chance I get so they can make 'orange juice.'" A snicker escaped his thin lips, and Fonda shivered. She'd done enough reading to know his reference to "orange juice" meant the Protestant paramilitary extremists. "Hey, would you like to join me and my lady? I have a few six-packs of Coors. We'll toast to the revolution."

Devin was very still. It was only the glacierlike ice in his eyes that betrayed to Fonda just how angry he was. Very slowly, he drew his hand out of the man's grip. Then, in a quiet, controlled voice, he said, "Let me tell you something, *brother*. Violence is not the answer in Northern Ireland. And it's Americans like you, *brother*, that assure there will never be peace in my country. Now, get the hell out of here. You make me sick."

The man's smile disappeared and he raised his hands appeasingly. "Hey, man, be cool. Guess I had you pegged wrong. Could have sworn I read somewhere you were R.C."

Devin spoke between clenched teeth, "I said, get the fuck out of my sight."

Fonda grabbed his arm. "Devin, don't let him get to you—"

"I'm going." The man backed away, still grinning uneasily. "Sorry, man, didn't know you were a fucking Unionist."

Fonda could feel Devin's arm trembling under her hand. It was the first time she'd seen him this furious. He turned and looked at her, his face like a stone carving. "You see why I get so disgusted with Americans? They're so quick to make assumptions."

Her hand tightened on his arm. "He's a jerk," she said. "Probably doesn't know anything about what's going on in Northern Ireland."

There was a long silence. When he finally spoke, his words were like a dash of cold water in her face. "And *you* do? What do you think you know about Northern Ireland? Just what you've read in the library books. No, Fonda. Don't talk to me about my country. You know nothing about it. Not a bleeding thing!" And he turned away from her. "I'm going for a walk."

He didn't return until long after the symphony had started to play. And when he did, he was cold and distant. As the music of Sousa bounced out into the cool July night, Fonda sat very still on the blanket and blinked back tears.

There appeared to be a cold front moving in.

23

THE STORM broke early in the morning with howling winds and torrents of rain. Jessie lay under the warm covers, listening to the din outside. It was ten o'clock before she managed to draw herself out of bed. Bleary-eyed, she gazed over at Fonda's empty bed and saw a note on the pillow:

> Gone to autograph signing at Tower Records with Devin. Your allowance is on the bureau. Don't get into any trouble with Laoise. See you at the sound check this afternoon.

Jessie dropped the note into the trash and walked over to the window overlooking the pool. It was a grim sight on such a gray morning. With a sigh, she turned away. Her eyes fell upon the spending money Fonda had left on the dresser and a slow grin lit her face. The mall! It was only a few bus stops away from their hotel. With a bounce, Jessie landed on the bed and grabbed the telephone on the nightstand.

"Hi. Can you ring Laoise Meehan's room, please."

"I'M TELLING you, Caitlyn, those weren't ordinary punks who did this to me. It's the UVF. Those Protestant extremists are all over this fucking country!"

Caitlyn's eyes were cold as she stared at Ian across the table.

The man was a mess. One eye was half-closed because of swelling and the right side of his jaw wore a ghastly bruise. "Don't be using that kind of language with me, Ian."

"Sorry." His fingers were trembling as he lit his pipe.

Caitlyn noticed. The man was falling apart right in front of her eyes. "Ian, I'm telling you. It's your imagination. No one knows you're connected with the armed struggle. It's ridiculous."

Ian leaned toward her earnestly. "I was being followed. I know it. They waited until I was alone and then accosted me."

Caitlyn sighed and glanced around the crowded food court in the Seattle mall. It was time to put the fear of God into this worthless excuse for a man.

"Why don't we cut the bullshit, Ian. You went to a gay bar to find a pickup. But you were unlucky. Out of the entire place, you chose a gay-basher." She watched Ian's face whiten. "Oh, come on. Did you think we didn't know? We make it a point to know everything about our people." She took a sip of her hot tea and smiled at the shocked look on his face. "Yes, love. I know everything about you. You joined the IRA after your father was shot dead by the UVF. They put you through Queen's University and sent you to England to set up a base of operations. That's when you had your little victory with Lord Mountbatten. That impressed us so much, we decided to bring you in to take over as Devin's manager." She smiled. "After Pat Sullivan's unfortunate accident. You didn't think you got that job all on you own, did you?"

As she talked, Ian's heartbeat accelerated. He felt naked and exposed. All these years, he'd thought his secret was secure.

"It's funny how accidents can happen." She snapped her fingers. "Just like that! And you're paralyzed and in a wheelchair the rest of your life. Or you're dead. Perhaps if you're more careful in the future, you won't have to worry about hoodlums." Her eyes hardened. "Stay out of the gay bars, Ian. As long as you're working for me. Otherwise, well . . . you heard what I said about accidents." She smiled into his alarmed brown eyes. "Now, what about San Francisco?"

IT SEEMED everyone in Seattle went to the mall when it rained. And everyone in the mall seemed, at that moment, to be in the Food Court. After standing in line for ten minutes to buy huge drippy slices of pepperoni pizza, Jessie and Laoise had circled around the large dining area looking for a vacant table. They were about to give up and eat their pizza standing up when a couple left a table just a few feet away. Laoise made a dash to it and plopped down her pizza and soda.

"Well, it's dirty, but it'll have to do."

Jessie sat down opposite her. She took a sip of her Coke and casually glanced around.

"See any babes?" Laoise asked, using one of Jessie's favorite terms for a cute male.

"Uh-uh. And I'm not looking. I can only think of one babe at a time." She blushed as she thought of her early morning fantasy of Ryan. Then she saw something beyond Laoise's left shoulder that put him right out of her mind. "Oh, my God!"

"What?"

Jessie's nails dug into Laoise's forearm. "Don't look now, but behind you. No! Don't look, I said! It's Ian Brinegar and he's sitting with a fox!"

Laoise's head whipped around.

"Laoise! He'll see us!"

But Devin's manager was much too busy at the moment to notice two teenage girls several tables away. He was engrossed in an intense conversation with a beautiful woman. She was tall and sophisticated, with sleek black hair cut in a short style that drew attention to her graceful swanlike neck. A real knockout! Even from a distance, the girls could see her eyes were a startling shade of blue.

"Witch-eyes," Laoise said. "Soulless, don't ya know?" She hunched toward her friend and lowered her voice. "How do you suppose Ian can attract a woman like that?"

Jessie shrugged. "His money?"

"You couldn't pay *me* enough to kiss up to that old idjeet. Hey, what do you suppose is wrong with his face? It's all black and blue!"

"Maybe she beat him up. But I doubt it. They look pretty cozy. I wonder what they're talking about?"

Laoise's eyes gleamed at her words. She put down her pizza. "There's one way to find out." She stood up.

"Don't you dare!"

But Laoise was already walking away. Jessie covered her eyes and stared down at the bubbles in her Coke. A moment later, she peeked up and saw Laoise standing at a trash can behind Ian Brinegar, seemingly glancing through a discarded newspaper. Jessie could barely stifle a giggle. The idiot Irish girl was wearing a pair of dark sunglasses. Like she thought she was some kind of spy or something. After a moment, Laoise folded the newspaper and tossed it away. Then she glanced furtively around, and casually walked back to their table.

"Okay, Sherlock, what did you find out?" Jessie asked when she'd sat down.

Laoise took a huge slurp of her soda. "One thing is for sure. The girl is Irish. She has a strong Belfast accent."

"Well, what were they saying?"

"I didn't hear much." Then she smiled wickedly. "But what I did hear is grand. They arranged a rendezvous in San Francisco. And for some reason, it's a secret. And I bet I know why! She's married. Probably on the run from her husband."

"You think so?"

"Sure." Her eyes widened. "Perhaps that was who beat him up. The husband. She's probably left Ireland to get away from him. There's no divorce there, you know."

"You're kidding!"

Laoise gave her a strange look. "Not at all. It's a sin, you know."

"Look. They're leaving. God, she's beautiful. What does she see in an ugly old man like him?"

Laoise took a bite of her cold pizza and chewed thoughtfully. "Lord knows. Jess, I just had an idea."

"Uh-oh. The last time you got that look in your eye, we almost blew up the sound stage."

Laoise grinned. "Don't worry. We'll never be suspected. I just thought of a way to put the fear of God into Old Pokerface Ian Brinegar."

"Tell me, quick!"

Her lips curved up in a sly smile. "We're going to send him a little gift from his lover's jealous husband."

FONDA, PERCHED on an equipment crate, wrapped her arms around her drawn-up knees and stared intently at Devin across the darkened stage. He and the band were in the middle of the sound check for the night's concert.

From the beginning, nothing had gone right. A scheduling mix-up had made Seattle's King Dome unavailable and the venue had been changed to a university football stadium, which automatically meant more problems than usual. The weather, for one thing, was a major inconvenience. The rain hadn't stopped, and from the look of the dismal gray skies, it wouldn't any time soon. To make matters worse, there was a problem with the lighting. Some of the special effect strobes had gone belly-up, and even now, technicians were busy trying to repair them in time for the concert.

The depressing weather, the always bad acoustics of an outdoor stadium, the damaged equipment not to mention the brutal attack on Ian Brinegar, had combined to turn the Seattle gig into a nightmare.

Right now, Devin was singing "S.O.S.," a song of war and destruction, one of the darkest songs of his career. Fonda shivered as she listened to his raw voice, spitting out the black lyrics with all the diplomacy of a machine-gun attack. She knew the bitter song had been written in the months after Caitlyn's death, and her heart ached for the pain so obvious in his voice. Yet she couldn't help but feel jealous, too. Could he ever love her as much as he'd loved the Irish girl?

It was that horrible scene at the park yesterday, of course. Although Devin had apologized for lashing out at her, he'd been remote ever since. Earlier, when she'd accompanied him to the Tower Records autograph session, he'd barely acknowledged her presence as she shot a few candids with the Minot. Uncharacteristic, too, had been his cool, almost brusque treatment of his fans. He'd rushed through the two-hour session like a demon, not bothering to stop and chat with his admirers. Although lines were still gathered outside in the pouring rain, at noon sharp he'd signed his last autograph and stood up. Even the crestfallen face of the teenage girl next in line hadn't touched him. Fonda didn't think he'd noticed it.

A deafening crash came from the back of the stage, sending a jolt through Fonda's heart. Devin stopped singing and whipped around. In an echoing whimper, the lead guitar trailed off. A few seconds later, the bass and drums stopped.

A pained look crossed Devin's face. *"What in the name of Christ is going on back there?"*

A shamefaced crewman stared at him glumly. "Sorry, Dev. I lost me grip on that amp."

Fonda held her breath as Devin glared at him. His mouth had thinned into a grim line; his eyes glowed like black coals. The look on his face was almost exactly like the one he'd worn yesterday when he'd responded to the Irish patriot.

Finally, he exploded. *"Jaysus!* Am I surrounded by a bunch of clowns?" Violently, he shoved the mike stand to the stage floor. "Fuck this! I'm outta here!"

With a bound, he jumped from the stage and headed out into the rain. Fonda scrambled up from the crate.

"Devin, you can't go out in the rain like that. It's freezing out there!"

He kept walking. It was as if he couldn't hear her. Fonda moved to follow him, but Bram was suddenly at her side, his hand clutching her arm.

"He needs some time alone, Fon."

Fonda turned to him. "But I can't stand to see him like this."

"It's just his Celtic blood brewing, love. Happens to all of us now and then." He gave her arm a quick squeeze. "The best thing to do is leave him be for a little while."

Leave him be. It went against Fonda's nature, but what else could she do? With hours to kill, she took a taxi back to the hotel to check up on Jessie. She and Laoise had come back from the mall wet, bedraggled, but in high spirits just before she'd left for the sound check. Hard to tell what kind of mischief those two were cooking up.

Fonda inserted the key into the lock and walked in. Jessie whirled round and stared at her guiltily, clutching what looked like a small corsage box. Her fair cheeks were stained crimson.

"What's that?" Fonda asked.

"Nothing." Jessie crossed the room to the mini-fridge and pushed the box into its depths. With a slam, she closed the door and turned back to Fonda. "Nothing important, I mean. See, it's Darcy's birthday and Laoise's dad bought this flower for her, and well, he didn't have anyplace to put it, and it's a surprise, see, so I'm keeping it for them until they need it. Her birthday is tomorrow, not today, did I say today? It's tomorrow." She stopped abruptly, as if waiting for Fonda to respond.

Fonda rubbed her suddenly aching temples. "I'm going to lie down for a few minutes. If Devin calls or comes by, wake me."

But when Fonda awoke, she found there had been no word from Devin. She didn't see him again until hours later when he arrived on stage for the night's concert.

THE STAGE was dark. Suddenly, a beam of blue light pierced down onto the drum paraphernalia, and the crowd began to applaud. The low tone of the synthesizer vibrated through the air, growing gradually in volume. There was movement on the stage. The drummer, Barry Pearse, climbed onto his stool, and immediately began to swish his drumstick against the cymbal in a slow steady rhythm. An instant roar erupted from the crowd. Two other shapes moved on stage, Seamus MacBride, the lead guitarist, and the bass player, Liam O'Toole. With a practiced touch on the strings of his guitar, Seamus's signature riffs fueled the stadium. The crowd noise intensified. There was more movement on stage. Devin!

Fonda caught her breath. She'd never seen the beginning of the concert from this angle before. Center-stage, several rows back. Next to her, Bram, who'd suggested she watch the start from the crowd, flashed her a grin. Like her, he was caught up in the excitement of the moment, even though he'd been through more concert openings than he could count.

Fonda couldn't keep her eyes off the shadow of Devin's lithe figure, dressed completely in black. A spotlight shot down from above, capturing Devin in its circle. The crowd roared their approval, and he acknowledged them with a wave. He moved back and forth on stage, his body in harmony with the building music as he waited for the intro to end. When it did, he launched into the opening lines of "Eclipse," and the floodlights flashed on, illuminating the crowd. A deafening roar shook the stadium, and Fonda realized she was on her feet with Bram, yelling as loud as everyone else. How easy it was to become a fan!

When the first song ended, Bram grabbed her arm and shouted over the noise. "The man is *on* tonight, for sure."

Fonda could only grin back at him. There was no use trying to talk. She could never make herself understood in this noise. Her eyes returned to the stage. Devin was singing one of his early hits, "The Forgotten." She snapped a couple of photos, then slung the camera strap onto her shoulder.

How different it was seeing the concert as a fan, instead of as part of the crew. Somehow, it was more electric, the excitement of the crowd almost palpable. They fed off Devin's presence, who, in turn, caught their intensity and gave it back ten-fold. Like a voltaic creature, the atmosphere in the stadium writhed and twisted, moving from person to person and row to row, back and forth from the front of the stage to the highest "nosebleed" seats. It was the most incredible phenomenon Fonda had ever experienced, this dynamic power generated by one man. Devin.

The crowd erupted in applause with the last note of "The Forgotten." Abruptly, the spotlight went out, leaving the stage dark.

Except for sporadic whistles and shouts, the stadium was quiet as they waited to see what he would sing next. There was the sound of a guitar tuning. A soft lavender light beamed on Devin as he played the first notes of a plaintive, haunting melody on the keyboard, one all too familiar to Fonda. It was "S.O.S.," the song he'd been rehearsing during the sound check just before he'd stalked out. Fonda's chest tightened. Caitlyn's song—the one that mourned her death. Years had passed since he'd performed it in concert. *Why* was he singing it now?

His voice was ragged, almost hoarse with emotion as he belted out the somber lyrics. Even from this distance, Fonda could see the naked pain on his face, and inwardly, she wept for him. Why wasn't her love enough to make it go away?

> *"Can't you see*
> *I'm falling under now*
> *I reach for you*
> *You're not there."*

With every word he sang, Fonda felt as if he were hurling darts into her heart. Suddenly Devin stopped singing, but the band played on. What was wrong? Had he forgotten the words? Devin released the microphone from the stand and moved toward the edge of the stage. He motioned for the band to soften the music, and for a moment, he stared out into the crowd, his face a mask of anguish.

He lifted his mike to his mouth and spoke: "Hello, Seattle!" The crowd roared. He waited for the applause to die down and went on, "I had the great opportunity to celebrate your Independence Day here in your grand city. And I met some of you who welcomed me with kindness. Indeed, I'm grateful for that. But there was a black moment when one American came up to me and asked me to drink a toast with him. To celebrate the revolution in Northern Ireland."

"Oh, *no*, Devin," Fonda whispered.

He was slapping one hand against his thigh, over and over, and with every word he spoke, the rhythm began to pick up. "'A toast,' he said. To celebrate the killing, the bombings, the *horror* that is Northern Ireland. He made an *assumption* that because I'm Irish, and because I'm Catholic, I believe in the violent methods of the resistance, that the end justifies the means." His words rang with contempt, bristled with anger. "I say to him, and to you, that the men who join these organizations—and we all know who I'm talking about—are bloodthirsty animals! They don't care about Ireland. Power is what it's about, my friends. Money and power! And to some, *killing* is what it's about." His hand stopped pounding his thigh, and he stood very still. His voice dropped. "America . . . stop believing in these people. There are a lot of idealists out there. I know. I was one of them. Perhaps I still am. But *killing*—and helping the killers with money and arms—will never save Ireland. Only the Irish can do that, by peaceful means. By legislation. By sitting down and talking with the people we don't agree with. Peaceful methods. It's the only way!"

Devin turned and walked offstage. The silence in the huge stadium was almost eerie. Finally, the applause came, followed by fans screaming for more. Fonda, shaken by Devin's ferocity, turned to Bram and was startled to see his blue eyes glinting with fury.

"Jaysus, the bloody fool is committing suicide!"

"What do you mean?" Fonda asked. Her stomach churned. She'd never seen Bram so deadly serious.

He stared at her. "If Devin tries to go back to Derry after that, the Bogside boys will put out a price on his head. His life won't be worth a pint of Guinness!"

For a moment, Fonda felt a fear so sharp, she couldn't bring herself to speak. Finally, she swallowed hard. "You're kidding aren't you?"

His face remained grim. "The Irish don't kid about the Bogside."

The crowd roared appreciatively as the band began to play the opening to one of Devin's hard rock songs. Fonda pushed her way down the aisle. She had to get backstage and see Devin between sets. If it was the last thing she ever did, she *had* to get him to talk to her. Tell her what was tearing him up inside.

Following her, Bram called out. "Wait, Fon. I'm coming, too."

Fonda kept going. Bram's angry words had shaken her. God, she hoped he was exaggerating. Surely, Devin wouldn't be so foolhardy as to speak out like that if it were really dangerous. Then, again, when he was in one of his moods, he didn't seem to care about the consequences.

At the stage door, Fonda flashed her pass to the minder and entered. As she jogged down a short flight of stairs and into the tunnel leading to the area behind the stage, she heard Devin's gravelly voice belting out the lyrics to the rock hit. It was as if the interruption of "S.O.S." had never taken place. But as soon as she reached the stage wings, she knew something had changed.

It was the crowd. The noise was different; it reminded her of the sound a crowd made once at an air show when the Blue Angels performed a dangerous maneuver overhead. Their faces were turned upward as they stared at something above the stage. Some were pointing upward excitedly. From her angle, Fonda couldn't see what they were looking at. Bram appeared behind her.

"Oh, bloody hell!" He pushed her aside and stepped out onto the stage.

"What is it?"

When he didn't answer, Fonda moved forward. Her heart lurched at the sight that met her eyes. *"Devin!"*

He was balanced on a narrow catwalk twenty-five feet above the stage, crooning into his mike.

Bram grabbed her arm. "It's okay, Fon. He used to do this sort of thing in the early days. Always caught hell for it afterwards, but he knows what he's doing."

Fonda turned to him, her eyes frantic. "But why now?"

Bram nodded, his eyes betraying his concern. "It does appear he's going through some kind of crisis."

Fonda's eyes returned to Devin teetering on the catwalk, one booted foot propped on the tiny rail at knee-level. Then, from stage right, she saw another man inching onto the catwalk. Jacky O'Brien, who was handling Devin's mike lead, had come to coax him off safely. Fonda turned to Bram. "Look. There's Jacky."

Bram had already seen him, yet his face remained grim. "Jaysus, the bloody ass! Doesn't he know that scaffold won't hold the weight of both of them?"

As if in answer to his rhetorical question, a loud crack split the air. Jacky scrambled back the way he'd come, but Devin, in the middle of the catwalk, froze uncertainly.

Fonda screamed and clutched Bram's shoulder as the frail scaffolding began to crack in half. A crescendo of horrified screams rose from the crowd. The band kept playing. From their vantage point, they couldn't see the danger. Devin's microphone fell to the stage floor as, finally realizing his danger, he clutched onto the rails of the catwalk as it began to break apart. Fonda buried her face into Bram's chest, unable to watch Devin dangling twenty-five feet over the stage. In a moment, seconds, perhaps, he would be lying broken, nearly at her feet. Bram's arms tightened around her.

"He's climbing, Fonda. Praise God, he'll make it back."

Fighting her fear, Fonda half-turned to watch. Devin was almost to the top of the crippled catwalk nearing the platform at stage left where Ian Brinegar waited, gesturing frantically. Fonda held her breath as Ian reached out for him. With one huge heave, he pulled Devin to the platform and the crowd gave a collective sigh of relief.

Just as Ian clutched Devin in a bear hug, the catwalk gave way, breaking completely and falling to the stage in a horrendous crash. Pandemonium broke out in the stadium. Fonda saw Seamus go down, hit by a large chunk of falling debris. Members of the crew rushed onto the stage to attend to him. Minders used their muscle to keep the crowd back from rushing the stage. Women were crying, calling out for Devin. Angry shouts filled the air. The concert had deteriorated into total chaos.

Still in shock from Devin's close call, Fonda stood clutching Bram's jacket, unable to move or think beyond the moment. From behind her, Devin scrambled down the stairs leading from the catwalk platform. Ian Brinegar thumped down behind him, his face scarlet with rage. "What the fuck is wrong with you? Is your arse where your brain used to be? You could've bloody killed yourself!"

Devin moved past Fonda, his eyes glazed with shock. "Not now, Ian. I have to see to Seamus."

Fonda pulled away from Bram and followed Devin. Seamus was sitting up, rubbing his hand ruefully over his shoulder. "Not to worry," he mumbled. "Sure, but it's just a bruise."

Devin knelt down next to him. "Christ, Seamus, I'm sorry, lad. Are you certain you're all right?"

Still looking dazed, Seamus stared at Devin. "What the hell happened, Dev?"

"I'll tell you what happened," Ian roared. "The bloody fool tired to kill himself, and in the process, take out the entire crew! What's wrong with you, man? Where's your common sense?"

Bram joined in the attack. "Jesus Christ, Devin, you know better than to pull a stunt like that! What were you thinking of, man?"

Devin didn't try to respond to either of them. Instead, he stood stiffly, his face stoic. But Fonda saw the pain in his eyes. It was as if he were wrestling with a silent demon, one determined to destroy him. As the haranguing voices continued, his eyes shifted and came to rest upon her. It was the signal that made her move.

"Stop it!" She strode up and grabbed Bram's arm. "I think he's got the point."

Ian stopped in mid-sentence and glowered at her. Bram took one look at her and then nodded. "She's right. It's neither the time nor the place. Come on, Ian. Let's get this mess cleaned up. Thank the good Lord no one was hurt."

The concert promoter was at the mike, calling for patience from the audience. The concert would continue after a brief delay, as soon as it was determined Seamus could play. As Ian and Bram moved away, Devin and Fonda stared at each other, both of them silent. Fans crammed up against the stage calling out Devin's name and holding up programs to be signed They might as well have been invisible. Devin's eyes were only on Fonda. She stood very still. There were so many questions in her mind, and they all began with "Why?"

But when she finally found her voice, she was startled by the question that came out. "Was Ian right, Devin? Are you *trying* to kill yourself?"

His face crumbled. And he was in her arms, holding her, rocking her back and forth. "Just hold me, Fon. I need you, girl, like I've never needed anything before. Just don't let me go."

Fonda held him tightly, feeling the tears build up behind her eyelids. How could she let him go, she wondered, if she'd never had him in the first place?

24

AFTER A brief examination by a doctor, Seamus was allowed to continue with the concert. But as Fonda watched from the wings, she realized something had gone out of Devin's performance. He was preoccupied and remote. Still, the enthusiastic crowd didn't appear to notice.

Fonda was relieved when Devin finished the last song of the encore, and with one last wave to the crowd, called out, "God bless you. Goodnight!"

He exited the stage and headed for his dressing room. As he passed by Fonda, he squeezed her arm and gave her a tired, lackluster smile, his eyes somber.

She didn't follow him. Perhaps Bram was right. He needed some space. God knows she didn't want to smother him. But forty-five minutes later when the limo drew up outside to take them to the hotel, Fonda went to his dressing room and found it empty.

Bram was on stage with the crew, supervising the dismantling of the sound equipment. Fonda caught his attention. "Bram do you know where Devin went?"

"Just a sec, love." He glared at one of the stagehands. "Hey, lad, go easy on that amp! Unless you want it taken out of your pay. Yeh, Fon, he took a cab to that church down the street from the hotel. Why don't you go to him?"

Fonda stared at him uncertainly. "Should I?"

He came toward her and nodded. "You're the best medicine for him. Don't you know that yet, girl?"

"But he won't talk to me," Fonda said in a near whisper.

"Perhaps he can't just yet. Give him time, he'll talk to ya. Just be there for him. I know, I know! Earlier, I told you to leave him be. And you did. But now, he needs you. Don't worry, love, you'll learn when to leave him alone and when to stick by him." His hands on her shoulders, he turned her toward the exit. "Take the limo. I'll find my way back to the hotel."

The limo stopped in front of the Catholic church on the corner. As Fonda gazed at the grand exterior of the building, she felt an odd peace invade her. It had been so long since she'd been inside a church. Maybe it was time.

"You don't need to wait for us," she told the driver. "We'll walk back to the hotel."

"But, Ma'am, it's pouring out."

She nodded. "It's okay. We may be here for a while."

It was quiet inside. Once the heavy oak doors closed behind her, even the sound of the rain was muffled. Fonda gazed around in the dim light. She was in a vestibule with walls frescoed in scenes from the New Testament. It was hauntingly beautiful, reminding her of photographs she'd seen of Michelangelo's Sistine Chapel.

Fonda propped her umbrella in a corner and turned back to the sanctuary. She could see Devin sitting in a pew framed by the light of flickering candles. Alone in the huge room, he was hunched over, his face resting in the palm of one hand. Fonda approached quietly, unsure of her reception.

He sensed her presence and looked back. Fonda bit her lip, not speaking. His face was solemn; nothing in his expression told her he was happy she'd come. Then, as he gazed at her, his eyes softened.

He stood up and came toward her. With a soft sigh, Fonda went into his arms. Relieved, she nestled her face against the scratchy wool of his jacket, and felt the comforting weight of his hand resting on her damp French braid.

"Oh, Devin," she whispered.

"I'm sorry, love," he said. "For the way I've been treating you. I don't know what gets into me sometimes. It's this rage, you see. It just builds up in me. My da used to call it 'wrestling with a demon.'"

"I'm just glad you're okay. I was worried."

His hand moved up and down the back of her jacket. "Ah, see what I do to you? The very thing I promised I wouldn't. Give you heartache and worry."

"Devin, let's go home. We'll forget this awful day."

He nodded, his chin resting against the top of her head. His hand slipped down to entwine with hers, and they began to move toward the vestibule.

"I lit a candle for us," Devin said. "And prayed that nothing will stand in the way for us."

"Stand in the way?"

He nodded. "You know, for a happy life."

Fonda looked at him and smiled. "You sound as if you've had a premonition of disaster."

His face remained serious. He didn't reply.

The rain was falling even harder than before. Fonda doubted the wisdom of her decision to send the limo away, but Devin assured her he didn't mind the wild weather. He smiled grimly. "Suits me personality these days."

They walked slowly toward the hotel, hand-in-hand, sharing the umbrella. At a corner, while waiting for the WALK sign, Devin turned to her, and with one hand around her waist, pulled her against him. Even through the thickness of his jacket and jeans, she could feel his arousal as his cold lips settled on hers. His plundering tongue was warm, electric. Fonda groaned, her hands sliding up the back of his jacket.

Suddenly, Devin released the umbrella. The brisk wind claimed it and sent it tumbling away down the sidewalk. His hands tangled in her hair, furiously releasing the pins from her braid. The rain beat down upon them, but in the ardor of his kiss, Fonda was oblivious. He dragged his mouth away from hers and began to nuzzle a spot just below her left ear. The rain splattered on Fonda's upturned face, but she didn't care. Her eyes were closed, her lips parted. Devin's touch was boiling her blood, dizzying her senses. His fingers entwined in her heavy wet tresses, tumbling them down about her shoulders. The tip of his tongue delved into her ear, sending sizzling shivers through her body to collide in the center of her groin.

"I want you, Sweet Thing." he whispered. "Like I've never wanted anything in my life."

Fonda clutched him to her. "Let's go back to your room."

With one more tender, soul-searching kiss, he pulled away from her. "Aye, love. Before I take you here on this wet sidewalk."

The umbrella had disappeared. By the time they reached the hotel, the rain had soaked completely through their clothing. In the elevator, they huddled together, shivering. Eyeing her, Devin began to laugh.

"Love, you look like a drowned Dublin river rat!"

Fonda pulled away from him and gave him an indignant look. Their erotic mood of moments before had turned playful. "How gallant of you to say so, darling. And I might add, you don't look so great yourself." To emphasize her words, she gave him a little push.

"Hey!" He pushed her back.

By the time the elevator reached their floor, they were engaged in a giggling shoving match. The doors slid open, and suddenly, Fonda felt eyes upon them. Still grinning, she nudged Devin and moved to step out of the elevator. A well-to-do middle-aged couple stood outside the doors, their haughty faces stiff with disapproval.

Devin straightened up, looked them in the eye, and spoke with solemnity. "Isn't it shocking? The riffraff they allow in these fancy hotels these days?"

The woman's nose lifted disdainfully. She gave an audible sniff and stepped into the elevator, followed closely by her husband. As the doors closed in front of them, the man gave a wink and grinned. Devin and Fonda looked at each other and burst out laughing.

"Will we ever be like that?" he asked, unlocking the door to his suite.

"Not unless you decide to run for Parliament."

The smile disappeared from his face. He looked at her. "Perhaps I will someday. Once the day comes that I can't reach people with my music." He pushed the door open, but when she started to step inside, he reached out and put a hand on her shoulder. "Could you handle that kind of life, Fon? If I decided to go back to the North and try to change things?"

"You're talking about getting a position in the British government? To help improve the lives of Catholics in Northern Ireland?"

He stared at her. "Something like that."

Fonda didn't hesitate. "Devin, I love you so much, I would go anywhere with you. Your life will be mine."

He leaned toward her and kissed her softly on the lips. Then he gestured for her to enter his suite. He made no attempt to turn on the lights When she heard the door close, Fonda turned to face him.

Outside the balcony doors, the rain slashed down out of the black skies, beating ferociously against the side of the building. The only light in the room came from the city outside, but it was enough for her to see Devin's face, just inches away.

The look in his eyes made her heartbeat accelerate. He reached out and pushed her soaked denim jacket from her shoulders. It fell to the carpeted floor. His fingers were cool against her suddenly warm skin as he began to undo the buttons of her blue chambray blouse. Then it, too, was gone. His eyes moved down to her lace-covered bra, damp from the rain. The palm of his hand spread against the front closure, and for a moment, he left it there, feeling the unsteady thump of her heart. Fonda's lips parted as she stared at his thin masculine lips, wanting to feel them on hers. But he remained still, his warm fingers just touching her smooth, damp breasts. Finally, he moved, releasing the catch of her bra. She gasped softly as she felt the straps fall from her shoulders. He gazed at her hungrily, but still denied himself her touch. His hands moved to the snap of her jeans. The sound of her zipper was loud in the room, almost drowning out the rain. Slowly, he pushed her jeans and panties down over her slim hips and let them fall to her ankles. She stepped out of them and reached for him.

He backed away. "Wait, love." And he left her to go into the bathroom.

Suddenly, Fonda began to feel the cold, now that Devin wasn't near to warm her with the look in his eyes. Long moments ticked by as she waited for him to return. Growing aware of the uncomfortable weight of her long wet hair against her back, she began to shiver.

There was a movement near the bathroom door. Naked, Devin walked toward her, carrying two huge bath towels. He didn't speak, but just wrapped one around her, then began to lift her hair from under it. Fonda helped him until all of it streamed down her back against the towel. Devin took the other towel, stepped behind her, and began to gently dry her hair. Sighing deeply, she leaned against him, loving the way he took care of her. Feeling as if no one had ever cherished her like this before. No one had.

"Do you feel it?" he whispered. "How much I want you?"

Oh, yes, she did indeed feel it. Hard and proud against the small of her back.

"Do you feel how much I want you?" Fonda asked, voice husky, eyes closed.

His hand slipped under the towel, brushing across her silky down, seeking the moist core of her.

"Aye, love. I do that."

"Devin. I don't want to wait any longer."

But he made her wait. Slowly, he drew the towel away from her body, and starting at the hollow of her throat, began to rediscover every inch of her skin with his lips, his tongue, and his hands. As his tongue dipped into her navel, Fonda's knees gave out. She dropped to the carpet. Devin went with her. His burning fingers ignited a trail of fire down the backs of her thighs and the sensitive spot behind her knees. She began to tremble. A volcano rumbled in the lower recesses of her abdomen; it would be mere seconds until it erupted. His tongue . . . God . . . his tongue . . .

"Devin!" she gasped. "I want—Oh!"

Finally, he was still, his face pressed against her belly. "Love you, Fon. I love you . . ."

She drew him up, up until his nude body was cemented against hers. Kissing his jaw, his mouth, his nose, finally, she was able to speak, but all she could say was his name. She felt his hardness against her thigh, and shifted slightly, silently communicating what she couldn't say with words.

He understood. "Now?"

She nodded and with the back of her hand against his head, drew his mouth down to hers. Slowly, so very slowly, he entered her. When he didn't move, she opened her eyes and stared at him. He was looking at her, his face so tender that suddenly, she wanted to cry.

"Devin?" she whispered.

"Stay with me forever," he said.

Her hands tightened on his shoulders. "Yes, Devin. I will, I will!"

His eyes closed and he bit his lip. Then, slowly, he began to move inside her.

For a brief moment, she wondered about his intensity. It was almost as if he were driven by fear. But soon, she stopped thinking. Because there was only the sweet, sweet sensation he aroused inside her.

JESSIE SAT up in bed and stealthily glanced over to see if Fonda were still asleep. She'd come in at ten o'clock last night, face flushed and eyes glittering oddly. It was the sex, of course. What else could make a woman look that way? It wouldn't be long before Ryan would put that very look on *her* face.

Having determined Fonda was in no danger of waking, Jessie threw back the covers and slid out of bed. After pulling on her jeans and Indianapolis Colts sweater, she cast another glance in Fonda's direction and tiptoed over to the mini-fridge. A minute later, she was out of the room and flying down the hall, the corsage box in hand. She tapped lightly at Laoise's door. The Irish girl opened it immediately and held a finger to her lips.

"Da and Ma are light sleepers," she warned, nodding her head in the direction of the connecting door to her parents' room. "You got it?"

"Yeah. Did you write the note?"

A smug smile crossed Laoise's lips. "Sure, but I did. And it's real professional. They'll never guess it was us."

"Let me see it."

Laoise drew out a folded note from her jeans pocket. Jessie's eyes widened at the newspaper-print block letters clumsily pasted on the sheet of paper.

"Wow! It looks like something a murderer would do."

"What do you think of the message? Won't it scare the bejesus out of him?"

"It should make him think twice before messing around with a married woman."

"Well, it might not make him stop, but it will certainly make him look over his shoulder now and then."

A trace of apprehension crossed Jessie's face. "Do you think the husband might really show up and go after Ian?"

"Ah, we'd never be so lucky. Wouldn't that be a bloody gas?" Laoise looked toward her parents' door. "Shhh! I think someone's getting up. Come on. Let's go."

At the door to Ian Brinegar's room, Laoise placed the corsage box down on the carpet and motioned Jessie to get going. Then she gave the door four hard raps and ran.

THE RINGING of the phone woke Fonda. It was Devin.

"Breakfast in my suite. Five minutes. I love you."

He hung up. Fonda laughed and threw back the covers. Now, she knew for sure the old Devin was back. "Jess?"

But Jessie's bed was empty. Odd. She was up early this morning. In Laoise's room, most likely. Fonda tied the belt of her satin robe and grabbed her hairbrush to try and get most of the tangles out of her hair. It was still damp from last night's rain, and more unruly than ever. After a moment, she gave up, thankful that Devin seemed to love her mass of hair. Perhaps she'd get him to brush it for her after they ate. Quickly, she scribbled a message for Jessie:

Having breakfast with Devin. Meet me in the lobby at 12:30 and I'll take you and Laoise to McDonald's for lunch.

She placed it on Jessie's pillow and left the room.

As she rushed down the hall toward Devin's suite, she couldn't manage to wipe the silly grin off her face. How different she felt from yesterday when Devin's black mood had her so on edge. Today, the sun was shining. Not just outside but in her heart, too. They'd been apart only eleven hours, yet she couldn't wait to see Devin again.

Ahead of her, a door opened and Ian Brinegar stuck his head out.

"Good morning," Fonda called out, smiling. Maybe if she tried hard enough, Ian would be friendly.

But he barely acknowledged her greeting. He bent down to pick up a white box in front of his door. "Did you leave this here?"

Fonda shook her head. "Not me."

He opened the box and peered into it. His bruised face whitened. Slowly, he looked up and glared at her with gray steely eyes. "Did you see someone knock at my door?"

An inexplicable shiver ran through her. The man looked as if he'd seen a ghost. "I just came out of my room," she said. "There was no one in the hall."

He slammed the door in her face.

CAITLYN FLINCHED as the whip bit into her naked buttocks. Her blood red nails dug into the satin comforter as the heat between her legs intensified. "Oh, Christ—that's enough, Cal." Languidly, she turned over onto her back and gazed up at the copper-skinned man at the side of the bed. Her eyes roved over his perfect nude body. "Lovely," she purred. "You have such a deft touch with the whip. Let's see what you can do with *that*." Her gaze fixed upon his jutting penis.

Cal smiled and tossed the whip aside. A sheen of perspiration covered his massive chest. Evidence that his workout had been a good one. Further evidence was the tenderness of her backside. She felt like a bruised peach in the bottom of an apple cart. It was just the way she liked it. Now would come the best part.

He was poised to begin when the knock came at the door. With dazed eyes, Caitlyn stared up at Cal's impassive model-perfect face. "Bloody hell," she muttered, and rolled out from under him. "Stay here. Whatever this is, it won't take long."

She pulled on a royal blue satin robe and strode into the sitting room, closing the bedroom door behind her. Her eyes were icy when she opened the door of the suite. Ian stood outside, his face flushed. For a moment, she was speechless with rage.

Teeth clenched, she managed to speak. "What are you doing here, man?"

He thrust a corsage box at her. "They're going to kill me!"

"What's this?"

"Open it," he demanded. "You'll see what I mean!"

Caitlyn studied him. His face was ashen, his body trembling. Was this it? Had the man finally gone over the edge? "Well, come in, if you must." Her face expressionless, she closed the door behind him. She crossed the room to the bar, her satin robe swishing as she walked.

"Aren't you going to open it?" Ian demanded, his voice shrill.

Ignoring him, she inserted a nail into the seam and opened the box. Her lips twitched in a humorless smile as she gazed down at the dead flowers and scrawled note, well aware of Ian's anxious eyes upon her. She looked up and stared at him with cold eyes. "What kind of silly joke is this?"

"For Christ's sake, Caitlyn. It's no joke. The UVF are out to get me. What is it going to take to convince you of that?"

Caitlyn moved to the bar and poured a finger of Scotch into a crystal glass. She held it out to him. "Drink this, you fool."

Ian's face reddened at her derisive tone, but he took the glass and downed it.

Caitlyn waited until he'd finished it before speaking. "That note was written by a child, you ignorant old man. Do you think the Ulster Volunteer Force has time to play sophomoric pranks like this? If they wanted you dead, you'd be fish food by now."

The color left his face again. "I think I'm going to be sick." He dropped to the sofa and put his head between his knees.

"Ian Brinegar, don't you dare upchuck in my hotel room." Dear God, what had she done to deserve such an imbecilic incompetent? If it weren't for the fact that she disliked him so intensely, she could almost pity him for his unmanly weakness.

After a moment, he raised his head to her, and with disgust, she saw tears in his eyes. "Send me home," he whispered. "I can't go on with this. I'm too frightened."

"So, the little lad wants to go home." Her voice was scornful. "Sure, I can arrange that. If you're positive that's what you want. But I can guarantee you something, *Mulligan*." The emphasis on his code name wasn't lost on him. "You'll have quite a welcoming party. Why, I wouldn't be surprised if all our friends in the North come down for it." With satisfaction, she saw the stark terror cross his face.

He was silent for a long moment. Then, very softly, he said, "So, you're telling me I don't really have a choice?"

She gave him a gentle smile. "Oh, not at all, Ian. You have a choice. Either stay here and do your job—or go home and live the rest of your miserable life in a wheelchair." She waited a moment, and then went on in a softer tone, "Only one more meeting, Ian. That's all we're asking of you."

He stared at her and then nodded. Caitlyn crossed the room and sat down next to him, draping an arm around his shoulders. Her lips twisted in amusement at his barely suppressed shudder. Tinkerbell couldn't stand the touch of a woman. Delighting in his discomfort, she began to knead the knotted muscles at the back of his neck.

"Ah, I knew you'd come to your senses," she said softly into his ear. "It'll all be over soon, love."

He jerked away from her and stood up. "I have to get back."

"Yes, of course you do."

Smiling, she led the way to the door. "See you in San Francisco."

He hurried out. Caitlyn closed the door behind him. In deep thought, she moved over to the bar to gaze down at the box of dead flowers. She read the words again with a cold smile: *We know what you're doing, and if you keep it up, these flowers will be on your own grave.*

She burst out laughing. "How very appropriate." She reached into the mini-refrigerator and pulled out a bottle of orange juice. Pouring herself a glass, she raised it into the air in a silent toast. "Thank you very much, whoever you are. I just may place those flowers on his grave myself."

After finishing her orange juice, she picked up the phone and dialed an international number. The phone rang once in far-off Belfast and was picked up.

"Drogheda," said the thick accent.

"Caitlyn here. We have a problem with Mulligan. He's gone completely off and is now a danger to all of us."

The Belfast voice sounded genuinely sorry. "Ah, 'tis a shame, is it not? He was quite a volunteer in the old days."

Caitlyn rolled her eyes. These old-timers were so bloody sentimental. "Yes, I know it's a pity, but there's no alternative. He can't be trusted any longer."

There was a long sigh at the other end of the line. "So, what do we do?"

"Tell your men to take him out after the San Francisco rendezvous." She paused. A smile came to her lips. "He told me he wants to come home. I'll see he does. Unfortunately, he'll be traveling cargo instead of first class."

When she hung up the phone, she was still smiling. She moved to the bedroom door and opened it. "Cal, love? I hope you haven't lost that hard-on. I'm hornier than ever."

As PROMISED, Devin had breakfast waiting for Fonda in his suite when she arrived. That had been several hours ago, and still, they hadn't gotten around to eating it.

With a contented sigh, she moved her hand up his muscled chest, delighting in the texture of the springy hair under her fingertips. He groaned softly and pulled her closer within the circle of his arms. Fonda kissed a spot just above his left nipple, and for a moment, allowed her tongue to taste the salt of his musky male sweat. "Breakfast is probably cold," she murmured.

"What breakfast?" Devin stirred against her, nuzzling her jaw. "Ah, woman, you don't know what you do to me . . ."

"I know what you do to me," Fonda said with a little laugh. "Twice already, this morning. What time is it, anyway?"

She felt his arm shift as he craned his neck to get a glimpse of his wristwatch. "It's almost eleven," he said, his hand moving lightly on the small of her back.

She made a move to pull away, but his arms tightened around her. "I promised to meet Jessie and Laoise for lunch," she protested.

"Is that a fact?" His lips pressed lightly against her forehead, but he didn't release his grip.

"And don't you have a sound check to get to?"

"That I do." He grabbed a strand of her hair and brought it to his lips, kissing it leisurely.

"Well?"

He dropped the strand against her breast and kissed her closed eyelids. "Well?"

"Shouldn't you let me get up?"

"I suppose I should." But he made no move to do so. His chin dropped onto the top of her head; he snuggled her even closer.

She relaxed. Only a few more minutes, then she really would have to get up. It was so peaceful here in his arms, so sheltered. It was no wonder she wanted to stay.

"Are you happy?" Devin asked softly.

"Can't you tell?"

"That I can. I've been so afraid I couldn't make you happy."

Fonda's foot moved leisurely against his hairy calf. "Being with you goes beyond happiness."

His eyes were dark, turbulent with emotion. "Ah, love, you don't know how grand that makes me feel. Because you're my life. You are that!" He hugged her, rocking her slowly against him, back and forth.

Fonda's fingers found the small scar on his upper left arm. She touched it lightly, and wondered, not for the first time, what had caused it. So many times she'd been ready to ask, but it was always at inopportune moments. Moments when passion had taken over, causing her to forget everything.

"This scar," she said now. "How did it happen?"

The muscles of his arm tensed under her fingers. "The one on my arm?"

"Do you have others?"

He gave an abrupt laugh, one that sounded forced. "Don't ya know Irishmen have scars all over, most of them on our hearts."

"Well, I'm talking about this particular one on your arm. It's strange. Kind of crescent-shaped."

Devin released her and rolled away to sit on the edge of the bed. "Jesus! Would you look at the time? And didn't you say you had to meet the girls?"

Fonda propped herself on her elbow and gazed at him. "You're evading the subject, Devin O'Keefe. Why won't you tell me how you got the scar?"

He stood up, stepped into his underwear and then his jeans. His back was to her as he drew up the zipper. "It's a gunshot wound."

Fonda was so startled she couldn't speak. He turned to look at her, his face grim. "It was nothing. Just a flesh wound."

"But how did you get it? What happened?"

"It's a long story." His voice was cold, emphatic.

Her heart thumped painfully in her chest. Abruptly, she rolled away from him and sat up. She didn't want him to see the hurt on her face.

"Fon." He was at her side, drawing her into his arms. "Don't look like that. I'll tell you all about it, love. But not now. It was a painful time of my life. And I find it difficult to talk about. With anyone. Please try and understand." He lifted her chin so he could gaze into her eyes. "Tell me you do, Fonda."

Fonda stared at his anguished face. His eyes were sad, pleading. Once again, he was the Devin that so frightened her. The stranger she couldn't seem to reach. Yet the stranger loved her, and she loved him. She closed her eyes and shook her head slightly. *Oh, dear God, please forgive me for this lie.*

"I do, Devin. I understand."

25

It was quiet on the flight to San Francisco. Fonda closed the novel she was reading and glanced over at Devin. He was still pretending to be asleep. Or maybe he really *had* fallen asleep now. Earlier, though, his play-acting had been painfully obvious. It cut into her heart like a steel blade—the fact that he felt he had to resort to such measures just to avoid talking to her.

She shifted restlessly in her seat, wishing they were closer to San Francisco. But arrival time was still more than an hour away. She put aside her novel and brought out the notebook she used to jot down ideas for copy to go along with her photos. Last night, as Fonda had readied herself for bed, Jessie had gleefully chattered on about Devin's out-of-character climb above the stage.

"You must've got some great photos, huh? Wow! Maybe you'll win a . . . what do they call it? A Pulitzer?"

Fonda had stared at her for a moment and then quickly turned away to hide her reddened face. The fact was, it hadn't occurred to her to get a photo of Devin's dangerous stunt. Her only thought had been for his safety.

Fat chance, a Pulitzer! Fonda stared down at the scribbled notes, smiling grimly. It was to the point where she couldn't concentrate on her job. Falling in love with Devin was wreaking havoc in her life. Not to mention her career.

And what *of* her career? Her dream to publish a music magazine of her own? A dream was a hard thing to give up, but what else could she do? She couldn't imagine a life without Devin. Not now.

She turned to look at him. His breathing was rhythmical, his mouth parted slightly. His eyelashes, like blackened arcs against his lightly freckled skin, were still. He was really sleeping this time. As Fonda gazed at him, she was overcome with such a feeling of love and longing that tears sprang to her eyes.

"Oh, Devin," she murmured. "If only . . ."

What? She shook her head. Only one thing was certain. Something was very wrong with their relationship. But how could she fix it when she didn't know what it was?

A FEW seats away, Jacky O'Brien sipped a beer and stared at the white billow of clouds outside his window. He wore a satisfied smile on his face because it had just come to him. How he was going to do it. It hadn't been easy trying to find a way to seduce a sweet crumpet like Jessie Blayne while her big sister was hanging around. Not to mention that sanctimonious monk, O'Keefe.

Jacky's lips quirked. Of course, even Saint Devin wasn't so pristine as he'd like to think. Everyone knew he was balling that photographer, and had been for quite some time. She was quite a piece herself, she was, with her cute ass and that long curly hair that almost reached it. Jesus, what man wouldn't want to tangle up in that hair. Still, it was her baby sister Jacky couldn't stop thinking about.

And he'd come up with the perfect idea. An impromptu party in his hotel suite. His eyes fastened on the blond spiked head sitting a few rows in front of him. Why not do it right now? Put the germ of thought into the young stud's mind.

Jacky swallowed the last of his beer and unbuckled his seat belt. He stood up, stretched, then ambled down the aisle to where Ryan Meehan was sitting, apparently engrossed in the latest *Rolling Stone*. "Hey, Ryan-boy, how ya doing?"

Surprised, Ryan looked up at the sound man. It wasn't often

O'Brien bothered to speak to a lowly roadie like himself. "I'm okay," he said warily, wondering what was up.

Jacky squatted down beside his seat, a "good-buddy" look on his face. "Hey, man. I'm having a bit of a thing in my suite tonight. Just a few select friends, you know, ones who know how to have a good time. I was hoping you might drop by with that colleen of yours." He saw the flush spread across the boy's face and went on, dropping his voice a notch softer. "There'll be plenty of good grass and booze. And if you have in mind a bit of privacy for you and the crumpet, you can have the use of my bedroom. I'll make sure you're not disturbed." Ryan's face turned even redder. Jacky stood up and grinned down at him. "I'll let you know the time and room number later."

Back in his seat, Jacky pushed the button to the recline position. Almost instantly he fell asleep, a satisfied smile on his lips.

JESSIE HAD turned down lunch with Fonda and Devin in favor of shopping at Fisherman's Wharf with Laoise and Darcy. Fonda and Devin decided to spend the cool and overcast afternoon in Sausalito, a charming town full of shops and cozy restaurants with a view of San Francisco's skyline across the bay. Devin wore his Stetson and dark sunglasses, and for once, most of the people they encountered were more interested in shopping than noticing incognito celebrities. Even in the Italian restaurant where they had a late lunch, the waitress had given no indication she recognized him.

Over his veal scaloppini, he gave Fonda an abashed grin. "Do you suppose I should be worried?"

"Only if no one shows up at the concert tomorrow night." Fonda grinned. "Personally, I think this is kind of nice. Having you all to myself for a change."

His eyes flicked down to her breasts and then back up to her face. His expression warmed her blood. "That's what I'm looking forward to. Having *you* to myself. Back at the hotel. Do you know how delicious you look in that jumper?"

"Oh, go on with ya!" Fonda said, mimicking his accent.

He laughed out loud, causing heads to turn at the table across the aisle. "Meryl Streep you're not."

Fonda grinned. How she loved the man when he was like this. So lighthearted and loving. Why couldn't he be like this always? What had happened to him in his past that turned him into such a stranger at times?

Their ferry arrived back at San Francisco along with the afternoon fog. It rolled in from the ocean, slowly but relentlessly painting the edges of Golden Gate Bridge with an invisible brush, leaving an illusion that the sweeping orange steel girders were floating on a heavenly cloud.

Because of the fog, the character of the city had changed, become more brooding. And like the fog, Devin's demeanor had also changed. Where before, he'd been laughing and carefree, now as they neared the city, the inevitable barrier began to drop between them. Fonda could feel it happening. His eyes were faraway, his expression bleak. She studied him as he stared out toward the open ocean, and somehow, she knew his thoughts were of home. *Talk to me*, she wanted to beg. But she knew it would make the gap between them widen. She shivered, and it wasn't entirely because of the cold wind that whipped around them.

What hope was there for them? she wondered. If she couldn't be the balm to ease his pain, what chance did they have to be happy together?

IAN STEPPED over a rusted railroad tie and peered ahead into the darkness. A blast of wind from the bay hit him and he shivered, pulling his Burberry raincoat tighter around him.

Jesus, it was bloody cold here in San Francisco. Or Oakland, if one were to be precise. He hated to think what it would feel like in winter. Sweet Mary, it didn't seem like the middle of July!

And why, for Christ's sake, did they have to plan these meetings in places like this? Yes, he realized the need for security, but did they have to choose the sleaziest, scummiest area in town? Thank the good Lord it would be his last meeting with these American thugs. Caitlyn had assured him of that, at least.

"Is that you, Mulligan?"

Ian's head snapped up at the sound of the thick Belfast accent. He hadn't been expecting to meet any of his countrymen here.

"Who is that?" he asked, his eyes focusing on a dark figure just ahead.

"Never you mind who I am. You've got the final payment for the lads inside?"

Ian lifted his briefcase. "Right here."

It was too dark to see the man nod, but Ian sensed his approval. "Inside with you, then." He pushed against a heavy sliding door to the warehouse and it creaked open enough to allow the two men to squeeze through. The Belfast man switched on a flashlight and scanned Ian up and down. All Ian could see of him was a dark wool jumper on a beefy chest and thick muscular thighs clad in black.

"Put the case down on the table over there," he instructed.

Ian felt apprehension mixed with relief at not having been met by Harlen, the repulsive hillbilly killer. For weeks, he'd been dreading another meeting with that psychopath. The events of the last one still caused him nightmares. Ian scanned the room as he placed the briefcase on the table, but all he could see were several shadowy figures. He felt a prickle of fear shoot between his shoulder blades. Something didn't feel right here. Every hair on his body was standing on end.

"You can count it, if you'd like, Harley," the Belfast man said.

Out of the dark came Harlen's grinning face. To Ian, it looked like the skull of a hobgoblin thirsty for blood, and he knew his fear was justified.

"Howdy, there, Mulligan. Haven't had any more accidents lately, have you? I hear them dry-cleaning bills are mighty high for a fancy boy like you."

The Belfast man spoke again, his tone unamused. "I said, count the money, Harley. We don't have much time."

Harlen shrugged and turned to the briefcase. Ian waited, wondering why the Belfast man was making him feel like an enemy. They were on the same side, weren't they?

"It's all there," Harlen said after a moment. "Payment in full." He grinned at Ian. "You done good, boy."

Ian glanced away from him in revulsion and spoke to the Belfast man, "That's it, then? I can go?"

The flashlight's beam moved to the door. "That's the way out."

Ian took a step in the direction he indicated, but the man spoke again. "Oh, Mulligan? Just one last thing. I have a message from Caitlyn for you."

Bloody bitch! A snide one, he was sure. "What's that?" Ian turned to look back. The flashlight shone full on his face, blinding him. He lifted his hand to shield his eyes.

"Just this." The beam of the flashlight dropped to illuminate Ian's chest, and at the same moment, another flashlight splashed a bead of light onto the Belfast man. Ian's eyes focused on the silenced .357 Magnum aimed directly at his heart.

This is it, then. This time, it wouldn't be a joke. The man from Belfast was smiling cruelly. It was the smile of a killer. A man who enjoyed killing, who savored it. Ian was surprised at how calm he felt. Perhaps because somehow, he'd known as he'd walked into the dark warehouse, he wouldn't come out alive. His chin lifted an inch. This time, he wouldn't piss in his pants. Not this time. Caitlyn, the devious bitch, would burn in hell for this. But he would die like a patriot.

Ian focused his eyes on the assassin's chest. "Fuck you," he said clearly.

Something in the man's eyes flickered. A semblance of human emotion. But was it anger or regret? The click of the hammer was loud in the silence of the warehouse. Ian closed his eyes and murmured: "Holy Mary, Mother of God, pray for us sinners . . ."

The gun emitted a belching whisper. Ian waited for the pain, but he felt nothing.

"Throw down your weapons and freeze!"

There was silence for a second or two and then the loud clatter of weapons hitting the floor. Ian blinked. The voice had come from the darkness behind the assassin. But the Belfast man was no longer there. Finally, in the dim light of a discarded flashlight, Ian's eyes focused upon his dark shape sprawled on the warehouse floor. As if he were moving in slow motion, he looked around. Harlen, face grim, held his hands in the air, staring toward the still invisible figure in the shadows. The other men too were motionless, hands raised.

A flashlight beamed onto the body of the Belfast man. Ian felt the bile rise in his throat as his eyes fastened upon the viscous mixture of blood and brain matter that smeared the floor around his head. But for the grace of God . . .

"He's dead," said a voice out of the dark. It wasn't a necessary statement.

"Pat them down. Harlen, there, likes to hide a Bowie under his pant leg."

Someone moved from out of the shadows. It was a man Ian had never seen before. He was armed with an automatic pistol. Face impassive, he stood in front of Harlen.

"Don't try anything, Harlen," the voice from the dark continued. "You saw what this baby did to your Irish friend."

Harlen's eyes were like dark stones as he scanned the man in front of him. "You double-dealing little shit. What the hell are you up to?"

Ignoring him, the man knelt to retrieve a knife from under his pant leg. Ian could see the hillbilly's desire to knee him in the groin, but his fear of the man in the shadows was too great. Pocketing the knife, the man stood up and moved back. With a quick professional pat-down, he searched the remaining two men and gave the all-clear.

The man in the shadows stepped into the light. Ian gasped.

It was the blond man with the flattened nose. The one who'd followed him to the gay bar in Seattle!

Ian took a step forward. "I don't care *who* you're working for. You saved my life! How can I thank you?"

The man grinned. "You can thank me by raising your hands above your head like a good boy, Mr. Brinegar." One hand was still holding a Mauser on Harlen while his partner covered the other men. His free hand reached into his jacket pocket and brought out a wallet. It opened to reveal a badge. "Federal Bureau of Investigation," he said shortly. "You're all under arrest."

AFTER DEVIN and Fonda returned to his suite at the Hyatt Regency, he made love to her with a desperation that brought to mind the sad rainy night in Seattle. Fonda clung to him, achingly aware of her inability to fill the void in him, the one he'd made so obviously apparent at the Seattle concert. He wanted her, needed her desperately, yet pushed her away at the same time with that cold withdrawal into himself.

As she lay in his arms afterwards, she could feel his brooding silence. If she'd been less secure in his love for her, she would've wondered if, somehow, she hadn't pleased him sexually. But it was only during that sacred act between them she had no doubts about him. His body, as it tenderly delved into hers, sanctified their love, and at those moments, above all others, she became one with him. Afterwards, when their climatic shuddering had eased, Fonda always found her hands clasped in his as if he were holding onto a fraying rope near the summit of a sheer mountain. With the simple release of her hands, she felt him withdraw from more than her body.

Under her left ear, she listened to his heart beating steadily. Her hand slid up his chest to touch the sterling silver Celtic cross he always wore around his neck. It was warm from their bodies. She traced its outline with her index finger, wondering if there was something she could say to get him to talk to her. But almost as if he sensed her thoughts, he moved under her restlessly.

"I'm famished! Why don't we order something from room service?"

Reluctantly, Fonda sat up and reached for the menu on the table next to the bed.

There was a sharp knock at the suite door. "Devin, you in there? We've got trouble, man!"

Devin gave Fonda a puzzled look and grabbed his jeans. Hold

on, Bram." He stood up and pulled them on. "What catastrophe is up now?" Leaning over, he planted a kiss on her lips. "Don't you move, darlin'. I won't be long."

Fonda propped two pillows behind her head and studied the menu. From the living room of the suite, she could hear Bram's muffled voice but couldn't make out what he was saying. Then, quite clearly, she heard Devin's cry of dismay. "Jaysus, Bram! This has got to be a bloody mistake!"

Fonda suppressed a sigh. Something told her whatever the problem was, it wasn't going to be easily solved. And that meant Devin would have to deal with it. She tossed the menu aside and sat up on the edge of the bed to search for her clothes. She was already half-dressed when she heard the door to the suite shut.

Devin walked into the bedroom, his face brooding. He scooped his black T-shirt from the floor and pulled it on. When his tousled head appeared through the opening, he looked at her and said, "I have to go downtown. Ian has been arrested."

JESSIE STEPPED out of the elevator onto the fourteenth floor and found Ryan waiting for her, all smiles. He was so good-looking, it almost made her dizzy to look at him. He was dressed in faded jeans and a sleeveless San Francisco T-shirt he'd obviously bought that afternoon. It revealed his well-developed adolescent biceps and the firm muscles of his chest. It was very sexy, as he well knew. Her eyes dropped down to the crotch of his jeans. She felt her cheeks grow hot at the memory of her hand pushing against that forbidden spot. How hard it had been! How very delicious it had felt! And now . . . tonight . . .

"Come here, girl."

Ryan wasn't one to waste time on needless words. His hands slid under her wave of copper hair as he drew her against him for a kiss, his tongue prying her lips open with a searching urgency.

A moment later, when Jessie pulled away shakily, she felt as if hot chili pepper was coursing through her veins. She knew, without a doubt, she would go through the rest of her life and never find a better kisser than Ryan Meehan.

"That's just to get you warmed up," he said, smiling into her eyes. "You'll have to wait for the rest of it."

Jessie laughed and with an index finger flicked at the tiny gold cross dangling from his left earlobe. "You're pretty confident, aren't you?"

He grabbed her finger and nibbled at it, his eyes devouring her. "You've kept me waiting long enough, love. And I can tell by looking at you, you want it as much as I do."

Jessie knew her face was beet red. "Come on, let's go to this party."

He took her hand and began to lead her down the hall. The thumping sound of rock music grew louder. But it wasn't loud enough to drown out the slamming of Jessie's heart.

JACKY WAS behind the bar, jovially playing host to the dozen or so guests who'd shown up at the party. Besides Ryan Meehan and his little redheaded crumpet, he'd invited several of the back stage crew and their women, all ones he could be assured wouldn't run and tell tales of forbidden wild parties to Devin. Ones who weren't part of the bossman's close-knit group. The last thing he wanted was to get in trouble with O'Keefe. Hypocrite that the man was! Him and his "holier than thou" attitude, and all the time, he was sticking it to the photographer. It made Jacky sick.

He stooped down to grab a Budweiser from the small refrigerator under the bar. With a quick twist, he had the cap off and was taking a long, thirsty swig. The bottle thumped to the bar. Jacky wiped his mouth and scanned the room, a slight smile on his lips. Everything was going just right.

From the stereo, Guns 'N Roses pumped out rock music guaranteed to make the girls wiggle out of their hot little silkies. A haze of marijuana smoke hung in the air, so much that no one had to actually toke it to get high. Later, it would be time to bring out the coke.

In a dark corner, a brunette with huge tits squirmed on a technician's lap. From the look of things, it wouldn't be long before she was on her knees, paying homage to the Goddess Fellatio. Others had paired off and were getting friendly. The youngsters, Ryan and Jessie, were sitting on the floor, hands entwined, their backs propped against the wall. They looked uncomfortable with all the action going on around them.

Jacky had purposely not invited any lady friends for himself. As soon as Prince Ryan was out of the picture, he would have all the female entertainment he needed.

He glanced at his watch. Eleven o'clock. It was time to get things going. He knelt in front of the refrigerator and pulled out a Coke Classic and another bottle of beer. When a quick glance around assured him no one was paying attention, he dug the small plastic bottle out of his pocket. Quickly, he shook two tiny pills into a frosty stein, then followed it with the foaming beer.

"Sleep well, handsome prince," he said softly. "And dream of me getting it on with your colleen."

26

"RYAN, THIS is really embarrassing. God! She looks like she's trying to suck his face off!"

"Jessie, if you're so embarrassed, why the devil do you keep staring at them?" Ryan's face was red, and had been that way since the girl with the enormous breasts climbed onto the crewman's lap.

"Because I'm fascinated. It's like watching an X-rated movie."

Ryan was very much afraid it was going to turn into an X-rated movie any moment now. And before that happened, he wanted to get Jessie out of the room. She was a sweet kid, and although he had no qualms at all about relieving her of her virginity, he didn't want to see her soiled by such filthy going-ons as were about to happen here. This had the makings of a full-fledged orgy.

He supposed he really had no choice but to make their excuses and leave. But damn! He'd been looking forward to some time alone with Jessie. For weeks now, just the thought of her lovely red hair and her sweet, sweet lips gave him a hard-on that threatened to burst his zipper. And tonight was to be the night.

He gave Jessie's hand a squeeze. "Jess, maybe we should go."

"You two are looking a wee bit thirsty."

Jacky was standing over them with a stein of beer in one hand and a glass of Coke in the other. He passed the drinks over and settled down next to Jessie.

"Drink up! It's free and there's plenty more."

Ryan took an obliging sip of the foamy beer. "We're not going to be able to stay too much longer."

Jessie remained quiet and sipped her Coke.

Jacky looked around the room. "Ah, I know what you're thinking! It's a bad lot we got here." He leaned toward Ryan with a leering grin. "But you see, that'll make it all the easier for the two of you to slip off and be alone."

Jessie's face flamed bright red. Ryan felt the heat rise on his own face. The bloody idiot! Didn't he know women didn't want their love lives advertised to the world?

"Tell you what. Finish your drinks and I'll take you two into the bedroom." He snickered. "Pretend I'm showing you my stamp collection if anyone asks."

Ryan placed his nearly full stein on the carpet next to him. "Why don't you show us now?" At the moment, he was more anxious to get Jessie out of here than he was to make love to her.

Jacky's eyes were on Ryan's beer stein. "Hey, man, I'm paying for that beer. Finish it and we'll go."

Ryan shrugged and reached for the stein. The quicker he finished it, the quicker he and Jessie could get out of this den of iniquity. He took a long draw and grimaced. Christ, it tasted like goat piss! "Hey, Jacky. Will you keep your eyes on Jessie here. I have to make a trip to the loo."

Jacky grinned at Jessie. "Right you are, Ryan-lad. Ya don't want to leave a lovely like this alone with a roomful of horny bastards like we have here. I'll make sure she isn't disturbed."

Ryan got to his feet, taking his beer stein with him. Jacky didn't notice. He was too busy leering at Jessie.

AFTER DEVIN had left for the police department, Fonda ordered from room service and parked herself in front of the big screen TV in his suite. There was no sense in going back to her own room. Jessie had earlier arranged to spend the night with Laoise. Besides, Devin had told her he probably wouldn't be gone long. He'd been wrong. Four hours had passed since he'd left.

She couldn't understand why he'd refused to let her come along, but he'd been adamant. Now, as Fonda watched the credits of *Pretty Woman* roll by on the Pay Movie channel, she began to face the fact that the situation with Ian was very serious. What on earth had the man done?

The Pay Movie channel began to show previews of other attractions. Fonda reached for the remote on the bedside table. No more movies. They would be wasted on her. She did a channel scan and stopped on the local news. Then she searched in the bedside table for stationery and began a letter to her mother.

Earlier pleas for her to change her mind and come to their wedding in Monaco had apparently been for nothing, but it didn't stop Fonda from asking again. She was in the middle of an eloquent passage guaranteed to make her mother weep gallons when warning bells sounded in her head. Had she just heard Devin's name on the TV?

She looked up at the screen just in time to see Devin getting out of a limousine with Kyle McKenna, Ian Brinegar's assistant. After they disappeared into an office building, the screen switched back to the news anchor: ". . . according to our sources, Ian Brinegar has been under investigation for several weeks for illegally selling arms to the IRA. Those arms are suspected to have been obtained from pro-Irish Republican groups in America. Although no charges have been pressed against Devin O'Keefe, unconfirmed reports say he is being investigated for possible collusion with Mr. Brinegar in the illegal arms sales."

"No!" Fonda stared at the screen, her heart pounding. With the remote, she switched off the TV and jumped out of bed. Her fingers trembled as she pulled on her clothes, her mind spinning with disjointed thoughts. They were wrong! Devin would never be involved in selling arms to the IRA. She ran out the door and raced down the corridor toward the elevators.

When the elevator stopped on the fourteenth floor, Fonda hurried to Darcy's room. The Irishwoman's ample frame was draped in a terry robe when she opened the door to Fonda's frantic knock. "Fonda! Dear Lord, you look frightful! What is it?"

Fonda stepped into the room. "Did you see the news?"

"No, I was watching a movie. Fon, love, what's wrong? You're trembling, child."

At the sympathetic look on Darcy's face, Fonda felt the tears well up in her eyes. "Oh, Darcy! They're investigating Devin. They think he has something to do with smuggling arms for the IRA."

Darcy's face paled. "Oh, for the love of Jesus, that can't be true! Not Devin!"

Fonda nodded and began to pace the room. "They've already arrested Ian, and now they think Devin is involved with him."

"Ian Brinegar has been arrested for smuggling arms to the IRA? *Our* Ian? I can't believe it! Why, the man is a mouse!"

Fonda's fingers massaged her temples where a headache was beginning to throb. "All I know is he was arrested by the FBI. And I would think they must have some pretty good evidence to do that. Oh, Darcy, how can they think Devin has anything to do with it? He's the last man on earth who would help the IRA!"

Darcy drew her into her fleshy arms. "They've made a terrible mistake, love. The truth will come out. Remember, we're in America, not the Diplock Courts in Northern Ireland. Here, a man is innocent until proven guilty. And our Devin is as true-blue as they come. You'll see."

For a moment, Fonda allowed herself to be comforted. Darcy was right. Probably by morning, it would all be over with. Devin would be cleared of any wrongdoing and everything would be back to normal. She *had* to believe that—because to believe otherwise—Oh God, she didn't want to think about it.

She drew away from Darcy. "I should get back to my room. Devin might be trying to call." At the door, she paused. "Oh. Do you think it would be too much trouble if Jessie hangs around with Laoise tomorrow? I know she does anyway, but I'd really appreciate it if you'd kind of keep an eye on her. If I don't hear from Devin by tomorrow . . ." Her voice trailed off.

Darcy smiled and put a hand on her shoulder. "You'll hear from him. No doubt, he's waiting for you in his room at this very moment. You'll wonder why you got so worked up. And don't you be worrying about Jessie. I'll take them down to Fisherman's Wharf again. I hear there's some great shopping on Pier 39."

"Okay." Fonda's eyes were watery again. "Thanks, Darcy. It's great to have a friend like you. I guess it's too late to go say goodnight to the girls? They're probably asleep?"

"Why, Laoise went to bed about half-ten."

"And Jessie didn't?"

Darcy looked blank. "What do you mean?"

"Well, you said Laoise went to bed. What about Jessie? Didn't she?"

"Love, I'm confused." Darcy's brow was furrowed. "Why are you asking me about Jessie?"

Fonda stared at her a long moment, wondering why Darcy would choose this time to joke around when she knew how unnerved she was by Devin's plight. Then, almost immediately, she realized Darcy wasn't joking. *Don't panic,* she told herself. *There's an explanation.*

"Jessie told me she was spending the night with Laoise," Fonda said quietly.

"I don't know a thing about it." Darcy shook her head, puzzled. "But there's one way to find out. Just a minute."

Darcy walked across the suite to the door that connected with the adjoining room. She was inside for only a moment. When she returned, her face was etched with concern.

"Laoise is in there, asleep. But the other bed is empty."

Fonda's heart began to race.

"I'm sure there's nothing to worry about," Darcy said. "Perhaps they had a spat and Jessie went back to your room."

Fonda had already turned to go. "I'm sure you're right," she said over her shoulder. "I'll go check."

The sense of foreboding was stronger as she hurried to the elevator. It seemed to take forever to get back to her room. Her hand trembled as she inserted the card into the lock of her door. It didn't work.

"Damn!" She'd put it in the wrong way. After reinserting it the correct way, she heard the lock click. She opened the door and fumbled for the light switch.

When the soft light illuminated the room, she stared in disbelief at the two empty beds, both of them as immaculate as the maid had left them that morning.

JESSIE MOANED and pressed herself against the long firm length of Ryan on the bed next to her. His tongue invaded the inside of her mouth, playing Tag with hers and sending delicious shivers running up and down her back. This felt so *good*. No one had ever told her it would feel so good.

His hand moved under her eyelet blouse and after a moment of fumbling, he released the catch of her bra. Jessie gasped as his fingers touched her naked breast. In a continuous motion, his thumb brushed over the nub of her nipple until it grew stiff.

"Ah, you like that, do you?" he whispered into her ear.

"Ryan," she whispered in awe, as her body instinctively ground against his. She could feel his erection against her stomach and when she pressed against it, she delighted in hearing him groan.

"I'm not going to be able to wait if you keep doing that," he muttered, and then drew her blouse and loosened her bra up above her breasts. His mouth lowered to one pink nipple.

"Oh, God . . . Ryan . . ." Jessie breathed, eyes closed. "Who taught you to do that?"

He didn't answer, but continued to nuzzle one taut nipple and then the other with his tongue, mouth, and teeth. Jessie squirmed on the bed, feeling the ache between her legs and the familiar wetness that accompanied it. His hand slid up her thigh and under her denim skirt. Jessie stiffened as his searching fingers reached the elastic leg of her panties. In sudden apprehension, she squeezed her legs together.

Ryan's lips lifted away from her breast. "Let me in, Jess. You'll like it. I promise."

She forced herself to relax. His fingers slid beneath the elastic and touched her wet center. Jessie jerked. It was as if an electric shock had shot through her body. Slowly, delicately, his fingers began to move and a new feeling ripped through her. Even her own touch on those late nights and early mornings of sexual fantasies hadn't made her feel like this. Her legs parted to give him more room. She began to pant.

"Jessie," he whispered. "Touch me. I need you to touch me, too."

In the semi-darkness, she heard the sound of his zipper, and she turned toward him slightly. The delightful touch of his fingers inside her panties disappeared. She murmured her protest, but then, his hands were taking hers and guiding them to what he needed touched. It was hard and very hot in her hands. Jessie found it strangely exciting. It seemed so powerful. It jumped to her touch as if it had a life of its own. How wonderful, Jessie thought. What would it feel like to have one? She supposed it was like having an outside force inside your pants, a greedy and demanding one. How would it feel to be controlled by such a thing?

He groaned as she moved her hands up and down his thrusting length. His hands moved back under her skirt and began to work her panties down. She helped him get them off and then spread her legs, hoping he'd touch her down there again. For a moment, he did. But it didn't last long enough. His breathing had quickened as she continued to caress him. Finally, he wrenched away and sat up, fumbling in his jeans pocket.

"I have to put it on," he said. "Jaysus! You're driving me crazy!"

Jessie sat up. "I want to watch."

Ryan grinned as he ripped open the condom package. "You're something else, you know that? I've never met a girl like you before." Quickly, he stood up and removed his jeans.

From the window, the lights of the San Francisco skyline glowed just enough so she could see his thing was bigger than she'd thought. He was going to fit *that* inside of her? Deftly, he slid the condom on and turned to her.

"You ready?"

"I . . . guess so."

Somehow, the shivery feelings of a moment before had disappeared. Jessie hoped he'd touch her again or kiss her breasts. Maybe the feelings would come back. But instead, he rolled over on top of her and she felt his hard length prod at her thighs.

"I don't think you're in the right place," Jessie said.

He grunted and readjusted himself. Now, he was too high. Jessie squirmed beneath him, trying to maneuver herself into the right position. He pushed and prodded against her.

"Oh, Jaysus," he muttered.

"Ryan, I don't think—"

"There."

He was in the right place, but still, nothing was happening. Jessie grimaced as he ineffectually pushed against her. Finally, it appeared that he'd made some headway, but no sooner than she'd thought that, a barrier seemed to be erected inside her. Breathing heavily, he pushed, once, twice, and then, "Oh, Lord Jaysus! I can't." He let out a loud groan and fell limp on top of her.

"Ryan?"

Jessie lay beneath him, wondering what exactly was happening. Finally, when he didn't move, she pushed at his chest to get some of his dead weight off her.

"What's wrong, Ryan? Are you giving up? I've read it's hard sometimes with virgins, but I'm sure if we keep trying . . ."

Slowly, Ryan lifted his head from her shoulder. "Oh, sweet girl, I'm sorry. I tried, but I couldn't hold on. Just give me a moment, love. I'll make it good for you."

He rolled away from her. Jessie tugged her skirt back down and turned on her side to look at him.

"Just a moment," he murmured, his eyes closed. "Just let me rest a moment."

Jessie watched him for a long time. If she didn't know better, she'd swear he'd fallen asleep.

LAOISE WAITED a few moments until she was positive her mother had sent Fonda on her way, then she moved. Quickly, she grabbed her jeans and stepped into them, pulling them up and zipping them in almost the same motion. As she grabbed for a T-shirt in the bureau and began to drag it over her tousled head, she slid her feet into a pair of slippers. Less than a minute had passed when she stepped out into the corridor and raced toward Jacky O'Brien's room. Her mind worked furiously.

The things she did for that girl! All so Jessie could lose her bloody virginity to that cocky brother of hers. And now, they were *all* going to pay for it. Of that, she was sure—unless she could warn her. What sort of defense Jessie could think up, Laoise didn't know, but it would be better than getting caught red-handed.

The rock music from Jacky's suite thumped all the way down the hall. It was incredible no one had called hotel management yet. She had to knock twice at the door before someone finally opened it. A scrawny man with carrot red hair grinned at her drunkenly.

"Well, come on in!"

Laoise pushed past him, barely sparing him a glance. "Where's Jacky?" She scanned the room, but didn't see him or Jessie and Ryan.

"Probably in the head," the man said, following her. "Hey, you look like you need some loosening up. Come on over here. I've got something for you that'll wipe that frown right off your pretty face."

"Get lost," Laoise said, her eyes on the bedroom door. That's where they were, of course. "Bloody hell!" She didn't know if she was going to be able to stomach seeing them all naked and sweaty. Whoever said sex was romantic was a bleeding idiot. Especially when it was your own brother who was engaged in the process.

She took a step in the direction of the bedroom. A hand closed around her upper arm. "Not so fast, luvvie. We haven't got acquainted yet."

Scowling, Laoise turned back to the creepy red-haired man. "I *said*, get lost, Turd-face!"

But his hand remained firmly locked upon her arm. His brown eyes scanned her up and down, finally lingering on her small bra-less breasts clearly revealed against the thin fabric of her T-shirt.

"Just what I like," the man murmured. "Jail-bait. With spirit."

In horror, Laoise watched as he moved closer. "Let go of me!" she hissed, and was surprised when he did. He smiled lazily and took another step toward her. Laoise backed up. She felt the wall behind her.

There was nowhere else to go.

27

DARCY OPENED the door of Laoise's room, flicked on the light, and stared in amazement at her empty bed.

"Holy Mother of God, you're right!"

Fonda stared over her shoulder. "Whatever she's up to, Laoise has gone to warn her."

Darcy turned and met her eyes. "Yes, but where?"

"I don't know, but I'm going to find out." Fonda whirled around and hurried out into the corridor. She looked up and down the empty hall. Her eyes moved to the glass elevators. Only one was moving, its only occupant a man. Fonda looked over the bannister to scan the floors below. No movement anywhere. It was impossible to recognize anyone in the lobby far below. Jessie wouldn't *dare* leave the hotel. She had to be here somewhere.

"Any ideas?" Darcy was at her side.

Fonda was about to answer when a door down the corridor opened. A backstage crewman, arms entwined with a woman sporting breasts the size of torpedoes, lurched down the hallway on unsteady feet. He grinned widely when he saw Fonda and Darcy.

"Hey, where've you two been? Jacky's throwing one helluva party, he is!" He stopped in front of them and put a wobbly finger to his lips. "Shhhh!" he said loudly. "Don't let Devin hear about this. He's not a big one for bashes like this, I'm told. Ah, but what he don't know won't hurt him, will it now?"

The buxom brunette giggled and snuggled up against him.

His bleary eyes fastened on Fonda and he peered closer. "Say, don't I know you?"

Fonda looked at Darcy. "I think he just gave me my first idea," she said grimly. "Come on, let's go."

JESSIE STARED down at Ryan. She couldn't *believe* it! He was sleeping like a little baby.

And here she was, clothes rumpled, panties nowhere to be seen, bra undone, and maidenhead still intact! Did anyone in the entire world have worse luck?

"You"—she muttered at Ryan's innocent, sleeping face— "are a first-class jerk!" *And you look stupid laying there, all limp with that little white bag hanging off your dong!* "If you think *I'm* going to take it off, forget it!"

She swung her legs off the bed and stood up. Her panties had to be around here somewhere. She found them under the bed and pulled them on. Turning, she glanced down at Ryan again. She couldn't leave him here like this. It was too embarrassing. Everyone knew how he'd been hanging around her all summer. Of course, it was possible he could come up with a good explanation if found naked in bed. But that used condom was a sure giveaway. She had to get rid of it.

She reached for it, her nose wrinkling in distaste. "Yuk!" She couldn't *believe* she was doing this. The condom was slimy and damp, and so was his penis. Ryan didn't stir as she worked it off. "God! I *really* put you out, didn't I? I wonder if that's good or bad?"

Carrying the soggy bag between her thumb and forefinger, she slipped into the bathroom, dropped it into the toilet, and watched as it flushed away. "Good. Now, the evidence is gone."

Back in the bedroom, she hesitated a moment, staring down at Ryan. A tiny smile came to her lips. He really *was* cute. And before all that pushing and prodding, his touch had really set her on fire. Jessie pulled the blanket up over him and decided she'd give him another chance. But if he nodded off next time, she would be very much tempted to make sure it was a permanent sleep.

She was struggling to refasten her bra without taking off her blouse when the bedroom door opened. Over her shoulder, she saw Jacky standing inside the room, staring at her.

"Hey! Do you mind?" she said indignantly.

He turned and locked the door. "No need to bother with that, love. You'll just have to take it off again."

Jessie stared at him, not sure what he meant.

His eyes flicked to Ryan on the bed. "Lover-boy all tuckered out already? It's a shame, it is. Perhaps you'll be needing a man with a bit more stamina."

Finally, Jessie understood. She took a leap toward the door, but he anticipated her move and blocked her way.

"Ah, now. Don't be like that, girl. You've seen me watching you. And you've been eating it up, haven't you, now? Well, honey, it's time for me to collect on all those 'come-fuck-me' looks you've been giving me."

"Don't touch me," Jessie said, trying to control the fear in her voice. "I swear, I'll scream."

"No, you won't. And even if you do, no one will care. They're all having a good time out there. They'll just think we're having a good time in here. And we will be. I can make you feel real good, honey. I know a lot more about making women feel good than that young punk does."

He'd closed the distance between them. Eyes darting frantically, Jessie backed up, and felt her knees against the king-size bed.

"I think it's kind of kinky, don't you? You and me doing it while your boyfriend counts sheep next to us?"

Jacky sprang, knocking her down onto the bed and falling heavily upon her. His mouth ground into hers, his tongue insinuating itself into her mouth like a writhing snake. Jessie bit it as hard as she could. He jerked back, cursing, and his hand tightened about her neck.

"You're a little hellcat, aren't you?" he said, his hand moving from her neck to pen her arms above her head. She bucked under him wildly, but instead of thwarting him, it seemed to excite him even more. "I know about women like you," he gasped, grinning. "You'll want it hard and rough." With his other hand, he pushed her blouse above her breasts, and lowering his head, fastened his teeth roughly onto her nipple.

Jessie screamed.

WITH A clenched fist, Fonda banged on the door to Jacky's suite. When there was no immediate response, Darcy began to pound on it, too.

"Open up in there, you slimy little twit! If you have my children in there, I'm going to make you the sorriest son-of-a-bitch in the world!"

Fonda turned to gape at Darcy. The usually mild-mannered Irishwoman had turned fishwife. Just as she started to beat on the door again, it was opened by a stringy-haired blonde with a spacey look on her face. Fonda and Darcy pushed past her.

There were about a dozen people in the room, most of them sprawled on the floor in a drug-induced haze. In the corner, a couple were cemented together, apparently dancing to the raucous strains of heavy metal. The music ended, but they continued to sway together. On the other side of the room, another couple appeared to be in the middle of a romantic interlude.

Fonda's eyes widened as she recognized Laoise with a scrawny redheaded man. He had her up against the wall, his arms securely holding her prisoner.

Suddenly, Laoise's knee came up and connected with his crotch. The blood drained from his face as he bent double, cradling his damaged scrotum. Laoise smiled down at him.

"How's *that* for spirit, Slimebucket?"

"Laoise!" Darcy gasped.

The girl looked up and her face went white.

A scream came from the bedroom.

Fonda clutched Darcy's arm. "That's Jessie!" She ran to the bedroom door. "Damn! It's locked!" She pounded on it. "Jessie! It's me! Let me in!"

There were noises coming from inside the room. Sounds of a struggle. Frantically, she turned to Darcy. "Call the police! And get help!"

Darcy whirled around and ran out of the room. Fonda continued to pound on the door. There was a click and it opened. Jessie, white-faced and rumpled, pulled her into the room.

"Help him, Fonda! He's going to kill him!"

Fonda's eyes went to the two men struggling on the floor. One was Jacky O'Brien. It took her a moment to recognize the blond one. Then, in a flash, it came to her. Ryan Meehan! He looked quite different than usual.

Buck-naked, he was much more grown-up.

"FOR GOD'S sake, do *something!*" Jessie screamed.

"Yeah, *like what?*" Fonda screamed back, at a total loss. The two men were scrambling about on the floor like possessed maniacs.

Suddenly, someone from behind gave her a push. It was Seamus MacBride, followed by a half-dressed Cary Meehan. In a matter of seconds, the two men had pulled Jacky and Ryan apart. Darcy appeared at Fonda's side, still gasping from her run down the hall.

"The police are on their way—Holy Mother of God!" Her eyes bulged as she recognized her naked son.

His teeth were bared in a snarl as he struggled against his father's hold to continue his mayhem on Jacky. Seamus had a tight grip on the sound man even though his eyes were rolling senselessly and his face was a mass of bruises.

"For the love of God, Cary, he hasn't a stitch on!" Darcy looked as if she were about to faint.

Cary pushed Ryan away. "Go get yourself dressed!"

With a last chilling scowl at Jacky, Ryan scrambled across the

254 • Carole Bellacera

bed, grabbed his jeans, and disappeared into the bathroom. Seamus released Jacky. The sound man slumped to the floor, holding his head in his hands. Jessie took a step toward the door.

"Fon, I want to go back to our room."

Fonda stared at her. "If you think you're going anywhere before we find out what's going on here, you have truly lost your mind."

Darcy turned to look over her shoulder. "Laoise Meehan, get your wee fanny in this room. I know you're in on the whole thing, too."

Shamefaced, Laoise appeared at the door. Jessie turned to Fonda. "She didn't do anything! It was all my idea."

"What was your idea?" Fonda asked.

Jessie blushed. Her eyes slid over to the rumpled bed and then to the bathroom door. The implication was as clear as if she'd spoken.

It was Fonda's turn to feel faint. "You mean you and Ryan?"

The bathroom door opened and he came out, bare-chested but clad in his jeans. His face was defiant. He came over to Jessie and put a protective arm around her.

"We're in love," he said, his eyes on Fonda and his parents.

There was a dazed expression on Jessie's face.

"And I intend to wed this girl in a few years." He looked down at Jessie. "I know we're too young now, Jess. But I swear to God, in a few years, when I'm out of school, I'm coming to get you. That I will."

Cary Meehan's face was grim. "You'd better hope you won't be wedding her in a few months. Considering the state we found you in."

Both Jessie and Ryan's faces turned crimson. Finally, Jessie gasped out. "But we didn't *do* anything! Not exactly, anyway."

Fonda decided not to pursue the conversation any further at the moment. "What about him?" She gestured toward Jacky. "Why were you fighting?"

Ryan's face contorted. "The bloody bastard tried to rape Jessie! I heard her scream and there he was all over her."

Darcy gasped and her knees buckled. Laoise grabbed her arm

and led her over to a chair. Fonda was feeling ill, too, at the thought of Jacky O'Brien's slimy hands on her little sister. She swallowed hard.

"How . . . how far did he . . .?"

Ryan's face softened as he looked back at Jessie. "Don't you worry, Fonda. He never did more than roughen her up a bit. I would've killed him if he'd violated her."

Fonda's eyes speared Jacky. "Not if I'd got to him first. What kind of subhuman are you? She's just a child!"

He looked up and met her eyes, a sneer on his thin lips. "With tits like that, she ain't no child."

In a heartbeat, Ryan was upon him. It took both Seamus and Cary to pull him away. When they did, Jacky was writhing on the floor, holding his belly where Ryan's vicious punches had landed. Squawk-box voices came from down the hall. The police.

In a matter of minutes, they'd handcuffed Jacky and led him away. But when they also clamped the cuffs on Ryan, Jessie began to cry.

"But he didn't do anything! He was protecting me!" She turned to Fonda, huge tears rolling down her freckled face. "Fon, you can't let them take him! He didn't do anything wrong."

Fonda put her arm around her sister. Just an hour before, she'd been thinking the very same thing about Devin. For the moment, sympathy for her sister outweighed her horror at the ugly situation. "Don't worry, honey. You have to go into the station to make a statement. When they find out what happened, I'm sure they'll let him go."

A squad car drove them to the station. During the ride, Fonda sat silently as Jessie snuffled beside her. The teenager refused to talk about what had happened. Fonda didn't press her; the whole story would come out at the police station.

But once inside the station when a policewoman prepared to take Jessie's statement, the girl turned to Fonda and said firmly, "I'd like to do this alone, please."

As Fonda sat in a noisy waiting room, she thought about Devin across town in another place like this. But of course, that was ridiculous. Like Ryan, he was innocent of any wrongdoing. By now, they'd probably cleared him of all suspicion. At this very moment, he was probably waiting for her in his suite.

In the haste of leaving, she'd forgotten to leave him a note.

AT FONDA'S insistence, Jessie pressed charges against Jacky O'Brien for attempted rape. It was the best thing to do under the circumstances. Fonda had no doubt that as soon as Devin found out about it, a felony charge would be the least of the sleazy Irishman's problems. This way, with Jacky safely in jail, Devin would have time to calm down after getting the news. With all this mess about Ian Brinegar and arms smuggling, Devin didn't need a murder charge on top of it all.

In the taxi on the way back to the hotel, Fonda reminded herself that the problem with Ian was no doubt cleared up by now, anyway. She leaned back in her seat and closed her eyes. What a night! It was after two in the morning before the police had said they could go.

Ryan had been released into the custody of his parents after giving his statement. To Jessie's relief, no charges had been filed against him.

Fonda glanced over at her, wondering if she ought to try to talk to her now. When she saw the girl's eyes close drowsily, she decided against it. Tomorrow would be soon enough.

Back in their room, Fonda tucked Jessie into bed and then made her way to Devin's suite. As she unlocked the door, she smiled, thinking how wonderful it was going to feel to slip into bed with him. To feel his warm length against her body. She felt like he'd been gone for days instead of hours.

She paused in the doorway of the bedroom. The drapes were open and the lights of a sleeping San Francisco spilled onto the rumpled bed. Fonda's heart lurched. It was just the way she'd left it.

Empty.

STUNNED, FONDA returned to her room. Her eyes stung with tears. There was no way she could sleep, not when her mind was spinning with ominous thoughts of Devin and what he was going through. Blindly, she reached for a tissue on the bedside table and then stared vacantly at the flashing light on the phone. Her heart gave a jolt. He'd left a message!

But moments later when she got the operator on the phone, she was disappointed to learn that the message told her nothing. "Don't worry. I'll be home soon." It had come in just after midnight. That would've been about the time she'd discovered Jessie with Ryan and O'Brien.

With nothing else to do, Fonda forced herself to try to get some sleep. Devin would be back when she woke up. He *had* to be.

But when she awoke and found he still hadn't returned, she tracked down Bram, only to learn he didn't know any more than she did. Fonda spent the morning pacing her room and occasionally making trips to Devin's suite.

Jessie awoke at nine o'clock and sullenly curled up on the bed to watch morning game shows on TV. Fonda thought about initiating a conversation about the events of the night before, but decided not to. In her worried state of mind, there was no way she could remain calm and rational with her younger sister. And what Jessie *didn't* need right now was a hysterical lecture. Once Devin was back—once he was okay—

At eleven o'clock, fighting a renewed sense of panic, Fonda went to Darcy for moral support. There was a distracted look on the Irishwoman's face when she opened the door.

"Come in, love. You've caught me in a bit of a frazzle."

Fonda looked around at the several pieces of open luggage on the sofa and the bed. "What's going on?"

Darcy chewed on her bottom lip, her blue eyes sad. "Cary has decided it's best we go home. Considering the problem with Ryan. Oh, love, I don't know what to say. We raised the boy better than that. I'm just overcome with shame, I am!"

Shocked, Fonda stared at her. "You're leaving? Laoise, too?"

"All three of us. But I want you to know, Fonda, I don't put any blame on your sister for this. And I don't want you to, either. She's just a wee lass. How could she help having her head turned by a boy like my Ryan? He's no better than a Casanova, he is!" She turned away, her eyes filling with tears. "It must be this lot he hangs around with. I told his father I didn't think it would be good for him to get mixed up with this music crowd."

"Oh, Darcy!" Fonda put her arms around the plump woman. "You can't blame it all on Ryan. It was both of them, you know. They're at that age. If it's anyone's fault, it's mine. I was so caught up in my work and Devin, I didn't do what I promised my parents I'd do. Watch out for Jessie. I should've seen it happening."

Darcy clung to her. "Oh, you're a dear friend. I thought you were going to hate me. I felt so ashamed of Ryan."

"How could I hate you? He's just a young man with a young man's urges. It has nothing to do with you."

Darcy pulled away, dabbing at her eyes with the tail of her shirt. "I just pray to the Holy Father that no baby was made last night." She looked at Fonda. "Not that I wouldn't be perfectly happy to have young Jessie as a daughter-in-law, you understand. I believe my boy when he says he loves her. But dear Lord, they're so young. I should know. It happened to me and Cary, but thank the good Lord, it worked out for us. But it's not easy."

Fonda nodded soberly. "Well, we have to hope they both acted responsibly. After all, I got the distinct impression it wasn't an impulsive idea."

"Did you, now? Well, perhaps you're right. Still, I think it's best we go. I hope Jessie will understand. Perhaps someday, when they're older . . ." Darcy turned away and began to briskly fold up clothes on the bed. "Ryan isn't taking it well, at all. He was like a madman when Cary told him. He tried to go to Jessie last night. It took all of our strength to hold him back. And Cary had to keep guard on him all night. He has calmed down some this morning, but he's still not speaking to any of us."

"And Laoise?" Fonda asked.

"Cried all the night through, the cheeky minx! She's daft about leaving Jessie." Darcy sat on the edge of the bed, her face glum. "I don't know if she'll ever forgive us for this. This morning, when we told her, she shouted that she hates us."

"You know that's just her anger talking."

"I know. Still, it hurts." Darcy looked down at her wristwatch. "We have about a half hour before we leave for the airport. Would you mind if Laoise went down to say good-bye? I think it might make her feel better."

Fonda nodded. "Why don't you tell her to go now? I'll stay here until she's back. That way, they'll have some time together."

Fonda waited while Darcy went to the connecting door and spoke a few words to Laoise. After a moment, the Irishwoman returned to her opened suitcase. "The girl didn't say a word. Still giving me the silent treatment. But she'll go. Now, what happened with Devin? Everything is all straightened up?"

At the mention of Devin, Fonda felt the now familiar lurch of fear in her heart. She knew it showed on her face. "He still isn't back. Oh God, Darcy! What does it mean?"

28

WHEN FONDA returned to her room, Jessie was sitting cross-legged on her bed, her red, swollen eyes on the TV where Laverne and Shirley cavorted around a hospital ward. The laugh track spilled out into the room, but Jessie's blank expression didn't change.

Darcy and Cary were right to send Laoise and Ryan home, Fonda thought. She should do the same with Jessie. Later, when she found out what was happening with Devin, she'd call the airlines and see about flights.

Now, she'd see what she could do about consoling her.

"Jess?" She sat gingerly on the edge of her bed.

The girl's eyes remained fixed on the television.

"Look, honey, I know how you feel. It's not easy to lose a first love and a girlfriend all in one day."

Jessie turned and looked at her. Her expression said it all. *You don't know anything about the way I feel.* But she remained silent.

Fonda tried again, "Look, it was the best thing. I take the blame for what happened. If I'd paid more attention, then maybe you and Ryan—"

This got a response. "What? Wouldn't have slept together? Oh, don't look so shocked, Fonda! Do you think you're the only girl in the world to have sexual feelings? I *liked* Ryan!"

"You *liked* Ryan?" Fonda said softly. "Jessie, you don't sleep with a guy because you like him. There has to be more to it than that."

"There was! I found him sexy. He found *me* sexy. Fonda, there was *chemistry* between us. I wanted him to be my first."

Fonda stared at her, at a loss for words. Finally, she asked the question that had been troubling her since last night. "And was he? I mean, did you have sex?"

A triumphant light appeared in Jessie's hazel eyes. "Oh, I'd say so. Up to a point, anyway."

"What do you mean?"

Jessie shrugged. "Well, I'm still a virgin. Technically, I guess. Does that make you feel better?"

It did, but Fonda decided to ignore the question. "I think it would be a good idea if you went home."

A stony expression settled on her sister's face. "What is it with you adults? Is that your answer to everything? Pack the kids off. Get 'em out of your hair. That was the Meehans' solution, wasn't it? How much did *you* have to do with that, Fonda?"

Fonda couldn't believe her ears. Where had this animosity come from? Their relationship had been so close. When had it started to change? "First of all, I found out about the Meehans just before you did. And secondly, let me remind you, if it weren't for me, you wouldn't be here. You wouldn't *be* my responsibility. So, don't try to make me feel guilty about sending you home. You know, I hate to say this, but it looks like Dad was right all the time. He didn't want you to stay with me because he thought it would be a bad influence. But I trusted you. And this is how you repay me."

Jessie remained stubbornly silent. Fonda saw the closed expression on her face and recognized it as the one every child wore in the middle of a parental lecture. It hurt to know she'd been the one delivering it.

She got up from the bed. "I'm going over to the stadium to see if the band has heard anything from Devin. Do you want to come?"

Jessie shook her head, her lips tight.

"Okay. You're confined to this room, Jessie. If you want to order from room service, you know where the phone is. I'll give you a call in about an hour."

The door closed after Fonda. Jessie used the remote to switch off the TV and then turning onto her stomach, buried her face into the pillow, and cried until there were no more tears left.

FONDA ENTERED Devin's dressing room at Candlestick Park and stopped short. Bram was sitting on a chair, tinkering with an electric guitar.

"Any news?" she asked, her heart accelerating.

"No, love. Not yet."

Blinking back tears, Fonda dropped to the sofa. "Oh, God. What's happening?"

He gave her a sympathetic glance. "It's useless for me to tell you not to worry, isn't it?"

She nodded. "Afraid so." Her eyes fastened upon the guitar across his lap. "At least you have something to do to keep you busy."

He snapped the amp off. "Yeh. Devin wanted me to fix this up so he could work on a new song here in his dressing room. But it won't work. There's just not enough voltage in here for the amp. He'll have to work in the tuning room."

"If he ever comes back," Fonda murmured.

Bram leaned the guitar against the amp and stood up. "I'll see if I can find out something for you."

She gave him a weak smile. "Thanks, Bram. You're a sweetheart."

His hand briefly touched her shoulder. "I'll be right back."

After he was gone, Fonda dropped her face into her hands and felt the tears seep between her fingers. She was so afraid.

"I told you I'd cause you pain, Fon."

Her heart lurched. She looked up to see Devin standing in the doorway, his face lined with fatigue and his eyes veiled with sadness. In a second, she was in his arms, burying her face into his warm musk-scented neck. He gathered her close and bent down to press his lips against her hair. Her hands moved up and down his well-muscled arms, as if assuring herself he was really there.

"I'm sorry I couldn't call again," he said. "Things got a bit intense there for a while."

Fonda pulled away slightly to gaze up at him. Her eyes were frightened. "They said you were being investigated for arms smuggling. Is that true?"

His face grew grimmer. "Then you know. Yeh, they think I knew about Brinegar and his shenanigans. But they've let me go pending the investigation. Don't worry, love. It will be straightened out. Everyone who knows me *knows* I'd never get involved with that lot. And the FBI will determine that soon enough."

"What about Ian?" Fonda asked.

His face tightened. "I'm sorry to say it's all true. He's admitted everything. They deported him to Northern Ireland this morning to face the charges. Kyle is going to take over management of the tour so we can finish up in L.A. next week."

Fonda clung to him. "Oh, Devin, how can they possibly think you're involved with the IRA?"

Devin's hands clenched down on her shoulders. "Thank God you believe in me, love. It was all I could think about. Fonda, tonight after the concert, we have to talk. There's some things you have to know about my past. I'd tell you now, but Kyle has set up a press conference in about fifteen minutes. I was told it's all over the news about the investigation and he thinks it best if we try to set things straight right away."

"I think that's a good idea," Fonda said. "I'll come with you."

He kissed her forehead. "Christ, there must've been an angel looking over me the day you entered my life. What would I do without you? Come on, then. The sooner we get this press conference over, the sooner we can get to a sound check for the concert."

Fonda stared up at him. "Devin, you can't be serious about performing tonight! You haven't slept in over twenty-four hours."

"I have to. Tickets have been sold out for months. I can't disappoint them, Fon. You know that." He lifted her chin and his mouth moved over hers in a gentle, searching kiss. "I missed you."

Of course, she *did* understand; Devin had to go on with the concert. If he didn't, he wouldn't be the man she loved. Besides, soon this nightmare would be over. The press conference would set everything right. The FBI would clear him of all charges and everything would be back to normal. It *had* to be. Fonda couldn't bring herself to think of the alternative.

A TEMPEST of clicking cameras and the blinding stab of flashbulbs greeted Devin as he took a seat in front of a microphone and stared out at the crowd of journalists from national magazines, newspapers, and television. He blinked and looked away from the flickering lights. His eyes found Fonda standing on the periphery of the crowd. In her hands, she held her camera, but had made no move to photograph him. Her face was apprehensive, her eyes haunted. He knew she was torn between her duty toward the book and her loyalty to him. It was almost as if he could read her mind. If she took a photo of him, it would be as if she were joining forces with the others against him.

And against him they would be, unless he could find the right words to get them back on his side.

He forced himself to smile at Fonda and then lifted his hands to pantomime a camera shot. She nodded and raised her camera. Devin looked down at the table and ran his hand through his hair nervously. God, if only he could get a few hours sleep. He was so exhausted he could barely think. How on earth was he going to get through this grueling press conference?

Kyle McKenna took a seat next to him and gave a nod. It was the signal to get started. Devin cleared his throat and looked up at the staring faces in front of him. Was it his fatigue that made them look like voracious wolves closing in for the kill?

"Thank you for coming," he began, but his voice was immediately drowned by cries from the press.

"Speak up, Devin!"

"Louder! Can't hear you."

Devin adjusted the microphone. "Sorry. Thank you for coming today." His eyes scanned the room and found Fonda. The tentative smile she gave him was just what he needed to go on. "As you know, my manager, Ian Brinegar, was arrested yesterday on a charge of gun-running for the IRA and was deported this morning. Because he has been accused and not convicted, at this time I feel it would be inappropriate for me to make any further statement about him." He paused, trying to get his thoughts in order. A chorus of questions arose from the crowd, none of them intelligible.

Kyle bent his head toward his mike and spoke. "Please— Devin will answer questions after he makes his statement."

Devin took a deep breath and began: "As you know, there was a report released last night that I'm being investigated in connection with my manager's alleged arms smuggling. I would like to say, unequivocally, I have not, nor have I *ever* been involved in such dealings. Most of you who know me know I have been vehemently outspoken against the IRA from the beginning of my career. I deplore their tactics, and as much as I want to see Northern Ireland given back to the Irish, I would *never* support violence as a way to accomplish it." He paused, and once again, the questions filled the room. Waiting until silence was restored, he went on: "I'm confident the FBI will soon clear me of suspicion. In the meantime, I hope all of you will pray for Ian. Innocent or guilty, I know he can use our prayers."

Kyle spoke into his mike. "Devin will answer any of your questions now. We have about ten minutes."

The explosion of questions began. Devin rubbed his forehead where it was beginning to throb. He tried to concentrate, but the noise was so great, it was impossible to distinguish one question from another.

"Please! One question at a time." Kyle pointed to a petite blonde wearing round tortoiseshell glasses.

"Dena Kohlhal from *Entertainment Tonight*," she said crisply, her eyes on Devin. "Devin, how is it possible that your manager could've been smuggling arms to Northern Ireland all this time just *under your nose?* Were you never suspicious?"

Devin closed his eyes. How was it possible to make them understand about his relationship with Ian? He'd never really liked the man, but he'd trusted him implicitly. For Christ's sake, Ian had been with him since Pat Sullivan's accident. His face blanched. During the confusion following Pat's surgery and subsequent hospitalization, Caitlyn had brought Ian into their lives. Had she been reaching out beyond her prison cell to orchestrate Ian's operation all these years?

His silence was being taken for guilt. He could feel the changed atmosphere. They were turning against him. He struggled to find words to answer the question.

"First of all, Ian has been *accused*. Nothing more. I hope it's all an ugly mistake. But should he be found guilty, I can only say that, yes, he did it under my nose, as you put it. I have no answer as to how it was possible. Except for the fact that I trusted him—" His voice broke, and for a moment, he couldn't go on. His eyes slid to Fonda's white face. He shook his head and said again, "I trusted him."

"Devin, Justin Tilmon from *Spotlight*. Isn't it true you grew up in the violence of Northern Ireland? You were from a Catholic family, discriminated against, hated by the Protestants. Are you telling us you somehow remained apart from the situation? You didn't choose to fight on the side of your people?"

Devin's head swam. Jesus! This was one thing he hadn't expected. If they were going to dredge up the past, they would be here the whole bleeding day. He took a deep breath and leaned toward the mike.

"I left Derry at the age of nineteen. When I did that, I left the Troubles behind. Whatever I felt as a child has nothing to do with my life now."

A man with a bandana and a long ponytail raised his hand and laconically got to his feet. "Hugh Holmes, the *Ulster Star*." His heavy Belfast accent gave Devin a smothering sense of foreboding. "It's a known fact, Mr. O'Keefe, that you were briefly married to one Caitlyn MacManus from the Catholic ghetto of Falls Road in Belfast."

Devin's stomach clenched. The room had gone deathly still. Devin's eyes focused on Bram standing at the back of the room. The roadie's face had tensed. Devin looked back at the Belfast reporter. "That's true. What is your question?"

The man's thin lips parted in a sneer. Again, Devin was reminded of a hungry wolf preparing to spring for his prey.

"And isn't it also true, Mr. O'Keefe, that the very same Caitlyn MacManus—or O'Keefe, as was her proper name at the time—died during an IRA bombing at a Belfast department store?"

The silence in the room was complete as if everyone held a collective breath, waiting for him to speak.

Devin closed his eyes. Christ! Would this conference ever end? "Yes," he said softly. "It was reported in all the newspapers and magazines at the time. What does that have to do with Ian Brinegar?" He knew very well what it had to do with Brinegar. But surely no one else knew of Caitlyn's IRA connections. That she was alive and in prison. His heart pounded. There was something about the self-satisfied smile on the reporter's lips that warned him of what was to come.

"Oh, I'll tell you, then, Mr. O'Keefe. Isn't it true that your wife was *not* an innocent victim of an IRA bomb, but was, in fact"—he paused, his face triumphant—"one of the individuals responsible for *setting* the bomb?"

A chorus of voices rose in the room, all of them shouting at once. Hugh Holmes's voice carried over them all. *"Your wife was an active volunteer for the IRA, wasn't she, Mr. O'Keefe?"*

WITH A grim smile, Caitlyn watched the TV screen as the press conference erupted in pandemonium. The guy who'd taken over for Brinegar stood up and waved his hands. "That's all, folks. Thanks for coming."

Caitlyn turned off the TV and paced the hotel room, massaging her forehead under her thick cap of black hair. Everything was falling apart. That bastard Brinegar! Getting himself arrested and screwing everything up. She should've followed her instincts and taken him out sooner. Maybe back in St. Louis when he'd first started coming apart at the seams. Now what?

If he talked—and the lily-livered gazelle *would* talk—it would be only a matter of time until the FBI came after her. If she was going to go out, she'd damn well do it with a bang. Something that would make the world headlines. And who better to make the world headlines with than Devin O'Keefe?

Devin. God, he made her sick! He could've been such an asset to the Cause. In his position, he had the press hanging on his every word. The perfect platform to stand up and tell the world of the atrocities the Brits and Protestants committed against the Catholics. The discrimination and verbal abuse. The sectarian murders engineered by the RUC. Devin could have made a difference if he'd chosen to.

But no! He'd turned his back on his heritage. The coward! And look how he was rewarded. Money, prestige, respect. Love and happiness. She frowned. That bitch, Fonda! How could he love a pampered American princess like her? What did *she* know about loss? About life in a war zone? How *could* he have fallen in love with a shallow entertainment photographer? God, how she'd love to teach that little bitch about loss.

She sank into a chair next to the window overlooking the Trans America Building and stared at the skyline thoughtfully. Devin had two concerts in San Francisco. Tonight's would be too soon to take action. She needed time to plan. Whatever happened, it would take place tomorrow night. Surely she could evade the FBI for another twenty-four hours or so. But what could she do? How could she get past security?

She rubbed her forehead, thinking. One thing for sure, she'd have to hit Devin where he was most vulnerable. Her lips curled in a satisfied smile. There was no doubt where that was.

Fonda.

THE BRIGHT lights from the press conference went out. Devin sat numbly, his head in his hands. It was beginning to look disastrous for him. How, for Christ's sake, had that Ulster reporter ferreted out that information on Caitlyn? Ian had been so thorough in covering it up. Why, now, had it come to light? No one except Ian and Bram had known about Caitlyn's IRA connection. Not even Fonda.

His head shot up. Fonda was standing stiffly in the middle of the surging crowd. Her face was a translucent shade of white; her eyes dark and full of horror. Devin's stomach dropped. Jesus! If he lost her on top of everything else, he'd bloody well go crazy.

Then, as if his soul was reaching out to touch hers, he saw her face change. It had been a nasty shock, but she understood. She would forgive him for not confiding in her.

Slowly, she approached the table where he sat.

He couldn't stop himself from trembling as he got to his feet. The long night without sleep and the emotional turmoil had started to wreak havoc with his system. Fonda came around the table. Her eyes sparkled with unshed tears as she reached up a hand to touch his cheek.

"You should have told me about Caitlyn," she said softly. "Oh, Devin. You have to learn to trust me."

He wrenched her to him, burying his face into the sweet scent of her hair. Her camera crushed against his chest. "Oh, love—I trust you more than I trust myself. I'm just a foolhardy man that can't let go of a dark past." His hand stroked her small, well-shaped head under the mass of curls. "But tonight, after the concert, I swear to you, I'm going to let go of it all. Then there will be nothing between us—no secrets," he amended, as a coldness settled upon his heart.

Caitlyn. She was between them. Would always be. Could Fonda forgive that? Could she forgive the fact that he had a living wife? That he'd intended to marry Fonda in spite of it? Because, of course, marriage would be impossible now. Fonda would never willingly commit bigamy.

That he could live with. But if she left him? If she refused to have anything further to do with him? Devin closed his eyes and pulled her pliant body closer. If that happened, it wouldn't matter if the FBI arrested him for conspiring with Ian to smuggle guns.

Nothing would matter.

29

THE VEINS in Devin's neck bulged as he neared the end of one of his personal favorites, "Lost," a song about victims of Chernobyl's nuclear disaster. He'd been singing for almost two hours, and Fonda, as she watched the monitor backstage, knew he couldn't go on much longer. The performance was taking everything out of him. His clothes were wet with the sweat that seeped from his body as he clutched the microphone and belted out the last lines. When his voice faded as he ran out of breath, Fonda felt an overwhelming pang of love for him. He gave so much to his audience, even when he physically wasn't able. He stumbled away from the microphone as the band played on. The crowd cheered wildly, unwilling to let him go. Fonda turned from the monitor to look toward the stage. She *wouldn't* let him go back out. Enough was enough.

Disoriented by fatigue, Devin staggered backstage, grabbing the towel from the wardrobe woman. Fonda hurried to meet him. He threw his arms around her, clinging to her like a drowning man clutching a lifeboat. She held his damp sagging body against her and stroked his soaking hair. "Somebody help me get him back to the hotel!" she called out.

He turned his head and his lips slid along her cheek. "The newspaper was wrong," he whispered. "They came." He went limp in her arms.

Bram and another stagehand appeared at her side and took him from her. Fonda followed behind them as they swept him outside to the waiting limo. The newspaper article *had* been wrong. They'd predicted that because of the IRA scandal, there would be hundreds of no-shows. But they'd underestimated Devin's fans. The stadium had been packed with supporting fans, many of whom carried posters proclaiming their belief in Devin's innocence. Fonda knew just how much that support meant to Devin.

As the limo drove back to the hotel, Devin spoke only once. His face was nestled against her neck, and for a brief moment, he opened his eyes and whispered: "Fon, I have to tell you . . ." His eyes closed again. "I . . . have to . . ."

She stroked his cheek. One finger followed the line of his nose, over the bump where it had once been broken. She kept forgetting to ask him how it had happened. "Shhh—you can tell me later."

He sighed and nodded. "Later . . ."

He didn't speak again.

A half hour later, she was helping him into bed. Immediately, he fell into an exhausted sleep. Fonda lay on her side, staring at the shadowed planes of his slumbering face. Her fingers ached to reach out and touch him, but she didn't, lest she wake him.

Just before falling into an uneasy sleep, her last thoughts were of Ian Brinegar and the investigation against Devin. Perhaps tomorrow he'd be cleared. It had to be soon. She didn't think Devin's health could take much more abuse.

THE RINGING phone broke the silence of the hotel room. Fonda bolted up and grabbed it before it could wake Devin. "Hello?"

"This is Jacky O'Brien."

For a second, Fonda was frozen in shock. Outside the room, a cart rolled by, a waiter bringing room service to an early morning riser. Her eyes slid to Devin, still cocooned in the sleep of exhaustion. In the turmoil of yesterday's events, she'd completely forgotten about O'Brien and his attack upon Jessie. She scrambled to the edge of the bed, turned her back to Devin, and lowered her voice. "What do *you* want?"

"Just a moment of your time. I was wondering if you could meet me in the coffee shop downstairs? I have something to show you."

Fury ripped through her. "Whatever we have to say to each other, we can say in court, you son-of-a-bitch!"

Behind her, Devin groaned and rolled over in his sleep. A waft of heather-scented skin, Devin's scent, washed over her. Fonda held her breath, mentally kicking herself for losing her temper. What Devin *didn't* need right now was more worry. "What're you doing here, anyway?" she went on. "I thought you were safely behind bars."

There was a soft chuckle at the other end of the line. "It's called bail, honey. And after we have our wee talk, I'm of the mind that you'll be dropping the charges entirely."

Fonda sprang up. "You've got to be out of your mind. After what you tried to do to my sister? Not fucking likely!"

"Ooooh! Such strong language from Saint Devin's intended." His voice was laced with amusement. Then it hardened, his Irish accent becoming thicker. "Get yourself down to the coffee shop, girl. I have some information that just might stop ya from making the biggest mistake of ya life."

The cozy warmth of the bedclothes and Devin's body next to hers could do nothing to stop the sudden chill that ran through Fonda. "I'm not interested in anything scum like you has to say, O'Brien. Now, if you don't mind—"

"Don't hang up, Fonda," he said grimly. "It might not bother you to become the wife of an IRA Provo. But do you fancy becoming a bigamist as well?"

THE CLATTER of silverwear mingled with the murmur of conversation in the hotel coffee shop as Fonda sat across from Jacky O'Brien. The sounds were no different than they were on any other morning, but she felt as if she were hearing them from inside a vacuum. The rich smells of fresh-perked coffee and frying bacon saturated the air, but instead of making her feel hungry, she felt nauseous. Uncomfortably conscious of Jacky's smug gaze upon her, she held the copy of the *Daily Mirror* between shaking hands, her eyes glued to the glaring headline:

BRINEGAR TELLS ALL, DEVIN O'KEEFE'S IRA CONNECTION

Jacky sipped his coffee as Fonda read the article in the London tabloid, the blood inside her veins growing colder with every vile sentence. She read how the teenage Devin had spent his weekends throwing petrol bombs at the British patrols—how he was continually involved in brawls against neighboring Protestants. But it wasn't until Devin met Caitlyn MacManus at age twenty-one that he became involved with the tougher elements of the IRA, the Provisionals.

Yesterday, she'd been shocked by the discovery that Caitlyn had been responsible for the bombing of the Belfast department store, but one look at Devin's stricken face had convinced her to forgive this omission of the truth. Now, according to Ian Brinegar's revelations, Caitlyn had been setting the bomb *on Devin's orders* when it had gone off, killing her and several others, including two children.

Even that, Fonda was inclined to dismiss as the hysterical ravings of Devin's embittered ex-manager. Nothing in the world would make her believe that her gentle Devin could order the cold-blooded murder of innocent people. But the next paragraph sent her brain reeling, and she had to read it twice just to make sure she wasn't interpreting it wrong.

Afterwards, she sat stiffly, her eyes unfocused. Conversation ebbed and flowed around her. Laughter punctuated the morning. How could people be laughing when her heart was breaking? She felt as if every drop of blood in her body had congealed into a solid mass.

A sour-faced waitress appeared to pour more coffee for Jacky. After a caustic look at Fonda for not ordering anything, she moved away. Jacky gave a harsh laugh. "A nasty bit of news, eh? Who would've thought that Caitlyn O'Keefe, instead of being blown to bits, has been rotting in a prison cell in Armagh?" His tongue clicked against the roof of his mouth in mock sympathy. "And what a shock it must be for you. Seeing as how you were about to become the second Mrs. O'Keefe. Quite rude of him not to tell you, don't you think? That the first one is still alive?"

Fonda pushed away from the table. His hand clamped upon her arm. "Not so fast, love. There's the matter of an attempted rape charge we need to discuss. I've done you a favor by alerting you to O'Keefe's plan to turn you into a bigamist. Now, can you find it in your heart to drop the charges against me?"

Fonda stared at Jacky's weasel face, finding it increasingly difficult to breathe. She was still reeling from the shock of discovering Caitlyn was still alive. It *had* to be a mistake! A fantasy of delusion woven by the obviously unbalanced Ian Brinegar.

And now this idiot wanted her to drop the charges against him.

She summoned up the strength to speak. "Enjoy your days of freedom, Jacky. I don't know where I'm going to be when your court date comes up, but it doesn't matter. If I have to, I'll crawl over hot coals to see that you're locked away." She slid out of the booth and stood up.

Somehow, she made her way out of the coffee shop. As she waited for an elevator, she could no longer ignore the shrill voices inside her head. *Devin lied to you about Caitlyn. What else has he lied about?*

No!—she wouldn't listen! Devin would explain everything. He would tell her the British newspaper had it all wrong. They'd printed nothing but lies. Cruel, vicious lies that had no foundation in fact. He *would* do that.

For the sake of their future, he *had* to do that.

DEVIN SCRAPED the razor down his gaunt cheek, humming a new tune that had been floating in his head when he'd awakened. Mother Mary, the sleep had done him good. He felt optimistic this morning, ready to face the press, the FBI, and anyone else who was determined to cause trouble for him. Thanks to Fonda. Although last night's events were murky in his mind, one thing was crystal clear: Fonda had stuck by him; she'd been there every moment.

Today, they would begin their new life together. With no shadows of the past between them. He glanced at his wristwatch. The ferry for Sausalito left at nine-fifteen. They would have breakfast at that quaint little café overlooking the harbor. And there, he'd tell her the truth about Caitlyn.

It would be a shock at first, of course. But she'd understand. He'd *make* her understand.

The door to his suite opened. "Is that you, love?" Devin rinsed the razor under the running faucet.

Fonda appeared in the doorway to the bathroom, but she didn't speak. In short, practiced strokes, Devin finished shaving under his chin and turned to look at her. His ready smile froze when he saw her face. He dropped the razor into the sink, his heart a leaden stone inside his chest.

"What's happened now?"

"This." She held out the London newspaper.

He took it and began to read. She watched his face, waiting for some sign of reaction, but his expression remained blank. From the suite next door came the grind of pipes and then the hum of the shower. Voices murmured through the wall. After a long moment, Devin folded the paper in half and turned away from her. Silently, he took a towel from the rack and began methodically wiping the shaving cream from his face.

Fonda stared at him incredulously. "Devin! For God's sake, say something!"

Finally, he looked at her. She recoiled from the pain in his eyes. "It's not true, is it?" she whispered, still clinging to a swiftly fading hope.

He brushed past her out of the bathroom and strode to the window overlooking the Bay Bridge. His voice was low when he spoke, but she heard every word.

"Some of it's true. Some of it's not."

Fonda's tight rein on her emotions snapped. "What's true? You're an IRA bomber? Or just your everyday ordinary bigamist?"

His face paled. "Please, Fonda. If you're to understand, I have to start at the beginning. It's something I should have done a long time ago."

"Damn right! What about your childhood in Derry? Is it true you were involved in gang violence against the British?"

His lips cracked in a bitter smile. "What an innocent you are. Every Catholic child in Derry was involved in violence against the Brits. I've told you about the petrol bombs. And yes, once I was arrested for joy-riding with an older friend who had an IRA connection. It was the one and only time. The Provos frown upon that sort of thing, you see. Once they threatened us with kneecapping, we didn't do it again. You probably don't know what that is, do you?" His face had grown hard. It was a stranger's face. "That's when they shoot your kneecaps full of bullets. Not to kill ya, but to cripple ya for life. Now, I hear they have a new way of doing it called 'tooling.' They use a power drill. Saves on bullets, you know."

Her vision blurred as the dizziness swept over her. Was this her Devin speaking so coldly about such things as "kneecapping"? And his face! She'd never seen such a remote expression on his lean features. It chilled her to the bone.

"Oh, God." She sat down abruptly on the unmade bed and dropped her face into her hands. She felt him next to her, inhaled the fresh-scented cleanliness of his body, wanted him in spite of everything, but when he touched her arm, she jerked away. "How could you lie to me like this? You and your protest songs, your pleas for world peace, and all the time, you're IRA."

"No!" He grabbed her arm and forced her to look at him. "I *never* became a volunteer. But there was no way to escape their influence. Not when you live in the Bogside. But when I finally made my way to Dublin, I thought I'd left that life behind forever. And I had, until I met Caitlyn."

"And what about Caitlyn?" Fonda lashed out. "You lied about

her, too. You let me believe she was dead. Is it true, Devin? Is your wife still alive?"

His hand clenched upon her arm. "Yes, she is. But let me start at the beginning." Devin took a deep breath, then began to talk quietly. "First of all, I *was* going to tell you everything. I tried once, the night at Sun Devil. But you didn't want to hear it then, and I guess I really didn't want to tell you. I was too afraid of losing you. But when all this happened with Ian, I knew I had to come clean." He looked at her, his face ravaged with the pain of memory.

"You don't know what it's like to grow up in Northern Ireland. Every night when you go to bed, you hear the rioting in the streets. The gunshots. The breaking glass. You've heard of Bloody Sunday? I was ten years old. I was there in Derry when the British paratroopers opened fire upon the crowd. Innocent anti-internment marchers. That word may not be familiar to you, an American who's never had to worry about her father being put in prison for no other reason than the fact that he's a Catholic." His voice was cold, almost scornful. "'Lifted,' we call it. That's what the people were there to protest that day. You see this scar?" He pointed to the tiny crescent-shaped mark on his bicep. "I took a British bullet. If it weren't for a friend who risked his life to drag me from the street, I might not be here today. My sixteen-year-old brother, Glen, was killed that day. And yes, I hated the Brits for it. I wanted revenge upon Glen's murderers, and upon the Protestants who'd persecuted us for so long."

Devin stood up and walked over to the window. To Fonda, his voice seemed to be coming from a great distance. "But after my father was released from prison, I began to realize how very senseless the violence was. I knew it was gaining us nothing—except hatred around the world. There was a girl . . ." He paused a moment, lost in memory. "Mary Marie. We were both young. Too young, probably, to feel the way we did about each other. But I was set to marry her as soon as I turned eighteen." He looked back at her, his eyes bleak. Their expression sent a shiver through Fonda. "But she didn't make it to my eighteenth birthday. The IRA saw to that with a bomb meant for the security forces. Instead, it took out a bus full of Christmas shoppers. Mary Marie was one of them. That was when I knew I had to get away from that life. I wanted nothing more to do with it."

"But then you met Caitlyn." It came out accusingly. She couldn't help it.

His eyes closed, hiding his pain. He gave a short nod. "Then I met Caitlyn." Again, he turned away and gazed out the window. "How do I make you understand what it was like for me with her? Mary Marie had been the only girl I ever loved. When Caitlyn came into my life, she consumed me. I couldn't think when I was around her. I didn't want to think. I only wanted to love her."

Fonda felt a rush of jealous rage wash over her. Oh, she'd known Devin had loved his wife. But she'd never felt she had to compete with a ghost. Now, it was altogether different. Caitlyn O'Keefe was alive, and imprisoned or not, she was Devin's legal wife.

"And do you still love her?"

The blood drained from Devin's face. "How can you ask me that?" he asked quietly. "Do you not know me at all?"

Fonda bit her lip. She wasn't at all sure she did. "Go on with your story."

He ran his hand through his damp hair, causing it to stand up in spiky tufts. "Ah, what's the use? I feel like I've already been condemned and ordered in front of the firing squad." But he shook his head and went on. "I didn't find out she was an IRA volunteer until just before we were due to be married. It all came out when her younger brother was shot by the UVF. An illegal Protestant paramilitary force. I broke off with her. But I admit it, I still loved her. I thought she was misguided, warped by the life she'd lived on Falls Road. But I think if she hadn't tried to commit suicide, I would never have seen her again. I was that dead-set against her activities. But when she swore to me she would give up the IRA for me, I allowed myself to believe it." He was silent for a long moment, his forehead resting against the glass of the window. "The bombing of the department store happened while I was in America for my first tour. Afterwards, Ian insisted we cover up the truth. That my IRA wife was alive. I fought him on it, but not for long, I admit. He insisted the truth would kill my career. I allowed him to convince me of that."

"Do you see her? At the prison, I mean?"

"Only once. Right after it happened. I couldn't believe what Ian told me was true. The only way I would accept it was for her to tell me to my face."

"And did she?"

A bitter laugh came from him. "Oh, yes. She did that. She called herself a patriot—and called me a Brit-loving bastard, among other things."

"And you haven't seen her again?"

"Once was enough."

Fonda stared at the droplets of water on his smooth back, wishing she could forget everything that had happened and just go over and wrap her arms around him. She wanted to kiss the mole on his right shoulder . . . to touch the scar left by the bullet. But she knew she couldn't do it. He'd *lied* to her. He'd meant to marry her, knowing very well he wasn't free to do so. How could she forgive that?

He turned around. "I fell in love with a very clever actress. I never knew the real Caitlyn."

"Just as I don't really know you." She hadn't meant for the words to come out, but they did. Their eyes met and the pain she saw in his forced her to turn away.

"But you do," he said, his voice just above a whisper. "You're the only person in the world who really knows me. And I need you, Fonda."

When she didn't respond, he came toward her, his eyes pleading. "Don't let this come between us. We have something special. Don't throw it away because of the mistakes I've made in the past."

Moments passed in tense silence. Then Fonda said, "Why would Ian lie about all this? Why would he say you ordered Caitlyn to plant that bomb if it weren't true?"

Devin shook his head. "I've been blind to everything, it seems. When I went to bail him out the other night, I wasn't prepared for his reaction. He literally *spewed* venom at me. I found out how he has really felt about me all these years. Because I believe in peace, he thinks I'm a traitor to my country. Why the lies?" He shrugged listlessly. "I suppose he believes it's the only way he can hurt me now. Ruin my career." Devin looked straight at her. "And drive away the only woman that means anything to me. Are you going to let him win, Fonda?"

"I can't think straight here." She stood up. "I've got to go some-where—away . . ."

Devin finished the sentence for her. ". . . away from me. Yeah, perhaps you should. Just one thing . . ." He reached toward her, but stopped short of touching her. Almost as if he were afraid. "Whatever you decide, I want you to remember one thing. Everything I've done—every lie I've told has been because I love you. And because I've been terrified of losing you."

Fonda turned away, a crushing pain in her heart. As she reached the door of the hotel room, he spoke again.

"Do you remember how you felt when you lost Michael? It was like that for me. With Glen, Mary Marie—Da and Mam, and finally, Caitlyn. Don't you go, too, Fonda. I'm begging you . . ."

Without looking back, she left the room. The door closed quietly behind her.

PART FIVE

Inferno

30

THE DOOR to Fonda's suite slammed. Her head snapped up, and through her tears, she saw Jessie's sturdy form standing just inside the room. It made her cry harder. Jessie, the little sister who'd always come to her for comfort, had come this time to give it. Fonda's chin dropped to her chest. But Jessie couldn't comfort her. No one could.

"I just came from seeing Devin. Do you know what you've done to him?" Jessie's voice was anything but sympathetic.

Fonda looked up at her sister. Had she heard right? But the tight-faced expression on Jessie's pale face told the story. Fonda shook her head slowly as if trying to dislodge water from her ears. "What I've done to *him?*"

"You've deserted him." Her voice was icy. "All you had to do was stand beside him. That would've given the world a clear message that he's innocent of wrongdoing."

"I wish I could have," Fonda said haltingly. "But I'm not sure he *is* innocent."

Jessie's face grew even whiter. "Fonda, you don't really mean that!"

Fonda stood up, angrily brushing the tears away. "What am I supposed to think? You tell me *what*. The man has been lying to me from the beginning." She moved over to the table near the window and stared down at the folded copy of the *Daily Mirror.* "Jessie, he made wedding plans with me, and all the time, he had a wife in a Northern Ireland prison cell! You tell me what I'm supposed to think?"

Jessie crossed the room to the table and picked up the offending newspaper. "Well, seeing as how I'm so inexperienced in matters of love, I couldn't possibly say anything that might make any sense to you. But if you ask me, you don't listen to what's in *this*." She flung the newspaper to the floor and tapped her chest, her face mutinous. "But what's in here. Or are you so distracted by everything happening outside that you don't listen to your heart anymore?"

For a moment, Fonda stared at Jessie. Her reddish eyebrows were drawn over her eyes in a straight line. Each freckle stood out like a little light in her pale face. It was as if the sixteen-year-old in front of her had aged by ten years. But almost immediately, Fonda realized it wasn't wisdom talking but idealistic youth. She turned away and stared out the window at the mid-morning sun sparkling on San Francisco.

"You're just a child. You can't possibly understand what's happening here."

"I don't need to understand," Jessie said crisply. "I know Devin. That's enough for me."

The pain in Fonda's chest twisted. God, why couldn't it be that easy for her? Abruptly, she turned back to the table and grabbed her purse. "I have to get out of here for a while. When I get back, I'll make arrangements for your flight home."

Jessie was silent until Fonda reached the door. Then her voice came, cold and very unchildlike. "Why is it everyone has to be perfect for you to love them?"

Fonda felt her head go light. She turned around. "What?"

Jessie wore a cold smile on her lips. "You heard me. Take me, for instance. I was your sweet baby sister up until night before last. But when you found me with Ryan, I fell off that tidy little pedestal you've put me on. And yes, you still love me, but it's changed, hasn't it? You don't feel the same as you did before."

"Jessie, don't be ridiculous."

"But Michael? He's still up there, isn't he, Fon? On that precious shrine you've made for him. His own special pedestal. You won't let yourself believe the truth about him, will you? You're too afraid you'll stop loving his memory if you do."

Fonda's body had stiffened at the mention of Michael. Jessie was going too far now. "What do you mean by that? What truth about Michael?"

"That he was weak. That he allowed Dad to force him into police work when all he wanted was to work with animals. No. You'd rather blame it all on Dad. It's easier for you to do that than admit Michael wasn't strong enough to insist on doing what he wanted."

Fonda was speechless. How could Jessie turn on her like this? They'd always been together on everything. Why, now, was she attacking her?

But she wasn't finished. "You know what your problem is, Fonda? You expect too much from people . . . especially the ones you say you love. And when they don't live up to your expectations, you either walk away or blame their shortcomings on someone else. Are you going to walk away from Devin now? When he really needs you?"

Fonda began to tremble. She *wouldn't* listen to any more of this. *Oh, Jessie, when did you become so vicious?* Fonda whirled around and opened the door. It slammed behind her as she ran down the corridor toward the elevators.

THE HOURS of the day melted by in a melange of colors and noise. When Fonda left the entrance of the Hyatt Regency, she began to walk along the streets of San Francisco. At Market and Sutter, she caught the cable car to Fisherman's Wharf. Through the jangle of the car's bells, she tried to concentrate on the conversational antics of the spirited operator, grateful for any diversion that would drive away the voices inside her head. Devin's voice. Jacky's. Jessie's. They were all pulling her in different directions. And then, of course, there was the ugly, sneering voice of Ian Brinegar, quoted by the *Daily Mirror.* How much of his voice told the truth?

All too soon, the cable car reached Fisherman's Wharf. For a moment, she stood in the milling crowd, wondering what to do. Finally, she began to walk along the wharf side of the street.

It was one of those crystal blue San Francisco days with a cloudless sky, and as always, a cool brisk wind whipping in from the bay. Fonda pulled her jacket closer around her.

Seagulls wheeled low in the sky over the harbor, calling out in raucous song. Fonda reached the renovated Pier 39, a shopping area teeming with tourists. It was exactly what she needed at the moment. Noise and bustle. Even the sound of rap music from a passing boom-box was welcome to her . . . anything to drown out the voices.

She walked all the way to the end of the pier, pausing now and then to stare into the shop windows. She lost count of the times she found herself thinking, *Devin would like this,* or, *I'll have to bring Devin back here to show him this.* Each time, the morning's event came back with a crushing blow.

At the end of Pier 39, as the afternoon sun beamed its warmth upon her face, she leaned against the rail overlooking the harbor and watched the ferry from Sausalito carve a swath through the water. Behind the ferry crouched the island of Alcatraz. Even in the bright sunlight, it seemed menacing. Although the prison was closed now, it was as if ghosts lingered around it, forever haunting its boundaries.

Or was Devin's Irish superstition rubbing off on her?

How ironic that a penitentiary had existed in San Francisco Bay just a stone's throw from one of the loveliest cities in America. Was it like that for Caitlyn, too, in her prison in County Armagh? Was she surrounded by rolling green hills and beauty, a piece of heaven that existed just outside the gates of hell?

Why did she care? This unknown woman was the cause of her heartbreak today. If it weren't for her existence, she and Devin could . . . could what? Go on as before?

For the first time, she thought about it. What if there *were* no Caitlyn? Suppose everything else had happened as it had? Ian arrested, accusing Devin of conspiring with him to supply the IRA with arms. Would she be here now? Or would she be with Devin, supporting him? Believing in him? Wasn't she basing her doubts and confusion about Devin on one lie? A lie he'd told for the simple reason that he loved her and was afraid of losing her?

Not for a moment could she really believe Devin was involved with the IRA. She thought of all the videos in which he'd sung the protest songs. How could he fake that emotion? That night early in the tour, she'd seen tears in his eyes as he'd sung about a murdered little boy. *He cared.* God, he cared about those victims. He could *never* give support to a bunch of fanatics, not now when he was old enough and sane enough to know better.

Suddenly she remembered the afternoon when they'd first made love. He'd been overcome with sorrow over the deaths of four British soldiers. Was *that* characteristic of an IRA supporter?

"It was in the past," she whispered. "How can I punish him for being young, for falling in with the wrong people?"

But then, Fonda's eyes filled with tears. The man she loved was *married!* In the eyes of the world, she and Devin could never be man and wife. Was she prepared to go through life as his woman, never his wife? Fonda hadn't been to church in years, not since before Michael died, but still, her Christian beliefs ran strong in her. No matter how much she and Devin loved each other, they wouldn't be married in the eyes of God. Could she live with that?

Better that than living without him. She turned away from the harbor, tears streaming down her face. Eyes looked her way and then veered off, embarrassed for intruding. She had to find a phone!

But when she did, the phone in Devin's suite rang five times before the operator picked it up to say the obvious. "There's no answer, miss. Can I take a message?"

Fonda looked at her watch and was stunned to see it was almost six o'clock. The sun sinking toward the horizon over the bay confirmed the lateness of the hour. Where had the afternoon gone?

She asked the operator to ring her room. If she could get a message to Jessie for Devin, she would feel better. But Jessie didn't answer either.

Fonda gritted her teeth. Where was that girl? Hadn't she told her to stay in the room until she got back? If Jessie thought she was in trouble before, she'd seen nothing yet.

When the operator came back on, Fonda left two messages. "The first one is for Devin O'Keefe. Tell him Fonda is coming home. And the second one, for Jessie Blayne. Write this down. Pack your bags to head east tomorrow."

Fonda hung up the phone. For the first time since she'd heard Jacky O'Brien's hateful voice that morning, she felt a lightening in her heart.

She and Devin were going to get through this. That is, if it wasn't too late. What if her lack of trust had turned him against her forever? What if Jessie had been right? Was it true that Fonda expected too much from the people she loved?

She began to walk briskly toward the cable car turnaround, overcome by an urgency to get to Candlestick Park.

But it seemed fate was against her. It was after seven o'clock before a cable car arrived, and it quickly filled to capacity. Fonda could only stand with the others and watch it go. Her eyes had been scanning for unoccupied taxis, but none had passed. When another twenty minutes went by without a second cable car arriving, Fonda decided to walk uphill, hoping she'd find a taxi closer to town. But it was almost eight o'clock before she found one.

Exhausted, she fell into the backseat and directed the driver to Candlestick. The concert would be starting soon. Fonda bit her lip and blinked back tears as the taxi drove onto Highway 101 heading south. She'd so wanted to see Devin before he went on stage. What if he tried one of his stupid dangerous stunts because of the way she'd treated him this morning? Oh, God! If something happened to him now, she'd never forgive herself.

Suddenly she became aware that the car had stopped on the highway. She leaned forward. "Is the traffic always this bad at night?"

The driver glanced back at her. "Naw! Must be an accident up ahead. Might as well sit back and relax, lady. This is gonna take a while."

JESSIE FLOPPED onto the bed, her eyes crossed. There had been times she'd thought she was bored in Indiana, but never had she had such a brain-numbing day as this one stuck in this hotel room.

Behind her, the TV droned on . . . Oprah Winfrey on some kick about women giving birth when they hadn't even known they were pregnant. Must be a special breed of women, Jessie thought. Either they were as fat as houses anyway, or more likely, their porch lights had burned out.

She'd been imprisoned in this fancy cell all day, watching one maudlin soap opera after another, and now, these stupid talk shows. And it was all because of Fonda's thickheadedness. Where on earth had she stormed off to, anyway? It was after four. The least she could do was call.

Jessie rolled over onto her stomach and rhythmically tapped her forehead against the mattress. God, how she missed Laoise! Almost as much as she missed Ryan. What were they doing now? Had they made it back to Ireland yet or were they still flying? Whatever, it was a sure thing that *Laoise* wasn't bored shitless.

A commercial for Pizza Hut came on and Jessie's stomach growled in response. She sighed. She'd probably starve to death here before anyone found her. Room service food sucked, and she was damned if she'd eat any more of it. She was lost in a heartbreaking fantasy of a distraught Fonda discovering her lifeless body when a knock came at the door.

"Well, it's about damn time," Jessie muttered and rolled off the bed. Fonda had gone out in such a huff, she'd probably forgotten her key. Maybe they could stop at Pizza Hut on the way to the concert. If, that is, she was going to be allowed to go. The way things had been going . . .

"You're always lecturing me about forgetting my key," Jessie said, as she crossed to the door. "It's nice to know you're not . . ." Her voice trailed away as she stared at the stranger in the corridor.

The woman smiled, revealing straight white teeth framed by mismatched lips that gave a whimsical quality to her attractive face. Immediately, Jessie knew she'd seen her before, but couldn't remember where. It nagged at her like a dream that wouldn't stay buried in her subconscious.

"Can I help you?" Jessie asked.

Something about her appearance wasn't right, though, but what? Her trim body was clad in stonewashed jeans and a heavy fisherman's knit sweater. A sheen of blond hair skimmed the turtleneck in a neat pageboy. That was it! Her eyebrows were dark, almost black. For a second, Jessie visualized a black cap of hair, glossy and thick, giving her a clear picture of what this person was supposed to look like. But it disappeared before she could remember where she'd seen her.

"May I come in?" Her accent was Irish, but it wasn't the dialect that Laoise and Ryan spoke. She wasn't from Dublin.

Jessie made no move to let her in. "I'm sorry, but I'm . . . well, grounded. I can't let anyone in."

"Grounded?" Her eyebrows furrowed.

"You know, under restriction. In trouble."

"Oh, I see. Well, it's just that I have a message from your sister. I thought perhaps you'd rather hear it in privacy."

In privacy? Jessie felt like laughing. She hadn't heard anyone say it like that since she'd seen Prince Charles on TV. That time, she and April had almost bust a gut laughing. She couldn't hide a grin. "Are you with the tour?"

"Of course. Haven't you seen me around? Please, Jessie, let me come in. Fonda has some very important instructions for you."

Jessie stepped back and opened the door wide. "Where is she?"

The Irishwoman walked in. "On her way to the stadium. And that's where she wants me to take you straightaway. Do you have your backstage pass?"

"Yeah, it's in my purse." Jessie stared at the woman. She was looking around the hotel room intently, almost as if taking a mental photograph. Jessie felt the hairs rise on the back of her arms. Something was wrong. She knew it! "What's your name?"

The woman looked startled. Then she said, "Just call me Kate. Why don't you grab your handbag and we'll be on our way?"

Jessie remained standing in the middle of the room. "Isn't it kind of early?"

A flicker of steel entered Kate's blue eyes. "Not if you have to battle traffic. The stadium isn't just next door, you know."

"But I'm hungry. I was just about to call room service."

"We'll get something on the way." Her voice had changed. Become impatient. "Grab your handbag, Jessie."

Jessie didn't budge. She still didn't know where she'd seen this bossy lady, but one thing was for sure. She wasn't going anywhere with her. "How do I know Fonda sent you?"

The woman's eyes locked with Jessie's. She no longer tried to conceal their hardness. "Because I told you so."

Jessie went to the bed and sat down. "Sorry. I'm not going."

Kate shrugged. "Have it your way." She opened the clasp of the shoulder bag she carried. A moment later, she held a small pistol in her hand. She smiled coldly. "Jessie, go get your handbag and make sure your backstage pass is in it." Her voice was steely as she enunciated each word.

Jessie's heart plunged to her stomach and at the same instant, the memory flashed in her mind. The mall! Ian Brinegar sitting with a dark-haired woman. A beautiful woman with a long, graceful neck. Ian Brinegar, who was now in a prison cell in Northern Ireland . . . who was involved with that bunch of thugs Devin had told her about this morning. Jessie sat paralyzed and lightheaded.

"What do you want?" she whispered, her heart racing.

"You know what I want. I just told you."

But Jessie couldn't move. She felt as if lightning had struck her, burned her onto that spot on the bed. Kate took a step toward her. Jessie's eyes centered on the tiny hole of the pistol's barrel, knowing that in a matter of seconds she could be dead. How many other victims had stared into the mouth of the weapon she held?

Almost as if reading her thoughts, Kate smiled. "I've killed children younger than you. And they were of my own blood and religion. Do you think it would bother me to plug an American?"

31

THE SUDDEN glare of the spotlight streamed down into Devin's eyes, momentarily blinding him. Just seconds before, he'd thought he'd seen Fonda's slender form on the periphery of the crowd. Stupid of him, really. She wasn't coming back. Not tonight. Maybe not ever. Still, when the bombardment of flashing lights subsided into a soft blue glow, he looked again in the direction where he'd imagined seeing her. He saw nothing but vague shapes, all of them bouncing to the music and singing along with him.

"Take it away, Seamus!" Devin called out, hooking the microphone to its stand. The crowd roared in appreciation as the spotlight fixed upon Seamus and the guitar bridge swelled out into the stadium. The guitarist loved these moments of being in the limelight. Quiet and retiring backstage, he became a different person when he soloed on guitar. But as always, at the end of the bridge, he'd happily turn the attention back to Devin. Tonight, for the first time ever, Devin didn't want it. Dejectedly, he moved back to a makeshift table and took a sip of water to relieve the dryness in his throat.

Christ, were they only into the fifth song? Already, the sweat was trickling down his face and saturating his sleeveless denim shirt. How, for God's sake, was he going to get through this concert tonight when all he could think of was Fonda? *Where is she? What is she doing now?*

The bridge was coming to an end. For a frantic moment,

Devin couldn't remember which song they were doing. The music was familiar, of course, but still his mind drew a blank when he tried to focus on the lyrics. Finally, seconds before the lead-in of the third verse, it came to him.

> *"Mountains*
> *Mountains majestic like*
> *The deepest soul*
> *Of man's darkest pagan shadow."*

This passionate ballad was one he'd written before he'd met Fonda. It had poured out of him one night in an Amsterdam hotel room during one of his lonelier moments. The woman he'd written about hadn't existed; but now, as the next verse came up, he realized how uncannily the lyrics described his feelings for Fonda.

> *"Our love, like an eclipsed summer*
> *Pictured in your frame*
> *I am the wind that dances upon your waves*
> *Singing out your secret name*
> *Still an apprentice to your silhouetted ways."*

The stadium rumbled with applause and howls of approval. Devin moved back to the water carafe as Seamus swung into "Eclipse." As the soothing water slid down his parched throat, Devin thought of the last line of "High Summer."

That's what he'd done, of course. Drowned beneath Fonda's wave. If she didn't come back, he'd never come to the surface. Would have no desire to.

FONDA FLASHED her backstage pass at the stone-faced minder. He waved her in just as she caught sight of Bram directing two crewmen moving a dolly loaded with lighting equipment. From the stage, she could hear Devin singing "Eclipse." She wanted to rush right out to see him, to reassure herself that he wasn't going to do anything foolish. But the more immediate worry about Jessie overrode her desire. As soon as she'd arrived at the stadium, she'd phoned the hotel again, thinking that perhaps when she'd called earlier, Jessie, despite orders, had gone down to the restaurant for something to eat. When the phone rang several times with no answer, a cold dread filled Fonda's heart. Something was very wrong.

"Bram! Have you seen Jessie?"

He turned around, a distracted look on his handsome face. "Oh, hi, Fon." He ran a hand through his disheveled hair. "Jessie? No, as a matter of fact, I haven't seen the lass. But I do know where she is."

"You do? Where?"

"Yeh, she's in Devin's dressing room. She called one of the roadies earlier and asked to have a pizza and some Cokes sent back."

Fonda's mouth tightened. "Why, that little . . . brat!"

"Oooh!" Bram said, a wry grin flickering about his lips. "Glad I'm not little miss Jess." There was a loud crash from the dolly. He whipped around, the amiable look disappearing from his face. "For Christ's sake, I shoulda left you two in Limerick where you belong!"

Fonda made an about-face. "She's going to be *more* than sorry her name is Jessie Blayne." Just as she took a step toward the hallway leading to the dressing rooms, "Eclipse" ended on stage to the intensified roar of the crowd. Then Fonda heard Devin's melodious voice. Her step faltered. What was he saying? She turned back to the wings as he continued to talk.

For the moment, all thought of Jessie disappeared from Fonda's mind. Devin's grave voice had captured her. She had to listen. When she reached the wings, she saw him standing in the middle of the stage, lit by a soft pool of amber light, his left side facing her. He had his acoustic guitar strapped over his shoulder.

". . . and mistakes are made that change the course of your life. Mistakes that can never be corrected, no matter how much you wish them so. Heartfelt though your apologies might be, they may not be enough to grant you forgiveness. This next song is an apology. I can only pray it's accepted. It's rough, I know, for it was only written this very morning. Try and overlook that, if you will. It's called 'Broken Man.'"

Fonda caught her breath as he began to strum the guitar. Softly, he sang, his voice hauntingly sad.

> *"Broken man, I am*
> *Your hurt mirrors in your eyes*
> *And shatters upon my wounded heart.*
> *I can't understand*
> *How I could be so lax*
> *About our love."*

Fonda bit her lip as Devin poured out his anguish into the ballad. Years ago, she'd wondered what it would feel like to be the inspiration for a love song. Now, she knew. By the time Devin reached the final verse, tears were streaming down her face.

> *"Give up*
> *Give up the past that holds us.*
> *Think back about our love.*
> *Your love*
> *Your love will never doubt me."*

The stage went dark. Too late, Fonda saw Devin exiting stage right. Frantically, she fought her way through the thick crowd of stagehands and crewmen as they readied for the encore.

"Devin!"

He didn't hear her. Helplessly, she watched him disappear into the shadows. She picked her way through the crewmen and followed. A hand touched her shoulder. It was Bram.

"Fonda, I'm sorry I was a bit distracted earlier."

Hastily, she wiped the tears from her face. "No problem, Bram. Look, I have to see Devin."

He smiled easily. "I understand. A bit of intermission celebration, am I right? Mind, don't you two hole up in there all night. These folks are expecting an encore."

Fonda's brows furrowed. What on earth was the man going on about? The last thing in the world she wanted to do was celebrate. Although her feelings for Devin had been resolved, there were still plenty of problems looming.

Bram's face grew serious. "That's a heavy load off your slim shoulders, isn't it, now? Having the investigation dropped?"

Her mouth fell open. "What? He's been cleared?"

"You haven't heard? Ian Brinegar retracted his statements from this morning's *Daily Mirror*. Under the knife, he admitted he's embellished the facts of Devin's childhood in Derry, and out and out *lied* about his involvement with the Provos. With what was left, the FBI realized they had no case against Devin."

"Oh, Bram! I love you." Fonda threw her arms around him, burying her hot face against his cotton shirt. She was relieved, but at the same time ashamed that she hadn't believed in Devin from the beginning. Could he ever forgive her that?

Bram's arms tightened about her. "I love you, too. You and Devin are two of my favorite people in the world. You deserve happiness."

Fonda drew away and looked up at him. "I ran out on him this morning after all that came out in the papers. I deserted him when he needed me most."

His blue eyes were soft. "And now you think perhaps you've killed his love?"

She nodded. "I don't deserve his love . . . or his forgiveness."

"Lass, didn't ya hear that song he sang out there?" His voice roughened. "He's asking for *your* forgiveness. Now get yourself going."

Still, Fonda hesitated. "I knew in my heart he couldn't have done those things Ian accused him of. But when he admitted Caitlyn was alive, I was crushed, knowing Devin and I can never be married. But even that, I can deal with now. I love him that much."

Bram stared down at her, his eyes troubled. "Fonda, love." He stopped and shook his head. "Aw, it can wait. Go on with you now. Go to your man." He gave her a gentle nudge toward the corridor leading to the dressing rooms. "Go forgive each other. Just don't take the whole bleedin' evening to do it."

DEVIN TOOK the towel from the wardrobe mistress and began to wipe the sweat from his face. She was an angular woman from Dublin who'd been with his crew for the last two years. Little or nothing ever disturbed her quiet equanimity, but tonight there was a spark of fire in her brown eyes.

"Your young sister-in-law-to-be has locked me out of your dressing room, she has. Been holed up in there for hours and wants to see no one but yourself."

Devin touched her shoulder. "Thanks, Bridget. I'll take care of it. There's soda in the fridge, right?"

She shrugged. "It was supposed to be delivered. As I couldn't get in, though, I can't swear to it."

"No problem." Devin reached his dressing-room door and tapped. "Jessie? It's me. I'm alone. You can let me in."

For a moment, there was silence on the other side of the door. Then Devin heard her footsteps. The door opened a crack, just enough so he could see one hazel eye and half a nose. "Jessie?"

"Just you, okay?" Her voice was strained. The door opened wider, barely enough for him to squeeze through.

He grabbed her thin shoulders and stared into her huge, frightened eyes. "Christ, lass! What is it? You look as if you've seen a ghost."

A hollow laugh came from the bathroom. "She has, Devin. A ghost from County Armagh, to be exact."

Devin's heart plunged to his toes. He didn't have to look up to know who'd spoken. Her voice had haunted his nightmares every night for the last four years. But look up, he did. Caitlyn, in a blond wig, emerged from the bathroom. In her hands, she held a gun. Her brilliant blue eyes were bright with excitement. But her smile was cold.

"Lock the door, Devin. And get on the phone to call your new manager. I'm afraid you've been taken ill and won't be able to finish the rest of the concert."

FONDA'S HEART beat fast as she stopped in front of Devin's dressing-room door. Now that she was here, she was almost afraid to go in. Even with the reassurance of the song he'd written for her imprinted on her mind, she couldn't be sure of her reception. Oh, God! What if he thought she'd come back because she'd heard of Ian's retraction? Could she convince him she'd done so even before she'd heard of it?

She *had* to. Besides, Bram could convince him of that, if she couldn't. She took a deep breath and knocked. "Devin? It's me. Fonda."

There was an awful silence on the other side. Fonda stood stiffly, waiting. He *had* gone in there. Bridget had told her so. Her stomach tightened. *He didn't want to see her.* But on the heels of this thought came another one. *He's gone into the bathroom. Maybe he's showering. Maybe he can't hear me.*

But Devin never showered before his encore. No, he was in there, and he had to have heard her knock. Anger surged through her. "Okay, Devin. I know I hurt you this morning, but the least you can do is let me talk to you face-to-face. Don't pretend I'm not here."

His voice came then, rough and almost recognizable. "Go away, Fonda! You made it clear this morning how you feel. There's nothing more to be said, is there?"

Paralyzed, Fonda gaped at the door. She felt as if she'd been hit by an out-of-control garbage truck. Even her apprehension hadn't prepared her for total rejection. Still in shock, she backed away from the door and turned to stumble back the way she'd come. But then, she stopped. Why the song? Why the *hell* had he written a song about forgiveness, yet he wouldn't give it?

She swung around and marched back to the door. Her fists crashed against it. "Goddamn you, Devin O'Keefe! Open this door before I break it down. Or if I can't do it, I'll damn well find someone who can! I *won't* let you do this to us!"

The door opened a few inches. Through the crack, Devin peered at her, his face pale and tense. "Christ, Fonda," he said softly. "Why couldn't you have just gone away?"

"Invite her in, Devin," said a voice behind the door. "I'm most interested in meeting your new lady."

"Who is that?" Fonda asked.

Devin made no move to open the door further. "Go away," he said, again in that strained whisper.

"I said, *let her in!*"

Devin wrenched the door wider and pulled her in. The door slammed behind her.

"Devin! What is—Oh, my God, *Jessie!*"

Devin's arms fastened around her as she lunged toward her sister. "No, Fonda. She won't hesitate to pull the trigger. I know her. She's a monster."

Eyes wild, Jessie stood frozen in the blond woman's grip, the barrel of the gun pressed against her right temple. Dark spots danced in front of Fonda's eyes as she fought the dizziness that threatened to engulf her. Her pulse, already galloping from anger, became thready and rapid. The room tilted crazily, and for a moment, everything began to spin out of control. Then, through it all, she felt Devin's hands, warm upon her arms, and drew reassurance from his strength. It wouldn't end now, not when they'd finally found each other again.

Her eyes fastened on the exquisitely beautiful woman with the flinty blue eyes. "You're Caitlyn."

A cold smile came to the woman's oddly shaped lips. "Why, she's not only pretty, she's smart." Her amused eyes went to Devin. "You've done well for yourself, Devin. Ian told me you were planning a wedding and everything."

She spoke in that curious Belfast lilt that always sent the last word soaring above the rest of the sentence. A charming trait, Fonda had always thought. Until now.

Caitlyn laughed. "A wedding! But surely not in the church, Devin. The last I heard, the Pope frowns upon bigamy."

"Damn you, Caitlyn!" Devin shouted. "Why are you doing this? Haven't enough people suffered because of you?"

Her smile disappeared. "Oh, no, Devin. Not enough. Not nearly enough. That's why I'm here. Brinegar, the bloody fool, has blown everything. They're closing in on me." She wore the shining expression of the martyr; it sent a shiver of horror skidding down Fonda's spine. "I always said I'd go out in style."

"At least let the girl go. She's just a child."

"That means nothing to me. But then, you wouldn't know that, would you? You don't really know me at all. Not what I've become since my little holiday in Armagh. But you know something? I'm *glad* they put me there. Because whatever I felt for the Cause before . . . whatever my loyalties were, they were only strengthened by my time in jail. I'm stronger now. And more dedicated than ever to a reunited Ireland."

Fonda felt Devin's hands release her. He took a step toward Caitlyn. "But don't you see, involving innocent Americans in this can only hurt your cause. You'll lose whatever support you've found here if you hurt one of their own."

Her blue eyes were like ice. "Don't come a step closer or I'll blow her brains out, Devin. You know I will." Devin stopped. "Now, that's better. Go over and lock the door like a good boy. Okay." Slowly, she released Jessie and pushed her down into a chair along the wall. "You, girlfriend. Go sit yourself down on that sofa. Devin, go call your manager like I asked before your little crumpet arrived. Tell him you're sick and you won't be able to do an encore."

"They'll never believe it," Devin said. "I don't get sick, and if I did, I'd make myself go on. Do you hear that crowd out there? They're chanting for me. They won't take no for an answer."

Clearly, through the closed door, Fonda could hear the cries of the crowd. "Dev-in. Dev-in. Dev-in."

"Besides," Devin went on, "if I tell them I'm sick, they'll send in a doctor. You might as well give this up, Caitlyn. It won't work."

"Christ!" Caitlyn began to pace, waving the gun erratically. "Tell them you have a fuckin' headache! I don't care. Just tell them you don't want to be disturbed. All I need is a few moments, anyway. Just to get my thoughts in order."

Fonda watched as Devin picked up the phone. She knew what he was thinking. He'd made a huge mistake by telling Caitlyn that his crew wouldn't believe he was sick. But somehow, incredibly, Caitlyn hadn't caught the significance of it. If Bram or the new manager could be warned that something wasn't right . . .

Fonda looked at Jessie. The girl sat stiffly on the chair, her face translucent with fear. Her eyes were fixed upon Caitlyn, as if she were morbidly fascinated by her tormenter. Fonda wished she could offer a word of reassurance to her little sister, but what could she say? It was obvious they were in the hands of a woman who was, if not psychotic, then fanatically obsessed, which amounted to the same thing. Mortal danger. Fear was so thick in the room Fonda could smell it.

Nervously, she moved her sweaty hands up and down her denim-covered thighs. She took a deep trembling breath and spoke. "What's going to happen to us? What are you going to do?"

Caitlyn's soulless eyes turned to her. A cold smile twitched on her lips as she pointed the gun on a direct line with Fonda's forehead. "That's a very good question, Yank. You're the first one to ask." She settled herself on the edge of the long table that held the remains of a pizza and several Coke cans, keeping the guns leveled at Fonda. One booted foot swung back and forth leisurely. Fonda found herself staring at it. Back and forth, it swung. It was the only way she could keep her eyes off the gun.

Caitlyn gave a short harsh laugh. "I'll tell you what I'm going to do. I'm going to kill all of you. You first." Her voice was pleasant as if she were describing a day of sightseeing. "Then your little sister and then Devin. Or should I kill *him* first so you can see it?" She shook her head, her eyebrows lowered. "Decisions, decisions—they drive me mad." She gave a soft shrug. "Whatever—I'll kill myself last. I'll die a patriot's death for Ireland, just as I've always known I would. Like my two brothers before me." Her smile widened. "But let's not talk of that now. We have plenty of time. First, before I kill you, we're going to have some fun."

"DEV-IN. Dev-in. Dev-in."

Bram had to yell to be heard over the sound of the frenzied chanting of the stadium crowd. "What the *bloody hell* do you mean, he's sick?"

Kyle McKenna ran one hand through his thatch of carrot red hair and yelled back, "Christ, Bram! That's what he said. It's not like him, is it? Refusing to do an encore? What should I do? That crowd will raise holy hell if I go out there and say the concert's over. Listen to them!"

"Don't do it," Bram shouted. "Something's fucked up here. And I'm going to find out what. I've been working with that man for eight years, and he's never once canceled an encore for a bloody headache!"

Leaving Kyle shaking his head, Bram strode down the corridor toward Devin's dressing room. "Christ!" he muttered. The chanting was growing louder and more insistent.

He reached the door and tried the knob. Locked. His beefy hand crashed against the wood. "Goddamn it, Devin! I don't know what you and Fonda are trying to pull, but you can't let down your fans like this. Open the fucking door!"

The door opened. A pair of familiar blue eyes stared at him. He blinked. Christ! A ghostly face from the past.

"Come in, Bram," said a musical Belfast voice, one he knew immediately. "Join the party."

32

BRAM TOOK in the situation at a glance. He saw Devin, grim-faced and stony-eyed, sitting on a chair near the phone. Fonda was on the sofa across the room from him, her face bloodless. Little Jessie was on a chair a few feet away, biting her lower lip and trying desperately to be brave. Bram's heart twisted for her. Poor wee one! What was Caitlyn thinking of?

Caitlyn. Christ! It had been years since he'd seen her. He should've killed her when he'd had the chance.

She was staring at him with a look of cool amusement. Had she read his thoughts? Bram used a mental trick he'd learned back in Galway to ease the tension from his body, picturing himself free-floating in calm waters. If they were going to get out of this alive, he had to keep his wits about him. Gradually, his heartbeat slowed to its regular rhythm, as did his breathing. He gazed back at Caitlyn steadily, his lips forming a disdainful smile.

"Well, aren't you going to say anything?" she asked, clearly un-nerved by his indolent composure.

He took his time, allowing his eyes to scan her body from top to bottom. "Yeh," he said finally. "You look like shit in that blond wig."

"Fuck you." She gestured with the gun. "Sit yourself down over there next to Devin's 'light o' love.'" Abruptly, she pulled off the wig and flung it into the trash can next to the coffeemaker. With one elegant hand, she combed through her short black hair, try-ing to get it into some kind of order.

Still a beauty, Bram mused as he sat down next to Fonda. What made an idealistic girl like herself go off the deep end like this? There had been a time when he'd understood her aims. Indeed, had believed in them himself. It seemed like a hundred years ago. When had he started to change?

Devin, of course, had influenced him. But Bonnie had been the real reason. All those nights of sitting up debating the situation up north. Pro-revolutionary tactics verses political action. Gradually, he'd come to see her way of thinking. And he'd realized Bonnie was a woman who could bring about a change for the people of Northern Ireland.

Would he live to see her do it?

At the morbid thought, Bram shook his head. No more thoughts of Bonnie. There would be time for that later. His eyes scanned the room. An opportunity would come up to distract Caitlyn. He had to make use of it any way he could. He gazed at the mess on the table. No knife that he could see. Were there any other potential weapons at hand?

He stretched his long legs out in front of him, consciously trying to give Caitlyn the impression he wasn't taking all this too seriously. "So, Caitlyn—what's up?"

She stared at him a moment, then her lips twitched. "You're some cool customer, aren't you, Bram? You know, in all the years I've known you, I don't think I've ever seen you angry. You're just good old easygoing Bram. It's such a fuckin' waste!"

Bram's stomach tensed. With an effort, he managed to keep his face expressionless. His eyes settled on the Fender Telecaster guitar leaning against the super amp he and Devin had been experimenting with. A flicker of an idea went through his brain. He looked back at Caitlyn, who'd perched herself on the edge of the table. She was staring at him, her lip curled in a contemptuous sneer.

"You could've been such an asset to us, you know. But instead, you chose to flirt with the outer edges of our struggle. We could've used a man like you inside. A man with brains and courage. But maybe you don't have any courage, Bram? Maybe underneath all that macho veneer, you're just another wimp!"

"For God's sake, Bram, what's she talking about?"

Bram looked across the room into Devin's shocked face. "It's old history, Devin. And I'm not exactly proud of it."

"What?" Caitlyn scoffed. "Not proud to be a volunteer in Northern Ireland's struggle for independence? I should kill you right now for saying that."

Bram could feel Devin and Fonda's astonishment. He felt deeply ashamed, even now, years after his interest in the organization had cooled. Why hadn't he been able to tell Devin? God knew there had been plenty of opportunities. Caitlyn was right. He was a wimp. He met Devin's eyes.

"I'm sorry," he said softly. "When I was a lad in Galway, the Troubles up north might as well have been a million miles away. That's how much concern I had for politics back then. But when my parents were blown up by a Protestant bomb in Belfast, I went crazy." Bram swallowed hard, the memory of that horrible day still fresh in his mind, even though it had happened ten years ago. "They were incinerated within moments."

The room was silent. There was only the low hum of noise coming from the stadium, punctuated by occasional shouts and shrill whistles. The chanting for Devin had stopped. For a moment, Caitlyn appeared visibly moved by Bram's admission. She was the first to speak.

"Christ! We have all lost so much because of that infernal place."

"For God's sake, Bram," Devin said, his voice anguished. "Why did you never tell me, man?"

"Because you made it clear how you felt about our fighting back. But don't you see, I had to do something? I had to avenge my parents' deaths. So I went to Belfast with some college friends and met with some volunteers. I never actually went 'active,' you understand. I just helped by giving money, making contacts, arranging safehouses. Non-guerrillist activities."

Caitlyn's face had hardened. "As I said, a wimp."

Devin was staring at her. "You and Bram—he introduced you to me. It was all intentional, wasn't it?"

Bram got to his feet. Caitlyn jumped up, swinging the gun at him. "What the hell are you doing?"

"I'm thirsty." Bram went to the refrigerator and opened it. The back of his neck felt exposed. He could feel the gun centering upon it. "A beer, Devin? Fonda?"

"Yes, thanks." Fonda said quietly.

Bram grabbed three Coors and a Coke for Jessie while scanning the interior of the refrigerator for a possible weapon. Nothing. "Caitlyn, you want something?"

"Just get what you want and sit down. Hand it to them slowly and don't try anything."

Bram's eyes met Devin's as he passed him a beer. *Just stay calm, man. We'll get out of this somehow.* Jessie's hand shook as she took the Coke from him. He tried to reassure her with a smile, but she lowered her eyes without responding. Bram sat down again next to Fonda and handed her a beer. She peered at him, her hazel eyes frightened. *What's going to happen to us?*

He popped the top on the can and took a swallow. "The meeting was arranged by people at the top. They saw you had the potential to go far, and decided to use me to get one of their top volunteers into your life. I knew what they wanted, of course. I just never guessed you'd fall so hard for her. In fact, I'd argued against the whole thing. I told them you weren't interested in women at that point in your life. Your career was everything to you. They wanted to know if you were gay. When I scoffed at that, they told me not to worry about it. Caitlyn would take care of everything."

Caitlyn had moved over to the refrigerator. Keeping her eyes on the room, she opened it and reached in for a Coke. "Yeah, you were putty in my hands, Devin. You made it so easy, even I couldn't believe it." She had the Coke in one hand and the gun in the other. She looked down at the pop top and then moved to Jessie. "Here, kid. Open this for me."

Devin's face had grown ashen. Bram felt his gut wrench. Christ! What a thing to find out after all these years. And *he* was responsible. Things could never be repaired between the two of them, even if they got out of this mess intact. But right now, the way Devin felt about him wasn't important. Watching Devin's wounded face, Bram vowed he'd do what he could to get them out. Even if it meant sacrificing himself.

"You never loved me at all, did you, Caitlyn?" Devin asked softly. "It was all a game to you."

Caitlyn stared at him. "It was never a game to me. It was my life. But that's something you can't understand, can you? *You* of all people should, but you can't." She paused, her face contemplative. "As for love . . . there was no room for love in my heart. Still, there were times I came close to loving you." Her eyes hardened. "But that didn't last. Not when I saw how you were rolling in the money, and you weren't giving a cent to help your people in the North. You could've done so much for them, Devin. Instead, you chose to help the starving in Ethiopia." She spat out the words as if they were an obscenity. "Or the prisoners in South America. Why not *our* prisoners, Devin? Why not the men and women in the H-Blocks? People like your own father? You didn't lift a finger to help them, did you, now?"

Devin sat woodenly, his head bowed. From the stage came the sound of his voice; how long had they been playing the *Eclipse* album? Bram had no doubt they'd put it on to pacify the crowd. Would it work? Out of the corner of his eye, he saw Fonda raise a hand to her mouth. She was crying soundlessly, her eyes upon Devin. Bram put a hand on her knee. *Steady, girl. Sure, he's in pain, but he can take it.* She didn't respond to his gesture of reassurance.

After a moment, Devin looked up at Caitlyn, his eyes emotionless. "Why were you so insistent upon marrying me? You had me where you wanted me. Why did you have to make it legal?"

Bram started to speak, but Caitlyn interrupted. "*You* wanted the marriage, remember? It's all you talked about. A house on the seashore, a passel of kids. I heard it so much, I was bloody sick of it. I never had any intention of marrying you, if I could help it. But then, when my brother was killed, I lost it, went crazy on you, didn't I? It all came out about my sympathies. And you were gone." She gave a cold smile. "The leaders didn't like that a bit. You were just starting off on your first American tour. There were thousands of pounds to be made. Orders came down that I had to get you back or else. That's when I decided desperate measures had to be taken."

"So you faked a suicide." His voice was flat, toneless.

Her eyes bit into his. "Not faked, Devin. What do you think? The entire hospital was in on the conspiracy? No, I took that bottle of pills, praying all the time you loved me enough to come to me. And you did." She shrugged her slim shoulders, took a sip from her soft drink, and placed the can on the table. "You pretty much know the rest of it. Except that after we were married, my doctor recommended I stay in Belfast for a few weeks instead of traveling off to America with you. He was paid off to say that, of course, because the organization had a mission planned for me. It was my first big one. A reward, you could say, for bringing you back to me."

"The bombing at Cave Hill," Devin said, still in that distant voice.

"Yes. I still don't know what went wrong with that. The timer was off. I managed to just get out, but my partner was killed. There were times after the Brits got me, I wished I was the one who'd died." Her face twisted in anger. "Inhuman bastards, they were! If you only knew some of the things they did to me . . ."

Devin's face was cold. "Children were killed by your hands at that shopping center that day. Who's the inhuman bastard, Caitlyn?"

"Shut up!" she yelled, losing her composure for the first time. "Just shut up, you sanctimonious son-of-a-bitch! You should be ashamed to call yourself a Derryman. You've been away so fucking long, you've completely lost touch with the reality of life there. We're in a war, goddamn it! Innocent lives are always lost in wars." Her free hand covered her ear in an incongruously childlike manner. She began to pace. "Now, leave me alone. I have to think."

Bram watched her. Across the room, Devin's eyes smoldered. His shock had worn off and his anger was beginning to take control. Bram knew something had to be done soon. Devin was thinking about trying to jump her. And that, Bram knew, could lead to a bloodbath. It was time to throw some ice onto the fire.

Slowly, Bram began to clap his hands. Caitlyn whirled around to face him. He could feel the others' stares. He smiled, his eyes on Caitlyn.

"Grand story, Caty. However, there's an omission in it. Not your fault, of course. Because this is something you couldn't have known." He took a sip of his beer, relishing in making her wait.

"Well, get on with it!"

"After Devin kicked you out of the house in Malahide, I heard a rumor from one of the boyos. He had a habit of flapping his mouth when he was in his cups, you understand. Poor old sod. The IRA finally caught on to him and 'tooled' his kneecaps. But he told me orders had come from the top for you to get yourself married to Devin however you could. When the call came from your roomie about your suicide attempt, I knew what was expected of me." His eyes moved to Devin. "I had to get you to Belfast, but even so, I was sure you were so disillusioned with her, you'd never fall into the trap of marriage. I almost fell over when you told me to find you a priest. Christ, I wanted to tell you the truth so bad. That she didn't love you, that it was a setup. But I couldn't, Devin. I was so fucking scared of crossing the Provos. Still, you were my best friend. I loved you, man, and I didn't want to see you tied to that witch for life. When she told me to find this priest from Falls Road, I lied to her. Said he'd been called away to perform a funeral mass. Instead, I found another one. Father Cruise Connelly. He was the brother of a friend of mine from Dublin. He agreed to come to Belfast to perform the marriage ceremony. There was only one minor problem."

"What are you talking about?" Caitlyn glared at him.

He threw her an enigmatic grin. "He wasn't a priest. Just an actor from the Abbey."

"MOTHER MARY! The marriage was illegal?"

It was Devin who spoke. He stared at Bram incredulously before flashing a triumphant glance at Fonda.

Caitlyn too stared at Bram, the blood draining from her face. Finally, she spoke. "You're lying, you bloody bastard."

Bram grinned. "You think so, huh?"

With a strangled scream, she hurled herself at him, the gun swinging. Bram tensed and tried to ward off the blow, but the gun slammed across his left temple. Pain exploded, and the room darkened. He slumped to the sofa. Through layers of cotton, he heard Devin and Fonda screaming, and then Caitlyn's savage order:

"Sit yourselves down now, or I swear, I'll put bullets through the lot of you."

Then there was only the sound of Jessie sobbing.

"Shut up, kid!"

Gingerly, Bram's fingers went to his head and came away sticky with blood. With an effort, he pulled himself up and groggily focused his eyes on Caitlyn. She'd resumed her former calm. "It doesn't really matter now anyway, does it?" She gave a harsh laugh. "We're all dead—or *will* be soon."

"I thought about killing you, you know," Bram mumbled, hearing his own voice as if it were coming from a deep tunnel. "When I heard the plan of you marrying Devin. I'd lay in bed at night and fantasize about putting a bullet through that lovely head of yours. God, I wish I had. But when it came right down to it, I didn't have the guts."

"Yes, that's so typical of you," she said with a sneer. "So, you used deception to defeat me. Trouble is, it didn't work, did it? Look where we are now." She turned to Devin. "You and your American lover will never live to be together. I have the gun, don't I? Now, all of you, be quiet. A plan is coming to me."

Bram stared across the room at Devin. His body appeared to be coiled like a spring. Jesus, what was going through his mind? Did he really think brute force was going to defeat Caitlyn? She was a well-trained Provo soldier. There wasn't a chance in hell they could get that gun away from her without one of them getting killed—unless they could distract her. His eyes swept the room again. How? How could they do it? Again, his gaze stopped on the Fender Telecaster across the room. So far away. Could he make it without being shot?

Caitlyn's sudden laugh peeled through the room. Her blue eyes sparkled maliciously. "I've got it. Oh, this is too good." She turned to Devin. "Go call your manager. You've miraculously recovered and you're ready to go back on stage."

As if to underline her statement, the last song from Devin's album came to an end. A low rumble began to grow from the stands. The stomping of thousands of impatient feet. The shouts were growing angrier.

Bram met Devin's confused gaze. What was this all about? Whatever, they both shared the same sense of foreboding. If she were willing to risk letting Devin go back on stage, she surely had something horrible planned. An icy feeling crawled along Bram's nerve ends. Bloody hell! She wasn't thinking of gunning Devin down in front of his fans?

He knew the same thought had entered Devin's mind. A resigned look came to his face as he turned to Caitlyn. "I'll do whatever you ask if you promise to let the others go. I know what you want, Caitlyn. Just let the others go."

She stared at him and then gave an amused laugh. "Oh, but you have me wrong, Devin. I'm not going to kill you. In fact, if you'll do this one simple thing for me, everyone walks out of here alive."

A shocked silence fell in the room. Caitlyn pointed the gun at a television mounted to the wall across from the sofa. "Will that thing show what's happening on stage?"

Bram nodded. "Yeh, that's what it's there for."

"Good. Now, Devin, this is what you're going to do." She paused a moment, thinking. Her mismatched lips curved in a Mona Lisa smile. "Oh, yes, this is perfect. I want you to go out on stage and make a little speech. You're good at that, aren't you? Ian told me all about that temper tantrum you threw in Seattle."

Devin gazed back at her silently, waiting.

"But this time, you're going to go out there and admit to the world you're an Irish patriot. You're going to tell them how you've supported the Republican cause all along. That your money has gone to purchase arms and equipment for the IRA *with your knowledge.*"

Devin jumped up, his face contorted with rage. "You're fucking crazy, woman!"

Her face hardened. "Sit down. I'm not finished. You're going to tell them about the atrocities you've witnessed since childhood. Atrocities committed by the Brits and the Prods. Devin, you've been blessed with eloquence. Your mother must've made love to the Blarney Stone when she was pregnant with you. You sway people. You move them. Christ, your voice could wring tears of sorrow from the devil himself. If you go out there and tell them *why* there has to be a revolution in our country, why armed resistance is the *only* answer for Irishmen to regain their freedom, they'll listen to you. Our movement throughout the world will grow so huge that the Brit government will have no choice but to get out of Ulster. All it takes is a man on our side who has the power to influence millions. You, Devin."

Statuelike, Devin sat on his chair, his face so cold it seemed to be carved from marble. When he spoke, his voice was low, furious. "I won't do it."

Caitlyn was silent for a moment. Finally, she shrugged. "Okay." She began to pace. Everyone watched her, knowing it wasn't over. She stopped, her eyes fastening on Fonda. Fonda met her gaze, her chin rising in defiance.

"She's so lovely, Devin," Caitlyn said. "All that hair and delicate skin. What a perfect couple you make. Much better than you and I did, you know. You really love her, don't you, Devin?"

"Don't you touch her, Caitlyn." Devin's face had become human again. His fists were clenched in fear and rage. "I swear to all that's holy, if you hurt her, I'll kill you."

"You're not in a position to threaten me," Caitlyn said mildly. She crossed the room and closed her free hand upon Fonda's upper arm, pulling her to her feet. Jessie screamed and both Bram and Devin jumped up.

"*Don't!*" Caitlyn ordered. The barrel of the gun rested against Fonda's temple. Caitlyn maneuvered Fonda in front of her. "She will be the first. Then the other two. It's your choice, Devin. Make the speech and walk out of here with Fonda. Or go out there and raise the alarm, then hold yourself responsible for three deaths. And the third choice, of course. You can stay here and watch them die. I'll leave you alive so you can live with the memory of it for the rest of your life."

Devin stared at her. Bram watched, his head throbbing where the gun had smashed against it. He could see Devin was wrestling with a decision.

"She's lying, Devin," Bram said flatly. "She won't let any of us walk out of here alive. No matter what you say. If you go out there and proclaim your support for the IRA, your career will be ruined. And she'll kill us anyway. It's not worth it, man."

"I don't give a fuck for my career," Devin said. He stared at Caitlyn. "Do you promise to let them go if I do it? Do you swear on the Holy Book that you will?"

Caitlyn gazed back at him steadily. "I swear it. In God's name, if you do what I ask, I'll let the others go."

Devin stared at her for a long moment. The crowd outside had started chanting for him again. He looked at his watch. Bram could almost read his thoughts. Nearly forty minutes had passed since he'd walked into the dressing room and faced the deadly viper hiding there. How much longer could they expect to hold on without someone getting shot? If one of them could get out . . .

But Bram had a bad feeling about this. It wouldn't work. As long as Caitlyn had Fonda in here, Devin wasn't about to do anything that could endanger her. At least, if he stayed, perhaps a chance would come up to jump Caitlyn. With her guerrilla training, it would take two of them to do it.

"She's a liar, Devin," he said. "Don't you see, man? This is her way of ruining you without actually putting a bullet through your brain."

But Devin was already picking up the phone. There was a resigned look on his face. After a few seconds, he spoke. "Kyle? I feel better now. I'm going out."

33

THE ROAR of the crowd intensified as Devin walked on stage, bathed in a pool of light. He stood center-stage and waited for the noise to abate.

In the dressing room, all eyes were fixed upon the television monitor, except Bram's. He was staring at the Fender Telecaster near Jessie. If he could get across the room and turn the amp to maximum, it would surely blow a fuze, and perhaps provide just enough confusion to jump Caitlyn. But could he get across the room to it before getting blistered by a bullet? Fucking unlikely. She was just too close to it. Perhaps if she were distracted enough by Devin's speech, there was a slim chance he could do it. Out of the corner of his eye, he glanced at Fonda. She was sitting stiffly, her hands curled around her Coors can, her eyes centered on the image of Devin on the television screen.

A wave of pain burned through Bram's gut. He cleared his dry throat, wondering how he could possibly get a message across to Fonda. For his idea to work, it would take two people, one to get to the guitar and amp, the other to jump Caitlyn. Obviously, he should be the one to go after Caitlyn. But how was Fonda to know about the amp? She had no technical knowledge. Jessie, although she was closer, was an even worse choice. Anyway, it would be too dangerous for her. He couldn't risk the child's life even if he could, by some miracle, get a message across to her. No. If it was going to be done, he'd have to try to get to the amp and jump Caitlyn immediately afterward. The possibility for failure was high. And in this case, failure would mean death. For all of them.

Another wave of savage pain twisted through his midsection.

FONDA'S FINGERNAILS dug into her palms as she stared at the image of Devin on screen. She licked her dry lips, wondering why the inside of her mouth felt like it had been mopped with a dustcloth. Even the beer she'd tried to drink had done nothing to wash the taste of fear away. *Oh, Devin, what's going to happen to us?*

The camera focused upon Devin's face. It wore a haunted look. Couldn't the crowd see something was terribly wrong? He still hadn't spoken. Instead of quieting the crowd, his silence appeared to be having the opposite effect. Their frenzy was intensifying. Fonda bit her lip. Caitlyn couldn't have come up with a better form of revenge in getting back at Devin. To force him to go against his principles in front of the very people who'd made him what he was today, a superstar with a social conscience, would be paramount to destroying his career. To his fans, it would be a betrayal of everything he stood for. It would be unforgivable.

Caitlyn stood stiffly in the middle of the room, her eyes on the television monitor. To Fonda, she looked wired. Ready to go off like an arrow quivering on a bow string. A shiver of fear ripped through her stomach as again she realized just how dangerous their situation was. The woman was obviously teetering on the edge of madness.

Still, it was impossible for Fonda to face the fact that she could be living her last moments on this earth. She *had* to believe they were going to get out of this alive. Because if she didn't, she was afraid she'd start screaming and never stop. Her eyes moved to Jessie. Dear God, why wouldn't the woman let her go? She was a mere baby, had her whole life ahead of her.

Fonda thought of her parents. It brought another shaft of pain spearing through her. What if Caitlyn *did* kill her and Jessie? How on earth would her parents cope? First Michael, then two of their three daughters.

She thought of the last time she'd talked to her dad on the phone. She'd been furious with him—had said some cruel things. *Oh, Daddy, I'm sorry.* Jessie had been right when she'd accused her of using her father as a scapegoat after Michael's death. *It's all true, Daddy. I couldn't blame Michael. He was dead, and you were there. I couldn't be angry with my dead brother, so I took it out on you.*

Would she ever be able to tell him how sorry she was?

"Christ!" Caitlyn muttered, her eyes on the TV. "Why doesn't he get on with it?"

In unison, the crowd had begun chanting again: "Dev-in. Dev-in. Dev-in." Devin stood motionless on center-stage, scanning the fans. His eyes were bright. To anyone else, Fonda thought, it would appear that he was overcome with emotion by the adulation of the crowd. How could they know the real reason behind it? That he was about to kill his career to save the lives of people he loved?

"Hey, lady," Jessie spoke up in a defiantly brave voice. "Can I please sit next to my sister?"

Caitlyn turned a pair of distracted eyes upon her. The girl squirmed uneasily on her hard chair.

"My butt hurts."

Caitlyn studied Jessie coldly, then suddenly, she turned to Bram and gave the gun a jerk. "Trade seats with the girl, Bram. No tricks, now." She watched sharply as he stood up and stretched.

"Happy to oblige." He gave Jessie a smile as they passed each other.

The girl scrambled onto the sofa and immediately threw herself into Fonda's arms, whimpering. Fonda held her close and stroked her copper hair. "It's okay, baby. We're going to get out of this."

"Quiet!" Caitlyn barked. "He's starting to talk."

Fonda drew away from Jessie, but continued to hold onto her hand. Her eyes focused on the TV screen. Devin had raised his hands to calm the crowd. His face was a mask of pain and determination. At first, Fonda had believed he'd never be able to convince the crowd of the pro-IRA sentiments Caitlyn had ordered him to deliver, but now, she wasn't so sure. She'd seen that stubborn stint to his jaw before. The day in the Seattle park came to mind when he'd confronted the Irish American who'd so openly supported the Provos. And the night of the Seattle concert when he'd lashed out at him and his cohorts. Only this time, he was going to be on the other side. He'd convince them, Fonda realized. If he thought it would save their lives, he would put on a performance that would leave no doubt in anyone's mind.

His voice rang out, rich with Irish flavor. "As most of you know, I was born and raised in a town called Derry in Northern Ireland." He spoke slowly and clearly, as if making sure his words would reach every ear. At the mention of Northern Ireland, the crowd roared. Devin waited a moment, then went on: "I emphasize the name, Derry . . . not Londonderry, as the Brits call it. That is a name that we Irish will *never* accept. They—the British—invaded our country *eight hundred years ago*. They stripped us of our heritage, they forbade us to speak our language, they destroyed or carried away our artifacts. And if that wasn't enough for them, they murdered us in droves." He paused, staring hard at the crowd, every muscle in his body taut. His voice lowered, yet it was so quiet in the stadium that his every syllable was as clear as if he were shouting. "It was under the bloody tutorage of Oliver Cromwell that British soldiers played the savage game of throwing Irish babes into the air and skewering them onto the tips of their swords. Why, you ask? How can one group of people be so bloodthirsty toward another? Well, you see, for many centuries, the British didn't believe the Irish *were* human. In fact, historians have found old letters that document the British belief that Irish men and women had *tails*—like animals!"

"Jesus Christ!" Caitlyn exploded. "What the fuck is this? A history lesson?"

Fonda met Bram's eyes. He gave a brief nod, as if reassuring her that everything was under control. How could it be? she wondered. It was obvious Devin was stalling. What good did he think that would do? Sooner or later, Caitlyn would grow impatient. What then?

The camera followed Devin as he moved to the back of the stage and reached for his water glass. After taking a sip, he went on. His voice was still soft, yet it vibrated with emotional intensity that couldn't help but reach out and enclose the listener in its grip. "The British invoked the Penal Laws, outlawing education for the Irish. In spite of bloody consequences, schoolmasters taught the children in hedgerows while a brave lad kept an eye out for the soldiers. Those laws forbade the Irish from owning land in their own country; from fishing in their own streams. During the Great Famine, Irishmen were imprisoned and tortured for catching illegal fish to feed their starving families. And during this famine, while the Irish were dying by the hundreds of thousands, the British government was *exporting* foodstuffs to England. Why?" His voice rose in rage. "Because if that supply were cut off, the poor Englishman would have to pay a higher price for his corn!"

Caitlyn glared at the television monitor. "For God's sake! I told you to announce your support for the IRA, not describe every bloody crime the Brits have enacted against us since Henry the fucking Second!"

Bram's sudden movement toward the amp at his right drew Fonda's attention. Before she could formulate a thought, several things happened at once. A low hum echoed through the room. The lights flickered. Caitlyn whipped toward Bram. For a second, time seemed to freeze. Through the brownout, Fonda saw Bram's white face as he stared at Caitlyn, his expression a mingling of triumph and dread.

The room went black.

"You bastard!" Caitlyn hissed.

There was a whisper of sound from the gun. Fonda didn't think. Just acted. She jumped up. The beer can she'd held between her thighs hit the floor with a crash, spewing liquid. With all her strength, Fonda threw herself forward to the spot where Caitlyn had been standing. The impact drove the breath from her body. Caitlyn grunted as they crashed to the floor, entangled. The gun skittered across the room with a noisy clunk.

"The gun!" Fonda screamed as she fought to pin down the thrashing, cursing Caitlyn. The Irishwoman was much, much stronger than she looked. "Find the gun, Bram!"

Razor-sharp fingernails pierced Fonda's face as the two of them rolled on the floor, Caitlyn trying desperately to free herself from Fonda's deathlike grip. Like a bucking horse, she threw Fonda off and began to scramble to her knees.

"Oh no you don't, you bitch!" Fonda's hands closed upon Caitlyn's hair. She pulled with everything she had.

Caitlyn screamed, struggling to get loose. Fonda held on grimly. "Bram! Please!" Oh, dear God, couldn't he find the gun? "I . . . can't . . . hold her!"

But she didn't loosen her grip. She hooked one leg over Caitlyn's squirming buttocks to hold her more securely. From behind, she heard Jessie sobbing and screaming out her name. A groan came out of the darkness from Bram's direction. *Oh, God! Had he been hit?*

"I have it." Bram's voice was weak and pain-wracked. "I can see you, Caitlyn. And I won't hesitate to kill you. Now, be still."

Caitlyn stopped struggling. Still, Fonda held onto her hair. No way she was going to trust the ruthless bitch.

"Jessie, pull yourself together, lass, and go get help," Bram said. After a moment, the dressing-room door opened and Jessie's panicked footsteps clattered down the dark corridor and disappeared. "That's a good girl," he said softly.

Fonda felt a stab of fear. He sounded so weak, as if he might pass out at any moment. Apparently sensing the same thing, Caitlyn gave a jerk. Fonda wrenched her hair savagely. She howled in anger.

"Don't try anything, woman," said Bram. "It would give me great pleasure to put a bullet through that pretty skull of yours. After the lives you've ruined."

Caitlyn gave a harsh laugh. Although Fonda couldn't see her face, she imagined her derisive sneer. "You know what I think,

Bram? I don't think you have the gun at all. I think you're conning me."

His voice was cool. "Are you willing to bet your life on that?"

Caitlyn remained still, obviously thinking it over. Fonda heard a shuffling movement in the darkness, then just barely, she made out Bram's dark form in front of them. He moved, pressing the gun barrel against Caitlyn's temple.

"Go ahead, Caty," he said softly. "Try something."

A burly shape filled the open doorway. "Where is she?" A flashlight bounced around the room and then focused upon the three of them on the floor.

"Right here," Bram said to the minder. "Have you called the police?"

"On the way."

A second minder followed the first one in. "You'd better help me with her," the first one said. "She looks like a hellcat."

Fonda still had Caitlyn by the hair. She didn't let go until the first minder grabbed her shoulders. "It's okay. I've got her. You can let go."

Even then, Fonda found it difficult to make her stiff fingers work. She felt as if she'd been holding onto Caitlyn for hours. Finally, she untangled herself from the woman and got to her feet, her limbs shaking. The two minders hoisted Caitlyn to her feet just as a uniformed cop appeared in the doorway, his gun drawn.

"Backup is on the way. Is this the terrorist?"

"Yeah. The girl said she's been holding these people hostage for the last couple of hours."

Even in the semi-darkness, Fonda felt Caitlyn's hate-filled eyes burning into her. "Well, you and your kind have won again," she said, her voice seething. "You know, it's inconceivable to me how Devin could have fallen in love with a pampered piece of milk-toast like you."

The policeman jerked her toward the door. "Come on. Let's get this spitfire someplace where we can keep an eye on her."

But Caitlyn wasn't finished. "A spoiled American, that's what you are! Raised with a silver spoon stuck in that pretty mouth of yours. How could you possibly understand what it was like for someone like me? And you!" She twisted toward Bram as the policeman dragged her to the door. "You call yourself an Irishman! I wish I'd blown your bloody head off!" She was gone.

The other minder hesitated at the door. "You two okay?"

Fonda nodded. Her entire body was trembling now with aftershock. She looked at Bram, who was still huddled on the floor.

"I think I've been shot," he said quietly.

With a cry, Fonda dropped to the floor next to him. "Where, Bram?"

"It's just my shoulder, I think," he said, grimacing. "But it hurts like bloody hell!"

"I've already called for an ambulance," the minder said. "It shouldn't be long."

Fonda fumbled for Bram's wound. "We've got to stop the bleeding." He flinched as her fingers touched stickiness. It was his left shoulder. Thank God it hadn't been a few inches lower and to the right. "You're going to be okay." She slipped out of her button-down sweatshirt and pressed it against the wound. "You saved our lives, you know that, don't you? I really think she was going to kill us all."

In the darkness, she heard his wry chuckle. "She was right, you know. About conning her. I couldn't find the gun."

Fonda caught her breath. "But then . . . what . . .?"

"This." He lifted a weak hand and waved an object in front of her. She could barely make it out in the darkness. Her fingers touched the hard plastic and followed it down to where it ended in a smooth round table.

"What is it?"

Bram's voice grew weaker. "The mike cable." He gave a feeble laugh. "I was shaking in me boots and praying she'd believe it was the gun." He swayed against her.

Fonda caught him just before he would've slumped to the floor. "Somebody help me! He's passed out!"

One of the minders stepped in with his flashlight. "Lie him down and keep him still. The ambulance will be here soon."

The pale light from his flashlight revealed beads of sweat on Bram's face. Fonda knew if she could see properly, his color would be ashen. He was in shock. She stroked his sandy hair away from his damp face, being careful not to touch the crusty wound where the gun had smashed into his skull. She felt an overpowering rush of love for this man who'd given them back their lives. Who'd purposely seen to it that Devin wouldn't irrevocably tie himself to a monster of a woman for life.

Bram's eyes opened suddenly and he grasped her hand. "Devin!" he said, his voice stronger than before. "You have to stop him."

She stared down at him. "The ambulance is coming. You'll be okay?"

He nodded, but his hand tightened on hers. "Fonda." He fought to keep his eyes open as once again, his voice waned. "You were the brave one tonight—if you hadn't jumped her, she would've finished me off. Now, go to Devin, love. Go to your man."

Fonda bent down and kissed his clammy brow. She scrambled to her feet and for a moment, swayed unsteadily. After the wave of dizziness passed, she stepped out into the corridor.

"Fonda!"

Jessie's face was streaked with tears. She threw herself into Fonda's arms. "They told me you were okay, but they wouldn't let me in to make sure."

Fonda hugged her tightly. "It's over, honey. We're safe."

Jessie pulled back, her freckled face pale and blotched from crying. "And Bram? Someone said he was shot. Is he going to be okay?"

"I'm pretty sure it's just a flesh wound." Fonda disengaged herself from Jessie's tight grip and placed a kiss on her forehead. "Why don't you go in and stay with him until the ambulance gets here? He keeps drifting in and out of consciousness. I have to get to Devin."

Her face paled. "Yes, go! I'm not sure what this is all about, but I know *she* wanted him to say things he doesn't believe. Stop him, Fonda. I'll stay with Bram."

Fonda was already flying toward the stage. She could hear Devin's voice. Earnest, forceful. Was it too late? She reached the wings and paused. If he'd already proclaimed his support for the IRA, she'd go to the mike herself and tell the crowd the truth. That he'd been coerced. That it was all a lie.

"When Glen was shot down that day in the streets of Derry, my whole world caved in upon me. It was even worse than the day my father was lifted. In the months Da had been in prison, Glen had become more than a brother to me. He'd become a father, as well. And when I saw his blood seeping out onto the cobblestones that day, I was filled with hatred and a need for vengeance against the barbaric murderers who'd shot him dead." His voice choked. He grew silent, struggling to regain control.

Fonda took a step onto the stage. She had to stop him before he went any further.

"Devin?"

At first, she didn't think he'd heard her. He stood stiffly, staring down at the floor of the stage. But then, slowly, almost as if in a dream, his head lifted. He turned to her, his eyes glazed, still lost in the memories of the past. Fonda moved toward him.

"It's over, Devin," she said. "Caitlyn is in custody."

Someone in the crowd gave a shrill whistle. It was the signal for the others. The stadium, unusually quiet during Devin's monologue, came alive.

"Get on with the music!" a voice cried out.

"Yeah! Enough politics! Let's rock!"

The glazed look disappeared from Devin's face as reality sunk in. For a moment, his eyes closed in relief. The noise of the crowd grew to a deafening roar. Fonda stopped, hesitating to go further. Devin had a show to perform, and she shouldn't be here. But all she wanted at this moment was to feel his arms around her. Just for a moment. Tears welled in her eyes as she smiled at him across the stage. The nightmare was over.

He took a step toward her. The stage was huge. Too big to cross quickly. But Fonda hadn't counted on how fast Devin could move. He folded her into his arms, his face buried into the ripples of her hair. The crowd went crazy, obviously thinking she was a fan who'd somehow found her way on stage. Fonda clung to him for a long moment, crying openly now. He brushed her hair away from her ear and kissed it softly.

"I prayed, you know," he whispered. "Prayed the whole time I was up here that He wouldn't take you away from me."

Fonda drew away to look into his eyes. "Bram was shot, but it's not serious. Just a shoulder wound, I think. He saved our lives, Devin. I don't think she ever intended to let us go." She squeezed his arm. "But now you have to go back to that mike. Tell them how you really feel. You can't leave them with Caitlyn's message of hate."

He stared down at her, his thumbs brushing the scratches on her face left by Caitlyn's nails. "Did she do this to you?"

"Devin, please! You can't leave it like this."

"You're right. But I want you with me."

The minders at the front of the stage were struggling to hold back the crowds as several daring fans tried to fight their way on stage. The chanting of Devin's name had started again:

"Dev-in. Dev-in. Dev-in."

Fonda glanced at the band behind them. They were staring at the two of them, faces confused, hands idle on their instruments as they had been for the last hour and a half. Of course, they had no idea of the drama that had taken place in Devin's dressing room. What could they be thinking about his long break and the rambling speech about the history of their country? And now, to top it off, Devin was engaged in an emotional confrontation with his fiancée on stage when he should be performing.

His hands slid down her arms and fastened upon her wrists. "Come, luv."

Devin led her across the stage to the mike. He unhooked it from the stand. "You've been very patient, but please, bear with me a moment longer. I have to share this with you."

He paused, his eyes scanning the thousands of fans before him. "For many years of my childhood, hatred filled my soul. Then one day I was in a shop in my hometown of Derry. Fifteen I was, and full of spit and fire. And I heard an IRA man talking to some wee lads. He was telling the lads about killing a young Brit with his bare hands. He described how he plunged a knife into the soldier's gut, felt the blood spilling onto his hands, and *relishing* it. 'He was just a babe, not much older than youse,' the man said to the lads. 'He still had peach fuzz on his face.' As I listened to the IRA man, I felt sickened. And ashamed. But then the real horror set in when the lads clamored for the IRA man's autograph. And I knew then that those lads would grow up to be just like him. Because of this vicious circle of killing and violence. And what does it really get us?" Devin's eyes moved to Fonda's for a brief moment. His hand squeezed hers. "Nothing but tragedy! Violence begets only violence. That is why I've spent my life trying to get my message of peace across to the young people—the future of our world. We *can* change things for the better. And we can do it without violence!"

A cheer rose from the crowd. Devin put his arm around Fonda's shoulders. "Just one more thing before we get on with the show. I want to share with you someone who is very special in my life. This . . . is the woman I love."

The crowd roared. Devin grinned and squeezed her arm. He replaced the mike on the stand and turned to her, both hands on her shoulders. As the noise of the crowd grew around them, he looked into her eyes and spoke for her ears alone.

"Fonda, will you marry me in Dublin—say, in about a month's time?"

She nodded, unable to speak because of the huge lump in her throat. But it was enough for him. He bent down and kissed her lips softly. "I have to give these people what they paid for," he said. "But know this. Every song I sing tonight is for you. And for you only. Now, go. In a little while, the night will be ours."

Fonda squeezed his hand and then let go. She felt his eyes upon her as she left the stage. It wasn't until she stepped into the darkness of the wings that he turned back to the mike.

"Okay! You came here to rock. Let's rock!"

The drums began. Seamus sprang to life, his agile fingers playing the opening riff to one of the hit singles from the *Eclipse* album. Once again, Devin's familiar husky voice rebounded through the night air around Candlestick Park.

And the stadium began to rock.

EPILOGUE

September 1991
Dublin

"You heard me, Liam. The Fat Lady Sings for the cover story instead of Sting." Grinning, Fonda held the telephone away from her ear and waited until the indignant voice of her managing editor died down from deafening to merely shrill. When he finally paused, she cut in, "Yes, I know I'm daft. But have I been wrong yet? Remember, Liam, *European Spotlight* 'spotlights' the up and comers, not the ones who've already made it." She smiled into the phone. "Trust me. I know what I'm doing."

"Giving old Liam a hard time as usual, love?"

Fonda looked up to see Devin leaning against the doorway, his dark eyes amused. Tucked in the nook of his arm, he held a stuffed white seal.

"Devin! Who's your friend?"

"His name is Elroy."

With a delighted grin, Fonda got up from her desk. Devin met her halfway across the room and pulled her into his arms. They exchanged a tender kiss.

"Mmmmm—that's nice." Fonda drew away and touched the plush stuffed seal. "Is this for me?"

"Don't jump to conclusions, love. This is for the *other* woman in my life. *This* is for you." And he kissed her again, slowly and surely.

After a long, breathless moment, Fonda murmured, "So, what are you doing in this part of town—besides getting me all hot and bothered?"

He grinned, the dimple near his mouth flickering. "Can't a man stop in to see his wife now and then? Or is the editor-in-chief of Dublin's hottest new rock magazine too busy for a romantic moment with her husband these days?"

"Never too busy for you," she said, snuggling her face against his neck and inhaling his fresh male scent. "How's the recording going?"

"Not bad. You'll be proud of me. I've only tried to strangle Desmond Scott twice this morning, the pompous young idiot. Lucky he's such a genius when it comes to producing a record."

Fonda giggled. "Just watch yourself. I don't want to see *The Irish Times* headlined with 'Rock Star Murders Producer During Recording Session.' It might look bad for your career, you know."

Devin sighed. "I'll keep that in mind. Actually, I stopped in to remind you we're having tea with Bram and Bonnie tonight. Bram said to tell you it's a great honor, you know. Being the first guests of the newlyweds."

Fonda groaned. "Good thing you reminded me. Jeez, it's been so crazy lately. I thought once we saw Mom and Dad off at the airport, life would get back to normal."

"What's normal?" Devin rocked her gently in his arms. His lips brushed her ear. "Is she awake yet?"

Fonda smiled. "Why do I get the feeling you came here to see *her* instead of me?"

"Do I detect a wee bit of jealousy in your voice, love?" He took her hand and walked toward a closed door in her office. His voice lowered to a whisper. "Let's go see. I promise I won't wake her."

He opened the door and peered into the adjoining room. "Sleeping like an angel, she is." Gingerly, he walked toward the crib, pulling Fonda with him. "Christ, she's beautiful, Fon. Such a wee thing." A delighted laugh escaped his lips. "Look at her! She thinks she's nursing."

Fonda felt a tingle in her full breasts. "Yeah, it's almost time. She'll be waking up screaming any minute now."

Devin gazed down at the sleeping infant, his eyes tender. "Can you believe it, Fon? A month old today." He placed the stuffed seal at the foot of the crib. His hand reached for Fonda's and squeezed it tightly. "I feel like the luckiest man in the world. All because of you and wee Michaela here."

"*We* are lucky," Fonda agreed.

So many good things had happened in the last year. After the San Francisco concert, Fonda had gone home to Indiana, her mind ringing with the validity of Jessie's vehement accusations. She'd faced her father, admitting to him that she'd held him responsible for Michael's death, and she'd been wrong to do so. Her confession had led to a heart-to-heart talk, one she'd never believed was possible between them. She'd been astonished to learn that his reserve toward her and Michael had been because he'd always felt shut out by their closeness to each other.

"Sandy was so easy," he'd admitted, his eyes misting with undisguised emotion. "In her eyes, I was Santa Claus, the Easter Bunny, and Jesus all wrapped up in one. But you and Michael were so different. I thought you didn't need anybody except each other. But I was wrong. You *did* need me. And I wasn't there for you."

During that visit home, a tentative bridge had been built between Fonda and her father. It would always be a bit shaky, perhaps, but at least it was a start. Her parents and Jessie had flown to Dublin for the wedding last August, and then again after Michaela was born, staying for nearly a month this time. Fonda had been amused at how her father could barely keep his hands off his newborn granddaughter. Mom, on the other hand, was captivated by Devin and his Irish charm. During the visit, Jessie had spent a lot of time with Ryan, and by the time they left for home, she'd made up her mind to apply for entrance into University College Dublin after high school graduation. Amused, Fonda wondered how her parents would react to the news of another Irish son-in-law.

Yes, it had been quite a year. And not the least of it had been the birth of *European Spotlight*. Devin had surprised her with the Grafton Street offices on the eve of their wedding. During her visit home, he'd been negotiating with Kari Jarlsberg to buy the Swedish magazine. Since the first Dublin issue hit the newsstands in early 1991, the magazine had been a huge success, rivaling Ireland's *Hot Press* in sales during the last few months.

Fonda took a deep breath and gazed down at their sleeping daughter. "Oh, how I wish Michael were here to see her," she whispered.

Devin's hand pressed upon her shoulder. "He's here," he said softly. "Can't you feel it?"

She met his eyes, and smiled. "Yes, I think I do." For a long moment, they gazed at each other silently.

From the next room, the intercom beeped. It was Laura, Fonda's secretary. "Fonda, they need you down in the photo lab— pronto!"

At that moment, Michaela stirred and whimpered. Fonda looked down at the baby and then flashed a glance at her office. The baby gave a long indignant wail. Helplessly, Fonda stared at Devin, her breasts tingling in anticipation of Michaela's feeding.

He shrugged. "I'd volunteer, but I don't think I have the right equipment."

Fonda scooped up the squirming baby and strode into her office. She spoke into the intercom. "Tell Jackson he'll have to handle it himself or wait an hour. I have something more pressing to do."

Back in the nursery, Fonda settled herself into a rocking chair and unbuttoned her blouse. Smiling, Devin took a chair nearby and watched as Michaela greedily locked onto Fonda's right nipple and began to suck noisily.

A new melody flowed through Devin's mind, and softly, he began to hum.